MW01254794

Emma: Ancestors' Tales Book One

By

Paula Shablo

© Copyright 2017 by Paula Marie Shablo
All rights reserved.
First Edition 2017
Cover photo by Paula Shablo

This is a work of fiction. Characters are purely the invention of the author's imagination, and any resemblance to persons living or dead is coincidental. Many of the historical references and many of the locations are real, but they have been used in a fictitious manner. Liberties have been taken with locations and their actual layouts and histories.

The author acknowledges the trademarked status and trademark owners of various products or locations referenced in this work of fiction, which have been used without permission. The publication / use of these trademarks is not authorized, associated with or sponsored by the trademark owners.

All rights reserved. No part of this book may be reproduced in any form or by any electronic or mechanical means, including information storage and retrieval systems, without the written permission of the author. Reviewers who wish to quote brief passages may do so.

This book is dedicated to my parents, Paul and Joyce Shablo.

Thank you for the true stories, the histories, the rich narratives of your lives that I was blessed to hear from both of you.

Thank you for the laughter and the tears.

Thank you for the strong foundation.

I am here because of you. More than that, I am happy to be here because of you. The love and support have made me strong enough to get through the tough times and have provided me with the good humor necessary to laugh through some of the darkest days.

Thankfully, the dark days have been few, and most of the laughter has been the result of the zaniness of life, which you raised me to recognize and appreciate.

I love you both so much.

Prologue

1965

1.

Emma leaned into the open doorway, ready to dart out of sight if anyone turned.

She needn't have worried. The adults all had their backs to her, their attention focused on the elderly woman in the bed: The Great-Grandmother.

Emma knew every person crowded into the room. They included her mother, her aunts and uncles, and her grandmother. The Great-Grandmother was her grandmother's mother, and she was very sick.

Emma had heard her aunts whispering about it earlier: Cancer. What a terrible word. Emma was only four, and even she knew it was a terrible word; a word for a very terrible thing; it had long since gained upper-case status in her mind.

"It's nearly over," Aunt Tilda had said. "The Cancer is everywhere now."

"What can we do?" Aunt Sondra had asked.

"There's nothing we can do," Aunt Sheryl had replied.

"Except wait." Aunt Tilda's final word on the subject was firm. The women had all nodded and gone off to do chores around the Great-Grandmother's house, and Emma had hurried off to join her sisters before she was discovered eavesdropping.

Now they were all gathered in the Great-Grandmother's bedroom, hovering over her and whispering urgently.

"Emma." Her grandfather's hand came down on her shoulder, gently squeezing. Emma jumped, startled nearly out of her wits. He bent and lifted her into his arms. "Let's come away from here, now," he whispered, somehow sensing that Emma didn't want to be caught watching the scene in the bedroom.

He carried her off into the dining room and sat her down at the table. "What are you up to, little lady?" Grandpa asked.

7

"Nothing," Emma replied meekly.

"A sick room is no place for a little girl," Grandpa declared firmly.

"I know, Grandpa," Emma admitted. "But she looks so...so bad. Can't somebody fix her?"

"I'm afraid not. No one knows how to fix this sort of illness, honey."

Emma stared down at her feet. Her left shoe was untied, so she lifted her foot in her grandfather's direction, and he knelt in front of her to tie it. "You fix lots of things, Grandpa," she said. "But, I guess...not this, huh?"

"Not this." He finished tying her shoe and patted her foot. "I wish I could." And he really looked like he did wish just that.

Emma felt bad for him. "I'm sorry I was snoopy, Grandpa," she said. "Don't feel bad, okay?"

"I guess we all feel a little bad right now, sweetheart. But that's okay; that's the way it is when someone you care about is leaving you."

"Where's she going?" Emma was four, and death was not a familiar concept, so she was genuinely interested in where the Great-Grandmother might be going when she clearly felt so sick. "To the doctor's again?"

"Not this time," Grandpa told her, shaking his head. "It's time for her to go home."

"But—she is home!"

Grandpa shook his head, at a loss how to continue the conversation. This was a talk her parents should be having with her; he didn't know how they wanted to handle it, and felt it wasn't his place. "Emma," he said. "Please run along now, outside with your sisters and your cousins. You should look out for the little ones, now. There's my big girl."

Emma looked at her grandfather's face, lined and sad, and decided she certainly was a big girl now, and should look out for the little ones as he'd asked. "Okay, Grandpa," she agreed, and jumped down off the chair and headed for the door. Then she turned back, crawled into his lap and planted a kiss on his cheek before heading outside.

Grandpa looked on as the little girl pulled open the screen door and trotted down the steps to join the other children.

There were plenty of adults out there to watch them; the aunts and uncles by marriage, a few friends who had come by to pay their respects. He shook his head, feeling old and sad, and wandered into the kitchen to sit with his father-in-law.

Emma found her father sitting under a tree in the yard, holding the baby. He was brand new, and the only boy in their family. He was sleeping, wrapped in a blue blanket and looking like a little angel. Emma knew he wasn't really an angel—he cried until his face turned red sometimes and pooped in his diapers just like her youngest sister still did—even though she was already one year old and should probably quit that. But when he was asleep—angel face!

Emma loved babies. Even one-year-old babies who still pooped in their diapers. Her other sister was three, and she didn't wear diapers anymore, but Emma loved her, too, because she was also still a baby, as far as Emma was concerned.

"Hi, Daddy," Emma said. Plopping down on the ground, next to her father, she leaned in and kissed the baby on the forehead.

"Hi, pumpkin." Her father gave her a tired smile.

"Grandpa says I'm a big girl now," Emma informed him.

"That's true."

"So, I better look out for the little ones."

"That's a great idea." He smiled at her. "Your sisters are over there." He nodded in the general direction of a group of little ones who were playing "London Bridge" with her older cousins.

"The Great-Grandmother is going home now," Emma announced, jumping to her feet.

Her father looked up at her, startled. "What?" he demanded, loudly enough that some of the other adults looked their way.

"Yes," Emma declared, nodding decisively. "She's going home. Right now. That's good, Daddy." Emma patted her father's shoulder comfortingly. "Home is good."

From inside the house, there came a wail of anguish, followed by the sound of many women crying.

9

Emma's father looked at the house and watched as Grandpa came out. Grandpa gave him a slight nod. He nodded back, and then he turned and stared at Emma as she skipped away to join the children at their game.

He wasn't the only one staring.

2.

Grandma and Grandpa's house was not as big as the house the Great-Grandmother and Great-Grandfather lived in, but it was closer to the cemetery, church, and funeral home, Mama said, and that was why everyone had come there. Emma's father and her uncles had brought folding tables into the living room after moving the sofa into one of the bedrooms. They had lined the whole back wall of the living room with tables, and then Aunt Tilda had covered them with fancy plastic tablecloths.

Aunt Sondra put paper plates and plastic cutlery at the far end of the first table, and Aunt Sheryl set up a big electric coffee pot at the end of the last table. Then Emma's mother came in with a big tray filled with paper cups and a pitcher of Kool-Aid.

Emma watched wide-eyed as her father and grandfather moved the living room chairs out of the room and her uncles began setting up a lot of folding chairs.

Then came a steady stream of strangers, most of the women carrying covered bowls and trays. The tables began to fill up with food, and when there was no more room, the extra offerings were taken to the dining room and kitchen.

When someone goes home, Emma discovered, the people they left behind have to have a funeral. As far as she could tell, a funeral was a big party where lots of people you'd never seen before bring tons of food to your Grandma's house and everyone stands around talking about the person who wasn't there anymore.

Sometimes the people ate the food, but many of them didn't touch a thing. That was curious; it was really good food!

Everyone seemed to know each other, and the ladies hugged and asked about children and everyone said how sorry they were.

Sometimes people cried. A lot.

It wasn't an especially fun party, Emma decided. If it was a party at all, no one seemed to be enjoying it much. There were a few smiles; then the sad faces would come back and stay.

But there really was a lot of tasty food to try, and so many desserts! Cakes, pies, cookies, pudding; and no one paid any attention to how much anyone was eating; a kid could pretty much have whatever she liked.

Emma helped herself to a cookie and went looking for her Aunt Rose.

Rose was in her bedroom. Cousin Suzi was with her, and so were Emma's sisters Melody and Dana. Rose was brushing Melody's hair, and Suzi was putting a barrette into Dana's curls. She looked up when Emma came in. "Hey, Em! Where were you?"

"I was watching the grown-ups," Emma said. "There are so many people here!"

Rose nodded. "Grandma was a very nice lady," she said. "She had a lot of friends."

"The Great-Grandmother, you mean?" Emma asked.

"Yes. She was your great-grandmother, Emmie-love, but she was my Grandma. My Mom is your Grandma."

"I know, I know!" Melody sang.

"You don't know nothin'." Emma declared.

"Emma," Rose warned.

"Sorry!" Emma wasn't sorry. Melody didn't understand the grandma and great-grandma stuff. She had a hard time understanding it herself, and she was older. She pulled away from Suzi. "I don't need my hair combed!"

"That's what you think, smarty-pants!" Suzi handed her a mirror. "Have you seen yourself this morning?"

Emma studied her reflection dubiously. Okay, yes; her hair was messy. But— "I don't want my hair combed!"

"Tough," Aunt Rose said.

Aunt Rose was young, not a grown-up yet. But there was no arguing with her; she could be bossy, and the grown-ups

11

would back her up. Emma folded her arms and sighed loudly, "Fine!"

"That's right, fine." She applied the brush briskly, and then asked, "Where did you get so much hair? My goodness!"

"It just growed there! Ouch!"

"It grew there. And shush, no one's hurting you."

"That's what you think, smarty-pants!"

"Emma!"

"Gosh!" Emma tried to hold still, but she hated having her hair brushed. It was thick and course and tangled easily. "Why are all these people here?" she asked.

"Well, some of them are family, and some are friends, and they have all come to say good-bye to your Great-Grandma."

"The Great-Grandmother went home. She's not here anymore, so they can't say goodbye to her," Emma explained reasonably.

"Well, people have their traditions, and funerals are one of them." Rose began to plait Emma's hair into a thick braid.

"What's a tradition?"

"It's something people do over and over again. Like Christmas and Thanksgiving celebrations; going to Church on Sundays; saying grace before you eat. There are lots of things that people do that make them feel good. When someone dies, we get together to say goodbye. We do it to remember them, and to make ourselves feel better, I guess."

"You're really smart, Aunt Rose," Suzi said. "I think it makes my mom feel better having all these people here."

"I know it helps my mom," Rose agreed. "It helps just knowing how many people loved her mother."

"They still can't say goodbye," Emma argued. "She already left."

"Her spirit left her body," Rose agreed. "But she may still be around, watching over us and knowing that we all came together to remember her."

"Where is she, then?" Emma demanded.

"Heaven," Suzi declared firmly.

Emma was quiet then, thinking it through.

Heaven. That's where you go when you die; at least that's what they said in church. Finally, she twisted around to face

12

her aunt, jerking the braid out of Rose's hand. "So, she died." She announced this firmly. "She had the hour of her death, amen."

Rose gently turned Emma's head and resumed braiding. "Yes," she agreed quietly. "She died."

"Why'd Grandpa say she went home, then?"

"Because Heaven is home."

"Then where do we live?"

Rose sighed. "I'm going to yell at Jill," she muttered.

Jill was Emma's mother's name.

"What? Why?" Emma demanded. "You can't yell at my mama!"

"I'm not." Rose sighed again. "Emma, when we're alive, we live with our families on earth. When we die, we live with our families in Heaven. They are both home."

Emma was silent. It must be awful to grow up and have to know all these things, she thought. It makes my head hurt!

Or...oh yeah! That could just be Aunt Rose, with her hair brushing and braiding and tugging making my head hurt!

"Are you done with me yet?" she demanded. "Cuz I want to take these babies and show them all the food!"

Rose twisted a rubber band into the end of the braid and nodded. "We'll all go have something to eat," she said. "Then we'll be staying here while the grown-ups go to the services."

Suzi lifted Dana into her arms. "What's services?" Melody asked, taking Rose's hand.

"Church."

"We don't go?"

"Not this time. We're going to stay here and eat and play games."

Emma shook her head. "I wish we could always do that," she said, "instead of going to church and being quiet."

"When have you ever been quiet in church?" Suzi laughed.

"I do! I do!" Melody sang.

Melody sang everything. It was like their parents had known she would sing when they named her!

The grownups left in groups and soon it was just Aunt Rose, Uncle Danny, Emma, Melody and Dana. The baby,

Matthew, had gone with Emma's parents. Emma had considered demanding to go, too, if a little baby was allowed, but decided it wasn't worth the argument. Besides, she was getting hungry, and there was so much food!

Rose put food on paper plates for each of the children, and then loaded a plate for herself. Danny helped her carry everything to the dining room table, and then went back to get a plate for himself while Rose got everyone Kool-Aid.

Once everything was ready, they all sat around the table and Danny said grace. At the end he added, "And please welcome Grandma into Heaven and into Your loving arms. Amen."

She couldn't let it go, it seemed. "Why did all the cousins go to church, but not us?" Emma asked.

"Your mom and dad feel that you're too young for funeral services," Danny replied.

"They took Matthew," Emma argued reasonably.

"He's just a baby and needs his mother," Danny explained. "Besides, he's too little to remember anything."

"Well, I'm older than Jenny—two whole weeks! She'll remember, and she went."

"Her mom and dad decided she could go."

"But—"

"Emma!" Rose scolded. "Your mom and dad decide what you do, and Jenny's mom and dad decide what she does. Period."

"Okay! Jeez!"

"Watch it, missy."

"Sorry!" Emma scowled at her plate.

"Eat your lunch."

"Look at it this way," Danny said. "We get first dibs on all the desserts."

Emma brightened instantly. "Good point, Uncle Danny!"

Honestly, Emma didn't know why she felt so left out by being excluded from the funeral services. Except for never having been to such a thing before, she probably wasn't missing anything good. After all, a lot of people had been crying all day; how much fun could it be?

14

She ate her lunch. Then she had a piece of chocolate cream pie and decided that it would forever be her favorite.

After lunch, she announced her intention to go pee, and went to the bathroom.

And that's where she saw her.

The Great-Grandmother.

Chapter One

1984

"Wait a minute—your first encounter with a ghost was in the bathroom?" Jacob stared at her, incredulous.

Emma laughed. "Yeah, go figure." She tossed a stray lock of hair back over her shoulder. "I can't even believe I'm telling you this."

"Why?"

"I really don't talk much about this stuff... except to my family. And they only know because I was so young when it all started that I didn't know enough to keep my big mouth shut."

Jacob laughed. "Is that really how you feel about it? Like it should be a secret?"

Emma pursed her lips and thought about it. "Well, no," she admitted finally. "Not from everyone. My family's always been cool about it. Well... mostly cool with it—once they got used to it. If nothing else, I keep them entertained. I've had a lot of stories to tell them."

"I want to hear them all!" Jacob was a believer, although he'd never seen a ghost himself. Nor had he ever had an experience that could be deemed even remotely supernatural. But he wanted to. The very idea had always fascinated him.

"Stick around long enough, and you're likely to." Emma wanted to take the words back as soon as they'd left her mouth. What was she trying to do, jinx a new relationship?

"Don't think I won't," Jacob replied casually. Like it was silly to think that he wouldn't.

Emma's heart did a weird little flip in her chest. Whoa, girl, she thought. Don't get excited.

"Anyway, over the years I've met a few people who...er...get it? I mean...well, if it's never happened to you, it's hard to believe, I guess."

Jacob shrugged. "It's never happened to me, but I've always believed it. I really, really wanted to see my grandfather after he passed, but...I guess you either have it or you don't."

"It?"

"The gift. The sight. The, uh…"

"The 'Shining'?" Emma suggested, giggling.

Jacob frowned and shook his head decisively. "Worst movie ever," he declared firmly.

Emma nodded in agreement. "Poor Stephen King," she said. "Writes a great book and some schmuck ruins the movie version."

"I know. I can't believe people like it! Didn't they read the book?"

"Probably not."

"Anyway—" Jacob decided not to pursue the book vs movie debate. He wanted to know more about Emma. "You have something, though," Jacob insisted. "What do you call it?"

"Me? I've always called it 'Emma's little problem'." She shook her head, and the lock of hair tumbled back into her face. She tossed it away again. "No, not really. Well…yeah. Really—but not all the time." She stared into the fireplace, thoughtful.

Jacob watched her. She was lovely in the firelight, her auburn hair fighting the flames for his attention. The hair was winning. He reached out to push that errant lock back behind her ear. "Why is it a problem?" he asked, sincerely curious.

Emma bit her lip. "Why is it a problem?" she repeated. "Why wouldn't it be? There's no controlling it—at least not for me. You'd think it would be great, being able to ask the questions that occur to you about what kinds of food people ate in eighteenth century Texas or when someone first saw a car. But I can't choose who I see, or when. People just…show up. And never at convenient times, either, I'll tell you that!" She laughed.

"So, you're not like those people on t.v. who go places and talk to spirits?"

"Oh, hell no! I wish!" Emma laughed self-consciously. "I always find myself thinking that they're all fakes, though," she admitted. "If I was to wander into a 'haunted' location and call to the spirits…nothing would happen. Oh, sure, I'd probably feel something, if there really were spirits around.

17

But…well…for me, it has always been a relative, or someone associated with a relative, and they don't cooperate with me on demand; they do whatever it is they—hmm…I was going to say, 'whatever they want to do', but I don't think that's right. I think they do what they *have* to do at any given time. So, the psychics and mediums I see on t.v. or in the movies? I want to believe, but…"

Jacob nodded his understanding. "I know," he said. "It's some sort of gimmick, right? They're just in it for the money. But…I still think it's real. Sometimes."

"Sometimes," Emma agreed. "And I always hope I'll meet someone who can really…you know…do it."

"Like you."

"Better than me," Emma said. "Someone who can make the choices. Call whoever they want."

"So, do you feel like some poor chick in a scary movie? You know: 'I saw a ghost! No one believes me!'?"

"No. No." She shook her head, and the hair flopped free once more. "Dang it! Time for a haircut!"

Jacob cringed at the thought of scissors cropping those lovely locks, but held his tongue. Her hair, her choice.

Emma continued, "After the first couple of times, I realized I didn't have to be scared. Not one of them has ever had any intention of hurting me. But with my great-grandmother…well…it was the first time; I was four; it was my first experience with death, and that was pretty freaky."

"Tell me the rest of the story." Jacob settled back in his chair. "So, you went to the bathroom…your great grandmother was in there…and then what?"

1.

1965

Emma trotted down the hallway and through the bathroom door, where she stopped short with a "skree" of shoes on linoleum. She was not alone.

Emma stared at the great-grandmother, genuinely shocked. She shook her head and closed her eyes tightly.

She opened her eyes again; the great-grandmother was still there, now smiling with apparent amusement.

Emma frowned. "You're not supposed to be here, Great-Grandma," she whispered.

The old woman turned to more fully face Emma and her smile deepened. She was sitting on the edge of the bathtub, and dressed in a long, flowing white dress. There were shiny white shoes on her feet and a strange looking white hat with a lacy veil on her head.

She didn't look sick at all, Emma noted. Her hair was done in an upswept fashion under hat and veil, and was a rich brown instead of silver. Her cheeks were rosy with good health. Her eyes sparkled.

She looked…young. Maybe even younger than Grandma!

That was weird!

"Great-Grandmother? Why are you here?" Emma whispered. Her heart was pounding hard; she was unpleasantly aware of it: thump, thump. She didn't just feel it; she could actually hear it.

"So you'll understand," the Great-Grandmother replied. "So you can explain."

"Un—understand?" Emma repeated. "Explain? Explain what?"

But there was no reply. The Great grandmother was gone!

Emma stood in the doorway, staring into the now-empty room. She was breathing hard, and at first, she couldn't seem to move. She put out a hand to grasp the door jamb and support her weight, sagging a little with shock.

The Great-Grandmother was here! She was here!

She couldn't have been here.

Well…

She wasn't here now. Except for Emma, still standing in the doorway, no one was here.

Am I crazy? Is this what it's like to be a looney-tune?

I'm not crazy. She was here!

Emma turned on her heel and fled from the room, yelling, "Aunt Rose! Aunt Rose! The Great-Grandmother!"

Rose came running, frightened by the tone of her niece's cries. Her heart was pounding wildly in her chest. "Dear God in Heaven, child!" she gasped, dropping to her knees in front of Emma. "You scared the life out of me!" She grasped Emma by the shoulders and gave her a little shake. "What's the matter with you?"

Emma was trembling. "The Great-Grandmother was in the bathroom," she said, her eyes wide with wonder.

"Of course, she wasn't," Rose declared firmly.

"Oh yes she was!" Emma argued, indignant.

Rose stared at the child, at a loss as to where to go next with this conversation. Finally: "Did you pee?" she demanded, changing the subject.

"What? No!" Emma shook her head. What on earth was wrong with her Aunt? "Didn't you hear me? She was in there!"

Rose stood up and grasped her hand firmly. "Let's go pee, and we shall see," she chanted. "I'm a poet and didn't know it." She laughed, a little shrilly.

"I don't want—"

"Do you have to pee, or not?" Rose didn't want to encourage any further discussion of dead women in the bathroom.

"Yes, but—"

"Then let's go."

Emma resisted the tug on her hand. "Can't I just go outside?" she asked meekly.

"Have you lost your mind? Of course not!" Rose stared down at her niece, exasperated. She sighed heavily. "I'll go in with you," she offered. "You'll see; there's nothing in there."

"Not anymore," Emma grumbled. She allowed her aunt to lead her back into the bathroom.

It was empty.

Of course.

Emma glared defiantly up at her Aunt Rose. "I can pee by myself," she declared through gritted teeth.

Rose backed out of the room and quietly closed the door.

Once they'd returned to the dining room, Emma sat quietly for a few minutes, sipping her Kool-Aid and thinking hard. She

20

wasn't scared anymore; she'd had time to process the experience, and it had already taken on the sepia tones of memory. The great-grandmother had scared her, yes; but not because she was scary.

She was just so...unexpected.

Best of all, she'd looked well. Pretty; fancy in her dress; skin rosy. Not like what Emma would have expected a dead person to look like; no, not at all.

Finally, she looked up at Aunt Rose and said, "Her dress was so pretty."

Rose started, nearly spilling her own drink. "What?" she demanded. "What did you say?" She'd reacted calmly—well, relatively calmly—to Emma's theatrics, but she'd been shaken by them. Her insides were still quivering, truth to tell.

"Her dress. The great-grandmother's dress," Emma explained. "It was so, so pretty."

Rose and Danny exchanged a look that Emma couldn't quite understand. "What did it look like, Emmaline?" Uncle Danny asked.

Rose said, "Danny, I—"

"Shush," Danny ordered. "What did the dress look like, Emma?"

Rose aimed a kick at Danny's ankle under the table, missed, and stubbed her toe on the table leg. Hissing with pain, she glared at him. Danny grinned wickedly back at her.

"Well...it was white, and it dragged on the floor a little," Emma said, thoughtfully recalling the details. "It had little shiny things on it, here," she added, indicating her chest, "and puffy sleeves. She had on shiny white shoes and a funny hat. Well," she conceded, "it was a pretty hat, but funny." She put her hands up, near her face. "It was...scrunchy? Like flat and fluffy at the same time...and it had see-through lace that could come down in front."

Danny looked at Rose, who had gasped. "Did Jill take her to the funeral home?" he asked her.

"No! She and Jack didn't even want the kids at the service. That's why we're all here, remember?" Rose clasped her hands together, and then thrust them under her thighs, sitting on them to still their sudden shaking.

"Then how on Earth—?"

Rose shook her head. "I have no idea. Maybe she heard Mama and our sisters talking about it, or something."

"Maybe..." Danny looked thoughtful. "I guess Emma could have been eavesdropping; she's a snoop. But—"

"Hey!" Emma cried indignantly. "Quit talking about me like I'm not even here!"

Melody and Dana sat listening to the entire exchange. Dana scooped up the filling from the chocolate cream pie and smeared it all over her face and into her hair. Melody laughed and sang, "Pretty white dresses and chock-lit hair, shiny shoes and pies up to there!" Dana found that hilarious and burst into wild giggles, almost tumbling off her chair.

Rose scooped the toddler up, holding her out in front of her as she rushed to the bathroom. Danny laughed, and Emma rolled her eyes. "Babies," she declared.

"Yep," Danny agreed. "Sing it again, Mel."

Melody giggled, but turned her attention to her own pie rather than singing.

"Uncle Danny?" Emma whispered.

"Yeah?"

"The great-grandmother..." Emma paused, unsure how to explain what she wanted to say.

"What about her, love?" Uncle Danny encouraged her quietly.

"She was so sick," Emma said.

"Yes, she was," Danny agreed. "Very sick."

"She's not sick anymore." Emma sat silently for a moment, thoughtful. She was supposed to understand; she didn't, not really. She was also supposed to explain, and that was something she thought she might be able to do. "She looks...good," she added. "She's rosy. She looks really fine." And Emma smiled brilliantly.

Danny put a hand over his mouth, inhaling deeply. Then he made a loose fist and leaned his chin on it while he stared at his niece thoughtfully. Then he nodded decisively and said, "Good. That's really good, Emma."

2.

1984

"So, they believed you?" Jacob asked.

"Well...let's just say they were intrigued." Emma chuckled. "Take it from me, there were some serious interrogations—interrogations of my parents, grandparents and aunts—you know, to make sure this little pitcher with big ears didn't overhear descriptions of the clothes my great-grandma was buried in. It turned out to be her wedding outfit, actually."

"Ah." Jacob nodded. "So, then they started trying to figure out if you'd—"

"Seen pictures or something?"

"Yeah."

"Had you?"

"I don't see how I could have." Emma scratched her forehead thoughtfully and pushed her hair back yet again. "The few wedding pictures there were left by that time were stored in my great-grandmother's steamer trunk. She'd wrapped them carefully, so they'd be in the dark and not get bent. She never displayed them because she was afraid they'd fade."

"Smart lady." Jacob frowned, wondering about photographs in general. "Do they still exist somewhere?" he asked. "Does anyone have them now?"

"My mother and her sisters have had copies made," Emma told him. "The originals, though...I'm not sure who has those; maybe Grandma. Or her brother. But she's the oldest child, so probably Grandma."

"I'd like to see those sometime."

"Me, too, actually. It's been ages."

"So, they must be pretty old," Jacob speculated. "When did your great-grandparents get married?"

"1911."

"Wow, that was quick! You didn't even have to think about it!" Jacob was incredulous. He squinted at her quizzically. "Why do you even know that?"

Jacob was amazed; he wasn't sure he could tell anyone what year his parents had gotten married, let alone great-grand-parents.

Emma laughed. "Oh, Jake, you have no idea!" she said. "Over the years I've learned a lot about my family. I didn't really have a choice."

"Because...?"

"They insisted that I know."

"They?"

"My family."

"Your parents? I'm confused."

"Join the club." Emma laughed again. Then she took pity on Jacob and elaborated a little. "No, not my parents. Or, not just my parents."

Emma stared thoughtfully into space. This was going to take a while, she decided, but now that she'd started, she was all in. "Don't worry," she told Jacob, smiling gently. "I'll explain. That's what I do."

Chapter Two

In the Beginning

1.

John Francis Knight, known to one and all since childhood as Jack, met Jillian May Lange in the spring of 1957, on a blind date. Ironically, they were not dating each other; Jill had been paired with one of Jack's friends, and Jack was with a friend of a friend of Jill's on a fiasco of a date arranged by a fellow who had married a girl whose parents refused to let her see him again after they'd eloped one drunken weekend. The couple often arranged outings with the erstwhile bride's chums, so she could get out of the house for time with "the girls".

Jack and Jillian spent the evening ignoring their "dates"— who, God bless them, were taken with each other anyway, so no hard feelings—and talked of many things. Love at first sight was apparently a thing. After a whirlwind romance, they married in the late summer of that same year and moved to Colorado.

Jack had just finished his military service and went to school on the G.I. Bill. He figured they owed it to him; there were things he'd seen in Korea that he'd never talk about, but would certainly never be able to forget. He figured a degree in business management could take him away from manual labor forever; he never wanted to dig another ditch as long as he lived.

Jill went to work at a local hotel as a bookkeeper; she was a whiz with numbers. Jack went to school during the day and worked in the same hotel as a bellhop in the evenings a few days a week.

They both occasionally worked on Saturday afternoons, but Saturday night and all day Sunday were theirs.

Jack and Jill—yes, they know, they know! —were poor but happy. They knew how to have a good time without spending a lot of money; that was a good thing, since they didn't have any money. They had a tiny basement apartment, a used car, enough food to eat and each other; and that was enough.

Once Jack had finished school, the couple moved back to Jill's hometown in Idaho. Old friends greeted them warmly and asked about the baby.

"What baby?" Jack asked.

They were astonished—and amused—to learn that people had assumed they married so hastily because they were expecting!

Isn't it funny how people always seem to think the worst of you? Even the ones who supposedly love you or call themselves your friends often jump to conclusions that cast you in a less-than-perfect light. Apparently, the rumors had flown!

Luckily, the young couple shared a good sense of humor. They had a laugh at Jill's hometown's expense, and got on with living their lives instead of dwelling on it.

Jack was quickly able to find a full-time job at a drugstore as a cashier. It was not what he'd hope for, with his freshly earned Associates degree, but it was what was available, and one must do what one must do to earn a living and support his wife.

Soon enough, Jack was able to find various odd jobs, and after a time he found more steady part time as a mechanic.

Jill did bookkeeping jobs part time until she actually *did* get pregnant, and then she settled into "mama" mode.

Emmaline Meredith was born in 1960, the first of Jack and Jill's five children. Many have been the times when she has been asked if they went up a hill to fetch her.

(That little rhyme got old fast, but the Knight children would just have to deal with it. Apparently, the worse a joke is the more people are apt to tell it—and tell it—and tell it again!)

By 1964 the Knights had added three more children to the household: Melody, Dana and Matthew. Jack called them "the stair steps."

Until the early months of 1965, before her fifth birthday, there was nothing particularly remarkable about Emma. Except for the fact that she was already reading at over a first-grade level and had never attended any schools at that point in her life, Emma was a typical child. Jill attributed Emma's early love of the written word to her own love of reading and the fact that she'd made it a point to read aloud to the children at least once—and usually twice—each day.

Of course, Emma was the quintessential oldest child; she could be pretty bossy and would lord it over her younger siblings at times, but her parents didn't find that to be remarkable—just annoying.

Emma developed as any little girl at the time would have been expected to do. She made messes, played with toys, got frustrated with her attempts to tie her own shoes. She became the queen of "Why?" Nothing much could be said to her without eliciting a response of "Why?"

In 1964 Jill's grandmother became quite ill with cancer. It spread quickly, and she passed away in March of 1965, mere months after being diagnosed. The illness was a topic of many a "Why?" conversation, but there were no satisfactory answers; decades later, there are still no satisfactory answers to the questions of how and why someone might be cursed with the illnesses of Cancer.

Somehow, four-year-old Emma had known exactly when her great-grandmother had crossed over, although she was outside the house with her father at the time.

Jack was a bit intrigued by his daughter's announcement that The—Emma always referred to the greats as "The"—great-grandmother was going home, but didn't find it to be too unusual given the fact that her family members had been discussing the inevitable impending demise for days.

But then Emma saw the old woman in the bathroom on the day of her funeral, dressed in the very outfit she'd been buried in.

How does one explain that?

Still, they reasoned, it had been a stressful time in their family. Jill was attending to four children, one of them an infant still at breast; Jack was working two jobs and any side work he could get, and still they'd had to find time to help with the care of Jill's grandmother. Certainly, things had been discussed within the hearing of their children. It would have had to make an impression, and Emma was like a sponge, soaking up everything she saw or heard.

Jack and Jill decided to chalk everything up to stress and imagination.

There was nothing at all remarkable about Emma. She was just a normal little girl with a great imagination.

And so she was.

And so, also, she was not.

It was only a matter of time before they would have to admit to themselves that something was not quite—

Normal?

Regular?

—ordinary about their child.

People talked to her, you see. It would have been easy enough to write it off as the ever-popular "imaginary friend", but the people who visited her knew things no one else could know.

It didn't happen frequently, but it happened enough for the young parents to realize that they might have something serious to deal with in the future.

3.

In the fall of 1966 Jack received an offer he couldn't refuse. He and Jill packed their belongings, put their house up for sale, and moved the family to a small town in southwestern Wyoming.

Once again, it was a stressful time for the family. It was November, and already the weather was wintery. They made the trip by car, Jack maneuvering the automobile over icy roads, cursing the old tires with their poor traction. Jill read aloud to the children and tried to keep them as quiet as possible; Jack was nervous enough with the roads as bad as they were.

By the time they made it to their destination, the whole family was exhausted and cranky. Matthew started crying and kept it up for a couple of hours. Jack took the older children into a diner for hamburgers while Jill stayed in the car, motor running for heat, and tried to calm the toddler. He was sound asleep by the time her family returned to the car with a doggy bag full of food for her and Matthew. They checked into a motel, and Jill went into the bathroom and cried for twenty minutes before coming out and eating her meal.

Jack made his wife go to bed immediately after she ate and sat the older children in front of a television set that had a terminally ill horizontal hold. He fed Matthew when the child woke up, and then put all the kids to bed.

He sat, guiltily brooding, and watched his family sleep for quite a while before crawling into bed beside Jill and drifting off himself.

They spent a couple of days in a motel while looking for a house, and then they moved into a tiny box of a place. It was basically a square: living room and kitchen on one side, two bedrooms with a bathroom in between on the other side.

Emma took one look and declared it "Ugly with a capitol UG."

Jill had laughed and reassured her outspoken daughter that it wouldn't stay that way, but she also had her doubts.

Somehow, Jack and Jill managed to fit bunk beds, a toddler sized bed and a crib into the bigger bedroom. They took the small bedroom for themselves, and there was barely room to walk around their full-sized bed.

Jill was a skilled seamstress, and soon she had fashioned drapes for the living room windows and matching covers for the used sofa and chair she and Jack had picked up at a second-hand store. She made matching spreads and curtains for the beds and bedroom windows.

Ugly with a capitol UG had indeed been transformed; the little house was actually cute!

But they were still strangers in a strange land. Jack's new job kept him away from home a lot, and Jill wasn't comfortable yet driving in such snowy and windy conditions. There was snow in winter in Idaho, but somehow, the Wyoming wind changed everything for her. It blew up ground blizzards that obscured your vision and caused black ice to form on the road even when it was cleared of snow. It was more than a little daunting.

It was November; autumn, supposedly. Winter was officially still a month away! But there was already plenty of snow on the ground, and it was bitterly cold.

To top everything off, Emma had to change schools. This greatly distressed her; she'd barely settled into her first school. She spent a good deal of time uncomfortable, what with the possibility of uninvited guests. Of course, there had been a few; she couldn't escape them! Her classmates found her to be a strange little girl, talking to walls the way she did. She had had few friends in Idaho; but she was used to the ones she'd managed to make. Now she would have to start over.

New towns were scary.

New schools were scary.

Starting over was scary.

Emma didn't want to be scared; being scared made her feel angry with herself. She was determined not to be labeled a "fraidy-cat", even if she was the only one doing the labeling.

That first winter in Wyoming, Emma was only six years old. She'd dealt with her gifts for long enough, however, to know that being who she was and what she was could present problems. Still, she stubbornly decided to face her first day of school bravely, and was amazed when she survived it.

Soon enough, she had survived a whole week! She had no visitors in that time, for which she was grateful. She hoped enough time would pass that her classmates would get to know her before something happened that would forever mark her as "weird".

She knew it was only a matter of time. It had happened in Idaho; it would happen again.

Her teacher was a friendly woman who assigned different students to show her around and introduce her to people. Two of them were rather bossy, self-important girls who stuck together like glue and insisted that everyone do things their way. They were named Cherry and Candy, names Emma found secretly amusing; it seemed more than fitting that they should be best friends. Emma wasn't overly fond of them. They made her feel guilty for all the times she'd bossed her sisters around.

The other girls assigned to help her were Della and Lucy. They were both very sweet and Emma enjoyed being with them. They were best friends, however, and Emma often felt like a third wheel.

Like any little girl, Emma longed for her very own best friend.

That wouldn't come to be for several more years, however. She was an odd girl, a lonely child. She lived in her books and her imagination, and she talked more to her visitors than to anyone living.

The family celebrated their first Thanksgiving in Wyoming. It was strange and sad not to be with Grandma and Grandpa, Emma thought. But still, they managed to have a very nice day and a delicious meal.

After Thanksgiving the First-grade class began practicing for the Christmas program that the school presented every year. Emma was delighted to be chosen as the narrator of a small skit they would be doing, and rehearsed her lines faithfully every evening after school.

Her classmates were impressed with her during rehearsals at school, and she began to feel encouraged that she might be making some friends, instead of the acquaintanceships she'd been experiencing so far.

She was so excited!

Then a small tragedy struck: Emma became very ill. Jill was afraid to take her out; the weather had remained bitterly cold, and Emma was running a fever. It was high enough to make her lightheaded and dizzy; she needed help to make her way to the bathroom. Luckily, doctors in those days were more willing to make house calls, and the local M.D. came at once to see the ailing child.

Measles.

Vaccinations wouldn't become the norm for a few more years, and measles could run rampant in a community, sometimes with devastating results. Emma was a very sick little girl. Her fever made her delirious at times; at other times she was insistent that she was fine and ought to be in school, practicing for the Christmas play.

But that wasn't going to happen.

Emma was devastated upon learning the doctor's verdict: there would be no Christmas play for her! There would be no more school for her at all for the rest of the year!

It was Emma's first experience with personal disappointment, and she never forgot it. Later, she remembered only bits and pieces of the time of her illness, but missing the play had broken her heart. She'd worked so hard and looked so forward to it. She had memorized every line; she would never deliver a single word.

Worst of all, she was sure no one in her class would ever like her now; she felt she had let them all down. It never occurred to her at the time that she could be replaced.

Probably that was for the best; knowing she was expendable would have further devastated her.

She was very sick for the next few weeks, and didn't return to school until after the holiday vacation.

Emma's first Christmas in Wyoming passed in a blur; Santa made his annual appearance, but she barely noticed; she was feverish and itchy, and spent most of each day in bed.

All in all, 1966 ended on a rather bitter note for Emma Knight.

4.

It was January. Emma was back in school after a Christmas she barely remembered. She was still pale and had lost weight.

Emma was in her First-grade classroom, reading aloud to her classmates. Suddenly, distracted, she looked up from her book. "Great-Grandma?" she said.

The teacher, Mrs. Hall, frowned. "No, Emma," she said. "That's not what it says."

"What is it, Great-Grandma?" Emma asked, ignoring her teacher. She was staring past her classmates, looking at the wall behind them—or so it appeared to those in the room.

"Emma, what are you—?"

"Oh, no!" Emma cried. She turned to the teacher and said, "I have to go now," and ran to the door. As she flung it open and raced into the corridor, Mrs. Hall chased after her.

It was no use. Emma sped down the hallway, out the front doors and down the stairs. She'd left without her coat or snow boots.

Mrs. Hall watched as she ran down the snow-covered road, plumes of frosty air wafting about her head. She started to follow, then thought better of it and ran into the office to call Emma's mother. The child had just been extremely ill, and now she was out running in the cold with no coat!

She'd waved at Mr. Cory, the janitor, to follow her. He heard enough of the phone call to understand what was going on and ran outside, where he jumped into his truck and drove off after the runaway child. He quickly caught up to her, and rolled down his window. "Hey, smilin' girl!" He yelled. "Where the heck are you going?"

"Home!" Emma gasped, still jogging through the snow. Her cheeks were already bright red with cold and exertion.

"Why?" Mr. Cory could see that the child was upset, and wondered what could have gotten her into such a state.

"Emergency!" Emma cried. "I have to get home!"

"Get in here," Mr. Cory commanded. "I'll drive you."

"But—"

"Right now, before you freeze!" He threw open the passenger side door.

An undeniable voice of authority had spoken.

Emma got in the truck, aided by the friendly custodian, who quickly turned the truck's heater to its highest setting and pulled the child close to his side to warm her up.

Despite Mr. Cory's efforts, Emma was shivering uncontrollably by the time they got to her house. Jill was out front, hastily loading the little ones into the station wagon, on her way to find her child. "I got her," Mr. Cory called out the window as Emma flung open the passenger side door and jumped out.

"Oh, thank you! Thank you!" Jill cried as Emma threw her arms around her.

"Please call the school and explain this nonsense," Mr. Cory chuckled.

"I will," Jill promised, and waved as Mr. Cory drove away. "Emma, what the hell?" she demanded, giving Emma a little shake. She snatched off her coat and wrapped it around her daughter. "Have you lost your mind? Do you want to get sick again?"

"Call Grandpa. Call him right now!" Emma was sobbing and breathless.

"I can't call Grandpa; he's at work!" Jill cried, exasperated.

"Mama, please, please!! Something's wrong with Grandma!"

"What? How could you possibly—?"

"Now, Mama, now, hurry up!!"

Jill stared into her panicked daughter's eyes and believed. "Bring the kids in," she said, and ran back into the house.

5.

Grandma Lange had suffered a heart attack.

Jill had called her cousin, who lived right up the street from the family home. Cousin Laura had gone straight to the house and found her Aunt Elvira passed out on the kitchen floor.

Just as she'd arrived, Jill was calling on the phone. Cousin Laura had picked up and said only "I'll call you back," before hanging up and dialing the operator for help.

By the time Jack got home from work, Jill had spoken to her cousin and her sister Tilda, and knew that her mother had been taken to the hospital. She didn't know much else, but over the next few hours she was able to get enough information to know that she should go home as soon as possible. It was serious.

Within the week, the family had returned to Idaho. Jack stayed for the weekend and then drove back to Wyoming for work. He hadn't been with his new company long enough to take time off; he would have lost his job.

Jill put Emma back into her old school. Unsure how long their stay would be, she preferred not to have her child fall behind.

Emma felt a little jealous of her cousins. Martin, Phillip and Jenny had always lived in California and went to school there, so their mother decided not to try sending them to a new school while they were in Idaho.

Cousin Suzi had come with Aunt Sheryl and Uncle Norton, but they had already gone back to Arkansas within the first week. Suzi was in Junior High School now, and couldn't miss too many classes; since her father had to go back to work, anyway, Aunt Sheryl decided they would do fine on their own.

At first Emma was excited to go back to her old school, but she ended up in a different classroom with none of her former classmates. No one from her old class seemed to recognize her at recess or during lunch hour, which Emma found strange; she remembered all of them! But they ignored her. Then, remembering the times she'd spoken with visitors, she supposed she shouldn't have been so surprised that no one acknowledged her now that she was back. She decided she shouldn't have found it strange; what else could she have expected?

She was weird, that was all. The weirdo is back; let's pretend we never knew her. That was how it seemed to her after a couple of days back in school.

For the next few weeks she wandered about the playground alone or with her second-cousin Doug—when he'd stoop to hanging around with a lowly first grader. Emma suspected that Cousin Laura, Doug's mother, made him do it; he didn't seem pleased about it, that was for sure. Probably he didn't want anyone to know he was related to the weirdo.

It occurred to her to blame her mother, but that lasted only a short time; Jill was very worried and very busy, and Emma could only feel sorry for her. She wanted to be mad at someone for making her go to school with kids who ignored her, but there was no one to be blamed.

She supposed she could blame the ghosts, but that was too silly to contemplate; they couldn't help it if they were dead! If they needed someone to talk to, how could she deny them? Probably they were just as lonely as she was—more, even; no one could even see them but her!

In the end, she could only take it all one day at a time, just like everyone else. It wasn't pleasant, but she supposed she was glad she had something to do.

Every morning Emma went to school while the others stayed at their grandparent's house. Aunt Rose, who was in High School, had to go, too, and wasn't any happier about it than Emma was. They were both worried about Grandma, and being in school all day was hard. But there was no help for it; the grown-ups said they had to go. Uncle Danny would drive them, at least. It was too far and too cold to walk.

Emma did her school work and tried to study hard; she loved to read, and loved to learn, but she was worried and scared, and the days seemed endless to her.

Things were more interesting at her grandmother's house. People were there all day, talking about the family, looking at pictures, doing chores.

Emma wanted to be there, too. It seemed quite unfair to her that all the other children were playing and having fun without her. It was hard not to feel resentful of them, but as with funerals and things like that, the parents made the decisions for their children, and all the children could do was accept it.

Oh, but she had her moments! There were a few times when she told her cousins they were missing out, having to stay home all day while she had fun at school.

It was doubtful they believed that, but it was her only defense against their taunts when she had to leave each morning.

Every afternoon one of Emma's aunts or uncles—usually Danny—would pick her up after school, and then everyone would meet at Leonard and Elvira's house for dinner and news updates.

It was really amazing how many people could fit in her grandparents' house, Emma thought. It didn't seem much bigger to her than the little box house they had in Wyoming, but there were a lot more people staying there. Grandma and Grandpa and Uncle Danny and Aunt Rose lived there all the time, but Emma knew that once upon a time, her mother, Uncle Ronnie, Aunt Tilda, Aunt Sondra and Aunt Sheryl had all lived there with them. And right now, they were all back, plus some of the spouses and all their children! Jill told the children that if they needed to make more room she would just have to hang them all by their shirt-collars on coat hooks. Emma thought that would be pretty uncomfortable, but part of her still wished Jill would really give it a try—it would look pretty funny!

6.

After the first few days of being there, Emma was thoroughly sick and tired of being asked how she knew that Grandma was in trouble.

It was hard to explain, for one thing. For another, it was hard for people to believe. There was no doubt at all as far as her mother and Cousin Laura were concerned, of course; they'd been deeply involved in events as they unfolded.

For the others, it was a little more complicated. They got phone calls after the fact, and it was crazy to think that had it not been for a panicked little girl insisting that her mother make a phone call, Elvira would surely no longer be with them.

"It was the Great-Grandmother," Emma explained, first patiently and later not so patiently. "She came to school while I was reading and told me Grandma was very sick and I had to tell Mama. So, I ran away from school, and then Mr. Cory came and gave me a ride, and Mama called on the phone and Grandma got tooken to the hospital."

"Taken," Jill corrected her.

"Grandma got *taken* to the hospital, I mean. Sorry, Mama."

"No need for sorry, honey."

Day after day, it never failed: someone always asked her what had happened, and Emma had to repeat her story.

It was tiresome.

People looked at her funny.

Her cousins thought she was weird, and spared no opportunity to tell her so. "I bet you made the whole thing up," eight-year-old Phillip accused her.

"I did not! You ask my Mama!" Emma argued tearfully.

"She'd just lie," ten-year-old Martin declared firmly. "Moms always lie to protect their big fat liar babies."

Emma burst into loud sobs and ran away, closely followed by Jenny, Martin and Phillip's younger sister. "Don't cry, Emma," she begged, patting her awkwardly. "I believe you."

"Why?" Emma demanded. "Have you seen the Great-Grandmother?"

"No," Jenny admitted. "But I believe in ghosts. I do! And Mommy says if you didn't make your mom call Cousin Laura, Grandma would have died right here in the house, all alone by herself!"

Melody appeared then, and sang, "Wash up for supper, wash your hands, it's time for supper in all the lands!"

"How do you do that, Melody?" Jenny demanded.

"Do what?"

"Make up songs like that?"

"I love singing, yes I do, I love to sing for Em and you!" Melody danced along as she sang, and Jenny clapped. Emma smiled, feeling better in spite of her cousins' mean words. "So, wash your hands and come and eat, cuz Grandpa's cooking can't be beat!" Melody bowed theatrically, turned on her heel and dashed away.

"How old is she?" Jenny asked, taking Emma's hand and leading the way to the bathroom.

"Five."

"Were we that smart when we were five?"

Emma laughed. "I don't think I'm that smart now," she admitted.

Jenny laughed, too. "Me, neither. But don't tell Mel that."
Emma nodded firmly. "Never," she agreed.

Jill and her sisters were all there, but when their father announced his intention to cook dinner, no one argued. He made the best Schäufele anyone had ever tasted, and served it with potatoes, gravy and sauerkraut. It was a family recipe for pork shoulder roast, passed down from his grandmother and great-grandmother and so on and so forth from Germany. No matter how they tried, Jill and her sisters were never able to make it as well as their father did, and their mother refused to even try. Elvira always said that competing with a man's mother in any way was never a good idea. Leonard said that was a great excuse for not trying to make it better than he did.

Jill and Tilda had busied themselves that afternoon making a few dozen bread rolls, while Sondra and Sheryl did salads and pies.

Sheryl was pregnant, the kitchen was small, and the sisters teased her about how much room she was taking up. Despite the crowded work area, the women completed their meal preparations before their father got home.

Leonard had made arrangements to get off work early, and went to work immediately on the delicious roast dinner.

By five o'clock Danny and Ronnie were setting up folding tables and chairs in the living room to accommodate the extra people. While they worked, they discussed Danny's deployment to Viet Nam.

"My C.O. was nice enough to delay things for me, but I have to fly out next week," Danny said.

"Are you going straight there?" Ronnie asked. "I ended up in Saigon, and never did go to Nam."

"I don't think I'm going to get that lucky," Danny replied. "But, no, my first stop is Fort Polk, Louisiana."

"At least it's not snowing there," Ronnie chuckled. "I trained there, too. In July. God, it was hot! You have no idea how lucky you are."

"So you say," Danny groaned. "But getting drafted can't be lucky, sir."

Ronnie pursed his lips. "No, sir," he agreed. "It certainly can't. I pray they don't send you to Nam."

"Yeah..."

The family listened solemnly as the young men talked. Service with pride was expected in this family, but Viet Nam was controversial; no one was happy with the draft. Too many boys were dying, and no one could understand why.

War is Hell.

Emma was seated at one of the folding tables with Melody, Dana, Jenny, Martin and Phillip. Matthew, now two years old, sat in a high chair next to Jill at the long dining room table. The children were served their food first, and then the adults took care of loading their own plates.

The dining room and living room were really just one long room, so the children were able to hear all the conversations going on around them. Emma ignored her cousins and sisters in favor of listening to the grown-ups, and the other children soon gave up trying to talk and listened to the adults as well.

The conversation began with discussions about Grandpa's wonderful Schäufele. The meat was so tender it melted in your mouth, and the gravy was rich and creamy. High praise was meted out by one and all, and Jill demanded to know the secret to such delicious sauerkraut.

Emma watched her youngest sister, who was shoving sauerkraut away from her other food, and wondered how anyone could find it delicious. Hers kept sneaking into her creamy mashed potatoes and gravy, and she tried moving it away a little less obviously than Dana was doing it. Melody seemed to be enjoying hers, however.

Next the topic turned to Grandma's condition. She was doing well, and was scheduled to be released within the week.

Emma smiled. She didn't care at all about how Grandma had gotten help in time, or her own part in that; she was getting well and coming home, and that was all that mattered.

She looked up, and the Great-Grandmother smiled down at her from her position just behind Martin. "I know it doesn't matter to you," the old woman said, "but your part in this does matter."

Emma shrugged. "Why?" she asked.

"You've got a lot to do. You've got a lot to learn."

"I do?"

"Who are you talking to, weirdo?" Martin demanded.

"You do," Great-Grandma said. "You'll understand someday."

"I hope so," Emma muttered.

"You hope so, what?" Phillip asked.

"Who are you talking to?" Martin and Phillip turned around to stare at the empty space behind them.

"Shut up, Marty!" Jenny cried. She couldn't see anyone there, either, but was unshakable in her faith that Emma could and did.

"She's a weirdo," Martin scoffed.

"Leave her alone!" Melody cried, as Emma stared down at her plate.

Jill left her place at the big table and came over to the children. "Is there a problem?"

"She's being weird," Phillip tattled.

Sondra joined Jill and stared menacingly down at her sons. "And just what is that to you?" she demanded. "Do you believe you're any less weird in your own ways?"

Martin raised his chin defiantly. "I don't talk to the walls!" he protested.

Emma glared at her cousin. "Neither do I!" she cried. "Maybe if you shut up once in a while and listened, someone would talk to you."

"Now, Emma," Jill chided.

"But, Mama, he—"

"Two wrongs don't make a right, Emma."

"But I didn't call *him* names!"

"Ah," Sondra said, "but *you* will still have dessert, and these two bullies will be going outside to sit on the porch and think about how delicious it is and how sorry they are that they were cruel and now they don't get any."

"Mom!" the boys chorused, and Jenny nudged Emma under the table, grinning with glee.

"Finish your dinner," Sondra commanded.

41

"You think you're so special!" Martin growled at Emma, and Grandpa stood up from his place at the table.

"Uh oh," Danny said. Ronnie raised his eyebrows knowingly.

They all knew it was over for Martin, and Phillip cringed back in his chair, uncertain whether he'd get caught in the crossfire.

Grandpa strode to the children's table and held out a hand to Martin. "You come with me, young man," he said.

Martin sighed heavily, already in tears, and rose to take his grandfather's hand.

"Oh, dear," Emma sighed, feeling guilty and sick at heart. She hadn't intended for anyone to get into trouble. She looked at the Great-Grandmother and said, "Why now?"

Phillip whirled around to stare at—nothing. He then glared accusingly at Emma, although he knew he was still under scrutiny by his mother and aunt.

The Great-Grandmother shook her head. "It's not always up to me, now or later; I come and go as I must. There are things you need to know. All must seek understanding."

"Understanding, ha!" Emma muttered. "I don't understand anything." She shook her head, and tears slid down her cheeks.

The Great-Grandmother sighed. "I know you don't, sweetheart," she said. "But you will. I promise you, love."

"Okay," Emma whispered, and wiped a tear from the corner of her eye.

The woman was gone.

The family was silent. Listening. Waiting.

There was no speaking for several minutes. Emma picked at her food, and Phillip cried quietly. Melody ate silently while Dana piled sauerkraut on the table next to her plate, no longer content just to move it aside. Jill and Sondra didn't move from their places; they hovered over the children's table.

Finally, Grandpa and Martin returned to the room. Grandpa looked stern and Martin was pale and thoughtful. He went to Emma and offered her his hand. "I'm sorry, Emma," he said. "I'm sorry for the cross you bear."

Emma took his hand, confused, and he shook it. "I don't—" she began, but Grandpa was there now, and put his hand on her head.

"Worry not," he said. "We'll talk after dinner."

"Okay," Emma agreed, more confused than ever.

"Everyone, eat!" Grandpa ordered. "I didn't slave over a hot stove for nothing, you know!"

After dessert—which was delicious, and was missed by Martin and Phillip, as ordered—Grandpa beckoned Emma away from the table. After donning coats and gloves, he took Emma by the hand and led her outside.

"Did you spank Marty?" Emma asked as they walked away from the main house.

"No, ma'am, I did not," Grandpa said. "I've never thought much of spanking children, actually. I don't think it teaches a child much, in most cases. Last resort, child. I believe that punishment cannot take the place of instruction. One must first know why a behavior is bad before one should be punished for that behavior; don't you agree?"

Emma thought that over, and then nodded.

"Of course, once a child knows why he is being bad and then chooses to be bad anyway? Well, then one must consider the paddle."

"Yeah," Emma agreed sagely.

"I simply spoke with him about what it means to respect another person's specialness. Someday, he will appreciate those who respect him for the things that make him special— and I'm sure there are many special things about young Martin."

Emma looked dubious, but admitted, "I almost fell off my chair when he said sorry."

"A heartfelt apology is a treasure, you know. Keep it in your heart; such a memory will do you good in the future."

Hand in hand, they walked to the old well and sat on the wooden bench beside it. It was old, but it was varnished and polished, and splinter free.

"My father built this bench," Grandpa said, patting the armrest. "He taught me everything I know about building furniture."

"Do I know him?" Emma asked.

"I don't know," Grandpa admitted. "You certainly never met him when he was alive, because he died many years before you were born."

"Really? When did he die?"

"1935. A very long time ago, when I was a young man."

"I don't get it."

"Oh, I believe you do." Grandpa patted her head again. "I believe you are very much like my father was, and that you have a burden to bear in this life much like the one he bore."

"Grandpa, what are you talking about?"

"Who told you that Grandma was in trouble?"

"The Great-Grandmother."

"Has she told you anything else?"

Emma sighed. "Yes," she admitted. "She told me I have a lot to do. She said we all must seek understanding."

Grandpa nodded. "And so, we must," he agreed.

"I *don't* understand!" Emma cried, frustrated. "I see her sometimes, just watching me, and then she's gone. She doesn't talk to me much. She never comes if I call. And Grandpa," Emma added desperately, "she's *dead*. I *know* she's dead, and that's why no one else ever sees her and that's why no one ever believes me!"

"I believe you," Grandpa reminded her gently. "Emma, your Grandma is alive. She's getting much better and will soon come home, and that's only because you are able to see her mother." He looked off into the fields, thinking. "It's a gift you've been given, child, but it's a difficult gift. There will be times you'll wish it had never come to you, but I promise you, there's a reason for it."

"I love Grandma," Emma said. "I'm so glad Great-Grandma told me about her. But, Grandpa…I'm scared."

"My father told me once that we have nothing to fear from the dead," Grandpa told her firmly. "I have never seen a spirit myself, but I saw my father speak to them a few times."

44

"Your father had visitors, too," Emma marveled. "And he wasn't scared?"

"Nope." Grandpa was quiet, thinking again, and then added, "Well, he was never scared of the dead. But I have to be truthful and tell you that he was sometimes scared by things he heard from the dead."

"Oh, great," Emma mumbled.

Grandpa smiled at her. "Emma," he said, "were you scared when your great-grandmother told you about Grandma?"

"Well, of course, I was, Grandpa!" She stared at him as if she thought he might be crazy.

"But it all turned out well, didn't it?"

"Well, yeah, but—"

"Sometimes being scared isn't a bad thing, Emmaline. Sometimes being scared is useful."

"Yeah, well sometimes I would rather be just a regular girl, Grandpa," Emma declared.

"I'm sure you would," Grandpa smiled. "And I'm sure this won't be the last time you say that."

It certainly wasn't the last time she said that, and even more often she thought it; but the gift was not going away.

However, after that family dinner, no one in her mother's family ever teased her or expressed disbelief in her abilities again.

7.

Martin had avoided a spanking *that* particular evening, but he and Phillip were normal little boys who could find mischief with no trouble at all. By the next afternoon, they were deep in it.

Jill had borrowed Grandma's car to pick Emma up from school. As they arrived back at the house, they noticed that several people were gathered at the foot of the big tree behind the house. Aunt Sondra was there, and Grandpa, and Uncle Danny; Jenny, Melody, Dana and Matthew, bundled in their winter wear, stood behind them; everyone was looking up.

Jill and Emma joined them and looked up as well. There, in the high branches, sat Martin and Phillip.

Oh boy. Climbing trees in the winter couldn't be a great idea, Emma thought.

Martin called, "In the days of old we all lived in the trees, like the apes!"

"So," Uncle Danny shot back, "like the monkeys you are, you've decided to return to the home of your ancestors?"

"Yeah," Phillip grinned.

"Get your butts down here right now," Danny barked. "It's dangerous up there; there's ice on the branches."

"Come on up and get us!" Martin challenged.

"If it comes down to that," Danny warned, "I'll be warming your backside as soon as you're on the ground. This is your last chance."

"Ah, fuck off, Uncle Dan," Martin scoffed.

There was a collective gasp among the onlookers. Grandpa's face turned bright red.

"Now, Dad," Sondra whispered frantically, "he's just expressing himself—"

"Expressing himself my Nana's fanny," Grandpa said.

"Kids go through a period of self-expression through profanity—" Sondra desperately grasped at straws, now.

"Oh, yeah?" Grandpa snapped. "Don't give me any of your fancy California philosophy nonsense; it's not gonna fly. Talk like that is plain disrespectful and unnecessary for 'self-expression'. You once tried the foul-mouth talk yourself—how did that work out for you, Missy?"

Sondra's face went pale. Her mouth dropped open and her eyes widened. Wisely, she did not speak again.

"You'll put a stop to that behavior, young woman, or I'll be paddling your backside along with your son's!" He'd spoken softly up to this point. Now he raised his voice. "If you boys are not back on the ground by the time I count to ten, you will be meeting with the board of correction within mere moments from now. I will climb this tree myself and beat you all the way down to the ground and continue to do so all the way back to the house. Do you understand me? One...two..."

Both boys had immediately begun to climb down the second Grandpa had raised his voice. They were on the ground before he got to three. Grandpa took Martin by the ear, gave his daughter a warning look, and marched the boy back toward the house. Sondra grabbed Phillip by the arm and followed meekly.

"Oooh," Jenny moaned. "Marty's really done it this time."

"I imagine he's going to be introduced to a bar of soap pretty quick now," Danny agreed.

"I can't believe Sondra tried to defend that language!" Jill cried.

"Californians," Danny scoffed derisively.

"Wow!" Emma gasped. "Is it okay to talk like that in California?"

"No!" Jill told her firmly. "It is not alright to talk like that anywhere!"

"Oh."

"And it's not alright to talk back to your elders, either."

"Danny's not elder," Melody argued. "He's 'Uncle'."

"I'm older than you are," Danny told her firmly. "That makes me your elder."

"So, I'm Jenny's and Melody's and Dana's and Mattie's elder!" Emma declared. "And they can't talk back to me!"

"That's not exactly—"

"Neat-o. I can be the boss!" Emma was jubilant.

"No, you can't," Jenny said. She looked worried. Emma could be bossy, anyway; she certainly didn't need any rules to back up her bossiness.

"Emma, that's not how it works," Danny said.

"I'm older," Emma declared haughtily. "I'm an elder, and that means it's not okay for them to argue with me."

"You're a child; it doesn't count."

"You said you were older—"

"I am a grown up!"

"But—"

"I am much older. That's how it works. An older grown up. Not an older child."

Emma thought this over, a look of stubborn determination on her face. Jill was struggling not to laugh; she could clearly

47

see Emma twisting things around in her mind to make it okay for her to be the boss of the younger children. Finally, Emma narrowed her eyes shrewdly and demanded, "How old is grown up?"

Now it was Danny's turn to think things over. He knew his niece well enough to know that she could find a way to turn the tables on him if he wasn't careful. Quickly he calculated appropriate ages in his head to make sure she wouldn't end up sassing her younger aunts and uncles. "If someone is old enough to babysit you," he said, "you have no business talking back to them."

"That's not very pacific," Emma frowned.

"Specific," Jill corrected.

"That's what I said."

"That may have been what you meant, but it is most certainly not what you said," Jill told her firmly.

Emma sighed dramatically. "Uncle Danny," she said, "that's not very specific." She had carefully drawn out the word, as if to make sure not only that her mother heard it clearly, but that she herself would remember it in the future.

"Here's specific for you," Danny said, imitating her drawn out enunciation. "Don't talk back to me, or any of your aunts and uncles. Don't talk back to anyone who is in a position of power, like a teacher or a babysitter or a grandparent."

"Or a parent!" Jill interjected.

"Right."

"Who can I talk back to, then?" Emma demanded.

"Marty and Phillip," Jenny said. "They might be older, but they're not elders—anymore than you are!"

"Yeah," Danny agreed. "But be prepared to run at all times."

"Danny!" Jill cried.

"He's right, Aunt Jill," Jenny told her glumly. "They're big meanies."

"Great," Emma groused.

"Get bent," Jenny told her. "We don't need you bossing us around!"

"Hmph!" Emma stomped her way back to the house, and the others followed.

"I think Sondra's in trouble, too," Jill told Danny. "Did you see the look on Daddy's face?"

"Oh, yeah," he agreed. "No matter how old we get, Dad's the boss around here."

"Because he's the oldest elder!" Emma called back over her shoulder.

"So true."

Once inside the house, soft sobs could be heard coming from the interior. They found the boys standing in opposite corners of the dining room, faces to the wall. Grandpa was sitting at the head of the table, scowling at Sondra, who was pale and glum-looking. Jill took one look and ordered the children to go play in the back bedroom.

Emma looked back at the grown-ups as she and the others quickly left the room, and decided that she was going to try very hard not to talk back to elders as old as Grandpa; she didn't ever want to have the same look on her face that Aunt Sondra did at that moment.

Crying with your face in the corner didn't look to be much fun either. It was probably best to keep your mouth shut.

8.

Grandma's condition continued to improve greatly; the military would brook no further delay due to family issues and by the following week, Danny had no choice but to get on an airplane and go to Fort Polk for basic training. Grandpa and Ronnie drove him to the airport, and they let Emma go with them; the flight was very early, and she could be dropped off at school on the way back.

"Mom threatened to have another heart attack last night," Danny said glumly. "She's worried I'll be sent to Viet Nam."

"Yes," Grandpa agreed. "We're all worried about that."

"There's nothing I can do about it," Danny declared. "And now I'm worried that she really will have another attack."

"Dan," Ronnie said, "Mom's doing great. She's going to be fine."

"She can't help being worried," Grandpa added. "It's part of being a parent."

"I don't want you to go, Uncle Danny!" Emma cried. She felt hot tears gather at the backs of her eyes. "I don't like wars. They're stupid!"

"I'll write you letters every week," Danny promised. "Then you'll know I'm okay." He didn't tell her that he, too, thought wars were stupid, nor did he admit that he really didn't want to go. There was no point in distressing her further.

Grandpa, Ronnie and Emma were allowed to walk with Danny to the tarmac and they watched him board the small plane he'd be taking to Salt Lake City. Once there he'd be boarding a bigger plane bound for Louisiana.

There was a lot of hugging, and Emma finally gave in to her tears; she loved her uncle and didn't want him to go away. She didn't bother to brush away the dampness on her cheeks as she watched him go up the steps and into the plane. Grandpa wiped her face with his handkerchief once the door was closed after the final boarding passenger. "It's cold," he remarked softly. "Don't want these to freeze on your cheeks, do we?"

"No, Grandpa," Emma agreed glumly.

Grandpa watched Emma carefully as the plane taxied down the runway and lifted into the sky. He was relieved when Emma stopped waving and took his hand. She was clearly sad, but she'd shown no signs of fear; Danny's flight would be a safe one, Grandpa was sure.

He'd worry about Viet Nam later, he decided, and hoped it wouldn't come to that.

Chapter Three

An Interlude

1984

"Did it?" Jacob asked.

Emma was startled out of her reminiscences. "What?"

"Did it come to that?" Jacob elaborated. "Did your uncle go to Viet Nam?"

"Oh!" Emma nodded. "Yeah. He did." Emma shook her head. "He kept his promise, you know. At least at first, he did.

"Every week, I got a letter. So did Mom. They were short and to the point: he was fine, the food was good, and basic training was a pain in the neck.

"Danny was a good shot; he'd been hunting since he was a little boy. Once he got through basic, he ended up in infantry training."

"Oh," Jacob said. "Oh, crap!"

"Yeah. They made it sound like a good thing, but really...I later told him that he should have pretended to be a rotten shot.

"But, you know, Uncle Dan was never one to do anything less than his best." Emma sighed.

Jacob looked worried. "Was he—? I mean, is he—okay?"

Emma looked surprised. "Oh, yeah!" She nodded vigorously. "Yeah, he's alive and well. Look, I'll tell you his story, but...well..."

"Yeah, back to Idaho for now," Jacob agreed. "One story at a time."

"Right. Anyway," Emma said, "it was time for us to go home."

Chapter Four

Train Ride

1967

Once Grandma was well enough to come home, Tilda had arranged to stay at the house and help Grandpa get her settled. Tilda was a single woman with no children, and she lived just one town over, so it was easiest for her to stay for a while. She had continued working all through Grandma's confinement, mostly coming over to help in the evenings and on weekends, thus saving her vacation time until Grandma would need her at home.

Sondra and her children, Martin, Phillip and Jenny, were going home to California on an airplane. Aunt Sheryl was going back to Arkansas the same way.

Emma's family lived closest to Idaho, but there were no planes flying to Wyoming. Jill could never have been persuaded to fly at any rate; the very thought gave her the heebie-jeebies. Emma was disappointed, though. Since watching her uncle's plane rise into the sky she'd been hoping to fly on a plane herself. But that was not to be.

Jack had planned to drive and get them; it would take a while but was by far the most economical way to travel. But that was not to be, either. The wintery weather in Wyoming was harsh, the roads were icy and treacherous, and he decided it would be safer for his family to come home on a train.

Grandpa drove the family to the train depot early one morning and showed them all around. Grandpa had been a train engineer for many years, but now he worked in an office and was getting close to retirement.

Emma and Melody were very excited about riding a train, and Grandpa boarded with them and showed them the car they'd be riding in. "You have your own table and benches right here," he said, while the conductor smiled at them all and took their tickets. "And there's a bathroom right here, because the train doesn't stop for potty breaks." Emma and Melody giggled, while Dana just stared at him solemnly.

Jill laid Matthew, who was sleeping soundly, on the seat next to Emma and hugged her father. "Take good care," she whispered fiercely.

"I'm not worried a bit," Grandpa told her. "Emma will know if there's trouble."

Grandpa hugged all the children and kissed the baby. "You let me know what's up," he told Emma seriously.

"I will, Grandpa," Emma promised.

Then Grandpa was gone, and a lot of strangers were filing in and getting seated all around them. Soon the train car was very full, but Jill and the children were quite content sitting at their table on benches that reminded Emma of restaurant booths.

Emma and Melody went to the bathroom, marveling that they could walk around while the train was moving. They turned around on their seats and watched the world go by outside the big windows. It was snowing hard, but they could see hills and rocks and the occasional tree. There were a few stops, but they didn't get off the train.

"This is long," Dana complained after a while. "Are we there yet?"

"Not yet," Jill told her. She was unpacking a grocery bag that she and Tilda had filled with sandwiches, chips, pickles, boiled eggs and cookies.

"We're eating on a train," Melody sang, and bit into her sandwich.

"I want to be there now," Dana whined.

"Well, that's just too bad," Jill told her firmly. "We'll be there when we get there. Eat your sandwich."

"But I—"

"Now."

Dana poked out her lower lip and grunted a sigh, but she took the sandwich her mother offered her and said no more.

Jill poured milk from a thermos into paper cups, taking care not to fill them too full.

The children ate, drank their milk and watched the snow fall. Matthew got grumpy, and Emma walked him up and down the aisle a few times, so he could "burn some energy", as Jill said. A lot of the other passengers made a fuss over him, because he was a pretty cute little guy, and all the attention cheered him up.

Dana, on the other hand, remained grumpy and out of sorts, so Jill made her lie down. She fell asleep almost instantly, and Emma was glad. If she had whined one more time, she might have slapped her.

Emma wasn't perfect. She could be a mean big sister sometimes. She wasn't proud of it, but there it was.

Emma and Melody sat across from Jill, Mel leaning on Emma and singing to her doll. Emma was trying to read a book Aunt Rose had given her, but she was distracted by the man standing in the aisle watching her.

Finally, she looked directly at him and said, "Can I help you?"

The man looked surprised. "Who, me?"

"Yes, you," Emma snapped. "Why are you staring at me?"

"You can see me?" He was incredulous. "I had hoped you would, but..."

Sometimes the ghosts she saw appeared absolutely solid, as if you could touch and feel them; sometimes their clothing was close enough to modern that you didn't notice the difference right away. Sometimes she was fooled for a short time into thinking they were alive. She'd been fooled this time up until the time when he declared his surprise that she could see him.

"Of course, I can see you," Emma replied impatiently. "Why are you here?"

"I was just wondering if you knew..."

"Knew what?"

People were watching her now, as she appeared to be talking to herself, but Emma was oblivious.

Jill watched her too and listened closely.

Melody just kept singing softly to her doll. This was nothing new to her; just her sister, talking to a visitor. It didn't matter a bit that Melody couldn't see anyone; if Emma was talking, it was a visitor; Melody had never doubted it.

"We made this trip before, a long time ago," the man said.

"We did? I don't remember that." Emma stared at him, wondering who he was—or rather, who he used to be. "I don't remember you."

Emma didn't think she'd ever visited with this man before; she was sure she'd never been on a train trip before—surely her mother would have mentioned that!

"Oh, not we, you and me," the man chuckled. "We, your great-great-great uncle and me."

"Ah." Emma nodded. "Sit," she invited, gesturing. "Tell me."

The man, who appeared to be growing younger right before her eyes, sat cross-legged in the aisle, and put his hands—big hands—on his knees. Emma turned to face him fully. She didn't think for a moment that he would disappoint her; he'd been on a train before, and with a member of her family, and he would tell her about it; she would give him her full attention.

He deserved nothing less.

He told Emma quite an exciting story, while all around them the other passengers blatantly stared at the little girl who sat, obviously rapt, and appearing to stare at nothing but the aisle floor; they wondered what on earth had so captured her interest.

It was the sort of attention Emma would draw all her life, like it or not, and even at the age of six, she mostly ignored it.

1.

A Shepherd's Tale

"I used to work for your great-great-granddad and his brothers," the man told Emma.

"What's your name?" Emma asked.

"Willie Murphy. Wanna hear a story?"

"Yes, please." Emma settled herself at the end of her seat, and Melody rested her back against Emma's, still singing to her doll.

Jill rocked Matthew, leaning his body on the table top to ease her aching arms, and watched her daughter, but after that first exchange there was nothing more for her to hear; Emma listened attentively to whoever was speaking to her and didn't interrupt.

"I'm going to tell you a story, and every word is true," Willie Murphy said, smiling.

"Once upon a time, in the days before you were born, or your Mama was born or even your Grandma was born, your Grandma's Daddy was just a little boy named Craig whose own Daddy, Cary, was a mill owner. Do you know who your Grandma's Daddy Craig is?"

Emma nodded. She knew the Great-Grandfather very well, especially after spending all this time with the whole family in Idaho.

"Well, good for you! Yep, he's your great-granddad who loves you very much and is so happy that you helped save his daughter! But this story isn't really about him, and it's not really about your great-great granddad Cary, either. I just told you about them because I wanted you to know who your great-great-great uncle Joel was.

"Joel was your great-great-granddad's brother. He was one of the first white babies born in Idaho back when it was still just a wild territory, full of Indians. He became a sheep rancher when he grew up, and I worked with him.

"Sometimes, when things were less busy, I would work for his brother Cary in the mill, too. I had a lot of kids to feed in those days, so I worked as much as I could."

"In the fall of 1904—"

Emma gave a little start at that. 1904! That was forever ago!

"—Joel and I and another of his hands, Mike Gilligan, herded a hundred head of sheep into the pens and loaded them up for market in Chicago. We took the train, just like you're doing right now, but the train car we rode in wasn't as fancy as this one! Oh, no. We had wooden benches to sit on, and had to go to the dining car if we wanted to sit at a table.

"We went to Chicago and sold all those sheep. Joel negotiated a good price for them, and we were feeling pretty happy with ourselves; we knew our families would be fed all winter! To celebrate, we went to a fancy city restaurant and had us a good, hot meal, with beef and potatoes and vegetables. We were given lots of fresh, warm bread and sweet butter, and then we had pie for dessert! We slept in a nice hotel that night. Chicago was quite a change for us; a real city! We didn't have anything so fancy and nice at home. It was all ranches and farm land there.

"Now, Joel and Mike and I, we all had good wives and children at home, and it was November. We had planned to go on from Chicago to the World's Fair in Saint Louis, Missouri, as we had heard a great many wonderful stories about the goings-on there. The fair was going to close at the end of the month, and we'd never have the chance to go again. It was a hard decision, but in the end, we were worried about bad weather and our families, and decided it was best to go straight home.

"Emma...we should have gone to the fair!" Willie shook his head ruefully and pursed his lips before continuing his story.

Emma waited nervously.

"We boarded our train in Chicago, and due to an increase in wealth—because we successfully sold all the sheep—we were able to book seats in a nicer car than the one we'd come in. We were quite comfortable—until the time of the crash."

Emma gasped, her eyes wide.

Jill felt a pang of envy and hoped Emma would remember everything when it came time to share. It was frustrating to know that there was actually someone talking to her daughter and to be unable to see and hear them, too.

"It was near midnight, I was told," Willie continued. "We were all asleep. I was on one side of the aisle, Joel and Mike on the other.

"I'm certain neither of them ever knew what happened—it was so fast, and they were sleeping soundly. I know that for sure, because I was reading a very clever story by Mr. Mark Twain and so, I was still awake when my companions retired.

"Joel was sitting by the window, with Mike next to him. I was across the aisle from Mike, next to a rather portly man who snored outrageously, so it was fortunate that I had entertainment to keep me occupied until I dozed off myself.

"Next thing I knew, I was flung off my seat and tossed about until I found myself on the floor with people and debris piled on top of me. I struggled my way out of enough of it to breathe, but I couldn't see much.

"Then the fires started, and my first sight of anything was that of Joel's head."

Emma bit her lip. Willie paused in his story-telling for several seconds. Then he said, "I shan't describe to you the sight of my friends or any of the other passengers. You're just a little girl, after all..."

Emma nodded gratefully. Her imagination was enough; she didn't care to hear the details.

"Anyway, I'm sure you know well enough that my friends did not survive the accident. It was quite tragic: a freight train had hit us head on. I found out later that it was a scheduling error. A scheduling error! There was an investigation, of course. It could have been avoided, if anyone had bothered to compare notes. Schedules change hands a lot in the course of a day, child. When work shifts changed, someone didn't read the past worker's notes carefully, and a track route that should have been switched didn't get done on time. It was a matter of twenty minutes, all told, and those minutes made all the difference."

"How would they do that?" Emma asked, frowning. "Change routes?"

The little audience around her came to attention, but Emma was quiet again.

"When the tracks were built, there were places where they could switch from one track to another, so trains could pass each other going in opposite directions. If the switch wasn't thrown, the train would continue running on the same track, and the train that was supposed to pass on the other side would be coming straight at it.

"No one switched the track for the freighter that was supposed to pass us on the other side. That's why it was still on the same track we were on. That's why it hit us.

"And it happened because someone didn't do his job properly." Willy shrugged. "That's how accidents happen."

Emma was silent for some time, thinking about it. She could see the train tracks in her imagination, and picture the place where a switch could be made to another track. She could also picture the crash that would happen if the switch wasn't made. She winced, and her lips tightened.

Willie sat looking at her. Finally, she brushed away a single tear and breathed, "Wow."

Jill sat up straighter, listening. So did many of the passengers around the family, but Emma didn't notice.

"Indeed," Willie agreed, nodding.

"But you didn't die."

"No, I didn't die; not then. Not for many more years. I was taken to a hospital in Sweetwater County with a broken leg and a broken arm. I spent a good long time there; they took good care of me, but in those days, broken bones were very serious, and I was plenty sick with an infection. By the time I was able to go home, Joel and Mike had already been buried."

"You missed the funerals?"

"I sure did. I needed to get back to work, though, so I went home."

"Where? Idaho?"

"Well, Joel's sheep ranch was further south, near the northern border of Utah. We weren't far from Idaho; I was able to go back and forth to work in both places—the ranch in Utah and Joel's brother's mill in Idaho. I did that a lot. I had a lot of kids to feed." Willie stood up and brushed off the seat of his pants, as if he could actually get dirty.

"But what about you? What happened to you?" Emma cried, alarmed that he might be going before finishing his story.

"Oh, me? I still had the money from the sale of the sheep— the police came to my hospital room and gave me Joel's satchel, because my name was on a lot of the paperwork inside. I don't know why they didn't send it on with his body, but I was grateful; the money could have 'disappeared' along the way."

Emma opened her mouth to ask what he meant, but he raised a finger at her and she closed it. "Honesty is the best policy, Emma, always, but even so, not everyone is honest. Thank God, the policeman who brought me Joel's satchel was an honest man. God bless the honest among us!

"All the money was there; I offered a reward to the policeman, but he refused to take more than a smile and a handshake! When I was able to leave the hospital, my first stop was Utah, where I gave the money to Joel's wife. She made sure my family was well taken care of for the rest of the winter by paying me generously, and I went back to Idaho to my wife and children. After that I only worked in the mill with your Great-great Granddad Cary; after breaking my bones, I didn't do well with sheep herding anymore. And so, we all lived happily ever after.

"Or something like that."

"But—"

"No, Emma, look…this story was not about me. This story was about Joel. Joel is finished, and now, so am I." Willie winked at her. "Be a good girl."

And he was gone.

"Well, dang!" Emma said.

3.

Jill took notes as Emma recounted what she recalled of the story, and many of their fellow passengers leaned closer to the family to hear the tale.

Emma ignored them; it was no news to her that many of them would scoff and say that she was just making everything up. True, they would praise her for her great imagination; she'd heard that many times already, and she was only six! But most of them would simply refuse to believe that someone had actually been in their midst, recalling a train trip and its tragic conclusion.

Emma was a child, one who still had not completed the first grade, and so she was not entirely familiar with the concept of counties and border lines. To her credit, she remembered the World's Fair was in Iowa; she was able to verify that later, in fact. She remembered that the sheep were sold in Chicago, because it was described to her as a real city, and she could imagine the fancy restaurant and hotel.

She also remembered Idaho and Utah, where Willie lived and worked.

But the name Sweetwater County was unfamiliar to her, although she'd been living there for a little while. She knew the names of towns and states, but the county name, if she'd hear it at all, had quickly slipped her mind.

It would be years before she recognized that the train crash had actually occurred in Wyoming.

Chapter Five

Research & Discovery

1984

Jacob took a few moments to absorb it all. "Hmm," he said. "So, not everyone who talks to you is family."

"No," Emma agreed. "But everyone who talks to me wants to talk about my family. Only my family."

"They don't talk about anything else?"

"Not if they can help it. They take a..." Emma sighed deeply. "What would you call it? A supporting role, I guess. And it can be so frustrating, because I want to know their stories, too."

"What do they want?"

Emma shook her head. "It's been twenty years," she said, "and I still haven't really figured that out."

"Do you want to?"

"Of course, I do!" Emma gave him a little shove. "When I was four years old my Great-grandmother told me she was there so I would understand. So I could explain." She sighed, and tried to push her fingers through heavily sprayed hair. They got stuck. "Ugh!"

Jacob chuckled.

"Shut it!" Emma glared at him, disentangling her fingers from her hair.

"What a difference a new decade makes," Jacob remarked. "I miss Marsha Brady." He sighed dramatically. "Long and straight and silky," he reminisced, and Emma poked her tongue out at him, making him chuckle.

"Good grief." Emma rubbed her fingers, looking disgusted. "Hair spray is icky!"

The 1980s, decade of the big hair look; curled and teased and sprayed, big hair was all the rage, but Emma decided she missed Marsha Brady, too.

"Anyway," Jacob drawled. "Go on. What are you supposed to explain?"

"Sometimes it seems like all I ever do is explain," Emma groaned. She was rubbing her hands absently on the legs of her jeans. "But it's never-ending. New stories, old stories. Some told by the dead; lots more told by the living. You know, I take vacations and go to the libraries to look through old news stories."

"Really?" Jacob sat up straighter and leaned toward her. "Did you find the train wreck?"

"Oh, God," she groaned. "That story was hard to find. Which was just dumb, considering the best news article I finally found was under my nose the whole time."

"Huh?"

"I was six, remember. My biggest clue, which I missed, was that Willie went to a hospital in Sweetwater County. But I was looking for stuff in Utah and Idaho, during the very little bit of time I could get when we visited relatives or something."

"What the—?"

"He died here, Jake. In Sweetwater County."

"And you found the story—?"

"Last winter during Christmas break, when I came home from school."

"How did you remember the clue?"

"I didn't." Emma admitted, and shook her head ruefully. "I had to be told."

1.

Christmas Eve, 1983

Emma yawned and stretched. She'd had a long trip in from Denver, where she was finishing her final year of college, and now the family had stayed up late, sharing memories and catching up on each other's lives.

"I gotta go to bed," Emma groaned.

"You?" Matthew cried. "Since when are you the first in bed?"

"Since I was probably the first one up," Emma declared.

63

"You didn't get here until noon," Jack laughed. "Denver's not that far. Even if you got up at six and ran straight out the door, I was the first one up!"

"Busted!" Dana laughed.

"Okay, okay," Emma conceded. "No one gets up earlier than Dad. Noted. But," she added, "I'll bet he went to bed a whole lot earlier than I did, so he got the most sleep!"

"Busted, Dad," Dana cried.

Jack grinned. "Maybe so, but Emma can handle it." He laughed. "She never sleeps, anyway."

"Emma shouldn't have waited until the last minute to come home, anyway." Jill added.

"Last minute?" Emma protested. "I—"

"You've been out of school for a week!" Jill scolded.

"Four days," Emma argued. "Out of school, but not out of homework! Mom, I love the new library—"

"It's haunted!" Fred interjected.

"—at least as well as I can, since it's not really my library. But it's not as well-stocked as the one in Denver, and I have to finish the research for my final."

"Another thing you waited until the last minute for?" Jill asked cryptically.

Emma ignored her, and asked her little brother, "What do you mean, the library is haunted?"

Fred, the youngest child of the clan, had joined the family nearly eleven years before, in the winter of 1973. He looked pleased with himself as he told Emma, "It's true! You know they built it over an old graveyard."

"Yes, but they reinterred the bodies that were there in the new cemetery years ago," Emma argued. "Long before they decided to get rid of my library and build a new one." She frowned, clearly displeased.

"They didn't find them all," Fred informed her. "They found—what—six graves, Mom?"

"Six," Jill confirmed.

"Six bodies this year, when they put in the new landscaping." Now Fred was positively gloating.

"What?" Emma demanded. "How have I not heard about this?" She glared at her family members accusingly.

"You don't live here," Fred explained. "You left us!"

"And you couldn't be bothered to write me a letter about such a juicy story? Jeez, Freddie!"

"Can we go there while you're here?" Fred was completely unapologetic. He didn't write letters! What was she thinking?

"Are you kidding me? I'd go right now if it wasn't midnight on Christmas Eve."

"Maybe someone will talk to you!" Of all her siblings, Fred was the one most interested in the possibilities presented in communication with the dead.

"Don't count on it. We're not from here, so no one in our family could be there."

Fred pouted for a minute, and then grinned. "So, what?" he demanded. "They visit you all the time; and none of them are from here."

Emma nodded thoughtfully. "That's true," she agreed. "But I'd assume that anyone haunting the new library would be someone who had lived and died in the area. No one in our family ever lived and died around here. And I never ran across any ghosts in *my* library."

"You need to quit fussing about *your* library, Em," Matthew teased.

"Like heck," Emma groused. "I leave town for a little while, and when I come back, my library is an office building, my church is gone—who do these people think they are, making all these changes without even asking what everyone thinks?"

"People were asked." Jack said. "That's what city council meetings are all about."

"But I wasn't even here!"

Matthew chuckled. "You're just one little person," he reminded his sister. "I doubt you could have changed their minds."

"Yeah, well, I'd like to talk to some of those council people and ask them what they were thinking. Clearly the building was fine, or they would have torn it down! But no, they just turned it into an office. That's a crap move."

Jack yawned. "Well, you go on and talk to whoever you want, my dear," he said. "The only one I want to talk to right now is the Sandman. Sorry, folks, I'm out."

Jill looked at her watch. "Good God, it really is midnight!" she cried. Turning to Fred, she added, "How many times can Santa circle the town before he gives up on little boys who don't go to bed at a decent hour?"

Fred jumped to his feet. "Oh, my heck!" he cried. "I'm going, I'm going!" And he raced out the room. Jack followed, moving at a more sedate pace.

Emma laughed. "I don't want Santa to miss me, either," she said. "Will Mel be here tomorrow?"

Jill said, "She says she will. I don't know what time, though."

"She's so busy!" Dana said. She stood up, clutched the small of her back with both hands and groaned. "Ugh, I sat too long!" she cried, pushing her swollen belly even further out in front of her. "I have to get home. Tom's going to wake up and wonder where the heck his wife's gotten to."

"He'll just think you ran out for more Snickers bars," Matthew chuckled.

Dana laughed. "Shut up, you, and walk me to my car."

Matthew jumped up and went to fetch their coats.

"Mel's gig was in Casper tonight?" Emma asked Jill.

"Yeah. I'm glad it decided not to snow."

"No snow until she gets here," Emma agreed, although a snowless Christmas did seem odd.

"I'm going to check on Fred," Jill announced.

"I'm going to bed. It's time for me to go to sleep! Goodnight, Mom. Goodnight Dana. Goodnight, Matt."

Emma headed for the stairs, trotted down to the basement and shut herself into her old bedroom.

Where someone was waiting for her.

2.

"Okay, I guess it's not time for me to go to sleep," Emma said. "Hello."

"Hi." Emma's guest was an attractive woman, her brown hair artfully done with a thick braid woven in a halo around her head. Her blue eyes sparkled behind round wire rimmed

66

glasses. She was dressed in a simple dress that seemed to be almost military in style, possibly from the 1940's.

"Can I help you with something?"

"Me?" The woman smiled, amused. "I don't need any help, thank you. I've come to lend *you* a hand, however."

"Oh?" Emma smiled. "Well, great! I'll take all the help I can get. Who are you?"

"I'm Annie. Joel's daughter."

"Joel? My great-great-great Uncle Joel?"

Annie smiled. "The very same," she said. "I'm fairly new to all this," she added apologetically. "I hope you'll understand what I've come to tell you."

"You're...new?" Emma frowned. "What do you mean?"

"I—er...evolved—how's that for a word?" Annie giggled. "Yeah, evolved, I *like* that! — in 1978. How long ago was that?"

"Five years."

"Compared to however many? Yes! I am new."

"Yes," Emma agreed. "Maybe the newest I've ever talked to, except my great-grandmother. She came just days after, uh...evolving."

"Of course," Annie smiled. "That was a special circumstance, I believe. She was chosen."

"Chosen?"

"It's best for initiates to be instructed by someone they know."

"Uh...huh." Emma frowned. "So, she got to come to me...the initiate...because I knew her when she was alive?"

"Yes."

"Well, that was thoughtful of...of *some*one. I guess."

Annie smiled, but didn't agree or disagree. Instead, she said, "I have to make a confession: I've chosen to appear to you as a younger woman; why wouldn't I? I was over eighty when I passed."

"When I go," Emma laughed, "I will never appear over thirty."

So, despite having her interest piqued, they were going to talk about age? Well, that was fine. If there was to be no further discussion of initiates and familiar great-grandmothers, what could she do about it, anyway?

"You'd be surprised," Annie told her, "how many women actually peak in beauty in their fifties." She preened a little and gave a half-curtsy.

"You're not fifty!" Emma cried. "Wait—you're fifty? This is how you looked at fifty?"

"Why, yes, indeed!" Annie laughed. "Ah, I felt beautiful in the 1940's. My children were grown—I had grandchildren by then—and I had more time than I'd ever had to style my hair and sew clothes for myself. My husband Albert and I fell in love all over again." She sighed happily, a lovely smile lighting her face.

"That's wonderful!" Emma sat down on the bed and patted the space next to her. Annie sat with her. "I hope you had many happy years together."

"Oh, yes, many years!" Annie beamed. "Almost sixty! We were very lucky, Emmaline. Not like my parents."

"And that's who you're here to talk about, right?"

"Yes, indeed!" Annie smiled and patted Emma's hand.

Emma could see and appreciate the gesture, but felt nothing. That was one of the most disappointing things about her gift; an ability to touch would have been wonderful. There had been many a visitor over the years she would have liked to hug.

"I know everything that Willie Murphy told me years ago was true," Emma said. "There's no reason anyone would come to me and tell me lies; it doesn't work that way! I don't know what it is that's been driving me to find proof."

"I do." Annie looked at her thoughtfully. "You're a very intelligent woman, Emma. You've always been intelligent and intuitive. Even without your gift, you understand that you're quite capable of constructing tales, and you worry about it. You want tangible evidence, to prove to yourself that the things you learn from your family are real—not some stories you've made up for your own amusement."

Emma stared at her, astounded. "Well...we all have our 'what-if?' moments," she agreed, cautiously.

Annie laughed. "What six-year-old child concocts a "what-if" involving their grandmother's heart attack, or a train crash involving a three times great uncle she probably never heard of?"

"I don't know," Emma admitted. "But I do know I have quite an imagination! And you can believe me when I tell you that it has often gotten me in trouble!"

"Well, I raised seven children and they made up a lot of stories, but nothing like that!" Annie laughed.

"It has never been about what I believe or don't believe, anyway," Emma admitted. "And I know my family believes me..."

"Do you really know that, or do you just hope so?" Annie asked. What a remarkably forthright woman!

"I could talk to you all night," Emma remarked. She really liked her fourth cousin. "Yeah, I suppose I mostly hope they believe. I guess that's why I spend so much time searching for facts to back things up. I go on wild goose chases sometimes!"

"You won't have to do that this time," Annie said. "I'm here now to point you in the right direction."

"What do you mean?"

"I know you've been searching for something. A medical record or a death certificate; tangible evidence. Facts, as you said. But you're searching in the wrong places. My father didn't die in Utah or Idaho, Emma. He died here."

"What?" Emma gaped at her cousin. "What do you mean, here?"

"Sweetwater County, Wyoming. This is where the two trains collided. Not right here in town, but very nearby. My father died on impact. His injuries were horrific, apparently."

"Oh! I'm so sorry!" Emma gasped.

"Thank you." Annie smiled wanly, and then shrugged. "It was so long ago," she said. "But the accident was horrible; it would have made local news for sure. You should check out newspaper articles from around here."

"Wow! Thank you! I will!" The trip to the library with Fred was a sure thing, now. "Can you tell me anything about what happened?"

69

Annie shook her head sadly. "It was a terrible time for us," she said. "My mother was in shock. I don't know if you knew this, but Father was supposed to go to Saint Louis and visit the World's Fair. He'd been talking about it for weeks."

'Willie mentioned that. I remember that."

"Willie Murphy. Yes, he came to see us many weeks later. He'd been pretty banged up. He brought my mother money and told her that they decided not to go to the fair because they worried about their wives and children. I recall there had been talk about bad weather coming, but I don't remember if it ever actually happened."

"How old were you?"

"I was eleven."

"I'm so sorry."

"Well, I get to see him now, and that is a blessing."

"You do? Why didn't he come and talk to me?"

Annie laughed. "What could he have told you? He missed the whole thing, Emma!" she said. "Slept right through it, and then he was gone."

Emma stared at her cousin, mouth agape. Of course, he wouldn't know. Only Willie was there in the aftermath; that's why he could come and tell the story. Annie was there with her mother when Willie came and told them what had happened, so she could also pass on what she knew.

"Where was your father buried?" Emma asked. "Willie just said Utah."

"There's a family plot in Weber County, Utah."

"Are you there, too?"

"Oh, no. I was buried with my husband in Davis County. Also, in Utah."

"I have a lot of work to do." Emma was feeling a little overwhelmed.

"May I make a suggestion?

"Sure."

"I know you have been raised Catholic. I'm sure I don't know how that happened; we didn't even know any Catholics when I was growing up!"

"Both my parents were raised Catholic," Emma said. "I think my dad is a Mexican-Irish hybrid, or something. I don't know about my mother."

"I was raised a Latter-Day Saint, like everyone else I knew," Annie told her. "Much of your mother's family came to this country with the Mormon immigrants."

"They did?" Emma was astonished; she'd never heard of such a thing!

Annie grinned. "They did. And you'll discover much of that history for yourself at some time, because you won't be able to stop yourself from researching it."

"Sure, I will," Emma boasted. "I can stop researching anytime I want."

The two women looked at each other and burst out laughing. They both knew Emma would be like a dog with a bone, now that she had new information to investigate.

Annie studied Emma thoughtfully for a moment, and said, "You know, Emma, I've long since come to a conclusion regarding churches."

"You have? What's that?"

"God doesn't care. That's what I believe now. As long as you love Him, He's impartial to denominations. But..."

"But?"

"You *do* have friends who are members of the LDS faith, don't you? Mormons?"

"A lot of them, actually."

"You might want to visit with them. The Church does a lot of historical research. You'd find it interesting, I'm sure. I know I did."

"You did historical research?"

"I only did enough to build a family tree for my children. But it was fascinating. You should try it."

"I'll do that," Emma promised.

"Love and hugs to you, Emma." Annie smiled.

And she was gone.

Emma gaped at the empty space beside her. "Well, dang!" she cried.

3.

1984

"So, after Christmas I took Freddie to the library, and asked about seeing old newspaper articles while he went 'ghost hunting'," Emma concluded.

"Ghost hunting, huh? Did he have any luck?"

"Oh, the library is...uh..." Emma looked skyward and shrugged expansively. "Well, it is haunted."

"Really?" Jacob looked astonished. "Did you see anyone?"

Emma shook her head. "I never have, but lots of people tell stories. And..."

"And?"

Emma studied him quizzically. "Have you been there?"

"No, not yet."

"You'll have to go there. You can...feel it," she told him. "It's a feeling; I can't explain."

"And they have old newspapers there?" Jacob asked. "Like, 1904 stuff?"

"Well, not the actual papers, of course. But they do have microfilm all the way back to the 1890s."

"You're kidding." Jacob was surprised that a small-town library might have an extensive archive.

"Why would I kid? There aren't copies of every paper published back then, but it's amazing how many there are."

"The paper barely has any news now," Jacob declared, somewhat contemptuously. "What on earth did they have to report back then?"

"Believe it or not, Sweetwater County was a pretty exciting place back in the day."

Jacob, who came from New Jersey, gave that a few minutes of thought. "I guess I can believe it," he admitted. "I've seen westerns. Cowboys, Indians, train robbers—"

"Railroad construction, ghost towns, no lawmen around for miles and miles—"

"Oh! I have heard about the old coal mines—"

"—and the Chinese miners who were murdered? Have you heard those stories?"

"What? No! I guess I *do* need to go to the library."

Emma grinned. "It couldn't hurt."

Jacob shook his head. He'd been properly schooled; even small towns had their stories. "Well, anyway," he said, "what did you find?"

"Hang on." Emma jumped up and left the room.

When she came back, she was holding a notebook. She sat down and thumbed through the pages; handwritten notes on loose-leaf paper, computer print-outs, photographs in sleeves. Jacob longed to get ahold of it and spend some time just reading.

"Here it is," Emma said, and handed Jacob the open notebook.

Jacob took it and looked at the print-out of a scanned newspaper page. "'Terrible wreck near Granger'," he read aloud. "The Pacific Express number three and an east bound fruit special, both running at full speed, collided head on, causing one of the most disastrous wrecks in the history of Wyoming." He looked up. "I'm paraphrasing," he admitted.

"I know." Emma grinned. "I've read it a hundred times, at least!"

Jacob continued reading. "Well, here's your third-great uncle, one of twelve dead. Here's Willie Murphy among the injured…Mike Gilligan…jeez, this was awful!"

"Look at the next article," Emma said. "I found it much later, in a library in Salt Lake City."

"'Only Utah victim of train disaster laid to rest'," Jacob read. "Oh, man. Both arms, both legs and face badly crushed, neck broken. His brother claimed the body and took it home for burial…" Jacob's expression was sober. "Wow, Emma."

"I know."

"Was this what you were supposed to"—he made air-quotes with his fingers— "'explain'?"

"Maybe." Emma shook her head. "Probably; at least that time. But—see, there's always a new story, a new relative."

She grinned ruefully. "This is not my only notebook," Emma admitted.

"I'm intrigued," Jacob said. "Can I look at this?"

"Sure."

Emma was cautiously optimistic; at least he hadn't given her a strangely sympathetic look and excused himself. Like, forever.

Instead, he was intrigued.

Chapter Five

Emma and Jacob

1.

Intrigued was just the beginning of Jacob's feelings for Emma.

He'd met her in the library at the University of Colorado in Boulder. He'd been a student there and had returned for an alumni meeting.

The meeting, of course, was just an excuse to come to Boulder and go skiing with his old classmates. They'd schemed and planned for weeks; rearranged work schedules, flown to Denver, rented cars. But the weather was uncooperative; no snow at Eldora had the alumna wandering the campus and watching the weather reports.

Jacob had separated from the group and gone rambling on his own. In retrospect he could never explain what had led him to the library. "It had to be fate," he decided. "It's not like I was looking for something to read, or anything."

Emma was seated at a long table, alone. Spread out before her were several books, a couple of maps, and a few notebooks, plus pens, pencils and markers. Jacob noticed her first thing, and meandered his way around the library, watching her.

She glowed. That was the thing. There was a light around her.

Probably not literally, Jacob conceded. But for him, it was an instant attraction.

She didn't notice him at all.

Emma pored through books, making notes in her notebooks. She highlighted often. She drew on her maps. She never looked up.

Finally, Jacob could take it no longer. He walked straight to her table and said, "What are you doing?"

"Trying to figure out where the battle of New Mexico took place," Emma replied, still not looking up.

"For what class?"

"No class. I just need to know."

"Are you writing a paper?"

"Not really..." Emma looked up. Finally. And saw him.

"Just a history buff, huh?"

Emma smiled, and it lit up her whole face. Jacob grabbed the back of a chair to lean on, so he wouldn't fall on his butt. What on earth was going on here?

"I'm really not," Emma said. "Sometimes I just...I just have to know things."

"Okay..." Jacob was bewildered and befuddled. He felt like someone had gut-punched him; and it was just a girl with a bunch of books in a library, for God's sake!

In the meantime, now that she had finally looked up from her books, Emma was glad she was seated. Her legs suddenly felt like limp noodles, and she could feel her cheeks heating with an alarming blush. "I'm weird that way," she said, trying to look away from him and unable to do it.

"Well, we're all weird in one way or another," Jacob offered lamely. "But I just happen to know that there were many, many battles in New Mexico."

"I know!" Emma cried. "I'm very confused." She shook her head. "I'm going to have to wait...for more...insight?" Now she seemed to be talking to herself.

"I'm sorry?"

"No sorry necessary." Emma smiled absently.

"How about dinner instead?" Jacob could hardly believe the words as they tumbled unbidden from his mouth.

"I—what?" Emma couldn't believe them, either.

"Dinner." Firmly. He was in control of his mouth now, by God!

"Uh...okay?"

"You sound unsure. Was that a yes?"

"Yes!" What the heck. She could use a break, and this guy was...potentially...someone special.

76

How did she know that?

How does anyone know anything?

And Jacob was already hooked. He didn't even know her name! She didn't know his, either.

"I think I better sit down," Jacob said.

"Please do."

He sat across from her and folded his hands on the table top. "Hello," he said.

"Hello," she replied.

"I'm Jacob." He reached across the table to shake her hand.

She grasped his hand firmly. "Emma."

"Where do you want to eat, Emma?"

"I have no idea. This is my first time in Boulder."

"But you're—what are you doing here?"

"I'm actually finishing up at The Art Institute in Denver," Emma admitted, "but I needed a day away. A friend of mine told me they have a great library here, so I drove up."

"You're finishing up?"

"Graduation's coming up fast. You're studying here?"

"Well...I did study here," Jacob admitted. "Alumni meeting. Also known as 'excuse for ski trip'. Also known as 'complete failure as ski trip'. No snow!"

"Weird, isn't it?" Emma commented. "I was just home for Christmas. We never got any snow!"

"Where's home?"

"Wyoming."

"You're kidding."

"No."

"I'm starting work at the mines this summer."

"Coal or Trona?"

"Trona."

"Good job!" Emma cried, impressed. "Did you study mine engineering here?"

Jacob laughed. "Actually, I was a music major," he admitted. "I don't know how I ended up in a mine engineering class, but...well, I'm never going to get paid this well playing the sax, I guess." He shook his head. "I blame my dad." Jacob raised his hands to make air-quotes. "'Always have a back-up plan'," he added in a deep, gravelly voice.

Emma laughed. "I've done years of theater. My back up plan? Journalism and photography. So, my first degree was an Associates in English, and I'm about to get my bachelor's in graphic arts and photography, and if you think my job prospects are good in Sweetwater County—think again."

"You could teach."

"Like I said, think again."

"What? Why?"

"All these college credits, and I'd still have to go back to school."

Jacob rolled his eyes and they both laughed.

In an incredibly short time they went from complete strangers to a pair of friends enjoying easy conversation and laughter. They talked for a couple of hours about research limitations, home towns, job prospects—whatever subjects struck them.

Jacob had spent four years in Boulder, so he suggested a couple of places to eat. They took Emma's car and drove around in the winter's early dark, exploring the little town, sharing a meal and hot chocolate and more conversation.

A lasting friendship was formed well before Emma had to take her leave and return to her campus in Denver.

By midnight it was snowing, and Jacob went skiing the next morning with his alumni buddies. But he'd managed to get Emma's mailing address and her phone number. There was no way he was going to lose touch with her if he could help it.

Emma went to classes and by the time she came back to her room, she'd decided she'd probably end up waiting by the phone for a few nights before having to conclude that she'd had a great day, but she'd never see him again.

She hadn't even struggled out of her coat before the phone rang.

It wasn't always a bad thing to be wrong.

2.

In the early summer of 1984, Emma came home. She had now accumulated an Associate degree and a Bachelor's degree, and had no idea what to do with herself.

She applied for a job at the local newspaper, but they weren't hiring and gave her very little encouragement.

She applied at two different photography shops, but they weren't hiring either.

She got a job at the local fried chicken place in the daytime and a night job at the movie theater, and felt like a complete failure; she'd just landed work in the same two places she'd worked while in High school.

She was twenty-four and living at home. What a cliché.

But all was not hopeless and depressing.

Jacob had moved to Wyoming shortly before Emma's graduation. Since the two had forged their friendship in Boulder a few months before, they had continued to visit long distance. Letters and phone calls had kept them up-to-date in each other's lives.

Since Emma's return from Denver, Jacob had become a frequent eater of chicken, and a frequent viewer of movies. He worked shifts at the mine, so they coordinated their schedules as much as possible and went dancing or to dinner. By August he had met Emma's whole family. Her parents liked him, and so did her siblings. Even the dog liked him—and she hated everyone who wasn't family. The beagle-mix was fiercely protective of the children and tended to shun outsiders, but frequently she was found sitting on Jacob's feet and staring adoringly up at him as he scratched behind her ears.

Eleven-year old Fred had become Jacob's shadow. Jacob, the "algebra king", had somehow managed to help him make sense of math, and was now regarded as something of a hero. "No more summer school for me!" Fred declared. Besides that, Jacob was quite a good baseball player; hero material for sure.

All in all, the summer passed with ease. Normalcy was the theme of the season, and Emma was grateful for the time to get to know Jacob without any unwelcome drama.

It was September before Emma had any visitations, and by that time all she wanted was for this relationship to go on forever.

Ghosts could be the deal breaker.

Oh, God.

3.

In Sweetwater County there's an appeal to eating at truck stops, oddly enough. The waitresses are all top-notch, for one thing; you're practically guaranteed good service. But the main attraction is the food; it's good, and there's plenty of it. Truck drivers know how to eat.

Chicken fried steak, mashed potatoes and buttermilk biscuits: All-American fare. "Oh, my God!" Jacob cried. "I guarantee you, this is not kosher."

Early in the friendship, Jacob had revealed his Jewish heritage, and Emma had been trying to learn more about it. She often stumbled and suggested food choices that weren't exactly acceptable.

Jacob wasn't exactly diligent, either, so it worked itself out.

Emma lifted one shoulder in a half-shrug. "What is?" she asked, and grinned wickedly. "You could have a salad, you know."

"And miss this? Are you crazy?" Jacob forked another bite into his mouth and grinned. "Don't tell my mother."

"I promise." Emma grinned back and took a bite herself. "She's probably already upset enough that you're dating a shiksa."

"She's not that upset," Jacob argued. "She can't be, you know. Considering she dated a Methodist before she married my father."

"She did?" Emma found that surprising. Jacob was the youngest child of six in his family, and three years her senior. She did some quick mental arithmetic and concluded that his parents must have married sometime in the 1940s. "Did she get in a lot of trouble with her parents?"

"I'm told the fur did fly," Jacob laughed. "But she probably would have married him anyway, if not for the war."

80

"World War II?"

"Uh huh. He was killed in 1943. In Tunisia, I think."

"Oh, wow. That's terrible." Emma buttered a biscuit, and added, "I know next to nothing about the war, you know. Just...the camps..."

Jacob shook his head. "My parents' immediate families were already in America, thank God," he said. "They came with a lot of immigrants after World War I." He shook his head again, ruefully. "I really should know more about this than I do. I'm the quintessential spoiled American Jew: born in the United States, educated in public schools with a lot of Christian children, eating bacon cheeseburgers just to shock my family—you know." He grinned. "I had a lot of gentile friends, and demanded to know why we couldn't have a Christmas tree!" He shrugged, shamefaced. "I just didn't pay enough attention to my own history back then. It makes me feel a little ashamed of myself now."

"So...you didn't lose any family in the war?" Emma asked hopefully.

"Oh, I didn't say that," Jacob said. "When I said immediate family, I meant my mother's parents and my father's grandparents and parents. But they left behind siblings and grandparents, aunts and uncles, cousins...some from Prussia, some from Austria. Probably lots of other places, too." Jacob stared at her across the table, sheepish. "Wow. I really need to ask my parents about this stuff. Shame on me."

"Family history is pretty important," Emma agreed. "You should—oh."

"Oh?" Jacob threw a look over his shoulder, expecting to see someone.

No one was there.

No one he could see, anyway.

But Emma could see her just fine. Just behind Jacob stood a small woman; she was no more than five feet tall, if that. Her black eyes sparkled with unshed tears as she stared at Emma. "Tomaron mis hijas," she said.

Emma shook her head, frowning.

Jacob watched her closely, confused.

81

"Tomaron mis hijas," the little woman repeated. "Los Apaches."

"Apaches? I—what?" Emma looked pretty confused herself.

"Los Apaches tomó mis hijas en el ataque. Necesito encontrar las."

"I can't—I don't speak Spanish!" Emma protested. "English? Can you tell me in English?"

"Fine...babies. Lose my muchachas. G—girs? I no espeak...por favor!" The woman began to cry. "Sírvase encontrar mis hijas!"

Emma shook her head, tears welling in her eyes, making them look bluer than ever.

Jacob was completely flummoxed. She looked at him. "I—I can explain," she offered weakly.

"I can't wait," Jacob told her.

"I have to learn Spanish," Emma told him. "Right away."

"Wh—what?"

"Spanish." Emma shook her head, distressed. "Why didn't I ever take Spanish in school? What was I thinking?"

"Okay, we'll learn Spanish!" Jacob had no idea what was going on, but if Emma wanted to learn Spanish, he was game. "Hey, I took a class in college," he offered. "What—I mean—where did this come from? Maybe I can... help?" This was confusing, he thought, but interesting. He was convinced that Emma was speaking to an actual person, even if he couldn't see anyone.

He'd heard about things like this.

More intrigue.

Emma looked past him. "Say it again," she said. "About the Apaches." She listened intently and then repeated, "Los Apaches...tomaron...mis hijas?" She looked at Jacob. "What does that mean?"

"Emma, what the—?"

"Please, Jacob, do you understand, or not?"

"Yeah, sort of. It's...um...the Apaches—I'm assuming Indians? — they took my girls. Baby girls? Daughters?" He shook his head. "Something like that. What the—?"

"Oh, God," Emma moaned. "Oh, God! Okay, this is going to take some work."

"Emma?" Jacob looked bemused.

"Let's eat, Jake," Emma begged. "I promise, I'll explain everything when we get home."

"Oh...kay...?"

"Family history, Jake. Family history. It's important." Emma resumed eating. Jacob watched her, then followed suit. Whatever it was, she clearly didn't want to discuss it in public.

Whatever it was, it was bound to be interesting.

Emma chewed and swallowed without tasting her food. She'd explain, she thought. She'd tell him everything. At least he'd know the whole story before he told her he couldn't date a nut case and disappeared from her life forever.

She glanced behind Jacob. The little woman was still there, wringing her hands and staring at her imploringly. Emma nodded at her. "I will try," she muttered.

The little woman nodded. "Gracias," she said, and disappeared.

"Well, dang." Just a whispered sigh before she sipped her milk. "Dang."

4.

"And now, you know." Emma concluded the Readers Digest version of her life. "I'm the one who seeks understanding. I'm the one who explains."

"You're the one who's amazing," Jacob said.

"I'm the one who gets stared at and laughed at!" Emma cried, frustrated. "And I don't speak Spanish! How am I supposed to help this one? I don't even know who she is! The only other time I saw her, she said something about a battle in New Mexico, and—"

"And that's what you were looking for in Boulder!"

"Yes. I didn't know why—I still don't! Oh, why did I take French instead of Spanish? Ugh!"

It had been a long night; it was a long story, even condensed. Jacob had been engrossed from the first sentence: "I can talk with my dead relatives." He was amazed and elated.

Emma, on the other hand, was scared to death; she was falling in love with him, and now he was going to head for the hills as fast as he could run. And who could blame him? She couldn't make him believe the unbelievable. She surely appeared to be a raving lunatic. Ever since her first encounter with the spirit world, Emma had faced disbelief and ridicule, and hadn't really cared; but this time, it mattered to her.

It mattered more than anything.

Would she and Jacob be over soon?

The thought was unbearable. How would she go on?

"Jacob?" she whispered. "I'll understand…if you want to go now…"

She *would* understand; she'd be devastated, but she'd understand.

"Emma, stop right there. Please, don't say anything else about me leaving." Jacob crossed the room and grasped her shoulders gently. "You've been nervous all night, talking about this, but I want you to know this: I believe you. I believe everything you've said."

"You do?" Emma exclaimed. "Jacob, let me tell you something—something I rarely admit even to myself: I can count on one hand the friends I have who know about this and actually believe it. Real friends, you know. There are people in this town who, if you asked them, would probably claim to be a friend to me, but honestly? They can't be true friends when they know about the things I do, but just—I don't know—humor me?"

"I have no intention of humoring you," Jacob laughed. "However, you may find yourself humoring me. Because, I want to know everything."

"I don't know everything," Emma protested. "Sometimes I think I don't know anything!"

"Well," Jacob said, "then we'll learn about it together. I want to understand how it works. I want to help when I can. You may get sick of me hanging around, but unless you send me packing, I'm with you."

"Wow." Emma shook her head. "Really?"

"Really." Jacob grinned. "I always knew you were fascinating—I just didn't realize how fascinating."

"I'm not—I—"

"You are," Jacob told her firmly. "Just you, Emma Knight. I knew it the first time I ever saw you. All this—this mystery? Icing on the cake. And I want to be a part of it all."

Emma was stunned. She'd been so sure the next sight she'd see would be Jacob's retreating backside.

She'd been busily planning recovery tactics. Things like crying all day and eating lots of ice cream; spending too much money on long distance phone calls to cry on her best friend's shoulder; going on tour with Melody and toting the guitars; maybe running away to New York City to be a Broadway star—or, more likely, a bag lady.

But—he wasn't going anywhere. He believed her! He wanted to be part of it, part of her life!

It felt like a miracle.

"Are you sure?" she cried.

"I've never been more sure of anything," Jacob assured her, grinning.

"Yeah," Emma breathed. "I mean, okay, then. But you're going to be sorry!"

"Never." Jacob was deeply aware of every quivering nerve, every breath he inhaled and exhaled. What could he say to her that would make her believe he was sincere in his depth of trust and feeling for her? What could ever be enough for a woman who had faced ridicule and outright disbelief her whole life?

Finally, he said, "We may be in for a hell of a ride, but I wouldn't miss it for the world."

"You say that now," Emma declared. "My relatives are very demanding. They show up at the most inconvenient of times. And now it turns out that they don't all speak English! Just wait until you're knee deep in Spanish lessons!"

"Oh, whimper and moan, and groan, groan, groan!" Jacob burst out laughing. "You just wait until I make you learn Yiddish!"

"Oy vey!"

"Good start!"

They laughed. It really was a good start.

Chapter Six

Language Lessons

1985

"Oh, my good golly!" Emma cried. "Dad! I blame you!"

Jack looked up from his paper. "Me? What did I do?"

"You didn't teach me Spanish!"

"I didn't—oh, for God sake, Emma!" Jack laughed. "I'm the last person you want to teach you Spanish."

"You speak Spanish, Dad!"

"I speak mush-mouth," Jack argued. "I picked it up from my friends. Grandma and Grandpa were all about us knowing English and getting a good education. They didn't teach us Spanish."

"They should have!"

"I agree. They regretted it later. But how were they to know that being bilingual would turn out to be a good thing? They grew up in an age when not being Americanized was considered unpatriotic."

"They weren't American?"

"Yes, they were."

"I'm confused."

Jack shrugged. "Confused is my natural state," he said. "For most of my childhood, I thought we were Spanish. Well, we *are* Spanish, but…look, it never occurred to me that I wasn't American, even though my folks always acted like we had to become American." He paused, considering. "It came from them being raised with Spanish as their first language, and the disadvantages that it presented to them later in life. They were determined that we would start school with a good knowledge of the English language and never considered that it would be advantageous to us all to know Spanish as well." He shook his head. "You're a smart girl, Emma. You'll figure it out."

"I don't even know where to start yet," Emma groaned.

"You can start," Jill said, "by addressing these invitations." She gestured expansively at the cards and envelopes scattered across the table top and shook her head at her daughter, clearly frustrated. "You're getting married, Em. You're entitled to take a few minutes for yourself! I know you're working hard to find answers, but these invitations are not going to write themselves!" She pulled together an impressive stack, neatened it, and pushed it toward her daughter.

Emma sighed, and pushed her notebook aside. She knew her mother was right, but she couldn't seem to let it go. "Do you have any idea how many different battles went on in New Mexico?" she demanded.

"Of course not," Jill replied. She looked at her daughter as if she'd been confronted with a new level of crazy. Maybe she had. She didn't remember how she'd dealt with her own wedding preparations; everything had happened so fast! And Emma had a lot of extra stresses to deal with. Still— "All I know is these invitations will not address themselves."

"I'd say I should have paid more attention in History class, but I don't remember ever learning a thing about the Indian wars or The Mexican American Wars or even the Civil War, except that they happened, and some dates I don't remember, and that we won. Whatever that means; winning would imply that everyone was happy in the end, and...well..." Emma sighed dramatically. "I guess I need to focus on the Apaches..."

"You need to focus on these invitations!" Jill cried, exasperated.

The kitchen door flew open and Melody sailed in, followed by her boyfriend, Rob. "I'm here!" she sang. "I come armed with pens in all colors! I am ready to write!"

"Well, thank God!" Jill exclaimed. "Your sister—the bride—is only ready to hunt Indians."

"Mom!" Dana interjected. "That's offensive." She bowed her head over the pile of invitations she was addressing. "You mean 'Native Americans'."

"Well, I'm sorry!" Jill said. "But until your sister—again, I add, the *bride*—learns more Spanish—we can't really properly investigate this problem, now can we? And in the meantime—"

"I know, I know!" Emma laughed. "In the meantime, I'm getting married." She gasped, and her eyes widened. "Oh, my God!" she added. "I'm getting married!" She exhaled loudly, eyes wide and alarmed. "Holy crap!"

Jack stood up from the table and beckoned to Rob. They left the kitchen to join the guys in the living room watching the Dodgers clobber the Braves. Melody quickly claimed his abandoned chair and the women got busy addressing invitations, taking breaks in between to fawn over Dana's baby son, Benjamin.

Jack made himself comfortable in his recliner, which Matthew had relinquished the minute his father entered the room. "So, New Mexico battles, huh? What have you got so far?" he asked Jacob.

"Well," Jacob said, "her name is Maria--"

"Everyone's name is Maria," Fred interrupted. "Unless it's a guy. Then it's Juan or Jose."

Jacob laughed. "We got a little more than just Maria. It's Maria Manuela Garcia Abeyta de Gonzales."

"Okay," Jack said, "de Gonzales. So, her husband was a Gonzales. The "de" signifies that it's her married name. That's...helpful? Er—somewhat, I guess. Hmmm...my grandmother was a Gonzales. My father's mother. She was from New Mexico, too. So was my dad. I mean, he was born there. He lived there off and on; at least until his mother passed. Then the family stayed in Colorado. But there were Gonzales aunts and uncles there, too, who he kept in touch with."

"Yeah, no shortage of Gonzales families in New Mexico," Matthew chuckled cryptically.

Jack shot his son a withering look and then looked back at Jacob. Matthew snickered.

"Anything else?" Jack asked.

"She said something about the Battle of New Mexico. She's mentioned a battle a few times."

"Terrific." Jack laughed cryptically himself. "No shortage of those, either. There was a battle a week, probably."

"It was an Apache attack, near as we can figure out." Jacob scratched his head. "It's vague, but...two daughters were abducted, apparently. That's it."

"No wonder she's having a fit." Jack shook his head. "Imagine losing a child like that!"

"It'd be nice if Maria would show up in our Spanish class," Jacob complained. "Well...maybe not. Emma would be a little upset if that happened, I guess. I was just thinking it would be convenient to have someone to ask about words we don't know yet. Emma tries to write stuff down, but this Maria hasn't shown up too often, and it's like she's just—I don't know—there and gone!"

"Maybe she knows she has to wait," Fred suggested. "Maybe she somehow knows Emma's learning Spanish. Oh, and you, too, Jake," he added thoughtfully.

"I guess that's possible," Jacob said. "Emma can't get it out of her head, though. She feels like she's letting Maria down."

"Can't have that! There's a wedding to plan." Jack stood up. "The Braves are toast," he announced. "I'm going to go call my Uncle George."

"Why not call Grandpa?" Matthew asked. "It was his mother who was a Gonzales, right? Not Uncle George?"

"Yes, but Uncle George knows a lot more of the family history," Jack said. "He's interested in it; he's a story collector, that guy. Grandpa would just tell me to call him anyway!"

The young men watched him go, and Matthew said, "We won't see Dad for a while now. Uncle George really does know some stories!"

Jacob looked wistfully after his soon-to-be-father-in-law. He wanted to go listen to the stories instead of watching the Braves get demolished by the Yankees. But he settled back in his chair while Matthew jumped back into the recliner before

89

anyone else could claim it, and silently prayed that Uncle George might have some family history to add to the story of Maria and her lost daughters.

1.

Weddings are stressful, Emma decided. If you could make it through the planning stages, you should be fully equipped to handle marriage by the time the wedding takes place.

Adding to the stress was the effort to make it a Jewish-Catholic wedding, in a town with no Synagogue and a zero-Jewish population. It was a task, to be sure.

Luckily, Jacob's parents were up to the challenge, and Emma's parents were more than willing to help make it work. The local Catholic Priest dragged his feet for about five minutes before deciding that the world needed more cooperation and less conflict, and a Rabbi was successfully enticed into visiting rural Wyoming from Denver.

Father Frances Godfrey and Rabbi Zachariah Epstein were fast friends. Emma and Jacob felt blessed beyond belief.

There were so many things to do, so many things to consider! Emma was fortunate that the Parish Priest was well informed on dispensation forms and Church policy to make sure that the marriage was valid in the eyes of the Church.

The two officiants spoke often on the phone, formulating a ceremony that would incorporate the faiths.

Jacob's parents, Hannah and Ezra, arrived two weeks before the wedding. Jill was delighted to meet them and accepted their offers of help with gratitude.

Jack took vacation time, so he could be on hand to help as well; some of that help consisted of little fishing expeditions and a trip to the golf course, but who could blame the men for escaping from time to time?

Weddings are stressful!

Jill and Jack offered their new extended family members the use of their camper-trailer, so they could save on hotel

90

expenses. Their offer was met with happy acceptance; they could be on hand to help, and still enjoy some privacy.

The weather was surprisingly cooperative. The Knights were able to make good use of the patio, and the two older couples sat there often, conspiring together to figure out where best to focus their efforts. Neither family had dealt with a mixed-religious ceremony, and it was all very interesting and informative.

Emma and Jacob were content to sit back and listen to their parents' discussions.

"I've brought my mother's Chuppah," Hannah said. "It was made for her wedding by her own mother, and it was used also in my wedding."

"What's a Chuppah?" Jill asked.

"Oy, what am I thinking?" Hannah cried. "Of course, you don't know about the Chuppah. It's very simple. It is a canopy, very special, which the bride and groom stand beneath while they take their vows."

"The Chuppah," Ezra added, "symbolizes the future home of the couple. Friends and family members stand at each corner of the canopy, holding it up over their heads. This reminds us all that the only real thing in a home is the people it holds. It reminds us that friends and family may support us, but it is up to us, inside the home, to love one another and become a new family unit."

"That's beautiful," Jack said, touched.

"It is," Jill agreed, and Emma wiped a tear from her cheek.

"This Chuppah was used in the weddings of my brothers and sisters," Jacob said. "It can be held up by poles, or it can be held by family and friends."

"For some reason," Hannah added, "this one has never been held by poles. We have always chosen friends and family."

"I think," Jill said, "that that visible symbol of support for the couple is amazing. What do you think, Emma?"

"I think Jacob and I have already chosen who will support the Chuppah," Emma replied. "We appreciate the support of all our family and friends."

"I have brought for you, my children, the veil and top hat worn by my grandparents, my parents, and finally Hannah and me, at our weddings," Ezra said. "I hope you will want to wear them."

"I would be honored," Emma said, dashing away another happy tear, and Jacob nodded enthusiastically.

"We understand that there will also be elements of the Catholic ceremony," Hannah said. "And I'm so glad that you were able to find officiates willing to work together in harmony to do this! We would have been hard-pressed to do such a thing. We've been with the same Synagogue for decades, but I have never seen such a thing in all those years."

"Neither have we," Jill agreed. "Luckily, our Parish Priest is amazing; he's lived in several bigger cities, so he had heard of ceremonies, although this will be the first he gets to perform. He even helped us find a Rabbi! I just know this will all be beautiful!" Jill's eyes were brimming with tears of happiness.

Jacob made a mental note to add tissues to the shopping list.

The guest room at Jack and Jill's house was prepared for Jack's parents, and Jill's parents were going to stay at Dana and Tom's house. Emma was so excited that both sets of grandparents would be attending her wedding. She knew how lucky she was; Jacob no longer had his grandparents.

All in all, it would be a wonderful family reunion as well as a wedding; Emma was a bundle of happy nerves.

2.

"Ha-ray atah m'kudash li b'ta-ba-at—am I saying this right?" Emma cried.

"You're doing great," Jacob replied admiringly.

They sat side-by-side on Jacob's sofa, in his soon-to-be-relinquished apartment.

"I feel like I'm going to mix in some Spanish accidentally!" Emma sighed.

"You're doing great with that, too." Jacob said. "And, you won't! You won't!" he hastened to assure her. "Now, me…I'm not so sure about."

"Stop it," Emma scolded.

Jacob chuckled. "We'll be fine."

Emma sighed dramatically. "I'm so scared someone will show up during the wedding."

"Me, too," Jacob admitted.

"I swear—I promise you—I'll ignore everyone not involved in the ceremony." She raised her voice slightly. "Do you hear me, ancestors?" she called. "I love you; you're welcome to watch, but no talking to me while I'm getting married!!"

Jacob laughed. "Let's do this again," he said. "I need the practice, too."

"Whatever! You grew up with this language." She giggled. "We've said it so many times, we should already be married."

"Nope. It has to be done with the exchange of rings."

"And Rabbi Epstein is okay with both of us getting rings? I read somewhere that only the bride gets a ring."

"That's pretty old school," Jacob said. "He did insist on gold bands, but we were already prepared for that."

"It's the only metal I can wear, anyway," Emma grinned. "Lucky break!"

"Oh, hey! Rick called today and agreed to be the fourth corner of the Chuppah." Rick was Jacob's brother, and had been having some scheduling difficulties, but had, happily, managed to arrange for time off. It had been an iffy thing right up to the last minute, and Jacob was delighted to be able to make this happy announcement.

"Oh, that's great!" Emma cried. "So, it will be held over us as we take our vows…"

"Yeah. And then they can attach it to poles during the last part of the ceremony." Jacob burst out laughing. "And I get to wear a top hat!"

"This is really happening!" Emma looked amazed.

"Just try getting out of it, miss!"

"Never!" Emma kissed him soundly. "You're stuck with me now! You'll never be able to get rid of me."

"Thank God." He kissed her back. "Now, again—Ha-ray at m'k udeshet li...."

3.

"...b-ta-ba-at zo k-dat Mosheh v'Yisrael" Jacob said, solemnly placing the gold ring on Emma's finger.

"With this ring," Rabbi Epstein translated, "you are made holy to me as my wife, according to the laws of Moses and the faith of Israel."

Emma inhaled deeply and put the ring on Jacob's finger, reciting: "Ha-ray atah m'kudash li b'ta-ba-at zo k-dat Mosheh v'Yisrael.

"With this ring you are made holy to me as my husband, according to the laws of Moses and the faith of Israel."

"Amen," the gathered family and friends chanted.

Emma and Jacob stood under a beautiful hand-made Chuppah, their parents and attendants at their sides. Emma's brothers Matthew and Fred held corners on one side, Jacob's brothers Rick and David held those on the other side.

Father Godfrey nodded at the parents, and said, "Now, I would like to invite the mothers, Hannah and Jill, to light these candles. In lighting these candles, the two mothers honor the lives of their children, the lives they brought into this world." He motioned the nervous women forward and placed a beautiful candle into each of their hands. He then lit tapers from a large candle burning at the front of the altar, and handed those to them as well.

Hannah and Jill carefully lit their lovely candles, and held them up for all to see. Then they discretely blew out the tapers.

"The love of mothers for their children is a light none can extinguish. Though they give their children away today, that light will continue to shine for them forever." Father Godfrey presented another single candle to Emma and Jacob, and handed tapers to each of them.

"Please, light your tapers from the candles your mothers are holding," he said. "Now," he continued once they had done so, "light this single candle. The two smaller candles represent Jacob and Emma's individual lives and how each is unique and special. This larger single candle represents the new oneness they are choosing in marriage. The lighting of these candles symbolizes the joining of these two families."

Jill and Hannah beamed through their tears. Ezra and Jack also were struggling to contain themselves.

Emma was smiling brilliantly, her eyes bright with unshed tears, and Jacob looked like he might burst into wild giggles at any moment. Their emotions had never been closer to the surface, and it was hard to know if they would be able to contain them.

"In marriage, the self is not extinguished, and so, in order to represent that, all the candles will remain lit. Wholeness and fullness of life depend upon the balance of individuality and togetherness, and so today Jacob and Emma give these things to one another: light, warmth, guidance, and love."

The candles burned brightly, and the warmth in Emma's heart could not be surpassed.

Rabbi Epstein said, "Out of two different and distinct traditions, Emma and Jacob have come together to learn the very best of what each has to offer. You, their family and friends, have joined us here in this place of life affirming celebration, appreciating their differences, and confirming that this couple being together is far better than them being apart from each other.

"As we bless this marriage under a Chuppah—this beautiful wedding canopy—we wish for you all to understand that this Jewish symbol signifies that the bride and groom are joining together under one roof. It symbolizes the home of their future. Their own brothers stand at its corners to help support this structure, which symbolizes their support, the support of both families, and your—their many friends—support, of this holy union."

Father Godfrey addressed them: "Jacob and Emma, standing under this Chuppah, I want you both to know that this is the only true anchor of the marriage that will be—" he took each of their hands and joined them together "—you two, holding fast to one another."

95

Rabbi Epstein sang, "Baruch atah adonoy, eluheynu melech ha-olam, mi-kah deish amo Yisrael, al yiday Chuppah v'ki du-shin."

And Father Godfrey sang the translation: "Blessed are you, O Lord our God, King of the Universe, you sanctify your people under this sacred marriage canopy."

Jack and Ezra stepped forward. Ezra opened a bottle of wine and poured into a crystal wine glass. Jack lifted the glass and offered it to Jacob. Jacob offered it to Emma, who took the first sip, and then she watched, smiling, as Jacob drank in turn. Their hands remained clasped throughout.

Father Godfrey said, "You may find the wine you share now to be bittersweet. This is reflective of all lives. Our prayer for you is that you will as easily share everything in your lives. May this bittersweet taste remind you that the inevitable bitterness in life can be perceived as less bitter because now you have someone with whom to share. Better yet, the inevitable sweetness of life will be doubled because you will both be there to share the happy moments. Let this cup of wine, which sanctifies your marriage, be a symbol of unity as you approach the moment when you come before God and before these, your brethren, as husband and wife."

"You have come before God and this community of your family and friends declaring your vows and consenting to become one," Rabbi Epstein said. "May the Lord in his goodness strengthen your consent and fill you with his blessings."

Together, Father and Rabbi chanted: "What God has joined together, let no one put asunder."

Everyone said: "Amen!"

Jacob passed the empty wine glass to his father, who placed it in a cloth bag. Ezra held the bag up for all the assembly to see. He said, "This glass from which you shared a sip reminds us all that life, and marriage, are fragile. May the Lord in small ways frequently remind you to take no day for granted, for our time together in this life is precious."

Jack moved to stand beside Ezra and took his hand. He said, "We pray that you will be happy together, and be good to each other. May your home be forever filled with love."

Hannah stepped forward, still holding her candle, and took Jack's free hand. "May you always drink from the full," she said, "and crush the empty beneath you. May the Lord protect you and bless you with a home filled with joy. May He shine his light upon your hearts and bless you with long lives together."

Jill joined the parents, took Ezra's hand, and added, "May he bless you with a family to love and fill your home with laughter. And now, in keeping with ancient tradition, we wish that the years of your marriage be no less than the time it would take to fit the crushed fragments of this glass together again."

Ezra raised the bag again, and then put it on the floor. "Now, my son," he said, "crush this glass beneath your heel—and crush it well!"

Jacob stomped down on the bag and gave it a good grinding as well, pulverizing the glass within. He wanted to be sure it would be eons before those pieces could be put back together.

All the guests cried "Mazel Tov!" and cheered as soon as the sound or breaking glass was heard.

Jacob kissed his bride.

The officiates chanted in unison, "We present to you: Mr. and Mrs. Jacob Kramer." The assembled guests applauded.

The lovely opening strains of "The Rose" began and Melody broke into song as the rest of the wedding party filed out of the church. Her beautiful voice followed the bride and groom out the door, sending pleasant chills down Emma' spine.

There were several unseen guests present—well, unseen by everyone but Emma—but none spoke to her. They merely observed. Emma was filled with gratitude, joy and love.

It was a beautiful ceremony, and a beautiful day.

4.

Following the wedding, the two families joined as one and feasted in the back yard of Jack and Jill's house. It had been a joint effort as all the women had gotten together to prepare food that was both Kosher and not-so-Kosher. There were several tables laden with food set up around the perimeter of the yard, and people wandered from place to place, loading their plates, laughing and chatting.

Emma enjoyed visiting with her new in-laws. She'd never had older brothers before and felt quite blessed to finally be able to say, "And this is my big brother," when introducing Rick to her grandparents.

Late into the evening there was music and dancing. Emma and Jacob shared their first dance as man and wife, and the crowd was moved to tears when she danced with Jack; what can be more beautiful than a father's last dance with his baby girl, before passing her on to her new groom?

Emma never forgot the beaming faces of her parents, grandparents and parents-in-law as she and Jacob took their leave of the guests and climbed into an outrageously decorated car to drive away and start their honeymoon trip.

Chapter Seven

A Battle In New Mexico

1986

Emma was busy slicing beef into strips. "Uncle George is sort of the family historian," she said. "That man remembers stories no one else has ever heard of, I swear."

"Well, I know Dad's been talking to him a lot, since before the wedding," Jacob said, while expertly dicing an onion. "And a lot of the stories are fascinating. But what do we really know so far?"

"I keep waiting for Maria to show up," Emma complained. "It's been weeks! But, okay, so far, here's what I know.

"Uncle George says his mother told a story about a Maria who lost her daughters. It was the late 1700s, I believe. Maria was living in the Province of New Mexico."

"The 'Province'?"

"Uhuh." Emma poured oil into a wok and set it on the stove to heat. "At that time New Mexico belonged to Spain, but was no longer part of New Spain, and—or was it? The history is really confusing. It was Spanish at the time, anyway; Spain was in charge at the time."

"Okay, go on." Jacob added chopped bell pepper to his pile of chopped onion, and started on a tomato.

Emma put beef strips into the wok and stirred as she spoke. "So, I still need to figure out the actual place—all I've gotten from Maria is 'Sandia', and as far as I can tell, that may have been a church."

"Weren't the Sandia the first indigenous peoples in New Mexico?"

"Were they? I—hmmm. I have no idea. There might be a mountain somewhere there, too...or a range of mountains. More research."

"Was that by Albuquerque? But I think that was a tribe...never mind, I foresee a trip to the library soon. Did we learn this in school?" Jacob shook his head briskly. "Go on."

"Well, anyway, I don't know for sure where it happened, but one early morning, a small band of Apache attacked a few homes where Maria was living and killed her husband—or her father-in-law—I haven't gotten that straight, either. Remember, Uncle George heard it from his mother, who heard it from her family...anyway, this Gonzales man was killed, and some other men as well, and the women tried to hide, but the Apache found them and took several of the young women and children with them. Maria's daughters were among those captured."

"Wow. And now—what?"

"She wants to find them."

"But—that was almost two hundred years ago!"

"I know!"

Jacob carefully added the vegetables to the wok, then started slicing an avocado.

"I'm putting cheese on mine," Emma announced. "But I won't get it near yours. Are you cool with that?"

"That's not Kosher, Em," Jacob scolded. Then he laughed. "I'm so cool with that I want to add cheese to mine, too...but I won't."

"Kosher is hard," Emma declared.

"Yep. I'm feeling pretty deprived right about now."

"Traditionally, cheese isn't added to fajitas," Emma informed him.

"Tradition, tradition!" Jacob sang. "You would have broken Golda's heart."

"Nah. I would never try to serve her a bacon cheeseburger."

"Oy vay." Jacob rolled his eyes.

Emma sat across from Jacob, careful to keep her plate well away from his; a kosher meal never mixes meat with dairy.

And forget about pork. In a world of bacon cheeseburgers, biscuits with sausage gravy and pork green chili—Emma's world, in other words—Jacob had it tough.

Luckily, although Jacob really tried, he wasn't too obsessive about his diet. Emma tried, as well, to make it as easy as possible. But she loved cheese on everything; meat, eggs, you name it—everything's better with cheese.

It was hard!

What she'd found hardest was having separate pans, dishes and utensils for food preparation. Meat and dairy must never touch. Hannah, her mother-in-law, was teaching her a lot whenever they managed to get together, and mailed her recipes and suggestions fairly often.

Jack and Jill had also jumped on the kosher bandwagon—somewhat. They made sure that at family gatherings there was a good selection of foods and set them out on separate tables in observance of Jacob's needs.

It was a learning experience for everyone.

"You know," Emma said, suddenly changing the subject. "I don't think I'll ever get over the fact that the High School did a production of 'Fiddler on the Roof' the year *after* I graduated. Mrs. Clark knew I wanted to play Golda."

Jacob just had to sing "Tradition." Now it was on her mind for sure.

"Maybe the local theater will do it," Jacob suggested.

"Only if we can get more people involved," Emma groaned. "Right now, there's not a chance we'd be able to do a musical."

"Things will come together."

"I hope so!"

They both knew it wasn't very likely. It was a small town, and the theater group was tiny. Their budget barely covered three-act plays. Getting an orchestra and a cast large enough for a musical was something only the High Schools and the community college might have the budget for.

Emma sighed.

Jake wrapped beef and crisp vegetables into a tortilla. "How are we going to find Maria's daughters?" he asked, thoughtfully swinging the conversation back to the case at hand.

Emma sighed. "I need to talk to her some more. I have a million questions, I swear. I finally feel confident with my Spanish, and she hasn't shown up! It's frustrating."

"You know she's just waiting to show up while you're in the middle of a photo shoot or an interview."

"Bite your tongue!"

Emma had finally gotten a job with the local television station—such as it was. She didn't go before the cameras, but she was responsible for interviewing the police and local politicians regarding day-to-day life in small town Wyoming and writing stories for the on-screen reporters to tell. It took up about three days a week. In the meantime, she'd started her own small photography studio in the basement of their house.

Either job would be a terrible place to end up conversing with a ghost.

Jacob grinned at her and saluted her with his wine glass. (It was full of water.) "Tongue bitten," he said. "But..."

1.

Ghosts don't care if you're working; it was a true miracle that they'd respected the "no talking" request at the wedding, really.

The courthouse was a busy place; it served the whole county, and was the only building in town that had an elevator.

Emma was talking to the mayor, Bonnie Parker, who seemed more interested in asking questions than answering them. "When are you due?" was her first one.

"How did you—?"

"Oh, please, Emma! Your mother is walking on air!"

Emma laughed. "March," she said.

"And how are you feeling?"

"I feel great—in between bouts of projectile vomiting, that is. So, about the—?"

"And Jake? How's he taking this?"

"Bonnie, if my mother is walking on air," Emma giggled, "Jacob is looking down on her from cloud nine. Now, if we could—?"

"Are we thinking baptism or Bar Mitzvah?"

"Bonnie, really, I would love to spend all day talking about my baby, but I'm supposed to be asking you about the tree project."

"Oh, of course!" Mayor Bonnie giggled girlishly. "I just love the babies—as you know."

"Me, too," Emma agreed. "We are beyond excited. So...how did this project come about?"

"Well, Emma, as you may also know, I am from back east. You've lived here all your life, correct?"

"Pretty much. I was six when we moved here."

"Well, I grew up in Connecticut. Connecticut has trees. Trees of all varieties. And this little town? Oh, my!"

"It's a desert." And a bit ugly, truthfully, except near the river, Emma didn't add.

"True. But with trees, this town could be beautiful. And so, I proposed this beautification project."

"And how did that go?"

"Well, it was not without some opposition. Some of the other constituents—the Mayor just past, for one—objected at first; I reminded one and all that their arguments probably stemmed from the fact that they didn't think of it first." Bonnie giggled. "And now, it's really starting to come together!"

"I've seen the work crews with the grass and sidewalks going in on Mai—Maria?"

The little woman had suddenly appeared just behind the mayor!

"Maria? I—excuse me?" Mayor Bonnie said.

"Oh, sorry, I—morning sickness—it—it just can't seem to happen in the morning, I—will you excuse me a moment?" Emma was completely flustered. She added, "Ven conmigo," addressing Maria, and turned and fled to the public restroom, praying that no one was in there.

Ghosts could be pretty inconvenient!

"You just take care of yourself," Mayor Bonnie called after her. "Why don't you just call me?"

"Yes, ma'am," Emma called back. She really felt like she might vomit as she pushed her way through the door.

"Dear God, please don't let her follow me," she begged. The room was empty; a small miracle.

The bigger miracle: Maria was there. "Hola, Emma," she said.

"Hello, Maria," Emma replied, speaking very passable Spanish after her months of lessons and practice. "Where have you been?"

"What do you mean?" Maria asked.

"It's been ages!"

"Really?" Maria shook her head. "It is very strange, time. I cannot choose, I cannot know…very strange."

"I guess it would be," Emma conceded. "Please, I've been studying your language, the area where I believe you're from…I have so many questions…"

"Men are the problem, always," Maria said. "Men, with their greed for land and power. Always with the fighting…"

"Where were you, Maria?"

"What do you mean? Here, there. I don't know…what do you mean?"

"I mean, where did you live? Where were you when your children were taken away?"

"Sandia Pueblo. Uh, Corrales. We lived there with the youngest children. We were no longer young people in those days. Most of the children had married, but families often lived together on the ranches."

"So, Maria—"

"Por favor. I was never a Maria. Manuelita is what I was called. Your brother is right: everyone was named Maria. The name was given to honor the Virgin Maria. There were many Pueblo Indians in the area—my own people came from the Pueblo tribes, many of them—but the religion we were raised in was Catholic."

"You're a Pueblo Indian."

"In truth, I do not know; it was common to claim only the Spanish blood, and many of my family insisted we were Spanish. But I was also told by my cousins that some of the women in my family came from the Pueblo tribes in the area. Sandia Pueblo, almost certainly; it was closest to Corrales.

"In the first days of occupation, many men came from Spain alone. Single. They took wives from the local people. Some of my family was called Espanola, some were called Mestizo." Manuelita shrugged. "Records are few. I know that you seek them out, but..." she shook her head. "It was rare that people learned to read and write. We depended on the Priests to record special events; births, deaths, marriages. It wasn't always done. And many churches were destroyed over the years, by weather or by war, and so the loss of records was likely great."

"I can imagine," Emma said.

"Women in my day were very often sad and worried. I have much to tell you, Emma, but perhaps this is not the best place..."

The bathroom door swung open and Bonnie came in. "Are you feeling better, Emma?" she asked.

Emma went to the sink and rinsed her mouth. "Much better, thank you, Bonnie," she said, pulling a paper towel from the dispenser and drying her face and hands.

Bonnie patted her gently on the shoulder. "I know you need this story, but I have to run right now. Here's my home phone number," she said, handing Emma a card. "I should be home after seven. Give me a call, and I'll tell you the whole story. Men," she added, "are pretty dumb about beauty. They want to sit back and enjoy looking at it, but have no idea of the work that sometimes goes into producing it."

Emma chuckled. "That's why the cosmetics companies will always prosper. Thanks, Bonnie," she added. "I'm going to run home and eat some saltines, I guess. I'll call you tonight."

"You take good care of both of you!" Bonnie cried, and exited at a trot. "Gotta run!"

Emma turned back to continue her conversation with Manuelita.

She was gone.

"Well, dang!" Emma groaned.

2.

Emma arrived at home that day around 2:00 p.m. which was early for her. Jacob was on day shift at the mine and wouldn't be home until about six. As she pulled into the garage, she thought about making something special for dinner. Latkes sounded good.

Manuelita met her in the kitchen.

"Oh, good," Emma said. "I'm glad to see you."

"It is impressive, your Spanish," Manuelita said. "You have done very well to learn it."

"Thank you."

"Today, at last, I would like to tell you a story. It is a sad story for me, but in truth, it is not only *my* story. This scenario repeated itself many times over the years in New Mexico. If you were to talk to other women, you would hear much the same.

"I was born in Bernalillo, Province of New Mexico, which in those times belonged to Spain. I married a Juan Gonzales in the 1730s when I was fifteen years old."

"What do you mean, 'a' Juan Gonzales?"

"Oh, there were many Juan Gonzales men. His father was Juan, and his grandfather, and his great-grandfather. Their brothers had sons, and they were also called Juan Gonzales. It is confusing. Like Maria. I am a Maria. Two of my own daughters were called Maria. I really tried not to do it—name my babies Maria—but traditions are hard to break! There were baptisms, and you might say to the godparents, 'her name is Teresa', and then the godmother would say to the priest: "Maria Teresa'. But," she added with a laugh, "I did not name any of my sons Juan Gonzales! My husband was quite displeased with me, but I held firm. One was called Jose—of course. And then, along came my son Antonio, who turned right around and named his son Juan, so of course it is never-ending."

The two women laughed together. Emma started peeling a couple of large potatoes. "You married at age fifteen?" she asked.

106

"It was not unheard of to marry as young as thirteen in those days." Manuelita chuckled ruefully. "People did not live so long, generally. It was necessary to get on with it as quickly as possible. You could be an old maid at twenty and dead at thirty; it was the way of the world.

"We were lucky, in many ways. We were old, Emma; we had grown children, and grandchildren. Even a great-grandchild, which was most unusual.

"In those days, there were the Spaniards and the Mestizos living together, side by side with the Pueblo peoples. There were other tribes nearby; friendly Apache; Kiowa and Navajo, who were mostly peaceful, but not entirely trusted. Many had converted to the Catholic religion and attended mass in the chapel Nuestra Senora de la Concepcion at Alameda, or other chapels in the area.

"But all was not peaceful in the region; other Apache tribes were not so friendly. They resented the Spaniards and had no love for the Catholic Friars. They raided the ranches and villages, stealing cattle and sheep, and anything else they could find.

"And so it was the day they came to my home and killed my Juan Gonzales before my very eyes; this old man with more than seventy years, and I with over sixty, trying to defend our family from wicked savages!

"My daughters Maria Elena and Maria Juliana were taken alive from the house, and I was left there with my grandsons Dion and Antonio and my great granddaughter Victoria. We watched my daughters dragged kicking and screaming from the salon, while my sons engaged in battle with the Apache warriors outside.

"It was a small band of Apache, but even so, they killed my husband and the husband of my granddaughter. They took other women and some children."

"I'm so sorry," Emma said.

"It is the men, always the men," Manuelita said. "Whatever he has, he will always want more. Whatever he has, another man will want it—right down to his wife and daughters. It matters not at all whether the man is Espanola, Mestizo or Apache. The white men of France, the German men—they are all the same. Like children with sweets, they will fight among themselves and for no good end."

"Nothing has changed from your time to mine in that regard," Emma agreed.

"I always told my daughters," Manuelita continued, "the world would be a more peaceful place if women were in charge—unless you make them share their kitchens!"

The two women shared a laugh over that, while Emma grated potatoes into a bowl.

"The men of the Pueblo and the haciendas made haste to gather a posse and follow the Apache band," Manuelita said. "They gave chase but were unable to catch up with them. The Apache were nomads, always moving from place to place, and they knew every valley, every mountain pass, every arroyo, every place possible to hide. They would come into the area, strike fast and hard, and vanish!

"They took my daughters away, and they disappeared."

Manuelita stood for a time, her face covered, trembling with emotion.

Emma continued her meal preparations, quietly waiting for her to continue. Absentmindedly, she dashed away a tear or two.

Finally, the little woman continued. "I was distraught," she said. "I could not eat or sleep for fear of what might be done to my girls. They were the youngest ones, maidens, not yet twenty, the babies of my old age.

"I pray they were taken as wives; that was often the case. If they were taken as wives they would live, you understand." Manuelita nodded emphatically. "They would live!"

Manuelita sighed. "My daughters were not the only women stolen from among the settlements. Even children were taken from us.

"We heard tales from those who saw the tribes from afar that there were many Spanish women among them. Still, there was no way to know for sure. My time here came to an end before I was able to learn of their fates. My hope is that you can find them."

Emma cracked eggs into a bowl and whipped them with a whisk. She was deep in thought. "Manuelita," she said. "I can't make you any real promises; I'm sure you understand that I can only promise to do my best.

"Yes, I understand," Manuelita agreed.

"I will need as much information as you can give me."

"What would you like to know?"

"What was the name of your town?"

"We lived on a sheep ranch in Bernalillo, on land owned by my father-in-law. There he built a large hacienda with outbuildings, and many of our family lived there among us.

"It was all part of a land grant given by the King of Spain to a soldier named Francisco Montes Vigil. In those times, if you had land, you were required by Spanish law to reside on and care for it. Senor Vigil could not do that, so he sold it to El Capitan Juan Gonzales, who was already living in Bernalillo. These things my husband told me; it was part of his family's history.

"The area was called Corrales, because there were many corrals built along the river to pen the horses, cows and sheep. We grew wheat and vegetables. We raised sheep and sold them. I had chickens and turkeys; we sold eggs. We were not poor; we ate well.

"There were several families in the area; some called Griego—it was said that they were Indians, but I do not know for sure. I was told that some Griegos had come from across the big waters; I never saw any big waters, but my husband assured me they existed. I was told that the Gonzales family came also across the waters, but from other lands than the Griego family. There were other countries. It would take weeks to travel across the waters, and more weeks to travel from the shores to our land in Bernalillo. My Juan Gonzales told me so. He told that the world was very big, so much bigger than I would ever know, and I suppose that is true.

"The Bernal families settled there; Bernalillo was named for them. There were many Bernal families and many Gonzales families. Some married into each other's families; that is the way of the world. I cannot be sure, but I suppose the Griego family may have been part of our families as well. Surely, they must have been. There were many other families, of course, but these were some of the founders who came from across the waters, into Mexico and left the Federal District of Mexico, as ordered by the crown, to settle in the north and expand the boundaries of New Spain. This is what I remember my husband telling me.

"Of course, my mother's family must already have come to Bernalillo from somewhere; none of them spoke of lands across big waters, and so for this reason, I do believe that I come from the Pueblos. I believe, but I do not *know*.

"As I told you, many of my family—the same family who never spoke of lands across the waters—insisted that we were Spanish." Manuelita shrugged.

"I don't suppose it matters, does it? The church told us we all came from one couple, Adam and Eve. But I never understood that; how could it be? No one could explain; accept it, we were told. That is all.

"God is a mystery, is He not? His word is a mystery!"

Emma agreed that this was so. She didn't understand much about the mysteries of creation herself. She participated now in two different religions, but couldn't claim to understand the teachings of either. What the heck—she talked to ghosts; that was mystery enough for her at the moment!

"I know that there were bigger places," Manuelita told her. "Santa Fe was the biggest place I ever saw, but we didn't go there often. Traveling was difficult; the Apaches might attack. I don't know what more I can tell you."

"Thank you!" Emma assured her: "That's good information; that's a good place to start." Emma was pleased, although she knew that chances were slim that she'd ever find Manuelita's daughters. She washed her hands at the sink and dried them. Grabbing a notebook and pen, she quickly wrote down the information before she could forget it. "Please tell me your daughters' names again," she said.

"Maria Elena and Maria Juliana."

"And the year?"

"I am not certain. I know we were old people by then...I would say 1775, 1780; perhaps later." Manuelita looked embarrassed. "Women did not have much use for dates; we were very busy! I...I did not read or write," she added defensively. "But I was one among many who did not."

"I understand," Emma told her kindly. "You've given me a lot of good information. Now I just need to do some research. I hope I will be able to find your daughters."

"Most times," Manuelita told her helpfully, "the Marias were called by their middle names. We called my girls Elena and Juliana. Juan most often called them Ellie and Julia. He once told me 'Mani, sometimes a nibble is better than a mouthful'." Manuelita laughed. "He could be amusing, my Juan Gonzales."

"I guess my parents felt the same," Emma chuckled. "I was only called Emmaline when I was in trouble."

Manuelita looked at her gravely. "Anglos do not use so many names as the Spanish. Imagine your mother yelling at you: 'Maria Emmaline Juanita Consuela de Baca Gonzales y Gonzales'! Then you know you're in trouble!"

Emma giggled. "I'd say you are every bit as amusing as your Juan Gonzales," she said.

"We shared a great deal of laughter in our years together," Manuelita told her. "It is always the best way to forget the tears. I miss him."

Emma was startled. "What do you mean?" she asked. "Isn't he with you?"

"I do not know where he is now," Manuelita told her.

"I don't understand," Emma cried. "I've always been told we reunite with those we loved in life."

"I do not understand, either," Manuelita agreed. "It is not what I believed it would be, this 'afterlife'. I have not seen Heaven; I have not seen Hell. I believe they are there, but perhaps it is not yet time for us to go. Here—I don't know—it is very big here. Sometimes there are many…people? Ghosts? Souls? I do not know what to call those who dwell here…but Spirits is as good a name as any, I suppose. At any rate, sometimes there are no others, and I am all alone. Sometimes I see family, or friends, and we spend awhile together; but in all this time I have not yet seen my Juan Gonzales. I would very much like to see him again."

"I'm told," Emma said, "that those who pass quickly, or violently, do not know what has happened to them, or any of the things that happened next. Did your husband know that your daughters were taken?"

"Oh, no! He was killed almost as soon as the Apache broke through the door—he was trying very hard to bar the door, but they overpowered him, and one brave slashed his throat!" Manuelita shuddered. "He was dead before he hit the floor! We were screaming and crying, of course, and I sought to hide the baby—my great-granddaughter—from them. Babies were often stolen and raised as savages. My daughters were trying to fight them off, trying to protect their nephews, who also could have been stolen away. And the Apaches dragged my girls off, but the rest of us in the house were left alive—except my Juan."

"I am so sorry!" Emma cried. "I really don't know how it works, but...perhaps your Juan has moved on because he didn't know what had happened."

"I do not know..."

"I hope," Emma said, "that finding some answers will help you find your husband."

"I pray that it will be so!" Manuelita cried. And vanished.

"Oh, dang!" Emma cried.

She put her notebook and pen away and went back to preparing latkes for dinner.

3.

"What's the special occasion?" Jacob asked, his eyes bright as he gazed at the dining room table.

"I got off work early," Emma announced, and added: "Maria paid me a visit. I felt like a celebration was fitting."

"Latkes, sour cream, apple sauce...ghosts should visit more often!" Jacob grinned. "Do I have time to wash up and change into some comfy sweats?"

"Heck, yeah! I'll join you."

"So, not a fancy-dress celebration?"

"No way, Jose. Let's be comfortable."

Dinner was a relaxed affair; latkes were a favorite. Simple fare, but delicious and satisfying.

"I have to call the mayor after dinner," Emma said. "Our interview got interrupted."

Jacob almost spat his water out as he burst into laughter. He grabbed his napkin to wipe dribs and drabs off his chin and chest.

"That's right," Emma continued. "You jinxed me!"

"Sorry!"

"Oh, sure!" Emma laughed. "Anyway, I'll have to call her now. Thank God she thought I was having morning sickness."

"That excuse might come in handy."

"Sure, if I stay pregnant for the rest of my life!"

"Well, I'll clean the kitchen while you work," Jacob offered, "since I jinxed you, and all. Although," he added, "I did contribute to your morning sickness excuse." He thought about that for a few seconds. "Er…scratch that last."

"I accept your gallant offer of KP duty," Emma giggled.

"Tell me about Maria."

"I guess she prefers to be called Manuelita," Emma said. She then filled him in on what she'd been told that afternoon.

Jacob listened carefully, and then said, "Do you remember your…what was it, a cousin? Anyway, she said you could ask your LDS friends about their genealogy research?"

"Oh, you mean Annie!" Emma cried. "I wish she'd visit again; I adored her." She looked thoughtful. "She did tell me that, and heaven only knows why I haven't done it. I've heard wonderful things about the research they've done."

"I wonder if we could just go to the church and talk to someone about it?"

"I can't think of a single reason why we couldn't."

"I'm on graveyards next week. What are your hours?"

"Flexible, as always. I'm so lucky! How did that happen?"

"Good genes."

"Right," Emma drawled.

"So, let's go see what we can find out."

"Let's do it!" Emma agreed. "Now, do the dishes!"

"Go get to work!" Jacob laughed.

Emma left the room to call the Mayor, and Jacob cleaned up.

Chapter Eight

Research

1.

"Salt Lake City, here were come," Jacob cried happily. "Road trip!"

Emma grinned, and then grimaced, trying to get comfortable in her seat. "I'm glad you're so tickled about it," she said, "but we penguins are having a bit of a hard time."

Jacob frowned, confused. "Penguins?"

"Ducks. Geese. Whatever waddles the most." Emma moaned. "Or...what animal pees the most? Cuz I can't seem to go more than twenty miles without searching the road signs for the next bathroom—and this is I-80! There's nothing every twenty miles!"

Jacob shook his head sympathetically. "I'm sorry, honey," he said. "Wyoming has the lowest population in the continental United States. I guess the highway department decided there weren't enough people to put in bathrooms."

"Dumb highway department. Low population or not, Interstate 80 gets a lot of traffic. They should have thought about the pregnant women driving through the state."

"I just hope it doesn't snow and slow us down—"

"God forbid!"

"How far is St. Mark's from the Family History Library?"

Emma peered closely at the map, trying to use the scale to figure it out. She hated reading maps; it was not her forte. "I don't know...I'm gonna say ten to fifteen miles. Wow! Salt Lake is big!"

"How did you ever get around in Denver?" Jacob laughed.

"Mostly, I stuck to my own area. I tried not to go too far south, where all the streets are one way. I took the bus and let someone else figure it out."

"You drove to Boulder," Jacob pointed out.

"I've decided that my decision to drive out of my comfort zone was a push from the fates so that we would meet, fall in love, get married, get pregnant and have to drive in Salt Lake today."

"I'm in no position to argue that." Jacob said. "I made that trip on a whim myself. If Jamie hadn't suggested an alumni meeting—"

"AKA the ski trip to end all ski trips—"

"Which it finally was!" Jacob grinned. "And if it had snowed the day before that ski trip, I never would have met you."

"Fate."

"Yep. We were meant to be." Jacob changed lanes and passed a lumbering semi. "But I have no interest in skiing right now, so please, God, no snow!"

"I wish we had more good doctors at home." Emma was feeling grumpy and whiney.

"It's going to be fine."

"I don't know why they want me to have this done." She was also scared; being pregnant and getting sent out of town for tests was not confidence-inspiring.

"Honey, it's a pretty easy test; and if anything needs to be done, they can take care of it right there."

"We really need some doctors at home."

"I know." Jacob agreed. He was cheerful and determined outwardly, but he was worried, too.   "Fort Bridger," he announced. "Wanna pee?"

"Silly question!"

Gestational diabetes and twins is a tricky combination. It was January, frigidly cold, and two months before the due date. Sending Emma to Salt Lake wasn't something anyone had taken lightly; travel was always a scary proposition in the winter. But Sweetwater County Hospital was not equipped to deal with premature births, and if the test results were iffy, the babies might have to be delivered early.

Emma had come packed to stay awhile, just in case. There would be amniocentesis tests and an endocrinology specialist would be seeing her to try to get her blood sugars to a reasonable level. Jacob had taken vacation time, and Emma

115

had asked for a leave of absence from the television station. Whether she had to stay in Salt Lake and have the babies there, or was allowed to go home, she would not be allowed to work during the rest of her pregnancy.

She was feeling a bit like a failure. Not to mention a burden on her husband.

Mostly, she was terrified.

To cheer her up, Jacob had suggested a visit to the Family History Library. It had been in a new location for about a year, near the LDS Temple, and they had been wanting to go for a while. Emma had visited the LDS church at home and been told all about the many, many records the church had gathered and cataloged over the decades.

Jacob had decided that the best thing to do was to come a day before the doctor's appointments, so they could really spend some time at the library—again, just in case they didn't get a chance afterward.

Just as they arrived at Salt Lake's Little America Hotel, it started to snow. Emma gave her husband a grateful smile, and said, "You did good, babe."

Jacob grinned. "We aim to please!" He leaned over and kissed her. "I'll get us checked in if you want to wait here."

"I better come with you," Emma sighed. "I have to—"

"Pee!"

They laughed. "I'd rather get you settled in a room right away anyway."

Jacob was a little ill at ease, noticing his wife's pale face. "You should rest a bit."

"Aren't we too early for check-in?" Emma wanted to go straight to the library.

"I booked us for an early check in."

"It's early, all right," Emma remarked, glancing at her watch. "How'd we get here before ten when I had to stop so many times?"

"I'm good!"

"True."

Check-in went quickly, and they were treated to bell-hop services; not an amenity most places still offer, but still done for guests in the tower. Their room was really nice. A king-sized bed, a desk, a sitting area with sofa, easy chair and tables, plus a good-sized television and a small refrigerator, coffee maker and microwave were all included in the room. It was a real home-away-from-home.

Little America is not on Temple, but it is close enough to Temple Square and all the historical sites that one can comfortably walk when the weather is good—provided you're not seven months pregnant. However, there are also buses and trolleys and plenty of parking options if you want to drive.

Emma started unpacking their things and stowing them in the closet, drawers and the bathroom. Jacob called the transit authority to double check the bus route to the Family History Library. It was less than ten minutes away, he discovered. "I'm going to go out and park the car," he told Emma, and gave her a quick kiss. "Then we'll get a bite to eat and go catch a bus!"

"Sounds great!" Emma agreed.

Little America in Salt Lake City was a nice place to stay. In addition to the very nice rooms, it had a restaurant and a coffee shop, a gym and a laundry area, an indoor swimming pool and free local phone calls.

Emma had purchased a phone credit card before leaving home, and used it now to call Jill and let her know they'd arrived safely. "It's snowing now, Mom," she said. "But it literally waited to start until we were in the hotel parking lot."

"Thank God," Jill exclaimed. "It's been snowing here for a couple of hours, and it's really piling up. How are you feeling?"

"Like I'll never be able to pass a restroom again for the rest of my life," Emma griped. "Plus…I'm really scared, Mom."

"I know you are. Twins are a big deal anyway, without this added issue," Jill said. "But you're going to some really good doctors down there."

"I just hope I don't have to stay! It's so expensive."

"We'll figure it out, if we have to. As long as you and the babies are safe, that's all that matters."

"Well, that's true." Emma was silent a moment, then asked, "Is Mel back from Los Angeles?"

"I'm pretty sure they flew in a couple of days ago," Jill replied. "Oh, why didn't I think of that? You could stay with her; she's pretty close by."

"Do you think she'd mind?"

"Are you nuts? She'd love it!"

"So would I," Emma admitted. "She travels so much now, I never get to see enough of her."

"I'm just glad she's not living in L.A."

"Me, too."

"Well, you just give her a call; I'm sure if you have to stay near the hospital, she'll be glad to have you around."

"Well, Jacob and I are here for the next week, regardless. We're going to the library right after lunch."

"I'd like to go to that library myself," Jill said. "I'd like to see if there are more records about my great-great Uncle Joel."

"Already on my list!" Emma laughed. "But you know the number one story I'm after right now."

"Bonnie—the Mayor? — she says the records there are the most extensive and detailed in the world."

"I know. I'm so excited. But it's not going to be easy—can you imagine how many Juan Gonzales families there must have been in that area? Manuelita said her husband's father and grandfather were both named Juan. Plus cousins, nephews—whew, I have got my work cut out for me!"

"I think you'll have to work backward. Start with Dad's grandmother, who was a Gonzales. By the way, your Dad is John—Juan in Spanish."

"Ugh! I need to think up some original names. No Maria, no John. No, no."

"So," Jill drawled, "are you telling me you're having one of each?"

Emma laughed. "No, Mama, I'm not telling you anything. We don't know; we asked not to be told, remember?"

"So you say, but what do you *think*?"

"If you're asking if I can just tell, the answer is 'no'," Emma informed her. "I wish it worked that way; I might be able to win a bet now and then. Nope, it would appear, even after all this time, that I only get insights into the past. I have to wait and see, just like everyone else."

"Bummer," Jill said.

"You'll get over it."

2.

"Wow!" Emma gasped.

"Yeah," Jacob agreed.

The Family History Library was huge. Huge. And quite beautiful, frankly.

They stood in the lobby, staring around, with no real idea of where to start.

Luckily, it was a matter of less than a minute before they were greeted by a lovely silver-haired woman with a name tag reading "Hello! My name is Lucy, and I'm a Volunteer."

"Hi, I'm Emma. And this," she gestured to her husband, "is Jacob."

"Hi," Jacob said.

"Welcome! I'm Lucy." She indicated her name tag. "How can I help you today?"

"I'm a total newbie," Emma admitted. "I'm very interested in finding some background on my family." She grinned. "An old, old family story has been passed down, and it's a bit of a mystery."

"Family history is so important, isn't it?" Lucy smiled. "And I'm sure you'll want to pass your knowledge down sometime soon..." She gestured at Emma's very round belly.

"I would definitely like to tell the whole story," Emma agreed. "I just hope I can find something."

"Well, you may or may not know that this building holds the biggest collection of historical family records in the world. Most of what we have here is on microfilm, but there is also much on microfiche. We also have books, newspapers and magazines; it's an amazing collection."

"I don't even know where to start!" Emma admitted.

"I'm dumbfounded," Jacob added. "Is everything here records of LDS families?"

"Not at all," Lucy said. "The records include all religions, all races on record. Anyone and everyone are welcome to come here and research. There's no charge for the use of the microfilm or microfiche viewers. There may be small charges to make copies, but really, the information you can find here is priceless."

"Do you think," Jacob asked tentatively, "that there would be any records of Holocaust victims and families?"

"There are many records here devoted to that," Lucy told him. "It's very important to be able to study the history and find family members. I personally know a family here in Salt Lake who found a relative they thought had died in Germany, but had actually survived and emigrated to New York."

"Oh, how wonderful!" Emma exclaimed.

"That must have been an emotional day for them," Jacob remarked. He looked thoughtful. "Would you mind very much if I—"

"Of course not!" Emma said. "I'd be disappointed if you didn't take advantage of the opportunity."

"Talk about not knowing where to start…"

Lucy smiled brightly at them both. "Let's start by looking at your grandparents," she said. "I'm assuming you know their birthdates and a little about them?"

Emma grinned. "It just so happens that I am hoping to start my search with my great-grandmother Anna Gonzales," she said. "I know she was from New Mexico. I'm really looking for information on her line today; as far back as I can go."

"It sounds like you're looking for something in particular?" It was obvious that Lucy was intrigued.

"A kidnapping," Jacob told her.

"Oh, how exciting!" Lucy cried. "I hope we can find something!"

"We do, too."

"And as for you, young man, I'd like to direct you to some records regarding World War II and the Holocaust. Do you know who you're looking for?" Lucy asked.

"My grandfather's siblings, perhaps," Jacob replied. "He came to the United States after World War I, and they stayed behind. He lost touch with many people during World War II, and so did my grandmother."

"Very ambitious searches!" Lucy led them to a bank of computers. "Let's get started…"

120

By entering names, birthdates and birth places into the computers, they were able to pull up search information. Lucy helped Emma pull microfilm records on the New Mexico Gonzales families while Jacob found a pay phone and called his mother for information about his great grandparents.

When he returned, he found Emma with her face pressed into the viewer, examining records and taking notes. He tapped her on the shoulder. "I think we're probably bankrupt after the long-distance charges," he told her good-naturedly.

"I guess I better get a second job," Emma quipped. She regretted it instantly. "Sorry," she said. "Considering I'm grounded for the time being, that was not funny."

Jacob shook his head. "I'm not worried," he said. "I was just shocked at the cost of a five-minute call to New Jersey!"

Lucy returned then with a few more rolls of film. "Oh, Jacob! You're back," she said. "What have you got for me?"

Jacob showed her his notes and she bustled him off to a new location, leaving Emma to her research.

Microfilm records are kind of a pain to work with, but Emma soon got the hang of loading the film reels and reading the records one by one. She had done the same sort of work researching her uncle's death in Sweetwater County.

The records here, though—they were so much more extensive, so much more detailed. If there was more to Uncle Joel's story, she'd undoubtedly be able to find it here someday.

New Mexico was full of Gonzales families. Juan was the most common given name, it seemed. There were fathers and sons, uncles, cousins; Emma felt quite overwhelmed.

"I'm just going to move backwards from Great-Grandma Anna," Emma muttered. She consulted her notes. Anna Gonzales; father, Juan Gonzales—no surprise there! But that Juan was too young, and he wasn't married to a woman named Maria Manuela.

Okay, next!

After an hour or so, Emma looked up from her notes and films, and realized she had no idea where she was. Of course, she knew she was in the Family History Library, and she was sitting at a bank of microfilm readers, but...where was the bathroom?

Emma chuckled. A woman who was seven months pregnant with twins should ask where the bathrooms were before anything else!

Jacob appeared by her side, seemingly like magic. "Where've you been, honey?" he asked.

"About two hundred years in the past," Emma replied. "And you?"

"More like forty years for me."

"Bathroom?"

"Let's go!"

They spent the rest of the afternoon at the library. Jacob had gotten several reels of microfilm and sat next to Emma, looking through old records of the war, emigrant records, death records and the like. He'd been able to start his search with his grandparents' names after getting birthday and birthplace information from his parents.

He looked grim; he wasn't interested in discussing anything yet; Emma was curious; still, she gave him his space. The information he was searching would hit a lot closer to home than Emma's search two centuries ago.

Emma was devoted to finding answers—explanations— within her family, and knew it was important to the spirit of her ancestor to know what became of her daughters. At the same time, she knew it could not compare to finding family members who had living relatives who still remembered them; who knew them personally. There was a very big difference in their searches.

Although the library was open until nine on Tuesdays, Emma was more than ready to call it a day by six. She'd taken copious notes and had print-outs of several things she'd found. Jacob looked drained and had printed out several records to take with him and go over.

One thing about it all—they'd not had time to worry about the doctors' appointments the next day.

They could think of no reason to eat anywhere other than the Little America restaurant, and found the fare quite satisfying. After dinner they returned to their room and pretty much collapsed with exhaustion.

Lying side by side on the bed, they clasped hands and stared at the ceiling. "I have a lot to tell you," Jacob said, "but I haven't quite processed the things I know, and I know so little..."

"Why don't you have a nice hot bath and relax?" Emma suggested. "I'm sure you're more than a little overwhelmed, and I can wait."

"Did you find anything?" Jacob asked.

"Quite a lot, actually, but I've got to go through it with a fine-toothed comb. So many, many Juan Gonzaleses! If there's a boy in me, he will not be a Juan or a John—no offence to my dad!"

Jacob laughed. "And if there's a girl in there, she's not Maria."

"Agreed!"

"I'm going to take that bath," Jacob announced, rising. "I promise not to use all the hot water; I know you want a good soak, too."

"I do," Emma agreed, "unless I fall asleep."

"It's not even eight," Jacob chuckled. "If you fall asleep this early, I'm alerting the media."

Emma yawned hugely. "You do that," she grinned.

Chapter Eight

Marking Time

"As I'm sure your doctor has already told you, multiparity— multiple births, like twins or triplets—is a high-risk pregnancy. Gestational diabetes increases the risk. Right now, your twins are within normal limits in size and development, but there is always a chance of prematurity in twins, and we certainly want them to get as much time in utero as possible."

"Of course," Emma agreed, and Jacob nodded.

Doctor Sanchez was a tiny woman, possibly as old as forty—but only based on her specialty. If she weighs a hundred pounds, Emma thought, I'll eat my hat. She stood barely five feet tall, and yet, in that moment, she was like a giant in the small room.

"Doctor Carlin has already given me his assessment and plan regarding your diabetic treatment," Doctor Sanchez. "Did he go over it with you?"

Emma nodded. "He gave me a monitor and some strips to test my blood several times a day," Emma said. "I have a ton of notes here…"

"Good, good. And of course, you'll be meeting with the nutritionist this afternoon to go over a good diet plan."

"Yes."

"We're hoping to be able to get your numbers down with diet, but I suspect that won't be the case." The doctor looked up from her notes and smiled. "Your present diet doesn't seem unreasonable to me—unless you've omitted a lot of cookies and cakes."

"We're horribly fond of our sweets," Jacob admitted, "but I don't think she's been overdoing it—have you?"

"I have the occasional treat," Emma admitted. "But, honestly, I went sweet-crazy in the first trimester and after that, it went back to the usual occasional candy bar and dessert after dinner."

"You realize that sweets are only part of the problem?"

"I remember my food pyramid," Emma said. "It seems like a good many of the foods we eat convert to sugar."

"That's correct. Do you eat a lot of carbohydrates? Bread, cereal, starchy foods like potatoes and beans, fruit—these are all carbohydrates and get converted to sugar. They are all part of a healthy diet, but need to be watched closely."

"Okay."

"You'll learn a lot about meal planning from the nutritionist. But here comes the hard part. You're not going to like it."

Emma and Jake braced themselves for bad news.

"I'd prefer that you stay in Salt Lake, if it's at all possible for you to do so," Doctor Sanchez said.

Emma and Jake both exhaled loudly; this was something they'd been prepared to hear. "We can make it work if we have to," Jacob said.

"I'm mostly concerned about the weather," the doctor continued. "The babies are fine, and so far, have not become bigger than they should be. As long as we can get your sugars under control, they should grow at a normal pace and—"

"Wait. I don't understand," Emma said. "Why would they get bigger? I thought twins were usually smaller than singletons."

"They are," Doctor Sanchez agreed. "But babies born to diabetic mothers whose sugars have been elevated for a long period of time can get pretty big. Carbohydrates—sugars—cross the placenta. It's how your babies get their nutrition. But extra sugar can cause them to grow too much, which leads to several risks—premature birth is already a risk and would increase with over-large babies. The larger size increases the odds of needing to have a cesarean birth. Prematurity increases the risk of breathing problems, and so does increased birth size.

"Clearly, these are things we don't want to happen. I'd like to do daily monitoring of your blood sugars over the next week, and if they don't come down to a safe level, Doctor Carlin plans to start you on insulin. I think this monitoring would be best done here, so treatment could begin right away."

"That makes sense," Jacob agreed. "We were planning to stay until next Tuesday, anyway."

"Would we be able to go home after that?" Emma asked.

"I want to say 'yes, of course'," the doctor said, "but all I can honestly say is 'let's wait and see how it goes'." She shook her head. "You live a few hours away; it's winter; you have an increased risk of premature birth and an increased risk of needing a cesarean. Your sugars could get better, or they could rise. Frankly, I want you close."

Emma felt like she might vomit; it was terribly frightening to hear someone make a list about all the risks involved in having babies. She'd never thought about it before; her friends and her sister Dana had popped babies out without much fuss.

Jacob, sensing her unease, put his arm around her protectively. "We'll make whatever arrangements we need to," he said.

"Melody lives in Park City," Emma added. "She's my sister. Is that close enough, or should I stay closer?"

"On a good day that's less than an hour away. That would be much better than three hours or more," Jacob added.

. "That sounds fine," Doctor Sanchez smiled. "But let's also keep an eye on the weather forecasts; if things look stormy, you might want to be closer."

"One day at a time," Jacob said.

"Exactly." Doctor Sanchez grinned. "Now that you're here close to all the great baby stores, do you want to—"

"No!" Emma and Jacob cried in unison.

2.

"Are you crazy?" Melody cried. "I would LOVE to have you stay with me for a while. For as long as you need. When? When?" Her voice blared from the telephone receiver.

Emma grinned. Melody was clearly beyond excited, which made Emma so happy she could cry. "Jacob will be here until next week," she said. I was thinking maybe he could drop me off there on Tuesday when he has to go home."

"Don't be silly," Melody said. "It's expensive staying in a hotel. I have plenty of room here—it's just me and Rob, and we have three bedrooms. The big guest room has a private bath. Check out of there and come here!"

"Oh, that sounds great," Emma cried. "I'll have to talk to Jake, but I think that might be a good idea. It wouldn't be tonight, though. I'm tuckered out from all the doctors and stuff; I'm already in my pajamas."

Melody chuckled. "I don't blame you; it's already dark, it's cold as a witch's tit, and you're carrying three people around!"

"I don't know if Mom told you," Emma said, "but I'm on a search for a pair of abducted great-great-infinity aunts."

"She did, and I'm super excited to hear all about them."

"We spent hours yesterday at the Family History Library, and the place is fascinating. I've found a lot of information, and I'd like to spend some more time there tomorrow. First, I have to go to a diabetes clinic and learn how to properly test my blood sugar, but that's early. Would you like to meet us at the library? I mean, do you have time?"

"You're gonna laugh, but…let me check my schedule."

Emma giggled. "We used to say that when we wanted to get out of doing things," she said.

"I know! But these days, I actually have a schedule that has to be checked. It's super annoying at times. Hang on a sec."

"Okay."

Emma could hear shuffling and rustling and the click of drawers or cupboard doors closing. "Aha!" Melody exclaimed triumphantly. "I found it. Okay, let's see…" She was quiet for a couple of minutes. "Okay. Tomorrow morning, I have to go into the studio for about an hour. That's at seven." Melody burst into giggles. "I wanted to be in this business because I wanted to stay up late and sleep in, and look what's happened!"

Emma laughed with her. "But it's wonderful, Mel. You've come so far! I'm so proud of you every time I hear you on the radio, and I always hope it'll happen when I'm with a bunch of people, so I can yell, 'Listen! Listen! That's my sister!'"

"You do not!"

"Oh, yes, I do!"

127

Melody laughed. "Believe it or not, that's the best compliment ever: my big sister is proud of me. That's better than friends, better than fans, even better than parents!"

"What—why?"

"I don't know if you know this, but I spent my childhood trying to get your attention."

"You mean by shrinking my favorite sweater after wearing it without asking and spilling chocolate milk on it?" Emma giggled.

"I meant *positive* attention." Even over the phone, she couldn't quite disguise the hurt in her voice.

"I'm sorry," Emma said, honestly contrite. "I guess when you're a kid, you just assume everyone knows you love them."

"I think I was just jealous of your ghosts," Melody admitted. "I wanted to see them, too."

Emma was quiet, not sure what to say. Could she ever explain how she felt about her gift? That sometimes it felt more like a curse, and it was a burden even while it brought her deep satisfaction at times?

"I'm over it, though," Melody continued, after a long pause. "It finally occurred to me how hard it must be for you. It hit me when you were planning your wedding; I could see you stressing about whether someone might show up during your vows or something."

"Oh, God, was it that obvious?" Emma cried.

"No, no. Only to us; you know, Dana and I, and Mom. We prayed and prayed that they'd all stay away and let you have your day."

"Well, it worked. They were there, but they just watched and smiled. So, thank you!"

"No problemo. Anyway, that's when I decided that you paid as much attention to me, and everyone else, as you could; you have more people than anyone I know trying to get you to pay attention to them!"

"I do feel overwhelmed at times," Emma admitted.

"So, anyway, what time is your appointment?"

"Eight."

"I can probably get to the library by ten if that will work for you."

"That'd be perfect!"

"You can check out of your hotel, and when we finish at the library you can just follow me home."

3.

So, they found themselves in Park City with Melody and Rob that Thursday evening, and within an hour of their arrival, it started snowing. And snowing. And snowing some more.

Jacob stood near the bay window in the living room, watching the storm. "Wow!" he said. "I'm glad we decided to leave when we did."

"I'm going to have to kiss my boss," Rob said, "for deciding that leaving early was a good idea today."

"Yeah, Mac will love that," Melody laughed.

"Maybe," Rob grinned.

"I'm awfully glad to be here," Emma smiled. "I just have one question—"

"Why is the Christmas tree still up?" Melody said.

"Yeah!"

Melody and Rob exchanged looks, and then grinned widely. "We got back from L.A. just a few days ago," Rob said. "Before L.A. we were at your folks' place for Christmas. It just—"

"It's like we haven't been home for ages. We came back from Chicago after Thanksgiving—"

"—and we put up the tree, thinking we might get to stay home for a while—"

"—and our manager called with the L.A. gigs, and we took them, broke for Christmas in Wyoming, went back to finish in L.A.—"

"—and when we got home, there was our tree!"

"And we just looked at each other and said, 'Let's enjoy it for a few days'! So, there it stands."

"Plug in the lights," Jacob suggested. Rob did so, and the tree was beautiful. "I can't believe it's not real!" Jacob said.

"I know," Melody agreed. "I found this a couple of years ago in New York City. It cost me more to ship it here than it cost to buy it! But I just had to have it."

Emma shook her head admiringly. "I can see why. It's gorgeous."

Melody jumped up, clapping her hands. "Rob! Set up the camera! Let's take a picture of us in front of the tree. Forevermore, we can say we had Christmas in January with my sister in our house."

After setting up a tripod and setting the timer, they posed for several shots in front of the tree. "One of these better turn out good enough for Christmas cards," Melody said.

"I hope so," Emma agreed. "Although my huge belly is going to be pretty tough to live down later."

"Yeah, I think you're twice as big as you were a month ago," Melody laughed.

"Really?!" Emma was aghast.

"No, silly! I'm just kidding!"

"It feels like it's true," Emma grumbled irritably.

"No, no, no. I'm sorry!"

"Prove it. Feed me!"

"Let's go see what we've got. I think pizza delivery is out tonight."

"Snow's really piling up fast," Rob agreed. "But that big ol' four-wheel drive of mine can make it to the store if we need anything."

Melody looked at Rob thoughtfully. "I'm sure we're okay for dinner," she said, "but just in case, it might be a good idea to go grab some supplies."

Rob and Jacob nodded at her and at each other. "The mighty hunters hear," Rob said.

"And obey," Jacob added. "Emma, where's your diet list?"

"Hang on, it's in my bag," Emma said, and started the expedition into the land of woman-purse.

Armed with a list, the men ventured out into the dark, stormy evening, and the women settled down in the kitchen. Melody had all the makings she needed for chicken soup, and it was nothing, she said, if not a soup night. "I don't need any help," she added. "So why don't you go through those notes and print-outs and tell me what you think you've got so far while I chop and slice and dice?"

"Are you sure?"

"Sure! The curiosity is killing me."

Emma got up. "Okay, I'll be right back." She went upstairs to the guest room Melody had set them up in. It was a very pretty room, with a queen bed, a chest of drawers and a dresser and mirror in light oak and decorated in soft peachy colors. Jacob had unpacked a lot of their things already—the room was furnished, but drawers and closets were unused, so they had plenty of room for their stuff. She found her notebooks and print-outs on the dresser and gathered them up.

Back in the kitchen, she told Melody, "I love this house."

"Me, too," Melody agreed. "I always thought I'd live in Wyoming, but the first time I did a show here, I saw this house from the road. And every time I was in the area, I'd drive up here and look at it. I don't know why, but I just fell in love at first sight."

"And it miraculously became available?"

"Pretty much!" Melody shook her head. "I drove up from Salt Lake after a show, and there it was—a beautiful, glorious 'For Sale' sign. Once I saw the inside of the house, I knew it just had to be mine. I made an offer the same day, and glory hallelujah, they accepted." She grinned. "Wanna know part two of the miracle?"

"Do tell!"

"By this time next year, that little bedroom is going to be home to a little song-bird."

"What? Mel! How long have you been keeping this secret?"

"Oh, about a week. I'm barely pregnant, man. But I'm always so regular that I just had to check! I'm due in September! We're so freaking excited! I didn't want to say anything, but—"

"Why?"

"Well, you're having your baby, soon, and—"

"No, no, no! If you haven't told mom, you get on that phone right now! She's going to be so happy! I'm so happy! They'll be really close in age—they'll be best friends! I—"

"Emma, wait." Melody sat down and took Emma's hands in hers. "It's not that simple...we're not married. It bothers Mom and Dad."

"But—"

"I know what you're going to say. We can get married anytime—"

"Well, you can! And—"

"I don't know if I want to," Melody stated flatly.

"Don't you love him?" Emma asked.

"Of course, I do," Melody admitted. "And I'm so happy about this baby. But..."

"But? But what?"

"I have kind of a crazy life, Em. What if Rob doesn't want to slow down enough to be a husband and father? I mean...huh! I don't know what I mean."

"Have you talked about this?"

"He asked me to marry him the minute we got the test results."

"And that's a bad thing because—?"

"Don't you get it? He never asked me before!"

Emma inhaled deeply and nodded slowly. "Ah. So, you're afraid—"

"That's the only reason he asked me? Yes." Melody shook her head again and squeezed Emma's hand. Then she jumped up and started skimming the chicken broth. "I never thought I'd be the one to end up feeling like this," she said. "I just figured all the conventional things—marriage versus living together—were going to be decisions that I'd make, and they'd stay made, you know? I was perfectly happy with the choice I made. I didn't need to be married. But now..."

Emma nodded. Babies changed things. We might think we know everything we need to know, but suddenly, our decisions include little people who can't choose for themselves. She understood that.

"But I don't want to get married because I have to—"

"Oh, Mel, it's not like Dad pulled a gun on him!"

132

"You know what I mean!"

"I do." Emma jumped up and hugged her sister. "I do, Mel, really. But did you ever stop to think that maybe he never asked before because he thought you really didn't want him to?"

"But why would he think that?"

"How many times in the past few years have you said you never wanted to get married?"

"Oh, gee." Melody grinned ruefully. "That."

"Maybe he believed you."

"Why wouldn't he?" Melody shrugged. "I meant it."

"Things change. People change."

"People get knocked up."

"Oh, Mel!" Emma squeezed her sister tightly. "What did you say when he asked?"

"I—nothing." Melody groaned. "I just sort of…stared at him. And then I ran out of the room to throw up."

"Oh, God. He may never ask again!"

"I know!"

After that, all they could do was laugh.

4.

"Ouch!" Jabbing your finger several times a day makes for some really, really sore fingers, Emma thought.

"I know, I'm so sorry." Jacob loaded the strip into the Accu-Chek II meter. The countdown started, and then displayed "142".

Emma was cleaning her fingertip with a cotton ball. "Damn it!" she cried. "Why can't I get down to 120?" She stuck her finger in her mouth. She yanked it out again. "Why can't I be under 100 when I get up? What am I doing wrong?" She tried, and failed, to stop the tears.

Jacob wrapped her in his arms. "You're doing nothing wrong," he whispered soothingly.

"I'm going to have to take shots, I guess," Emma moaned. "I can live with that—but will I still have to jab my fingers all day long?"

133

"I guess we'll add that to the question list," Jacob replied.

It was nearly time for Jacob to leave—he had to go back to work, so he could take time off again when the babies were coming. He hated the idea of leaving Emma, and was so grateful that she had her sister.

There had been plenty of questions, lots of information to absorb, and in the end, insulin was to be the great equalizer. Unfortunately, that didn't mean Emma got to stab herself any less than she had been.

The weather had been nasty all weekend and cleared up on Monday, and the trip in to Salt Lake City from Park City on Tuesday morning had been slick in spots, but nothing too drastic.

Now, however, Jacob would be traveling north, and darkness would be upon him before he got home. Emma was scared. The road reports sounded bad.

"I'll stop in Evanston and call you," Jacob promised.

"Okay…and after the Sisters?"

"I'll stop at the truck stop and call you again."

"I hate the Sisters!"

"Everyone hates the Sisters."

For the uninformed, geographically, Uinta County, Wyoming encompasses two separate watersheds: The Bear River and the Black's Fork of the Green River. They are separated by a series of low mountain ranges known to Wyomingites as the Three Sisters. Interstate 80 twists its way through these mountain ranges, and during the winter, it is a hellacious drive. The wind blows fiercely across the road, driving snow in ground blizzards resulting in very low visibility, and black ice patches.

Emma's fears were well founded. "I wish you didn't have to go!" she wailed.

"Me, too." Jacob picked up his bag. "I'll be back next week; I've got a seven-days-on, three-days-off shift coming up."

"That's weird." Emma followed him down the stairs.

"Yeah, I think Jim made it up just for me."

"Kiss him for me."

134

"Yeah, sure thing." Jacob chuckled. He stopped Emma before she could pull her coat on. "No, babe, don't walk me out—I might cry."

Emma's lower lip quivered, and the tears flowed down her cheeks. "Okay," she agreed. "I want you to be able to see where you're going."

"It's going to be fine." He pulled her into his arms and held her closely, then kissed her, pulled the door open, and walked down the driveway to the car. Emma stayed in the doorway until he pulled away, then closed the door and had a good cry.

This would be the first time since their wedding that they'd ever been apart.

Rather than sit around and feel sorry for herself, Emma took advantage of the prolonged stay and went to the library several times a week. Much of her time was spent researching the Gonzales family, but she also looked up her uncle Joel to see if there was more information.

Within a couple of days, she had discovered his, and several other family members', burial locations.

"Mel, they're all here in Utah!"

Melody looked up from the notes she was going over. They were sitting close together at a table covered with notes and print-outs. They'd become familiar faces at the library. "We should go."

Emma raised her eyebrows.

"Not today, silly. This summer, maybe."

"We could plan a family trip—before you get as big as me."

"Bite your lip, Laverne!" Melody laughed, quoting a favorite television show. "Laverne & Shirley" had kept them giggling once a week when they were teenagers, and some lines had become part of their shared vocabulary.

"It could happen."

"Never!" Melody shook her head. "I mean—how did this happen, anyway? Do twins run in the family?"

"Funny you should ask," Emma grinned. "I'm gonna say 'no'. In all this genealogy—so far—I've found exactly one set of twins. Just so happens, it was our great-great-great Uncle

Joel. He had a twin brother, who happened to live quite a lot longer than he did."

"Hmm. I haven't found any." Melody shuffled through the papers a bit. "What about Jake?"

"I don't know." Emma frowned. "We've just been so excited, and then so scared, that we didn't even think to ask."

"Has he said anything about his family search yet?"

"Not really." Emma shook her head. "I can't imagine having to search for that information," she admitted. "I think he needs to process things before talking about them."

"Or he just doesn't want to upset you right now."

"Probably. But that kind of makes me feel bad, you know?"

"He's a good guy," Melody said. "Let him be good. There's going to be plenty for you to talk about soon enough."

"True. I just hope he's talking with his parents a bit about it."

"He probably is. Ask him to ask them about twins," Melody added. "Now I'm nervous! What if it's all on our side?"

Over the next few weeks, Jacob visited when he could, Jack and Jill came down on weekends, and Emma grew and grew and grew.

"I look like a whale!" she complained. "And I feel like a pin cushion! And I'm going to cry—again!"

"Don't do that," Jacob begged.

They were sitting in an exam room yet again, waiting for Doctor Sanchez to come and give them a progress report. Emma had just gone through an ultrasound test, blood tests, and a pelvic exam where the doctor did a lot of "Uh huh" and "Hmm" and didn't say much else. She's left the room to get test results and to let Emma get dressed before sitting down to talk.

When she came back, she beckoned to them and said, "Let's go talk in my office."

The followed her down the hall and she got them seated before sitting behind her desk.

Jacob and Emma stared at her apprehensively.

"Here's the deal," Doctor Sanchez began. "We're three weeks out, and the babies look great. Realistically, you could go into labor at any time; it's the nature of twin births."

"So, I should come back here and stay?" Jacob asked.

"Well, let's talk about what's going on and then we'll get to that." The doctor shuffled through some paperwork in Emma's file. "First, Emma, your blood sugars are still a little high, but I don't want to increase your insulin dosage. Your blood pressure is also high today, and has been high the last few times you've been checked. Not dangerously high," she added, "but cause for concern.

"The babies are a little on the big side, but they're doing well.

"I think it's time to discuss inducing labor."

"But I still have three weeks!" Emma wailed.

"Convince us," Jacob added calmly.

"It's not really a matter of convincing you," Doctor Sanchez smiled. "I'm not going to force you to do anything. But I must advise you that Emma now has wandered into preeclampsia territory, and with everything else her body is dealing with, this can escalate very quickly.

"What is preeclampsia?" Emma asked.

"It's also called toxemia, and it's a condition caused by high blood pressure. It can cause problems with the placenta beyond the problems already possible with the diabetes.

"What I'm saying is, it's dangerous for you and for the babies. The decision is up to you, of course; we could try waiting. But I advise against it. I think the time has come for you to become a Mommy."

"What do we have to do?"

"Well, today I would like to give you an injection that will help mature the babies' lungs more rapidly. Tomorrow I want you to pack your hospital bag and get in touch with your family—make your preparations, in other words. The next day I want you to check into the hospital at six a.m. and we'll start an I.V. and get this party started."

"Wow." Jacob looked like he was in a state of shock. "I'm glad I'm here."

"I planned it like this just in case you weren't with her today," Doctor Sanchez informed him smugly. "Then there would be plenty of time for you to get here."

"I thank you," Jacob said.

"Me, too," Emma added sincerely. "So...you already knew?"

"I suspected last week," the doctor admitted. "But I was hoping. Still, you've done very well. It's not at all unusual for twins to be this early—earlier, in fact—and we've had very good outcomes." She handed them some paperwork. "You can take these home and fill them out. Give the hospital a call and pre-register, and take the paperwork with you when you check in. I'll see you Wednesday morning. Unless..."

"Unless?" Emma asked.

"Unless you go into labor on your own in the meantime."

"Thank you, Doctor," Jacob said. "We'll see you Wednesday morning."

A nurse arrived at the door with a loaded syringe. "Don't forget your shot!" Doctor Sanchez said.

"Pin cushion," Emma grumbled.

Chapter Nine

Honoring Ancestors—The Twins

"Oh...my...HECK!" Emma groaned. "No offense, honey, but I kind of want to punch you right now!"

Wednesday, February 11, 1987. It was early afternoon already, and Emma knew one thing; labor was tough!

"Let me know when to duck," Jacob said, his voice soft, his face pressed close to hers.

"Nah, it's gonna come...when you least...expect it. Whoo!"

The waiting room was full; Jack and Jill, Melody and Ron, Dana, Matthew and Fred took turns popping in to check on Emma's progress. Tom had taken time off to stay home with his and Dana's children.

The weather had been strangely cooperative. There had been no significant snowfall since the start of the month, so travel had been easy for the family.

Jack slipped quietly into the room. "Jake," he said. "Matt and I are on the way to the airport to get your folks now. We'll be back soon."

Jack leaned over to kiss Emma's cheek. "Try not to have the babies until we get back," he teased.

Emma groaned. "Shut up, Dad. This lady waits for no one!" She shifted her weight, trying to get comfortable while maintaining her modesty—no mean feat. "Seriously, no speeding. Be careful."

"I promise," Jack swore. "I'm on the lookout for crazy drivers."

Jill came in as Jack exited. "Want a break, Jake?"

Jacob looked at Emma. "Do I?"

"Of course!" Emma said. "Get some lunch, go potty."

"I'll hurry."

"I hate to say it," Emma sighed, "but I don't think there's any rush just yet."

Once Jacob was gone, Emma turned to her mother. "You know that line you gave me a few months ago? The one that goes: 'after they're here, you'll forget the pain'?" she asked. "I think you're lying."

Jill grinned. "I promise I'm not," she said. "Once you hold them in your arms, the pain will just fade away."

Emma glared at her mother. A contraction took hold and built up in intensity, and she inhaled deeply, then blew her breath out in short, sharp "Chee, chee, chees."

When it was over at long last, Jill wiped her daughter's flushed face with a cool cloth.

"This sucks!" Emma declared.

"But it'll all be worth it."

"I know, I know." Emma looked around then, and said, "Oh! Hello."

"Really?" Jill demanded. "Now?!"

The visitor was quite tall, thin but big-boned. She looked...strong, Emma decided. This woman looked strong. She looked around the room appraisingly. "Well! Things have changed so much," she told Emma.

"Changed since when?"

"Since I had my twins."

"Your twins—you're Joel's mother?" Emma looked at Jill. "It's Joel's mother!"

"Uncle Joel was a twin?" Jill asked.

"I forgot to tell you," Emma admitted. She looked back at the woman standing next to Jill. "Your name is Janette?"

The woman smiled, and her face was suddenly glorious. "It is!" she said. "I've seen you studying the past. It is good."

"And Joel's brother is Cyrus."

"Yes. When we went to settle the Idaho Territory, they were the first white children born in the area. I was very thankful not to be alone that day."

"Your husband—?"

"Oh, no, no, no!" Janette looked amused. "The men disappeared quite regularly during birth times in those days. They were not like your husband—they fled like frightened children at the first opportunity, then returned to brag of their accomplishment once the task was successfully completed." Janette laughed merrily.

140

"Why are you...huh...here?" Emma gasped, now in the grip of another contraction.

"I've been watching," Janette told her. "You're doing fine. I've just come to tell you that all will be well..."

She was gone.

"Well, dang!"

1.

Janette was right; all was well.

The twins arrived shortly after midnight on February 12th. It had been a long, long day for Emma, but she'd discovered something wonderful: her mother was also right; once the babies were placed in her arms, the pain receded from her memory.

"Oh, my God, Jacob!" she sobbed happily. "Look what we made!"

They were tiny; they were both breathing on their own. They were a boy and a girl; they were beautiful.

Their daughter had arrived first, and immediately howled her indignation with the outside world. Emma was allowed to hold her momentarily, and then she was whisked away to be weighed and measured and cleaned up while Emma returned to the task of delivering baby number two.

Their son put in his grand appearance eight minutes later. He didn't cry right away, which scared the life out of Emma. She held her breath until he finally squalled. He was allowed a brief visit with his mama, and then, he, too was whisked away.

Empty arms are not happy arms! Emma was impatient, waiting to hold them again.

The nurses efficiently cleaned mother and babies, put Emma in a huge and embarrassing diaper-like pair of panties and swaddled them all in clean blankets.

Again, Emma was allowed to hold her babies. The pediatrician arrived and took them away again. More measurements, temperatures, oxygen saturation tests.

Oxygen tanks arrived. The babies were fitted with cannulas and hooked up to the tanks. Emma and Jacob watched anxiously. One by one, the babies were placed back into her arms.

The pediatrician held a hand out to Jacob, who shook it. "I'm Doctor Schuster," he said. "Your babies are amazing; their oxygen saturations are a little low, but they're breathing very well, both of them. I don't think they'll be needing supplementation for long."

"Oh, good...?" Emma said, uncertainly.

"Yes, very good. Let's see, we have twin A, female. Four pounds, four ounces, sixteen inches long. Big girl!"

"Really?" Jacob asked.

"For a premature twin? Yes, indeed! Now, twin B, male, four pounds, one quarter ounce, sixteen and a half inches. Good, good!"

Emma was in tears. Everything sounded...well...good! The babies felt so warm and wonderful in her arms. But she was terrified, suddenly.

"Are you sure?" she cried. "Are you sure they're okay?"

"They are perfect," Doctor Schuster assured her. "They'll have to be with us for a few days, of course, but their hearts are beating away in perfect rhythm, their lungs are clear, their eyes are fine, they have all their fingers and toes—you're welcome to count for yourself, of course."

"Don't think I won't!"

"I don't doubt it for a second." The doctor chuckled. He reached down and plucked the baby boy from her, and turned to Jacob. "Let's introduce you to Dad," he said, and placed the infant in Jacob's arms.

"Papa," Jacob said quietly. "Hello son whose name will not be John or Juan," he said, and carefully placed a kiss on the baby's cheek, avoiding the cannula tube that was taped there.

Emma giggled. "And hello daughter who will not be called Maria," she added.

Doctor Schuster frowned in confusion, then shrugged. New parents said some funny things, sometimes.

2.

After a nice gurney ride, Emma and Jacob settled into a new room with their babies. The doctors were going to talk to the family and let the couple get comfortable before allowing any visitors.

"Before our parents come in," Jacob said, "I'd like to talk to you a bit about...well...my search. And...and some name ideas."

"I've been waiting," Emma told him.

"It was hard, Em," Jacob admitted. He hugged their daughter, kissed her tiny forehead, and looked at Emma with welling eyes. "I'm ashamed that I never had more interest before. Or maybe I was just scared."

"I can understand that."

"Okay." He blinked hard and sighed. "Well, you remember that my mother's parents came to the U.S. after World War I, right?"

"And your dad's parents and grandparents, as well," Emma added, nodding.

Jacob nodded. "I started my search with my mother's paternal grandparents. I guess her grandmother had already passed away before the war, but her grandfather refused to move when his son—my grandfather—asked him to."

"Oh."

This wasn't sounding good.

"His name was Avram. That's a Hebrew form of Abraham. He died at Auschwitz."

"Oh, God!"

"I'm not sure yet when or how, but his name is on the rolls."

"Oh, Jake!"

"I haven't told my mother; she never knew him. All she knows is that her father was keeping in touch with him, and then he stopped getting letters."

"I can't even imagine what that must have been like!" Emma wiped a tear off her cheek.

"I know. Me, neither. Anyway, I also looked for her maternal grandparents; they died, too, but in Warsaw. I don't know how they died, either. They were Dinah and Joram." Jacob kissed his daughter again. "I also discovered a great-great aunt who was executed at Belzec. Her name was Amalia."

"Avram and Amalia," Emma whispered. "Those are wonderful names. I like Joram and Dinah as well, but...you know...twins?"

Jacob chuckled. "Yeah. 'A' names. Do the next set get 'B' names?"

Emma's jaw dropped, and her eyes widened. "Bite your lip, Laverne!" she cried.

"What?" Jacob frowned, bewildered.

"Laverne? Shirley? Never mind." Emma shook her head. "You want another set of twins, you have 'em! I'm pooped."

"So middle names Maria and Juan?"

Emma groaned.

3.

The grandparents were ecstatic. Avram and Amalia were the first twins anyone could remember in the family. Nurses were in and out of the room, making sure the babies weren't passed around too much, and letting only two visitors at a time come in to congratulate the new parents.

It was amazing anyone got in at all; the sun was barely rising.

The grandfathers came in first. The nurse was very strict with them about holding the infants since they were premature. They sat the men down and carefully placed the babies in their arms. Ezra held Avram and Jack had Amalia. Both men were pleased with the names, and the reason behind the choices. Ezra brushed tears from his cheeks. "Your mother will be so gratified," he told the proud parents. "We could only assume...you know..."

"I know," Jacob said quietly.

The grandmothers were both tearful and joyous, each with a babe in arms and beaming through their tears.

The aunts and uncles were allowed a quick peek, but the nurses were adamant that too much cuddling was not a good thing for premies. Soon they shooed everyone away, and the families went off to Melody and Rob's house to rest and relax.

A lactation nurse came to visit with Emma just as she was dozing off. It's a hospital thing. Someone always shows up just when you're dozing off.

It was time for nursing lessons.

And then she finally got a nap.

Chapter Ten

Crossing the Atlantic

July 1987

"Are these things even safe?" Jill demanded, trying to figure out how to buckle the car seat into place in the back seat of her car. "They sure take up a lot of room!"

"It's the law, Mom," Emma groaned. She was on the other side, struggling with the second seat. "We had to buy them to bring the babies home from Utah."

"I know, I know," Jill conceded. "I just...ugh! —have such a hard time...getting them in here!" The seat belt snapped into place. "And then I'm just sure I've done it wrong."

"Me, too," Emma admitted. She looked up at Jill as she snapped the belt shut on her side. "Remember that contraption you had for Freddie? The one that just hung over the back of the seat?"

"Oh, God," Jill giggled. "It's a wonder that boy is still alive!"

"Yeah, it is!"

"If you girls keep having babies, I'm going to have to buy a bus."

"That's cool."

"Yeah, it is. I wish I had one now," Jill said. "Then Dana could ride with us."

"I wish the guys were going with us," Emma lamented. "At least Melody and Rob are meeting us in Hooper."

"This is kind of a strange route," Jill observed. "I was hoping to go in a loop, but that doesn't make sense, so I guess Hooper to Ogden to Huntsville...then back to Ogden and then home."

"At least they're not too far apart. Weber County is big; we might have had to make more than one trip for this."

"I really want to hit the other cemeteries one of these days, but these will do to start."

Dana arrived then, pulling in behind Emma's new station wagon.

Why Jill had insisted on taking the old Torino, no one could fathom. All she'd say was "I need to be the driver, and I want to drive my car."

"But, Mom," Emma had protested, "the wagon is brand new! I'll let you drive."

"No, no, I want my car. It's fine. Dad takes good care of it."

And that settled that. Arguing with Jill was like talking to a brick wall.

Emma trotted over to Dana's car. Dana opened the window. "Are we going to get lost?" Dana asked.

"Oh, no doubt," Emma replied with a giggle. "I was just wishing for a bus, so we wouldn't have to take separate cars."

"Memma! Memma!" Benjamin waved his arms. The toddler was firmly buckled into his car seat in the back. His baby sister's seat was next to his. Lena was sound asleep.

"Hi, Buddy!" Emma said, waving at her smiling nephew. To Dana she said, "I'm going to be so sad when he starts saying my name right."

"Me, too."

Fred leaned out the front door of the house and called, "Em, Ami's crying!"

"Coming!" Emma replied. "Dana, I know what a pain it is to unload, but I wanted to nurse the babies before we hit the road..."

"Tell Fred to come and give me a hand."

Fred said, "I'm already here."

They all laughed, and Emma ran for the house, with Jill on her heels.

1.

Anyone with small children knows that there's no such thing as getting an early start when traveling. At least, not as early has you might have planned.

It was almost seven by the time they hit the road, Emma and the twins riding with Jill, and Dana and Fred with her children following.

The plan was simple: visit three cemeteries in the course of the day, have a nice dinner and go home. Simple in theory; in practice, it was a little less simple.

Amalia did not like her car seat. She started crying the minute she was buckled in, and kept crying. Avram was indifferent to the seat, and to his sister's tears; he went to sleep almost immediately. But even as they were weaving their way through the Sisters, Amalia fussed.

"Oh my God!" Emma cried. "I'm sorry, Mom." She was in the backseat by now, trying to entertain the baby, calm her down.

"Maybe you should just take her out of that thing," Jill suggested.

"And you'll get a ticket," Emma said. "They passed the car seat law for a reason, Mom."

"I know, I know," Jill cried. "Maybe the buckle is too tight. Maybe something is pinching her."

"I already checked. There's nothing hurting her."

"I don't know how Abe is sleeping through this racket," Jill groused.

"Me, neither, but I'm sure glad he is."

Finally, Emma persuaded Amalia to take her pacifier, and the little girl went to sleep just as they entered Evanston.

"I need to pee," Jill said, "But I'm scared to stop!"

"Just do it," Emma told her.

They pulled off the freeway and into the Flying J truck stop. Dana pulled into a parking area near them. Fred practically flew out of the passenger side. He and Jill met on the sidewalk in front of the cars, grasped each other's arms and cried, "Babies! Whew!" Then they went inside to take care of business.

Emma and Dana faced each other through their windows and shook their heads at each other. Apparently, Lena had been at it, as well. They waited on Jill and Fred, and when they'd returned, both of them eased their ways out of their cars and fled.

In the bathroom, they both burst into giggles. "I just know they're going to wake up the second we get back on the road!" Dana gasped.

"I know!" Emma agreed. "And we've still got a couple hours to go."

"What were we thinking?" Dana locked herself into a stall, and Emma waited for the next available stall to open up.

"I'm pretty much hating the car seat law right now."

"It's a good thing, Em."

"I know. So is liver, but I hate that, too!"

"Shut up!" Dana giggled.

Some anonymous woman in a stall started laughing. "I'm sorry," came the voice behind the door. "My baby's not having a great travel day, either."

Dana and Emma laughed. A toilet flushed, a tiny woman emerged and gave Emma a bemused look, and Emma darted into the vacant stall.

Emma purchased coffee for herself and Jill and returned to the car. Dana had soft drinks for herself and Fred.

Once back on the road, the babies cooperated and slept. Emma and Jill were quite relieved.

"Are you nervous?" Jill asked Emma.

"About what?" Emma dodged the question nonchalantly.

"Don't be coy; you don't fool me," Jill said. "How much time have you ever spent in cemeteries?"

"None," Emma admitted. "You and Dad were never up for any of us attending funerals, and we've been extremely lucky not to have lost many people over the years."

"True. I never saw any benefit to taking children to funerals."

"I guess it's as good a time as any to discuss death," Emma suggested. "But I've been aware of death for as long as I can remember."

"So? Are you nervous?"

"I am...but I'm not. I mean, there's a part of me that just doesn't believe that the spirits of our loved ones hang around at their gravesites, you know?"

"Really?"

"If they did that," Emma reasoned, "how would they find me?"

"Huh! I never thought of that," Jill admitted. "I've always thought cemeteries were creepy, scary places; full of ghosts."

"We went through the cemetery once on a field trip," Emma said. "I think it was in fourth grade. I didn't see anyone; but no one related to us is buried there." She shook her head. "Freddie's always hoping I'll run into someone at the library, too, but I never have."

"Well, you know you're related to people in these cemeteries," Jill said. "You found that out in Salt Lake. So, what do you think will happen?"

"I have no idea, Mom," Emma admitted. She sipped her coffee. "This is new territory for me."

"Me, too. I hope you don't mind," Jill added, "but I'm going to Ogden first. Then we'll go over to Hooper from there. I'm scared we'll get lost if I don't head there from Ogden."

"Whatever works for you, Mama," Emma agreed. "We can have a late breakfast or early lunch there. I just know these babies are going to wake up soon, howling for sustenance. Lena and Benji, too, most likely."

"Good deal."

2.

After a good meal had been consumed by all, it was time to make the short jaunt from Ogden to Hooper. Amalia protested the car seat vigorously. Twelve miles never seemed so far!

Once they'd arrived and parked, Emma assembled her stroller, and Dana did the same. Whoever invented the twin stroller was their hero for sure! Benjamin was having none of it, though, and Fred took him by the hand to walk around the parking area while they waited for Melody and Ron to join them.

Jill went to the office to get a map from the sexton. By the time she returned Rob and Melody had arrived. Melody was carrying an impressive belly by this time, and Rob was especially solicitous of her.

They started walking down the path, and as they walked, they tried to make sense of the geography.

"I hate maps," Dana groaned. Lena was hopping in her stroller seat, chanting "Up, up, up!" as she did so, and shaking the stroller. Dana had tried unfolding the map on top for the stroller shade, but Lena's hopping made it impossible to read.

Jill took the map and spread it on top of Emma's stroller. "Fred, how are you at reading maps?"

"Topography is my scientific specialty," Fred declared. He led Benjamin back to the women, and Jill picked him up.

"UP!" Lena shouted.

"Lena, hush!" Dana scolded, which immediately prompted tears.

"Oh, boy, Mama," Benjamin said, watching his baby sister howl with an expression close to disgust. "Now you did it!"

"Oh, you hush, too, mister," Dana told him. She extracted the baby from the stroller. Lena quickly stopped crying. Fred took the map, put it on top of the stroller shade and started pushing.

Dana and Jill looked at each other; each woman with a child in arms simultaneously rolled their eyes and watched as the empty stroller was wheeled away, now a glorified map-holder. "Well," Jill huffed. "Don't that beat all?"

The women laughed and followed Fred, the king of the map.

Emma came to a sudden stop. "Guess I was wrong, Mom," she said.

Jill stopped, too. "Really?"

"Really." And then she said, "Hello, Annie. Good to see you again."

3.

Annie was not alone; there were several people with her. "You weren't wrong, Emma," she said. "We really don't hang around our burial places; what good would that do us? But we knew you were coming."

"How?" Emma demanded.

"How what?" Jill asked.

Dana and Fred, who had gotten ahead of them, turned back. "What's going on?" Fred asked. "Oh, never mind; we have company, right?"

Emma nodded. "How did you know we were coming?" she asked Annie.

Annie shook her head. "I don't know how we know. We just know. There's a connection between you and your family, Emma." Annie grinned. "I'm glad to see you again, too."

"Well, introduce us," Emma said, indicating the small gathering. "Um...didn't you tell me you were buried somewhere else? I'm confused."

"Like I said, we don't just hang out. I came to see you again. They came to see you for the first time."

Dana said, "I have cold chills," and Jill nodded at her.

Fred was looking every which way, just hoping for a glimpse of anything.

Benjamin pointed right at Annie and said, "Pretty!"

Annie said, "Thank you!"

"We'cum," Benjamin said, and then started wriggling in Jill's arms. "Lemme down, Grammy!"

Everyone stared at him, astonished. Jill sat him on the ground, which made Lena determined to get down, too. "Don't you move, young man," Dana warned, and then turned to Emma. "Did he—?"

"I think he did," Emma sighed. "Wow."

"I think I'm jealous of a toddler," Melody cried.

Rob nodded his agreement. "What are the odds our baby will--?"

Emma shrugged. "Or mine," she added.

"It's not unusual for children to see us," Annie said. "It's most likely he'll...hmm...outgrow it."

"Will he?" Emma asked. She looked at her sisters, and repeated, for their benefit, "Will he outgrow it?"

"Time will tell." Annie smiled at the little boy, who was looking around at the small gathering. "Most children do. You're a rarity, Emma.

"Shall we sit?"

Emma motioned to the others, and they moved off the path and into the grass. Annie and a few women moved close to the stroller and looked down on the twins, who stared back at them with wide, blue eyes. The women moved aside as a pair of men, obviously twins, came forward.

"Finally!" the first fellow spoke. "How many generations has it been?"

"For a living pair? Four," the second man replied.

"My father," Annie said, indicating the second twin, "Joel, and his brother Cyrus."

Emma nodded at each of them. "A pleasure," she said.

"The pleasure is ours," Cyrus replied, and Joel nodded, smiling gently. "Our father," Cyrus continued, indicating a third man, "John."

"John," Emma repeated, feeling slightly amused. Johns and Juans; it mattered little which side of the family, the Johns were abundant.

"I'm your great-great-great-grandpappa," the gentleman told her. He sported an impressive moustache. He indicated a tall, strong-boned woman. "My wife," he said.

"We've met," Emma said. "Hello, Grandmother."

Janette smiled warmly. "Did I not say all would be well?" she said, beaming down at the babies. "They are beautiful."

"Thank you."

Annie indicated a petite and pretty woman. "My mother, Mary Ellen."

"Hello."

The family, those seen and unseen, sat together in the grass under a huge fir tree. "Are we going to find the graves?" Fred asked.

"I don't think everyone here was actually buried here," Emma said. "I know Annie isn't."

"I'm not, either," Cyrus told her.

"Neither is Cyrus, Joel's twin brother." Emma added. "But John and Jeanette, who are our great-great-great-grandparents, and Joel and Mary Ellen, who are our great-great-great uncle and aunt, are here somewhere."

"Who else is here?" Jill asked.

Emma looked around at those assembled. Janette indicated a man and woman near her and introduced her brother Terrance and sister-in-law Janette.

"Oh, good," Emma said. "More duplicate names!"

There was general laughter. "It is the way with families," Joel told her. "We name our children after those we love; our

153

parents, aunts, uncles. Sometimes our wives or husbands inspire us to name our children after them." He grinned. "I had a sister and a cousin named Janette," he added, nodding at his mother and aunt, "after their mothers. I had a brother named John, named for my father, and for my great-grandfather."

After sharing this information, Emma asked, "And did you also have a son named Joel?"

"I did not. But I did have a son named after my grandfather. So did my brother." Joel chuckled. "They were close in age; it was confusing."

"I'll bet."

Joel smiled at her. "I'm sure you've wondered why we haven't met before."

"Yes."

"I had nothing to contribute; I was asleep!" At this Joel laughed, and it was a musical sound. "I thought I'd made a good decision, you know," he added. "Get home early, beat any winter storms." He shook his head. "I was feeling a little selfish, going to the World Fair without my family. The irony is not lost on me."

"None can know the hour or the day," Emma said. "Or something like that."

Joel grinned and shook his head. "It's a good reason to live your life well," he agreed. "Don't forget."

"I won't."

Joel's mother Janette spoke up: "There are many questions you'd like to ask, I'm sure." The woman had a lovely voice, and an accent that was an odd mixture of Irish and Scottish that Emma found enchanting. She smiled warmly at Emma. "But you have plans, and the day is short, as all days are."

"But—"

"It is well that we can be with you now," Janette continued. "You have learned already of the accident that befell my Joel; as your great-grandmother instructed, you have learned and explained."

"My great-grandmother—yes." Emma frowned. "But she's not your family; her husband, my great-grandfather was."

"My grandson, Craig—Jimmy was his father. Madeline was his wife, and a fine woman."

"But you never met her?"

"I never met Craig; I was not so very old when I moved on."

John said, "I knew him; he was yet a lad when I crossed over. A fine lad; a hard worker."

"Still, they are our family," Janette explained, "and we have watched when we could. We take an interest, you see."

During all the conversation, Emma kept her family informed of what was being said. After she passed on this latest exchange, Janette continued. "There is only one story we will share today, because it has been a matter of much speculation in the family over the years. Then you will see the stones you've traveled to see, and go your way.

"In my generation, we came to this country with the Latter-Day Saints. President Brigham Young and his Brothers in Christ developed a plan which allowed the Saints to travel to the New World in pursuit of freedom. In Zion—the Great Salt Lake Valley—our people were free to live as we chose, to build up a great family of Saints who would follow the teachings of the Church. A great many people worked together to build the fund that would pay the way for many poor families, who would emigrate and repay the favor when they were settled and established.

"There were ships leaving from England. We all qualified for fund money to assist us on our way. Soon enough— although it seemed to take forever! — we received our letters of instruction, our passage orders. We were fortunate enough to be assigned the same ship and traveled to England from Scotland together as a family; John and I, our four children, my brother and his wife and their five children. Their oldest son was fifteen and apprenticed to a cobbler; he stayed behind in Scotland. That was very difficult for the family!"

Her sister-in-law, also a Janette, nodded and said, "Although we knew he would do well in his work, it was hurtful to us all to leave him behind. But an apprenticeship meant he was indentured; he would have to repay his patron for his instruction once he was established. We could not afford to pay to have him released from his obligations." She shook her head. "He did very well for himself. He made us proud."

"Did he ever leave Scotland?" Emma asked.

"No, he married and settled there."

Here John added to the conversation. "We had a son who was called home before our conversion. He was not yet three years old at the time. Brother McAllister was very kind to baptize him and make him a member of the Saints, so he is with us always."

Emma looked around; there were no children, save the living, among them. "Where?" she asked.

Her third-great grandfather smiled at her. "Little children are innocent," he said, "and await no judgement. We will be with them all in time."

Emma nodded. She had so many questions! But it was true; they had a schedule to keep.

"We left Scotland together and traveled to England. There we stayed with Saints who were charged with organizing the travelers," Janette continued. "The day we boarded ship was a joyous one; all the Saints rejoiced with singing and laughter. Many came to see us off; the docks were swarming with Saints on that day!

"The trip was a difficult one for us, although most of the travelers managed without incident. We were fortunate to have booked passage in the spring; I'm certain things would have fared worse for everyone otherwise."

The other Janette—whom Emma would henceforth refer to as "Aunt Janette—spoke up again. "Before we had even left the harbor, a Sister had given birth. Four babies were born on that voyage, and such a blessing they were! There was no privacy; giving birth is a difficult thing in any case, but those mothers also did so with a captive audience. There was a midwife among us, and she did her best to preserve their modesty.

"We were blessed to add to our brethren, but there were also losses; three deaths, and two of those were from our number." Aunt Janette shook her head sadly.

Janette went on. "Our children were small; Jimmy was eight and Jeannie was seven. (Jeannie was our Janette). Little John was three and sweet Mary was not yet two years old."

Aunt Janette added, "My Janice was nine and Mary was seven. Tommy was four and Jenny—our Janette--was two. And the baby, Maggie, was only three months old! You must well know, Emma, how difficult travel with an infant can be!"

Emma passed this information on and agreed wholeheartedly that traveling with babies was a chore—especially after Ami's crying jag that morning. She couldn't begin to imagine the difficulties her ancestors had faced, traveling such a distance. She resolved to count her blessings and try not to complain so much about her difficulties in the future.

"Soon," Janette went on, "we were all very sick. The sea tossed us about continuously. There was never enough to eat, and the foods we were eating were not as nutritious as what was needed to keep a body well.

"Blessed were the days when we were well enough, and the weather fair enough, to go on deck into the fresh air! We tried most diligently to keep everything clean, but below deck were over five hundred Saints, many ill with infirmities of the stomach and bowels. Such a smell I had never before endured, and it added to my own illness, I declare!

"I was never before a woman to get sick, and I was disgusted with myself!" Janette shuddered. "I soon overcame the illness, as did Jimmy and Jeannie. Little Mary was still on the breast and fared best of us all; she suffered not one day of illness!"

"Tis truth, Sister!" declared Aunt Janette. "A mother's milk is a gift; for neither did my infant Maggie suffer a day."

Terrance spoke at last. "It is a most difficult thing, to watch your family suffer," he said. "I did my best to aid the other men aboard with watch and chores, cleaning and praying, but spent as much time as possible with my wife and children."

John nodded. "The men were assigned duties. We would stay on deck during the dark hours and keep watch. Daytimes we would clean the floors, look after our families and those others in our charge. Soon we began preparations for the long journey that would follow our landing in the New World. We would be walking into New Zion, and for that we would need provisions; the women aboard who were well enough began to fashion tents from bolts of canvas. We stayed quite busy every day."

"Yes," Janette agreed. "Our days began very early, and all the Saints who were well enough would meet for prayer each morning and evening. We prepared our own meals, sewed the canvas tents and watched our children. My Little John and Janette's little Jenny continued to be quite sick; they never had a well day aboard the ship. Their bowels ran continuously; their stomachs would not hold their meals. We both tried adding our own milk to their diets, but they could not retain even that, and they became mere shadows; their bones were displayed most prominently.

"At first, they cried, but as they weakened they merely moaned; worse yet, in the midst of his infirmity, John would yet smile tenderly at me. It broke my heart to see that sweet smile, knowing how he suffered so!"

"Jenny did the same," Aunt Janette agreed. "It was almost as if she was reassuring me! It yet pains my heart to think of it!

"In the darkness of the morning near the end of April, my Jenny and Janette's Little John died within hours of each other," Aunt Janette added. "It was a most horrible day!"

"Consumption of the bowels, they called it." Janette's eyes shone with tears. "It is a most fitting name, for they were indeed consumed by their illnesses.

"The news was announced at morning prayers, and all the Saints mourned. That afternoon, our babies were committed to the sea, their tiny bodies sewn into sheets. They were so little; there was hardly a splash as they were tipped over the side!"

The whole group, living and dead, was silent for a while after this exchange. Finally, Emma wiped away her tears and said, "I'm so sorry for your losses!"

Both Janettes nodded their thanks. "We know the time will come when we will all be reunited," Aunt Janette said. "But it was a fearsome test of our faith!"

Janette smiled sadly. "Even now, it is difficult to wait," she said. "But we know the reunion will come and there will be much rejoicing.

"There have been many stories of our passage to Boston, and the children we lost. Some say there was one child only; therefore, we have come to tell you that there were two; the cousins Little John and Jenny, son and daughter of sisters-in-law both named Janette."

Janette chuckled. "I can see now that honoring a loved one by naming your child after them can lead to a good deal of confusion. I do not envy you, Emma, in your duties to discover and explain, but I admire you for your willingness to use this gift.

"Rise now and visit the stones where none dwell nor linger. See the names engraved upon them and know that all are indeed in a better place than this, and will yet go on to still a better place. We will meet again. We leave you with our love."

Then Emma was alone with her living family. "Well, dang!" she said.

4.

After locating several headstones in the Hooper cemetery, they had gone back to Ogden and from there to Huntsville. Jill was using Ogden as her touchstone, and that was fine with everyone; no one wanted to get lost.

Once in Huntsville, they made a stop for more camera film, and then went on to the cemetery.

Like the grounds in Hooper, everything was well tended. There weren't as many family members buried here, and no one showed up to visit with them and tell stories.

As much as Emma loved her ancestors, she found this a relief today. Janette's story of crossing the Atlantic had left her emotionally drained. She was more grateful than ever that she lived in the times she was in. Six weeks at sea and then a walking journey across the country? No thank you! Jump in a car or an airplane instead? Yes, please!

"Oh, man!" Melody groaned as they started back along the path to the parking area. "I have so much respect for the pioneers now! All I want is for someone to push me in a stroller—right now!"

Everyone laughed, although they understood that Melody was more than half serious. Her ankles and feet were swollen and her back ached. "Is anyone going to be mad at me if I beg off the next cemetery?" she asked.

"Of course not!" Jill declared. "But please—if you're up to it—have dinner with us in Ogden before you go. Is that okay with you girls?" she added. "We can go home from the cemetery instead of from the restaurant."

Emma and Dana assured Melody and their mother that it was fine. Time had certainly zoomed by; everyone could use a sit-down meal before finishing up.

In what could be termed either a late lunch or and early dinner, the family was seated at a long table at the Village Inn. Emma draped a blanket over her shoulder to nurse Avram while Jill held Amalia. Dana was also taking the opportunity to feed Lena, while Fred tried to keep Benjamin entertained. The waitress helped by delivering crayons and a coloring page.

While they waited for their orders and nursed babies, there was a lot to talk about.

"I'm a little freaked that they don't have their children with them," Melody said, patting her tummy.

"Me, too," Dana agreed.

"Not me," Fred declared.

"Really? Why not?" Emma asked, honestly curious. She had her own thoughts on the matter; she wondered if Fred's would be the same.

"It's like they said: the children are innocents. There's no place for them there; they've moved on to the final place, I believe."

"Heaven?" Jill asked.

"Why not? I guess you have to call it something." Fred shrugged. "I picture a place full of laughing children and dogs."

"Sounds heavenly to me," Emma agreed.

"But there's no one to take care of them!" Melody fretted.

160

"I don't think that's so," Jill said. "If it's Heaven... Paradise...whatever...they're well taken care of."

"I want to believe that," Dana sighed. "But it must be so hard! They must have expected to see them..." She sighed again. "They've waited so long!"

Clearly everyone shared Emma's feelings on the matter. It would be difficult to wait to see your babies; but it felt right that innocent children would not have to wait for Heaven; why would they? No judgement awaited the innocent.

It was true that at this point, the dead had nothing but time; but the passage of time, if Manuelita was to be believed, was different where they were. Manuelita had once told Emma that she didn't know how much time had passed between visits. Emma could only assume it was the same for the Janettes, who were waiting to reunite with their little ones.

Finding Manuelita's daughters seemed more urgent to her now than ever.

"I sometimes feel," Emma said, "that the more I learn, the more questions I have."

Jill smiled at her. "That's true of everyone, sweetie," she said. "The older I get, the dumber I feel."

"It's not just that," Emma said. "We live in an age of information. Computers and telephones, television, books—all the things we take for granted now are things our families never had. It could take months to receive a letter. Travel took months as well, and was so dangerous it was a miracle if you arrived at your destination at all. Record-keeping took a back seat in many, many cases.

"We've been lucky here; the Latter-Day Saints were—and are—brilliant recorders of history. Even so, much has been lost in time. Janette said it herself—many believe that there was only one child lost on that journey. That's what compelled them to visit with us today, to set the record straight. But if the records aren't there, how am I to prove it? How can I explain?"

"Maybe the explaining has already been done," Rob suggested. "Does it matter on a larger scale? I mean..." he trailed off. "Oh." He shook his head. "There are so many more ancestors than just our family...I don't know what I was thinking, that just your immediate family needed to know..."

Everyone stared at each other. Jill smiled sympathetically. "You have a hard gift, Emma," she said. "Sometimes I feel sorry for you. But mostly," she added, "I just feel proud."

"You could have run from it," Melody added. "I'll bet people do."

Dana said, "Growing up, I was sometimes jealous of you."

"I still am!" Fred admitted. "I probably always will be. But I'm proud of you, too."

"I heard someone say, 'It's a blessing and a curse'." Emma giggled. "I don't remember who said it, or why, but the saying sometimes crosses my mind!"

"Food!" Fred cried. The waitress had returned.

"It's a blessing," Melody added, making room for the waitress to place her plate in front of her.

Rob laughed and moved his water glass. "Speaking of blessings," he said oh so casually, "Mel finally said yes."

Mouths fell open, and shrieks of delight followed. "A wedding!" Jill cried. "At last!"

And all conversation moved from past to present in an instant, and then moved to the future, as they discussed plans for a wedding for Melody and Rob.

After a good meal and much discussion—which was lively but resolved nothing—Melody decided she was recovered enough to visit the Ogden City Cemetery after all. It was a short drive, and for a wonder, Amalia didn't get into a snit until they were parking.

"I hope she falls asleep in the stroller," Jill commented.

"You and me both," Emma agreed. "I can't believe anyone so little can make such a big racket!"

"Avram has been pretty quiet all day," Jill said. "I'm afraid at some point he's going to have to put in his two cents worth."

"Oh, Lordy!" Emma groaned. "Bite your tongue, Mama!"

No one was in a hurry, and they strolled through the grounds admiring the statuary and the landscaping.

"I'm so glad you finally said yes," Emma told Melody. "It's about time!"

"Well, I did have to wait for him to get up the nerve to ask me again," Melody laughed.

"Hey!" Rob laughed. "You're not supposed to tell on me!"

"I think we were supposed to turn left back there," Fred said.

They turned back and took another path. "Who are we seeing here?" Dana asked.

"Emily. She was Janette and John's daughter; the only child who was born in Utah." Emma told her.

"What? I thought they lived here."

"They were sent to help settle Idaho Territory. Joel and Cyrus were the first white children born in that area—it was Indian country up until then."

"It still should be," Fred muttered.

"It was a different time," Jill said. It was an empty platitude, and she knew it. "Not that it matters," she added. "There will surely be a reckoning sometime for the wrongs done to the natives."

Fred scoffed. "With our Government?" he cried. "That'll be the day."

Ron gave Fred a playful shove. "Watch it, rebel," he said. "People have died for you."

"And I respect them for it," Fred declared. "But the government responsible for the deaths of millions? Not so much." Fred was adamant in his disdain. "It's all about the money," he added bitterly. "War is good for the economy."

"Fred!" Jill cried.

"He's not wrong," Emma sighed. "Theft and lies; more theft and more lies; Native Americans have never gotten a break from our Government."

"Aren't we Indians?" Melody asked. "I thought we were."

"Probably not on my side of the family," Jill said. "But your dad is almost certainly descended from the natives."

"Almost certainly?" Dana queried, her eyebrows arched.

"I don't think we can prove it," Jill admitted. "It's all family claims, rumors, stories."

"Manuelita told me that she was told there were Indians in her family. But she didn't seem sure of it," Emma said. "She said many of their family were called Mestizos."

"What does that mean?" Melody demanded.

"A mix of Spanish and Indian. Heaven knows which tribes."

163

"We're talking New Mexico," Jill mused. "I would imagine one of the Pueblo tribes."

"Maybe you'll be able to find out," Fred suggested.

Emma shrugged. "Maybe." She was doubtful. "Do you have any idea how many different tribes lived in that area?"

"Well, she told you Apaches stole her kids, so I'm going to say she wasn't an Apache," Dana said.

Rob was busy studying grave markers and the cemetery map. "Here she is," Ron called.

Emma pulled a small notebook from her back pocket and leafed through it. "She was a teacher," she said, "and also, the widow of a policeman. Look," she added, "I found her picture in an old newspaper obituary."

The family passed the picture around. "This is amazing," Jill said. "She passed away before I was born; I never even knew about her! She was your Great Grandpa's aunt; he surely knew her. I wonder if my mother did..."

"Maybe you could just ask him," Fred suggested hopefully.

"I'll call your Grandma when we get home, if it's not too late," Jill offered.

"But if Great-Grandpa knew her—"

"No one is here, Fred," Emma said.

"Can't you just call him?"

Emma shook her head. "It doesn't work that way!" she cried. "Not for me, at least."

"Kind of inconvenient, isn't it?" Melody remarked.

"Understatement!" Emma giggled. "Imagine all I could understand and explain if I could just ask!"

"You could be the next Jean Dixon!" Fred said.

"She's a fraud," Dana scoffed.

"Don't speak ill of the dead," Jill ordered sternly.

"She died? When was this?"

"This past winter; January, I think. Anyway, you don't know she was a fraud."

"She once said Nixon would beat Kennedy."

"She also said that Kennedy would die in office."

"She said cancer would be cured by the time I was seven," Emma declared flatly.

"Oops!"

164

"I think most psychics are frauds," Rob announced. "Like war, it's profitable."

"Do you think I'm a fraud?" Emma asked, honestly curious.

"I don't think you're a psychic," Rob replied, shrugging. "I don't even know if there's a name for what you are; but I certainly don't think you're a fraud. I think you're amazing. And kind of spooky."

"You think my sister's spooky?" Melody demanded indignantly.

"Sure! I know you've watched her do this your whole life. But I'm new to it. I spent my whole life believing there were no such things as ghosts. So…yeah. Spooky. But—" he added, grinning, "not in a bad way!"

Lena started hopping in her seat, chanting "Up! Up!" Dana lifted her out of the stroller. Benjamin was skipping in circles around a large tombstone, and she made him stop. "I find it comforting to know that we're being looked after," she said. "But I admit I'm feeling a little freaked out by Benji talking to them."

Emma shrugged. "If he doesn't outgrow it, you'll get used to it."

"I guess I'll have to." Dana reached into the pocket on the back of the stroller, and pulled out paper and a stick of charcoal. She handed Lena to Emma, and went to the grave marker to get a rubbing. Melody snapped a few pictures; so did Emma and Jill.

"What are your plans for those etchings you've been doing all day?" Jill asked.

"I thought we could make a little scrap book of our trip. Write up the stories we heard, put in the etchings and the photos, add copies of the obituaries we were able find and maybe have copies printed for everyone," Dana said. "I can't talk to them, but I'd like to do something to honor them."

"That's a beautiful idea!" Emma cried. "You come over sometime next week and I'll show you some of the information I have collected so far."

"I'll help," Jill offered enthusiastically.

"I wish I lived closer," Melody complained. "But I have my own ideas…"

"Yes?"

"Nope. It's a surprise." Melody grinned.

"Well, that's wonderful," Jill said, "but don't get as obsessed as your sister was while we were planning her wedding. There's a lot to do!"

"We could just sneak over the state line and get married in Nevada," Melody suggested.

"I'll kick your butt, young lady!" Jill cried.

"The baby's due in two months—"

"Which means we've got a lot to do in a short time—unless you want to wait?"

"I don't...know?" Melody drawled. "Call me when you get home, Mom, and we'll hash it out, okay?"

"Wyoming or Utah?"

"Wyoming!" Melody said.

"Los Angeles!" Rob said simultaneously. Then he burst out laughing at all the astonished expressions aimed his way. He held up his hands in mock surrender. "I was kidding! Jeez!"

They put Lena back into the stroller, and Benjamin agreed to ride behind her for the first time that day. By the time they got back to the cars, all four children were asleep.

They said good-bye to Melody and Rob, who were returning to Park City.

Carefully as possible, they buckled babies into their car seats. Thankfully, they all continued to sleep.

"Please God, let them sleep all the way home," Jill prayed. Dana and Emma nodded emphatically, and Fred crossed his fingers. Both hands. They got into their cars and headed for home.

The quiet lasted as far as Fort Bridger, where they stopped to use the restroom and nurse babies. Emma crawled into the back seat of Jill's car, squashed between the two car seats. Fred did the same in Dana's car shaking his head woefully. All the babies cried the rest of the way home.

Everyone arrived safely, though, and that's what counts.

Chapter Eleven

Spook

August 1987

When Emma entered the nursery, she found Manuelita standing over the crib, cooing at the babies. "Qué hermosos bebés preciosos!" she cried. "What precious beautiful babies!" She turned to face Emma and smiled brilliantly. "They are such a gift, are they not? And now, you understand more than ever."

"I do," Emma agreed. "I thought I understood before, but—"

"It is a special thing, a mother's love, no? One can understand, but not truly know the feeling until it is experienced."

"Yes."

"You have made much progress, I think," Manuelita stated. "But you have no answer yet for me."

"I'm sorry."

"I have nothing, if not time." She shrugged. "You haven't as much of that as I," she added, with a giggle. "But I know you are looking, and I do appreciate it."

"We are planning a trip to New Mexico this fall," Emma told her. "I'm going to go through church records and historical archives."

"It is a good plan." Manuelita looked pleased.

And she was gone.

"Well dang!"

1.

"Well, that was a quick visit," Jacob remarked when Emma told him a few minutes later. He took Avram from her, so she could nurse Amalia.

Emma settled into her rocking chair and offered the baby her breast. Amalia—now more often called Ami—accepted

167

eagerly and began to suckle. "I feel a little guilty," Emma admitted. "But she didn't seem upset that I haven't done much research lately."

"She's a mother; I'm sure she understands." Jacob tickled Avram—who was now almost always called Abe—and the little boy gurgled happily.

"She said something, though—something right; that I can better understand her feelings, now that I have children of my own."

Jacob nodded. "It is right," he agreed. "I really thought I got it before, but now...?" He shook his head. "It's kind of like how I thought I knew about the Holocaust; until I found the names of people connected to me—to me personally—I didn't know a thing! History lessons didn't cover jack crap, and nothing could have taught me about how I felt, seeing those names..."

"That's it, in a nutshell," Emma said. "I understood in my mind; now I understand in my heart.

"I've got to find them."

Summer was passing quickly, and plans for their trip to New Mexico started to come together. They wanted to drive, rather than flying; Emma loved to fly, but didn't relish a drive to Salt Lake, long term parking fees and the necessity of renting a car once they got to New Mexico. She felt more comfortable with the idea of being able to stop whenever they needed to, nursing in relative privacy and taking their own sweet time.

The one drawback to any travel plan was little Miss Amalia. To say that she hated her car seat was an understatement. She could carry on non-stop for miles and miles once she was buckled in, and nothing would console her.

Avram could care less; he ignored his sister, played with his toys, slept. Emma would swear there were times when she caught him rolling his eyes at his twin. He might have been only six months old, but he clearly understood the futility of crying over seating arrangements.

"I don't know if this is such a good idea," Emma moaned during a short outing one afternoon.

"Sorry, what?" Jacob asked. Amalia was squalling in the backseat; it was hard to have a conversation.

168

"This trip," Emma said, louder. "Maybe it's a mistake."

"Maybe we should just suck up the long-term parking fees and fly," Jacob suggested.

"What if she cried the whole flight?" Emma shuddered. "People would try to throw us out without parachutes!"

"It's the car seat; she wouldn't have one on a plane. We could hold the babies in our laps."

"Hmm."

"We could go Greyhound," Jacob suggested.

"Ugh!"

"Bus to Salt Lake, catch a train…?"

Emma sighed. "When I was a kid, you could catch a train here to anywhere," she said. "I will never understand why that changed!"

"I'll research the options," Jacob offered. "Driving might make us crazy!"

Emma chuckled tiredly. She twisted in her seat to watch her screaming daughter. Amalia showed no signs of giving up and falling asleep. She wailed despondently, her little face bright red, her fists clenched and flailing. Avram slept peacefully beside her.

She turned back and grinned at Jacob. "Abe would be fine."

"Good ole Abe," Jacob laughed. "I hope he'll always be able to sleep through anything like that!"

"I wish I could," Emma agreed.

"You can't sleep no matter what."

"True."

Jacob eyed her thoughtfully, then looked back at the road. "It's almost five hundred miles…"

"I might cry myself…"

2.

"Why don't you just leave the babies with me?" Jill asked— not for the first time.

"Mom, it's for a week!" Emma protested.

"Do you honestly think I can't handle them?" Jill looked hurt.

"Of course not," Emma assured her. "I couldn't handle them if it wasn't for you and all your help and advice." She sighed and shook her head. "I don't think I can handle being away from them for a whole week!"

Jill smiled. "I know that feeling well," she said.

"And Abe won't take a bottle!"

"We've got time to work on that."

"And the wedding is next week!"

"That's a whole different can of peas."

"No, it's not! What if Mel goes into labor while I'm gone?"

"Mel is due the week before your trip." Jill grinned ruefully. "I'm more concerned that she'll go into labor during the wedding."

"That would be two weeks early!"

"And that's impossible because…?"

"You're right. Oh, crap. What if she does?"

Jill shook her head and smiled. "If she does, we'll deal with it. If she goes over and has the baby while you're gone, we'll deal with it. Anything life throws at us, we'll deal with, Emmaline."

"Mom—"

"Em, don't be ridiculous. The babies will be fine. You and Jacob could use a nice vacation. You know you'll never get any real research done if you take them—the distraction will keep you from concentrating on what you need to do."

"Mom—"

"You know I'm right, Emma. If you really need to do this—"

"I do, Mom. I always need to—"

"Then you're going to have to learn to accept help when it's offered," Jill stated firmly. "The things you do—the souls you help—it's hard on you. I know it; I've always known."

"I have to—"

"I believe you do," Jill agreed. "But there have been so many times when I wanted to tell you to stop."

"Why?" Emma was appalled; she'd never dreamed that her mother might not want her to do the things she did.

170

"Because it's so hard on you!" Jill cried. "Do you think I don't know that you've never slept through the night? Not even when you were a little girl, Emma! They came to you, saying 'Tell my story, solve my mystery, explain my situation.' And time after time, you've done your best. And when you had trouble, you worried. You never wanted to let anyone down. And in between all of that, you had to go to school, and get good grades, and earn scholarships!"

Suddenly, Jill burst into tears. Emma gasped. "I wanted you to have a normal childhood!" Jill sobbed. "I wanted you to have friends; go to dances; have sleep-overs!"

"Mom, I—"

"You didn't, Emma. Your sisters did, and you joined in sometimes, but you were so...so...alone!"

"Mom, I promise you, I never felt alone!" Emma cried. "I had friends—"

"You had Sasha," Jill agreed. "And Marty. Until they moved."

"I still have them," Emma said. "I talk to them every week." She grabbed Jill's hands and squeezed. "Please don't cry, Mom."

"I'm sorry; I'm just...stressed out."

"Mom, just...you're going to make me cry, Mom!"

"Well, that would just suck, wouldn't it?"

"Did you just say—suck?" Emma burst out laughing in spite of herself, and Jill's sobs turned to giggles.

"For crying out loud, Mama!" Emma cried, snorting.

"Ah, shit!" Jill giggled. "I just wanted so much for you, and they work and worry you to death. It's not fair! I can't yell at them, I can't make them stop. And I can't even have a good cry over it—dang it, Emma!"

"If I let you babysit, will you knock this crap off?"

"Emma!" Jill gave her daughter a little shove. "I just can't tell you how happy I was—how happy your dad and I were—when you met Jacob."

"Imagine how I felt," Emma said airily.

"You shush. I'm serious." Jill wiped her eyes ineffectually. "Ugh!" she said, and got up to get a paper towel. She wet it under the tap and patted her face and eyes. "We saw the trouble you had with people not believing you, or thinking you were…uh…off a little. We saw how some of your classmates wanted to make a party-game of you."

"They didn't—"

"Emma, it's time to stop trying to protect those…those little…"

"Mom, they were just—"

"Little bitches."

"That was years ago…"

"Does it hurt any less?"

Emma tightened her lips and inhaled deeply.

Jack and Jacob were standing in the doorway. "What's going on in here?" Jack demanded. "Are you fighting?"

"Are you spying?" Jill countered indignantly; she hated to be caught crying.

"Hardly," Jack snapped. "We could hear you bawling from the back office. What the hell is going on? Did Emma make you cry?" He glared at Emma accusingly, and Emma stared back, jaw slack.

"No!" Jill cried. "Of course not, Jack, now stop it!"

"Good to know you're so protective of Mom," Emma commented dryly. "Also, good to know you guys have been wanting me to quit helping the ghosts for years."

"We never—I didn't—Jill!" Jack sputtered. "What have you been talking about?"

Emma was feeling stung by her father's accusation, hurt by her mother's disappointments and really just wanted to collect the babies and go home. She started to get up, but Jacob crossed the room, put a hand on her shoulder and gently pushed her back into her chair. He pulled up a chair and sat beside her, then beckoned to Jack to do the same. "This isn't a fight," he said quietly as Jack seated himself. "This is two women who are overwhelmed and overworked. So…what's the scoop? Mom?"

Emma blurted, "I really don't want to go into this!"

"You've never wanted to go into this!" Jill cried. "Those little brats hurt you, and you've never even admitted it!"

Jack said, "Oh."

"Oh?" Jacob glared at the trio. "What 'oh'? Someone better start talking."

"It was years ago," Emma argued. "It hardly matters now."

"Everything you deal with happened years ago," Jacob reasoned. "It all matters."

"Not that many years ago." Emma made a face. "In this lifetime, I meant."

"I don't care. Clearly, it's been upsetting your parents for a long time, whatever it is."

"She wanted to make me quit!" Emma cried, pointing an accusing finger at her mother. "She never told me that!"

Jack took Emma's hand across the table, maneuvering the pointing finger gently. "You have children of your own now, Emma," he said. "How would you feel if someone hurt one of them? How would you feel if people saw them and thought they were liars or fakes? Or tried to use them somehow?"

"Dad, I—"

"You would never tell us what happened. But we heard stories. We saw the pain you were in. We saw how your classmates treated you."

"They didn't really treat me like anything," Emma argued. "They just sort of..."

"Ignored you? Made you an outcast?"

"They got over it. We all did."

Jacob cleared his throat. "I'm lost," he said. "What happened?"

Emma groaned, but she knew it was time to tell her own story. To explain. "Look," she said. "We do have kids now, so you might as well know: there's nothing worse in the whole wide world than a group of twelve-year-olds..."

3.

1972

When children reach the age of twelve or so—say seventh-grade age—they should be institutionalized for at least a year, because they are such a mix of hormones and angst that they are certifiably insane.

Emma was no different than her peers in most ways; when she started seventh grade, her first year of Junior High School, she was a bundle of nerves. Over the summer her budding breasts had taken on some serious weight, and she was self-conscious about it; school clothes shopping had included her first real bras, the kind with actual cups. It was a shocker.

Her auburn hair was thick and very long; even braided, she could sit on it if she wanted to. She'd diligently stayed out of the sun to avoid burning, and the inevitable freckles.

Basically, she was every girl: worried about her body, her face, her hair, her clothes; worried that she might say or do something wrong; worried that she'd get lost in a new school building where for the first time she had to go to different classrooms for her classes; worried she'd be doing it all alone.

She fervently hoped to make friends; after six years, she really had no one she considered more than a school-only chum. Her classmates thought she was weird; of course, they did—she was the looney tune who had darted out into the snow in first grade, off to save her grandma. She was the one who carried on conversations with "invisible friends".

There was no one she knew who understood—or believed—that her so-called "invisible friends" had once been real, living people. No one cared that she didn't invite them; they showed up when they showed up, that was all. And the ghosts didn't care that she was in school, either; she had no choices.

There were other grade schools in town, two of them, and once you reached seventh grade, all the kids went to the same Junior High, which at that time housed grades seven through nine. She would meet some new kids this year, probably a lot of them, and she hoped they would like her.

The school year started out strange and got stranger. Suddenly, two girls she'd known since first grade—Cherry and Candy by name—wanted to be friends.

They started out by talking to her every morning and soon started walking the hallways with her before classes started, talking about boys, classes, parties and holidays. Emma was leery at first; they'd always been cold to her in the past, teasing about her abilities. In fifth grade they'd started calling her "Spook" and it had stuck. Even some of the new kids she'd met so far this term were starting to call her that.

"We never meant it to be mean," Cherry told her.

"It's mean," Emma grumbled.

"We'll tell everyone to stop," Candy offered. Then she started going on and on about some boy she had a crush on.

For a wonder, within a few days, everyone was calling her Emma! She started to hope that this would be the year that she'd actually be accepted and make some friends.

Once school starts in the fall, the first big holiday is Halloween. Emma had never really been a fan; dressing up and begging for treats didn't appeal to her. If she really wanted candy, she had her allowance to spend on it; she didn't need to ask the neighbors!

Halloween for others was all about the scares. But ghosts didn't scare her; she'd been dealing with them for real since she was four. And because she had a connection to the unseen world, witches and vampires and such hadn't made much of an impression on her. Monsters didn't have any impact on her life; if they were real, some ancestor would have warned her. She went out trick-or-treating each year with her younger siblings, but mostly because her parents believed in safety in numbers, and she was the oldest. She hadn't worn a costume since fourth grade.

But here were all these kids who should have been grown up enough to be over it, hyped up over costumes, tricks and treats, and the talk of the school, the Halloween party Candy and Cherry were having.

"My parents said we can have twenty guests," Cherry told her one morning as they walked the halls before class. "It's going to be hard to choose only twenty!"

Emma nodded sympathetically. She didn't have much hope in being one of the chosen; Cherry and Candy were really popular, and everyone wanted to go to this party.

"We'll figure it out, though," Candy added. "We already have a theme."

"That's good," Emma said.

"Yeah, it's going to be great!" Cherry cried.

"What is it?" Emma asked.

Lowering her voice, Candy chanted mysteriously, "It's a surprise!"

"Yeah, okay," Emma said. She stopped by the door to room 112. "This is my class. See ya!"

"But you're down, right?" Cherry asked.

"Wh—what?"

"You're down. For the party. Right?"

"You're—I'm invited?"

"Well, sure!" Candy said. "Of course! Why wouldn't you be?"

"I don't know, I just—" Emma was flabbergasted. "Thank you!"

"We gotta run. Details to come!" Cherry cried. They left her.

Emma went to class, floating on air. She'd been invited to the most talked-about party of the year! It was a glorious day!

Emma had been to parties before, but they were grade school birthday parties where the whole class had been invited. Small-town moms were adamant about not leaving anyone out of things like that, at least when the kids were little.

Junior High was a whole different ballgame; the seventh-grade class no longer included just twenty or so students; the numbers had tripled—more
than tripled, since two of the three grade schools had two classrooms of each grade, kindergarten through sixth grade. Even the most understanding of parents wasn't willing to host over a hundred twelve-year-olds for the evening.

Over the next week or so, those few lucky enough to snag an invite chattered among themselves about costumes, music and the surprise theme. It seemed no one save Candy and Cherry were privy to the information; it generated a lot of speculation.

Emma was beginning to get excited about Halloween for the first time she could remember. Jill was delighted to help her choose a costume; she was so happy for her daughter. It was rare for Emma to be included in things; she'd never slept over at a friend's house or been invited to visit after school. Jill had often felt sorry for her and worried about her.

"Candy said I should be a gypsy," Emma told her mother. She and her sisters were gathered in the kitchen, brainstorming. Jack and Matthew were out hunting with friends. Hunting season was—and is—a big deal in Wyoming.

"What do you want to be?" Jill asked.

"I don't know," Emma admitted. "I'm not really into this stuff, Mom."

"A gypsy could be fun," Jill said. "It wouldn't be hard to throw a costume together if you want me to make it for you."

"Really?"

"I didn't learn to sew so I could buy some cheap thing that will fall apart the first time you wear it," Jill declared adamantly.

"Cool!"

"Will you make me one, too?" Melody asked.

"Me, too!" Dana added.

Jill glared at the two younger girls, exasperated. "Why would you all want the same costume?" she demanded. "I happen to be a pretty talented seamstress! I can do other things!"

Melody giggled and sang, "She can sew a costume, she can sew a dress, she can make a bunch of things and make them all the best!"

"That's right!" Jill said. "That's exactly right!" She stood up and groaned dramatically while clutching the small of her back.

"You're getting pretty fat, Mama," Dana announced pragmatically. Not quite nine, she was still young enough to be tactless without malicious intent.

"Yeah, tell me about it," Jill agreed good-naturedly. "You make sure you let this little brother or sister know how messed up my body got while I was waiting, okay?"

"Okay," Dana agreed. "Hey!" she added, "Can I be a pregnant lady for trick-or-treat?"

Melody and Emma giggled. "I don't think so," Jill said. "That would be a waste of my talents. All I'd have to do is stuff a pillow up your shirt; that's not much of a challenge, now is it?"

Dana ran giggling from the room and returned with a pillow stuffed up her shirt. She swayed her back and marched around the kitchen. "Oh, oh," she groaned, "when will I ever have this baby! I can't wait!"

"I do not sound like that!" Jill protested, giggling.

"I can't see my feet!" Dana continued. "Are my shoes tied? I could trip and kill us both!"

"Dana!" All of them were giggling now. "Stop it! I'm going—"

"—to wet my pants!" Dana, Emma and Melody chorused.

"You're all grounded!" Jill gasped, laughing. "I'll be right back," she added, and fled in the direction of the bathroom.

The sisters collapsed, giggling uncontrollably.

"Oh, God, my tummy," Dana gasped.

"Her—tum—my!" Melody laughed.

"It's time!" Emma shrieked.

From the bathroom, Jill yelled: "Enough!" But she was still laughing.

True to her word, Jill was quite the seamstress. The completed outfits she constructed were worth their weight in gold, truly.

Dana had abandoned pregnant lady in favor of a lovely blue Cinderella costume. The real Cinderella had nothing on Jill's interpretation of the ice-blue gown. With a flowing full skirt, puffy sleeves and a beaded bodice, all she needed to complete the look was the little tiara that Jack picked up in Salt Lake City.

Melody opted for a rock-star outfit. Emma suggested Alice Cooper—her personal favorite—but Melody chose David Bowie. She loved Ziggy Stardust and the Spiders from Mars. Jill was simultaneously amused and appalled, but she did a great job with the outfit. She chose a wildly printed quilted material for the jumpsuit she fashioned. With the tapered legs, Melody was able to easily add knee-high boots. Jill drew the line at letting Melody dye her hair bright red, though. It was easy enough to spike and spray it; Melody was definitely rocking the look. She wanted to carry her real guitar with her, but Jack had picked up a good-sized toy guitar to complete her outfit.

Matthew was a pirate; tight striped breeches, knee high socks, a white shirt with flowing sleeves, head scarf and eye patch. "Arrrgh!" Jack's contribution for that costume was a stuffed parrot that Jill managed to attach to the shoulder of Matthew's faux leather vest.

But the gypsy costume was the most amazing of all, at least in Emma's opinion. Jill had found a rich violet paisley printed fabric and solid violet and blue fabrics and combined them into layered tiers in a full, pleated skirt.

She made a flounced underskirt to make it even fuller. She added a peasant blouse with puffed sleeves and a silk sash at the waist. She fashioned a lovely head scarf with the paisley fabric. Emma added long beads and bracelets, and gold hoop earrings, and carried her tambourine. Somehow Jack had managed to find a crystal ball to complete the ensemble.

It was a big deal; Halloween had never been a grand production in the past, but everyone in the family understood what it meant to Emma to be included with her peers. Even though they weren't going to the party, Emma's siblings were excited to have cool costumes; since they were all still in grade school, there would be costume parades.

Halloween was on Tuesday, and everyone would be dressing up then. Junior High students and even High School students were allowed to wear their costumes to school, and Emma was looking forward to that for the first time she could remember.

But because of the party, Emma would debut her costume a few days early.

Saturday the twenty-eighth arrived, and Emma was a nervous wreck. She alternated between excitement and anticipation, to fear and dread. What if no one liked her costume? What if no one talked to her? Or…what if they did? What would she talk about?

"Maybe I should just beg off," Emma suggested.

Jill put her hands on her hips. "The hell you say," she cried.

"I'm not good at this stuff," Emma whined.

"Just be yourself," Jill told her. "It'll be great."

"I've been myself for the last six years," Emma grumbled. But she finished dressing and adorned herself with the beads and baubles.

Jill helped her apply eye shadow and even let her use some mascara. "Wow, that violet shadow really makes your eyes look dark," she remarked.

Emma stood before the mirror and examined herself critically. Incredibly, she was pleased with her appearance. "Wow, Mom," she said. "I really look like a gypsy!" She turned and hugged Jill fiercely. "Thank you so much! It's great!"

Jill smiled, pleased.

Jack dropped her off at Cherry's house at seven that evening; the party was supposed to end at eleven, the latest Emma had ever been out.

Cherry's mother met her at the door and greeted her by name. "Everyone is waiting for you!" she told Emma excitedly. She waved at Jack, who was sitting in the car, and closed the door.

"Waiting for me? Why?" Emma asked.

"Don't be silly, dear! You know!"

"I—I do?"

The woman laughed merrily and led Emma to a door that opened to the stairway to the basement. "You look fabulous, dear! Down you go, now!"

So, Emma went down the stairs. Twenty-one faces stared up at her as she descended. She held her tambourine in one hand, her crystal ball in the other; she felt, for the first time, an actual moment of precognition: she'd been set up.

Cherry and Candy advanced on her, smiling brightly. "At last!" Cherry cried.

Candy added, "She's here! Now we can begin!"

"Begin...what?" Emma asked, dreading the answer.

"Gypsy fortune teller, Emma!" Candy announced, and all the kids applauded. "Here's your table, Emma," she added, leading her to a small, round table covered with a dark cloth and laden with fortune-telling paraphernalia: a deck of tarot cards, a crystal ball, and a pair of dice, feathers and rune stones.

"What is this?" Emma demanded.

"It's your table," Candy repeated. "You're the fortune teller—tell our fortunes!"

"I'm not a fortune teller," Emma protested. "I'm a gypsy."

"That's what gypsies do," Cherry explained. "It's okay, Emma," she added. "We all came prepared to pay, if you want us to."

"Pay for what?"

"Our fortunes!" Cherry pointed to the table. "We set it all up for you; it's our theme!" Gesturing grandly, she intoned: "'Talk to the dead and learn your fortune!'" She smiled winningly. "We just knew you'd love it; you can show off your power!"

"This is your theme?" Emma cried.

"Sure!" Candy smirked knowingly. "You're always talking to someone—at least you say you are—"

"So how about a little proof?" Cherry added.

"We've been watching you do it since first grade—"

"So, do it now, for us!"

"It doesn't work that way," Emma cried.

"Fortune tellers just call the spirits," Candy said. "So, do it. We want to ask them questions."

"It doesn't work that way!" Emma repeated.

"Just sit down, Emma!" Cherry whispered viciously. "You're ruining the party!"

"Cherry, I can't call the spirits," Emma argued.

"See?" Candy spat. "I told you it was all a fake, Cherry!"

"So, you don't talk to dead people?" Cherry demanded.

"Yes, I do, but—"

"Then do it! It's a party, Emma; just do it."

"Cherry—"

"She's a fake, just like I told you," Candy said. "I always said she was just talking to herself, trying to get attention."

"Attention is the last thing I want!" Emma protested.

"Look, Emma," Candy sneered menacingly. "We went to a lot of trouble to set this up. No one believes in your power, but we told them all you're the real deal. So, don't mess it up!"

"Is she ready yet?" a boy named Martin piped up. "I want to talk to my Grandpa."

Emma whispered frantically, "Why didn't you ask me first? I could have told you! It doesn't work that way!"

"You said you had powers," Candy accused.

"I never said I had powers," Emma shot back. "I talk to my family. My family."

"You're going to do this," Cherry told her, glaring threateningly.

"Oh, no I'm not!"

"Oh yes you are! Or we're telling everyone you're a big fat faker!"

"So, what? You've all been calling me that for years!" Emma retorted. "You think that's a threat?"

"If you are nothing but a faker, anyway," Candy reasoned, "then just fake it now. Who's gonna know the difference?"

"I will!" Emma cried.

"Told ya," Candy said to Cherry. "I told you she's a fake; I told you she'd wimp out."

"You should have told me," Emma said. "If I'd known, we could have—"

"Could have what? Figured out how to fake it better?" Candy sneered.

"Figured out a better theme," Emma muttered.

"You're wrecking the party, Emma!" Cherry said. "Is that what you want? To ruin the best party of the year?"

"No, but—"

"Then just sit at this table and tell fortunes. What's it gonna hurt?"

"Cherry," Emma growled through gritted teeth, "I have no idea how to tell a fortune. I don't get a choice when spirits visit me; they come when they want to, not when I want them to."

"Just fake it like you always do," Candy prodded.

"I don't fake it!" Emma cried. "And even if someone came, they don't tell fortunes. They talk about the past."

"She's a fake," Candy declared firmly. "I knew it."

"Hey!" Martin hollered. "Are we gonna do this, or what?"

"Shut up, Marty!" Cherry yelled. "We have to get ready."

"I'm not doing this," Emma said.

"Yes, you are," Candy replied. "I don't care how you do it; you do it. That's the whole reason we invited you."

"That's why? To humiliate me?"

"Big word, Emma!" Candy applauded sarcastically. "You even used it right! Mr. McKenzie would be so proud!" She poked a finger at Emma's chest, and Emma jerked away. "No, stupid! We invited you for you! Everyone says you're a fake; we were trying to help you. So, you could prove once and for all you have powers."

"I don't *have* powers," Emma hissed. "I have a damned *curse* is what I have. And I don't have to prove a thing—not to them, not to you, not to anyone!"

"Of course, you don't," Cherry agreed soothingly. "But we invited you to the best party of the year, Emma! Do it for us! We did it for you!"

"Cherry, I can't just—"

"Just pretend. Fortunes are just a game, anyway, right?"

"Just sit in the chair and pretend you see stuff in the crystal ball," Candy cajoled.

"Don't ruin our party," Cherry begged.

"We did it for you," Candy added.

"The hell you did," Emma spat. "You did it for yourselves! Either way, you're not the ones who end up looking bad!" But she sat down. She sifted through the things on the table top and shoved the tarot cards aside. "I'm not touching this crap," she added.

"I have a Ouija board," Cherry offered.

"Don't even think about it!" Emma shuddered. "You guys are going to hell," she added, muttering.

"What?" Candy demanded.

"If you missed that bus, you'll have to wait for the next one," Emma declared dismissively.

"*What?*"

"*Slow.*" Emma shook her head contemptuously. "I'll use the crystal." She glared at the girls. "You better hope this all stays fake," she warned, narrowing her eyes menacingly.

"You don't scare us," Candy said; but she looked worried, suddenly. She glanced at Cherry, now not so sure of herself.

Emma was furious; she wanted nothing more than to stomp up the stairs and call her parents for a ride home. There was also a part of her that was so hurt she wanted to curl up in a corner and cry. And the most vindictive part of her hoped that a ghost would show up—one who could bang on walls, rattle chains, moan dramatically and move things; one who could pull Candy's and Cherry's hair and make them scream; they deserved it!

That wasn't likely; ghosts, in her experience, just sort of stood or sat there and told you stories.

Still...one could dream. And if they wanted a fortune—well, by God, she'd give them a show, at least. If that made them really believe she was nothing but a fake, all for the better. She knew she wouldn't be hanging out with them after tonight, anyway.

She put her own crystal ball in her lap; the one on the table had an elaborate stand, and in spite of herself, she liked it. She sat her tambourine on the table, near her left hand.

She took a deep breath and let it out. She repeated the action. Then she frowned up at her former friends. "If you've got snacks and drinks, you better bring them. Fake or not, this requires a lot of energy."

Candy stared at her for a moment, and then darted off to the other side of the room. "Is it?" Cherry asked.

"Is it what?" Emma countered.

"Fake."

Emma stared at her, not blinking. "No," she said. "Or...is it?" She raised her eyebrows inquiringly.

"Emma, I—"

"Shut up, Cherry. Just—shut up."

Emma stared out into the room, a long recreation room decorated with small card tables covered with Halloween-themed cloths. A stereo was playing eerie music. In one corner there was a large tin tub; presumably, they'd be bobbing for apples at some point. In the other corner, a long table was set with a punch bowl and glasses, rows of caramel apples and popcorn balls, bowls of chips and dip and wrapped candies.

Emma took another deep breath. "Martin?" she called. "I guess you're first."

Cherry hurried off to help Candy.

184

Emma had a plate heaped with pumpkin muffins, chips and dip. Candy had filled a goodie bag with candy, a caramel apple and a popcorn ball. Cherry brought her a steaming cup of apple cider.

Emma sipped her cider and waved the girls away. They backed off and sat with their guests.

All eyes were on Emma. She was terrified; she was trapped.

Where's a good ghost when you need one?

Martin sat across from her. He looked as nervous as she felt. "So," he said. "You're a fortune teller, huh?"

"I'm a gypsy," Emma said.

"Candy says you can tell fortunes," Martin told her testily. "Can you?"

"I guess we'll find out," Emma muttered.

"I really need to talk to my grandfather."

"Why?"

"What do you mean, why?"

"I mean, why, Martin?" Emma sighed, exasperated. "Ghosts do not just show up; there has to be a reason, and it has to be important." She was flying by the seat of her pants, but this was something she knew for certain; if the reason wasn't compelling—and not to the living, but to the spirit involved—they had nothing to say.

"How do you know?" Martin demanded.

"My great grandmother came to me in the middle of a school day to let me know that my grandmother—her daughter—needed help right away," Emma told him. She'd never explained her abrupt departure from school during a snowstorm to any of her classmates before; Emma was not compelled to explain anything to anyone outside her own family. Martin was not one of the classmates who had been there, but several of them were here—Candy and Cherry, for two—and were hanging on her every word. "It turned out she had a heart attack," Emma continued. "We went back to Idaho for over a month while she got well. But if my great-grandmother hadn't come to me, she would have died, because she was home alone when it happened."

185

There came a sound of many gasps in the room, but Emma ignored it. "Do you think your grandfather has something important to tell you?" she asked. "Or do you just want to say hi and make him prove something to you? Ghosts aren't interested in proving to anyone that they exist."

"But they said—"

"I don't care what they said! All I care about is your reason for being here. Why do you want to talk to your grandfather, Martin?"

Martin stared down at his lap, muttering.

"What?"

"I said, because I miss him!" Martin cried, and his face told the story of someone still in the midst of grief.

Emma nodded. "It hasn't been long since he passed," she observed. "Less than a month, I'd say."

Martin looked impressed. "That's right!" he cried.

Emma studied him; she could make some guesses, but she felt badly for him and didn't want to make him feel worse. She forced herself not to glare at Candy and Cherry; she continued to make eye contact with Martin. He looked by turns grief-stricken, defiant and hopeful. Emma wanted to cry.

"He wasn't sick," Emma said. It wasn't a question; Martin exhibited all the signs of one who'd been completely taken by surprise by death.

"No." Martin agreed. "He was the healthiest guy I knew!"

"I don't think he'll talk to me, Martin," Emma said. "He has to come to terms with his death first."

"What do you mean?"

"Well," Emma said, "sometimes, when it's sudden, ghosts don't really know what happened to them..." Emma was thinking about a train crash and a ghost who had yet to visit her himself.

Martin smirked; it seemed self-protective, really; it made Emma sadder for him. "Then why did your great-grandmother come to you?" he demanded.

"It was different," Emma replied thoughtfully. "She had cancer. She was really sick for a long time; she knew she was going; she was ready to go. Once she did, it was all better for her." Emma sighed. "She came to tell me so—so I could tell my family. They needed to know she was better off."

"Maybe I need to know that, too!" Martin cried.

"You already do know that," Emma said.

"No, I don't! He shouldn't have—it wasn't—damn it!" Martin had tears in his eyes, and Emma felt awful.

"Accidents happen, Emma."

Emma looked up; her great-grandmother was there! Emma stared at her, hopeful for the first time that night. "What kind of accident was it?" she asked.

"Tragic," her great-grandmother said.

"Stupid," Martin said.

"That's helpful," Emma muttered.

"This is not a good idea, Emmaline."

"I know, Grandma."

"What—your grandma comes, but not my grandpa?" Martin cried.

"Martin—"

"Tell him to always check the safety."

"Grandma—"

"Tell him!"

"Martin." He was looking over his shoulder, trying to see...anything. Of course, he couldn't. She tried again, a little louder: "Martin!"

"What?" He swiveled back to face her.

"Always check the safety."

Martin's mouth fell open. "How did you—?"

"Tell him it was an accident."

"It was an accident, Martin."

"Tell him to stop blaming his friend."

"Stop blaming your friend."

Martin started to cry. "He's not my friend!" he moaned.

"His grandfather's friend," the great-grandmother clarified.

"He was your grandfather's friend. It was an accident. Stop blaming him."

"He—"

"Stop it, Martin!" Emma knew she could take it from here; her great-grandmother was gone, at any rate. "He already blames himself so much that your blame can never hurt him. It

187

was an accident!" Fully aware that every eye was on them, she leaned closer to Martin. He leaned in closer to her and she whispered, "If you don't let this go—if you don't forgive this man and go on—you're the one who will suffer. Holding a grudge is hard work, and never worth it, Marty. Your grandpa has moved on; he doesn't hold a grudge; he knows his friend would never have done it on purpose. He wants you to do the same."

"I don't know if I can!" Martin sobbed. "I love my grandpa!"

"I know you do. He knows it, too." Emma put a hand on his shoulder and squeezed. "And to honor him, you need to let it go."

"I'll try," Martin whispered. He got up, turned away from everyone and ran up the stairs.

Emma stood up and faced her seated peers, who were staring at her with a mixture of awe and fear. She pointed at Candy and Cherry. "You!" she cried. "I hate you guys."

"But you did it!" Cherry argued. "You—"

"She's a witch!" one of the girls gasped. It was Muriel, one of the kids Emma had known since first grade.

"Shut up, Muriel!" This came from a new girl; one Emma hadn't met previously.

Emma continued. "This was all your doing! Do you think that was fun for him?" She pointed at the stairway. "He's suffered a loss, and you made a game of his pain!"

"Who's next?" a boy Emma didn't know asked, oblivious.

"No one's next!" Emma shouted, furious. "I never should have done this in the first place!"

"But, Emma!" Candy cried. "The party's just getting started!"

Emma stared at her, jaw slack. "Are...you...crazy?" she demanded. "Or just stupid?"

"Hey!"

"I'm not doing this," Emma declared emphatically.

"Yes, you are!" Cherry argued. "We'll tell the whole school what a fake you are!"

A few of the other kids nodded, and Emma heard several say "Yeah, we will," and "Just wait and see," but she didn't care. She snatched up her crystal ball and her tambourine and stalked toward the stairs.

"Get back here!" Candy cried. "You're spoiling all the fun!"

Emma whirled around and glared at her, furious. "If you think using me to make a game of someone's grief is fun, Candy, you're one sick puppy."

"I didn't know—"

"You knew enough!" Emma spat. She shook her head, filled with contempt. "You should have known better!" She started up the stairs. She was startled to find the new girl right next to her. "What?" she cried. "What do you want?"

"I'm going with you," the girl said. "I don't want any part of this! Or any of that...that...mess!" She opened the door at the top of the stairs.

Cherry's mother stood there, looking distraught as Martin sobbed on the phone. "What did you do to him?" she demanded when she saw Emma.

"Ask your kid," Emma snapped. She regretted her rudeness immediately but offered no apology.

Martin hung up the phone. "She didn't do anything, ma'am," he sniffed. To Emma he said, "My dad's coming." He shuffled his feet, and his face reddened. "Do you want a ride home?"

Emma nodded, surprised. "Yes, please," she replied.

"We'll take you, too, Sasha," Martin offered.

The new girl smiled. "Thanks, Marty." She turned and offered Cherry's mother her hand. "Thank you for having us," she said.

The woman, caught off guard, shook hands with her. "Wait," she told them. "I'll get your treats!"

"That's not—"

She darted down the stairs.

"—necessary," Emma finished weakly.

"We'll be right outside," Sasha called to the woman, and the three of them went out the front door. "Whew!" Sasha added. "That was—"

"Hell, on earth," Emma said.

"Good enough," Sasha agreed. "Are you okay, Marty?"

"I'm sorry, Emma," Martin said. "I didn't know..."

"I'm the one who's sorry," Emma sighed. "I never should have let them talk me into that."

"Guilt you into it, more like," Sasha said disdainfully. "I heard them; they went behind your back and then made you feel responsible for the success or failure of their 'great'"—her hands rose, fingers making air quotation marks— "party. Hmph!"

"And I just made things worse," Martin added, "because I really wanted to talk to my grandpa."

Emma shrugged. "Everyone has someone they want to talk to," she said. "But—"

The door banged open. "Here are your bags!" Cherry's mother thrust goodie-bags at them. The kids took them from her awkwardly. They were stuffed with muffins, candies, caramel apples and popcorn balls. The woman looked flushed and harried. "Enjoy! Thanks for coming!" And she slammed the door.

The trio looked at each other, and wandered away from the porch to the sidewalk. "Well," Sasha said. "I'm thinking things might not be too pleasant in there." She nodded toward the house, eyebrows raised dramatically.

"Wish you were a fly on the wall?" Martin asked.

Emma toed the sidewalk. "Not really," she said. "The rumors will be flying on Monday. I can wait til then to find out what a fake and phony I am."

Sasha shook her head. "You're not," she said.

"No," Martin agreed emphatically.

"You wait," Emma told them. "There are a lot of kids in there. They'll find a way to make this my fault."

"Emma—"

"You'll see."

Martin's father pulled up next to them then, and they all climbed into the car. "Party's a bust?" he asked.

"And how," Martin agreed. He proceeded to tell his dad the whole story.

Stopping for a traffic light, Martin's father turned to look at Emma. "Well, well," he said. "I know your dad; he never told me you were so special."

"I'm not," Emma muttered, face flushing.

"Don't you worry." The light turned green and they moved on. "Being special just means you understand the hurts of others well enough to be helpful."

"Wow," Sasha breathed. "That's profound."

"Your grandpa was a wonderful guy," he told Martin. "He raised your mom right; that's how she's managed to be so great to us. Right?"

"Yes," Martin agreed.

"Your friend is right; he would never want you holding on to this. Let it go, son. His friend needs to let it go, too, but so far, he's not listening to us. Maybe…"

"I'll call him tomorrow," Martin said.

Emma started to cry. "Accidents happen," she whispered.

"Yes," Sasha agreed. "Yes, they do." She put her arms around Emma and patted her awkwardly.

True friendships really can be formed in an instant. The three of them formed their own circle that lasted throughout their school years. Emma had never since longed for a larger circle of friends; she had learned that if you have one or two who accept you and believe in you, it's really all you need.

4.

1987

Emma shook her head and wiped tears from her cheek. "I was right," she said. "Those kids concocted a story about how I'd bragged that I could tell fortunes because I was in touch with the dead, and then I talked Cherry and Candy into making me the center of their party. They claimed that I learned all about Marty's grandfather from newspaper stories." Emma laughed bitterly. "Never mind that I didn't know Marty before that night. Never mind that his grandpa died in Wisconsin. How would I have found a news story? I mean, never mind that he was Marty's mother's dad, and I would have had no way to know her maiden name, let alone anything else about him!"

"Those little—" Jill started.

"Twelve-year-olds," Emma finished. "Crazy people."

"You would never have done a thing like that!" Jill protested. "And *you* were twelve."

"I have a nicer family, I guess," Emma said. "No, no, I can't say that! I have no idea what their families are like; some really bad people have great families. I'm not even saying that they were bad people. They were twelve!" Emma rolled her eyes dramatically. "Are twelve-year-olds technically real people?"

"I've always thought most of them are abducted by aliens and replaced by clones," Jack commented dryly.

"Especially the girls," Jill agreed. "You get the originals back a few years later. In the meantime, you're thinking: 'Where's my child? Who's this stranger in my child's body?'"

"Great," Jacob groaned. "I look forward to that!"

"Anyway," Emma continued, "by the time Monday rolled around, the whole school had heard Candy and Cherry's version of the story. Most of the party guests went along with it. I mean, there were a few, besides Marty and Sasha, who denied things had gone that way; those kids ended up hanging out with us a lot, because Cherry and Candy made life hell for them when they wouldn't go along with the rest of them."

"Wow," Jacob sighed.

"There were kids in school—kids who weren't invited to the party— who believed Marty when he told them what had really happened, but mostly, we became the odd bunch. Well," Emma added, "I was already an oddity. They just joined me. Poor kids!"

"I worked with Marty's dad for years," Jack mused. "He never said a word to me about that night, other than letting me know he'd picked you all up."

"I asked him not to," Emma explained. "I didn't want you to worry."

"That's what parents are for, Emma!" Jack protested.

"Why would you keep it from us?" Jill demanded. "You've kept so much to yourself..."

Jacob shook his head. "Kids kind of suck! I'm so sorry, honey," he said.

"Me, too," Jack agreed. "I'd like to—"

"Let it go," Emma said. "I know it hurts when your kids are hurt," she continued. "I've always known it; you two have had to live in this town all these years and hear the talk about me. I'm so sorry for that!"

"What?" Jill cried. "You have nothing to be sorry for!"

"Well, I'm sorry anyway," Emma insisted. "But look: that night I met the best friends I've ever had. They fell in love and married each other. That's a beautiful thing!"

"I was so sad that they moved," Jill sighed.

"We're going to visit them in New Mexico if we drive," Emma said.

"We're driving," Jacob told her. "Grandma and Grandpa here have offered to babysit," he added.

"I know, but—"

"And we're going to accept the offer, aren't we, Emma?"

Everyone looked at Emma expectantly. Emma sighed loudly. "Fine," she said. "You can help me get Abe to take a bottle!"

Jacob grinned. "I'll do my best," he agreed.

Emma suddenly turned to Jill and glared at her ferociously. "You, Mom," she cried, "will not cry again to make me talk about my past!"

"I didn't—"

"And there will be no more wanting me to stop what I do!" This was directed at both parents.

"Emma, we—"

"Because I can't." Emma stared at the table top. She was quiet for a while, and no one said anything. "If you think you've wanted me to stop," she said finally, "you should know that I've probably wanted that more than you did, and so many times! But I can't."

Jack smiled at her. "We know," he said. "You've never had a choice."

"No choice at all."

Jill shook her head. "That really does suck," she said solemnly.

Emma burst out laughing. "Who taught you that word?" she demanded. "It's awful!"

Jill looked offended. "The word 'suck' has been part of the English language for more years than I could possibly count," she informed Emma haughtily. "This usage, however," she grinned, looking positively wicked, "I learned from your brother."

"Freddie? He needs a spanking!"

"That would suck," Jill said.

"Mom!"

"For Fred, at least," Jill added. "It would suck a lot."

"Mom!"

"And then I'd blame you, and Freddie would be mad at you. And that would suck for you!"

"Mom!"

"Jill!"

"And then—"

Chapter Twelve

A Wedding Delivery

September 5, 1987

Rock stars don't get married in small towns in Wyoming—until they do.

Melody had opted to get married in her own hometown, in her own church. Rob's family, all from Utah, made the trip up for the weekend.

Unlike Emma—maybe even despite Emma—Melody had always been a popular girl. She was outgoing and friendly, a social magnet. She was wildly talented. She'd had an entourage of friends and acquaintances from the time she started kindergarten.

There were a lot of guests coming.

From the beginning she'd been secretive about the wedding theme; Jill knew, because she was making the dresses, but beyond that, it was all hush-hush. So, when she modeled her dress for Emma and Dana, it became crystal clear to Emma why her mother had had the Halloween party fiasco on her mind lately.

"What do you think?" Melody asked, twirling about as much as her belly would allow.

"Wow!" Emma gasped. "It's like Dana's original request and my finished costume rolled into one!"

"What?" Melody stared at Emma. She stood before her sisters dressed in a flowing red and gold paisley print gypsy outfit. The skirting began not at the waist but just beneath her breasts and flounced to the floor. The underskirt was exposed on the left side, where the skirt had been bunched up and secured with a big bow. The white blouse featured poet's sleeves and exposed her shoulders.

"Pregnant lady and gypsy," Emma said.

"What are you—" Melody began, and then realization dawned, and she burst out laughing. "Oh! I was just channeling my inner Stevie! I didn't even think about…that's so crazy!"

"Stevie?" Dana asked.

"Stevie Nicks? Fleetwood Mac? Gypsy? Who are you? Where's my sister?"

"Oh, yeah, yeah, yeah."

"No, that's The Beatles."

"Will you girls please concentrate on the task at hand?" Jill cried, exasperated, as the sisters giggled.

Emma's dress was nearly a duplicate of the one she'd worn over a decade before; it would now accommodate a woman's figure and also featured off-the shoulder blousing. Dana's was the same, only instead of the violet and blue combo Emma's had, hers was magenta and pink. They both had silk sashes and scarves, but Melody's head was wreathed with rosy wildflowers.

"So, it's a flower-power wedding? A gypsy wedding?" Dana asked.

Melody shrugged. "When we were little, I wanted to be a hippie. Remember, Emma?"

"Yeah," Emma agreed. "Until the day we passed a group of them in the parking lot of the Safeway and caught a whiff of them, it was your big thing."

"Where was I?" Dana demanded.

"You were there," Jill told her. "But you were pretty little; you just don't remember."

"I sure do!" Melody giggled. "Phew! Were they stinky! I decided then and there that if I was ever a hippy, I would take lots of baths anyway."

"I'm sure they took baths whenever they found a place to do it," Jill offered diplomatically; she was sure of no such thing. "But they certainly were a ripe bunch."

"Anyway, these dresses are nothing like the Fleetwood Mac video, but I love the song; I did a cover of it on my new album. It just stuck in my head, so I mentioned it to Mom and ta-da! She can do anything!"

"And Rob?" Dana asked.

"He was down," Melody replied. "His brothers laughed their butts off at first, but they agreed."

"This is going to be great," Emma declared.

There's nothing so precious as an open-minded parish Priest; he barely reacted when Melody asked to march barefoot down the aisle. Her feet and ankles were quite swollen at this point and she'd been wearing house shoes or socks for the past month. His only comment: "Those floors are pretty cold!"

Emma and Rob's brother Mark led the procession down the aisle that day, and Emma beamed with happiness at her grandparents—both sets—and her mother on the bride's side of the aisle. It was good to have them all together again; the last time had been at her own wedding.

Melody's cover of "Gypsy" played on the sound system as Melody fairly danced her way up the aisle, clinging to Jack's arm. Rob's smile couldn't have gotten any bigger as he watched his bride approach, and Emma felt so happy for her sister that she thought her heart might burst with emotion.

As Melody and Rob took their vows, Emma looked toward the back of the church, where she saw her great-grandmother and, for the first time since his passing, her great-grandfather. They smiled at her; dressed in their own wedding finery, and looking much younger than when Emma had known them, they were quite a handsome pair. Emma smiled back at them in acknowledgement; she knew in her heart they were not the only unseen guests at this wedding; family gatherings attracted family, including those who had passed.

In any town there's a place where the large gatherings take place; here it was the Eagles Lodge. It was big enough for a large venue; it had a big kitchen, a small stage and plenty of room for dancing. There was even a bar, for those so inclined, but that was a separate room; no kids allowed.

Emma and Dana had had relatively small weddings and their receptions had been in Jack and Jill's back yard. Melody's wedding could never have been done that way; she and Rob knew too many people. So, the Eagles Lodge had been rented and decorated, and the guests filled the place. A long table at the front was filled with family; including the little ones, four generations!

Melody's band members had taken the stage to provide the music. The hall was a cacophony of sounds; laughter, music, chattering conversations. The food was home style; roast beef and chicken, mashed potatoes and gravy, vegetables and salads. Out of respect to the very pregnant bride, most of the guests had declined alcoholic beverages.

Just as things were winding down, Melody suddenly cried out: "Good golly Moses!"

"What?!" Rob said.

Melody stood up and said, "We just want to thank you all very much for coming." She looked at her new husband. "We have to be going now. My water just broke."

"Oh, my God!" Rob cried, leaping to his feet. "Thanks everyone! Looks like you're all on your own with the cake and such!"

Everyone followed them to the door and cheered as they climbed into the wildly decorated car. "Party on!" Melody yelled as she folded herself into her seat.

Numerous cans rattled against the pavement as they pulled away. The guests cheered again, and there was a lot of general laughter. Jill turned to Jack inquiringly. "Let's go change clothes first," he replied to her unasked question. "And we'll be on our way."

"Yay!" Jill said. "Now I don't have to worry that I won't make it to Park City in time!"

"We'll deal with the rest of this," Emma assured them.

"Yes, well," Jill said, "party on, like your sister said."

"We'll see you all soon," Dana promised.

The rest of the reception, sans bride and groom, continued for a couple more hours. Jacob and Tom shooed Emma, Dana and their grandparents out after a while, with the promise that they would see to the clean-up. Dana loaded them all into her new Suburban wagon and they headed for the hospital.

"I'm so excited," Grandma said. "We've never been in town when one of the great-grandchildren were born!"

"This day just keeps getting better," Grandpa agreed.

Grams and Papa, Jack's parents, were seated in the rear section, and Grams giggled. "We were here for Benjamin," she said. "Remember, Dana?"

"I do," Dana called over her shoulder. "What a treat for me, four generations in the recovery room." She laughed. "That sounded sarcastic, didn't it?" she added. "I'm totally serious; it was a treat! Great-grandson, granddaughter, son and father, all together in the room! And my mother and grandmother, too. I never felt so blessed! Now Mel will have doubles! It's amazing and wonderful."

Emma couldn't stop smiling. "Mel's going to be such a cool Mom," she said. "Imagine all the songs she'll be making up for this baby!"

"Oh my gosh!" Dana cried. "She'll end up with a children's album, I just know it!"

"That would be so cool!" Emma cried. "I didn't think of that!"

Once they got to the hospital they were directed to the maternity waiting room, where they all commenced pacing.

Jack soon joined them. "They just took her to delivery," he informed them.

"Already?" Emma and Dana chorused.

"Mel admitted that she'd been having contractions since this morning," Jack said. "She thought they were false labor pains, and ignored them."

"What the hell?" Dana said. "She must be one tough cookie! By the time my water broke, I was a mess!"

"Me, too," Emma agreed.

"Well, according to Melody," Jack reported, "the pain didn't start until the water broke. She was singing a pretty loud tune by the time they got here, I'm told."

Everyone chuckled.

They settled into uncomfortable orange plastic chairs, maneuvering them so they could face each other while talking.

"Where's Mom?" Emma asked.

"They let her go into delivery."

"Really?" Grandma gasped. "Where's Rob?"

"He's in there, too."

"I'm feeling a little jealous!"

"Me, too," Grams agreed.

"I don't get it," Dana said. "You want to go in? Didn't they just knock you out in the olden days? And the dads paced in the waiting room?"

Jack burst out laughing. "That's probably more accurate for when you were born," he said. "I was born at home, and Grams had her sister and grandmother there to help her."

"Jill was born in a hospital," Grandma added, "but not all of my kids were."

"That's right," Grandpa agreed. "And I delivered a couple of them myself."

"Ooh, not me!" Papa said. "I was a pacer!" He laughed. "But I was always close by, whether we did it at home or in the hospital."

Dana and Emma stared at their grandparents, jaws agape. Emma turned to Jack. "Did you go in with Mom when we were born, Dad?" she demanded.

Jack laughed again. "Hell, no!" he replied. "I was a big chicken. I did the pacing dad thing. I was going to go in when Freddie came along—I had totally talked myself into it--but I missed it. He came so fast that I didn't make it in from work. Thank God Lucy was there to drive your mom!"

"I remember that!" Emma cried. "It was snowing like crazy, you went to work, we all went to school, and the next thing I knew, you showed up at my school to tell me I had a new brother." She giggled. "I think I danced on air all the way back to class."

"Well, what you may not remember was that I was out in the field and got a radio call from the office saying Lucy had called and was taking your mom to the hospital, and to go ahead and get my butt over there." Jack laughed merrily. "I still run into the doctor sometimes, and he'll never let me forget how my wet shoes screeched on the linoleum as I slid around the corner and into the waiting room. He says he still can't figure out how I didn't fall on my ass." He shook his head. "Anyway, when I got there, Fred had already been born. I don't think Jill was there more than an hour. He was the fastest birth of all five of you—and the biggest!"

"Weird," Dana said.

"Who'd you deliver, Grandpa?" Emma asked.

"Aunt Tilda," Grandpa replied. "Ronald, too. The hospital was too far, and they came along too quickly to make it."

"For the record," Grandma added, "a model-T Ford full of kids is no place to have a baby!"

"That was Ronnie," Grandpa laughed. "Tilda—we didn't even try! We just stayed home."

"Wow!" Papa cried admiringly. "I don't know if I'm jealous—or just glad it wasn't me!"

"He's glad it wasn't him," Grams confided. "This man helped every animal on our farm give birth, but he'd have fainted dead away and been a useless heap if he'd had to help me!" She laughed her tinkling laugh, and they all joined her—Papa loudest of all.

Jack clapped his father on the shoulder. "Don't worry, Pop," he said. "I missed Fred's entrance, and all these years later I couldn't tell you whether I was mostly sorry, or mostly relieved."

"We'll be sure to ask Mom," Dana giggled.

Emma excused herself to find a payphone and check on Jacob and the babies. Fred answered the phone and told her he and Matthew were on baby duty while Tom and Jacob finished at the Eagles. The kids were all fine, he assured her, and Avram had even taken a bottle! "Thanks, Freddie," Emma said. "You're a life saver!"

"Tell Dana I think Lena's really Mel's."

"What? Why?"

"She just sings and sings. It's so cute." Fred chuckled. "I have no idea what she's saying half the time, but it's cute."

Emma laughed and rang off. She stopped at the vending machine and got sodas, then went back to join the family.

"Freddie says Lena's Mel's," she told Dana. "She just sings and sings."

Dana laughed. "I know," she agreed. "So, Freddie's at my house?"

"No, he and Matt have all the kids at my house," Emma explained. "Jake and Tom are on clean-up duty." She handed out sodas and sat down.

"Wow, Mel totally got us out of that. Yay, Mel!"

Jack grinned. "Don't forget to thank her for that," he said. "Seriously, though, did Fred say if they had any help over there?"

"No, Dad, he didn't say."

"I'm going to go call and check," Jack said, and wandered out of the room.

"I'm sure there are plenty of people helping out," Grandma offered. "That was quite a crowd!"

"Yeah," Emma agreed. "I'll bet there are quite a few folks there with them."

"Mel's band is there," Dana grinned. "They probably offered to provide music during clean up."

"That wouldn't surprise me a bit," Emma agreed.

When Jack returned he was grinning broadly. "Mel's 'party on' orders are being followed," he said. "Matt said the band has organized a 'dance with your broom party'. He's wishing he could have stayed! By the way, Kacey's there, helping out with the babies, too."

"Oh, cool," Emma said. Kacey was Matthew's girlfriend. They hadn't been dating long, but the whole family already loved her, including all the babies.

The wait wasn't long. Before they knew it, Jill appeared, beaming. "Rob and Melody are the proud parents…"

Everyone waited. Finally, Jack prompted: "Of?"

"A beautiful baby!"

"Jill!"

"Mom!"

"It's a girl!"

The room erupted in laughter and applause.

"She's getting cleaned up, and then everyone can take a peek," Jill promised. "I hope someone has a camera."

More laughter as everyone showed their disposable cameras. It seemed that everyone had grabbed one off a table at the reception, where guests had been encouraged to snap away and then leave the cameras for the bride and groom. "This was a great idea, Mom," Emma said, waving two of the little green rectangles at her.

"I've been known to have a few." Jill agreed.

Within the next hour everyone had had a chance to visit Melody, Rob and their new daughter, Natalie. She had made her appearance early and dramatically, as was fitting for a child of Melody Knight. Just under five pounds, she was the picture of health, with thick black hair and dark, dark eyes. Emma left Melody's room grinning from ear to ear. Melody's little family was settled in for the evening, and her last words to Emma as she was leaving: "I couldn't ask for a better honeymoon."

Chapter Thirteen

Road Tripping

October in Wyoming is a fickle month. On any given day, the weather is a toss-up. One day may be sunny and seventy degrees, and the next day you could get three inches of snow and twenty-seven degrees with forty-mile-an-hour winds.

Hunting season was in full swing. Orange was the fashion color of choice. Jack, Matthew and Fred were out every weekend after antelope, deer and elk. Fill the freezers and feed the family: The Knight creed. Tom joined them when his schedule permitted, but Jacob bowed out. He offered to pay for meat processing instead, as his contribution to the families' freezers; hunting was not his forte, he said. Crying wasn't considered manly, he told Emma, and he'd prefer that his in-laws not discover that he was a sissy.

"You're not a sissy!" Emma cried, indignant. "You're sensitive."

"I think in the Old West, those two words are synonymous." Jacob laughed. "I come up with excuses not to participate every year. At least the trip to New Mexico is a valid reason to miss all the fun."

"Oh, this trip," Emma moaned. "I'm going to cry my eyes out every day."

"You're not," Jacob declared. "We'll be very busy. And we'll get to sleep through the night! And make love whenever we want to! And sleep through the night! And drive without hearing a baby howling! And sleep through the night!"

"Wow, sleeping through the night has gotten you really excited," Emma commented dryly.

"It's up there with making love whenever we want."

"Which you mentioned only once," Emma pointed out.

"Well," Jacob drawled, "I didn't want you to think I was a horn-dog."

"Uhuh."

"And we get to sleep in!"

Emma grinned. "Yes," she agreed. "Yes, we do."

1.

For convenience, it was decided that Jack and Jill would stay at Emma and Jacob's place while they were gone. The twins would be able to sleep in their own cribs and all their various belongings would be easily accessible.

"You can use our room, Mom," Emma said. "You don't have to stay in the guest room; it only has a full-sized bed." She finished tucking in the top sheet on the King-sized bed.

Jill laughed. "I wouldn't even be able to find your dad in that bed!" she declared. "He's so skinny, he'll get lost."

"Mom!"

"We'll be fine in the guest room," Jill promised. "It's just right. I've already filled up the dresser drawers and the closet! I don't know what's wrong with me; it's a week, my house is five minutes away, and I think we just moved in!"

Emma giggled. "Have you seen all the bags I packed for Jake and me?" she asked. "It's like I can't believe there are laundry facilities anywhere once we leave town."

"You get it from me; so sorry." Jill grinned. "Mel and Rob brought so much stuff for the wedding and honeymoon that we didn't have to buy a thing while they were staying with us. Mel even had laundry detergent and diapers, and the baby wasn't due yet!"

"I'm so sad they had to leave," Emma cried. "I miss them so much."

"Me, too!" Jill admitted. "But as soon as Natalie hit that five-pound mark, the pediatrician said they could travel safely and they're so busy." Jill giggled. "Honeymoon with a newborn should be interesting."

"Oh, I imagine they're too busy working right now to really 'honeymoon', anyway," Emma said. "Mel said they spend so much time in L.A. that the novelty has worn off. They'll probably plan a trip in the spring."

"Maybe they'll let me babysit."

"If you do a really good job," Emma offered, "I'll put in a good word for you."

Jill gave Emma a swat on the rump as Emma tucked in the blanket at the foot of the bed. "Yeep!" Emma cried.

The car was loaded; the gas tank was full. Jacob and Emma were in the front seat, with their seat belts buckled. They were staring at the closed front door of their house, and both of them were fighting tears. Emma was losing.

Jack and Jill had just retreated into the house with the babies after wishing them a safe trip. Hugs and kisses had been exchanged.

The trip had begun; it was time to go; the car was running; they sat there in the driveway, staring at the door. Emma choked back a sob and Jacob sighed. "We can do this," he said.

"Yep," Emma agreed.

"Just have to put the car in reverse."

"Uhuh."

"I'm going to do that now," Jacob said, and applied the brake. He shifted gears.

"Take your foot off the brake," Emma said.

The front door opened, and Jack came out. "Shoo!" he hollered. "We got this!"

"Yeah, yeah, we're going," Jacob called, trying to grin.

"All our children are alive and kicking," Jack added.

Jacob backed down the driveway and into the street. He and Emma waved at Jack, who stayed outside waving until they reached the end of the street and turned the corner.

"Are they gone?" Jill asked, poking her head out the door.

"Yeah," Jack replied. "But I'm going to stay out here for a few—just in case they come back!"

Jill retreated indoors, giggling.

2.

Going back had certainly crossed their minds, but they didn't do it. They drove through town and hit the freeway. The trip certainly wasn't a short one; they would be driving for several hours.

Emma had taken a map last week and outlined two different routes. One would take them down Interstate 25, through Denver. The other would be a more rural route on state highways and possibly more scenic. "Should we take the interstate coming home?" Emma asked. "The weather is so nice today."

"That's what I was thinking," Jacob agreed. "The interstate will probably be the first plowed if it snows next week, and I do want to hit Denver at some point on this trip. I want to go to Cabela's and get your dad's Christmas present there."

Emma laughed. "You've got him all figured out, don't you?"

"I try to stay on the good side of the guy who gave me my wife."

"Excellent choice."

Jacob was silent for a few minutes. Then he said, "Did we bring some good tapes? It's really quiet in here..."

Emma stared at him, open mouthed, then burst out laughing. "Well, there's something we don't get to say very often!" She sorted through the various cassette tapes. "What do you feel like listening to?"

"Pretty much anything is okay," Jacob replied good-naturedly. "Let's skip the CCR for now, though," he added. "If we play 'Green River', I might really cry."

"I think that's about Utah," Emma told him.

"Doesn't matter," Jacob said. "I didn't think I'd be all homesick, and stuff, but—my mother was right. Kids change everything."

"Yeah."

Before reaching Rawlins, they turned south and headed toward Baggs. "Wow," Emma said. "I think the only time I've ever been this way was on the one hunting trip I ever went on."

"You went hunting?"

"You did note that I said, 'one hunting trip', right?"

"Bad?"

"Not for me," Emma laughed. "I got very nervous that we might actually find a deer, and someone would shoot it, so I became 'Miss Noisy'. I deliberately stepped on fallen branches—not that there were many of those out here. I whistled. I sang. I thought Daddy was going to kill me!" She laughed merrily.

"Oh, man!" Jacob chuckled.

"Anyway, no deer that weekend, and I never, ever asked to go again. I don't know what I was thinking!" Emma giggled. "Even if I had asked, Dad never would have let me go again after that!"

Jake looked around as he drove. "Not much to see out here, is there?"

"Not really. But when I went to the library to research our route, it said that once we get into Colorado, things get prettier."

"Maybe we'll get to see some fall colors."

Emma nodded. "That'd be cool."

Baggs was certainly nothing to write home about. They continued south and crossed the Wyoming/Colorado border. By the time they got to Craig and headed east on Interstate 40, Emma was worried that the library had it all wrong. It all seemed typically southern Wyoming-ish; dry, few trees, lots of brush.

Once they headed south again on Highway 131, the scenery began to change for the better. There were trees in various states of color changes, which became more numerous the further they went. The weather was cool, but the sun was shining brightly. They stopped occasionally to take snapshots; Emma was keeping a list of film frame numbers and writing locations as they took pictures. She explained to Jacob that she never seemed to remember where any particular photo had been taken and wanted to make sure she could identify the locations later.

Jacob had his doubts about the plan, but finally conceded that it might just work when Emma produced baggies labeled "film roll #1, film roll #2," etc.

At Walcott they changed roads to Interstate 70 East for a short while, and then got on Highway 24 South. "This is an interesting trip," Jacob remarked. "So many different roads! Are we lost?"

"Oddly enough, no," Emma replied. "We're getting close to Leadville. I'd like to do a little sight-seeing there, if you're up for it."

"I'm so ready to get out of the car for longer than a snapshot. Leadville, it is!"

It was nearly two in the afternoon by the time they reached Leadville, mostly because of their multiple stops. The town was advertised as holding the record for the incorporated city with the highest elevation in the United States, about twice as high as Denver, Colorado, the self-proclaimed Mile High City.

"Wow, the altitude! 10,152 feet! Honey, you got your inhaler?" Jacob asked.

"I'm fine, Jake," Emma assured him.

"But you have it, right?"

Emma nodded. "It's in my pocket," she replied. "Mom reminded me about fifty times."

"And the extras?"

"Holy cow, you've conspired with my mother!" Emma cried indignantly.

"You do have extras, right?" Jacob persisted.

"One in my purse, one in the suitcase, one in the cosmetics bag," Emma recited.

"Brilliant."

Asthma is no joke, and Emma had struggled with it since childhood. It was annoying, but she was grateful people cared enough to nag her.

They'd somehow managed to skip lunch and were starving, so the first thing they did was look for somewhere to eat. They decided to park on 10th street and walk through the historic district while keeping an eye out for a likely restaurant.

They started at Ice Palace Park. Emma had borrowed a tourist book at the library, and looking at it noted, "There was an actual ice palace built around here. It was built in the winter of 1895-96 and was made with over 5000 tons of ice!"

"Wow!" Jacob looked at the pictures in the tour book. "It had a huge skating rink. That must have been amazing."

Emma pointed northwest and said, "That's Turquoise Lake. The mountains are huge!"

"Hmm," Jacob nodded, and raised the camera. "Mount Massive, is it?"

Emma consulted the book. "Uhuh."

They walked to Harrison Avenue and headed south, taking in all the sights. The whole area was filled with historical buildings, and they took a lot of pictures.

"Did any of your family land here during the gold rush and silver rush days?" Jacob asked.

"I don't know," Emma admitted. "The truth is I'm a lousy researcher. I only go looking for things my family tells me about."

They mounted the stairs of the National Mining Hall of Fame and Museum. They paid the admission and went inside to wander through the many exhibits depicting mining life in the 1800's and the wild history of the town. It was quite a big place, well-tended and very interesting. But their stomachs were growling by now, so Jacob asked for restaurant recommendations and they headed out to feed their faces.

They found a quaint and casual place to eat. The food was good, the service friendly, and the prices were quite reasonable. The building's Victorian architecture was interesting, too, providing the feeling of stepping back in time while they dined.

"This whole area is Victorian style," Jacob remarked. "When was this area settled?"

Emma consulted the book again. "Mid-1800's when the gold rush started," she replied. "But that wasn't here in the town proper. Lemme see," she added, flipping pages. "Leadville was incorporated in 1878. A lot of famous people have been here. The Unsinkable Molly Brown was married here! This is where her husband made his fortune; she never would have been on the Titanic, otherwise. Doc Holliday lived here. Um, what else?"

Jacob forked a roasted potato, and shook his head. "This place is so...small, really. It's cool that it has such a rich history and has managed to keep its old-fashioned charm." He put the potato into his mouth.

210

"There are a lot of ghost-town related sights to see around here," Emma remarked. "We may have to come back sometime and do the real tourist thing."

"Let's do some more family history research and see if anyone came here," Jacob suggested. "That would make it a more interesting trip."

"I think there was some sort of notorious love triangle here, too," Emma said.

Their waitress appeared then to refill their tea pot with hot water. "That would be the Tabors," she said. "Sorry," she added. "I overheard that."

Jacob grinned. "What if we'd been locals talking about the neighbors?" he asked.

The waitress giggled. "I'd pull up a chair and beg you to dish!"

They all laughed. "I was referring to locals," Emma admitted, "but they're long gone."

"The Tabors," the waitress agreed. "Local legends."

"Dish," Jacob ordered, and the woman giggled again.

"Horace and Augusta Tabor came here in the 1870s, and Horace struck it rich by grubstaking some silver miners. Before that they worked really hard, both of them, and Augusta was never comfortable with the sudden wealth. Horace wanted to live it up, and she wanted to live a simple life where enough was enough, and too much was unnecessary. They were both pretty stubborn, and pretty soon he took up with "Baby" Doe, a divorcee half his age.

"Horace was really rich by that time, and put Baby up in nice hotels. He filed for divorce—I think it was illegal, the divorce he got—and took off with Baby Doe and married her.

"Augusta was really well-liked and respected, so people turned against Horace and he moved to Denver with his new wife. Augusta got a good divorce settlement and died rich.

"America switched to gold standard in the late 1800s and Horace went broke because all his wealth came from silver. He died broke, pretty much, and Baby Doe came back here and lived in a shack until she died an old, old woman." The waitress shrugged. "Folks at the time said it was what they deserved for doing Augusta wrong, but I don't know about all that."

"I'm sure there's a lot more to the story," Emma suggested.

"Oh, sure," the waitress agreed. "What I told you is probably less than the Reader's Digest condensed version!" She laughed. "There are books, and I think even a movie out there. Plus, the museums, and there's a tour of the shack she died in. You can get the whole story—I promise—but I have three other tables to get to. Dessert?"

Jacob and Emma laughed and ordered apple pie.

3.

Back on the road, they made good time on Highway 24 South and were soon on 285 South. "Isn't this the same road?" Emma asked.

"Basically." Jacob made a face. "Merge here, turn there, end up in the same place."

"I hate maps," Emma groused.

"I just watch the road signs and hope not to get lost." Jacob turned and grinned at her. "And if I get lost, I just call it an adventure and try not to panic."

"But you don't ask for directions," Emma speculated.

Jacob laughed. "That's a man-myth! I have no shame—I'll ask the first person I see."

"My dad would drive in circles for a month before asking directions," Emma giggled.

"Only if your mom was with him—we must preserve the myth!"

"You just told me it was a myth!"

"I'm trusting in your discretion."

"Oh, crap."

It was already getting dark—the disadvantage of autumn travel: short daylight hours. They'd taken their time and made several stops, and thanked the Good Lord for the good weather. They would have tried to make better time if there had been any chance that the roads would be bad.

"If we stay on 285, we can stay the night in Santa Fe," Emma suggested. "Then we can check out their library tomorrow and see if we have to actually research in Corrales."

"We can research both places," Jacob said. "And anywhere else in the area that strikes our fancy."

"Have I told you lately how awesome you are?"

"Nope."

"You're awesome."

"Thank you."

"I hope I get a few visitors once we're there," Emma sighed. "Research is great, but it's always nice to be able to talk to someone who knows whether the history records are correct. Look what happened with the babies on that ship from England."

Jacob nodded. "And those records are from the Latter-Day Saints," he added. "They have a great reputation for record-keeping, and even they were not infallible." He shook his head. "This is bound to be harder; there were so many non-readers. Certainly, the Indian tribes weren't recording family histories in their churches or Bibles or whatever; their shared histories, from what I've read, were passed down through stories, generation to generation."

"That's what I've read, too." Emma agreed. "And that makes sense. I mean, a lot of what I know about my own family has been told to me, not found in history books."

"Me, too. Except for the things I found in Salt Lake," Jacob said. "And for that, I have to thank the LDS people for doing all the research they do. Because my family lost contact with anyone who could have told them personally."

"Or lost them completely," Emma agreed, "without ever having a way of knowing they had." She sighed deeply. "What a horrible, horrible war."

"Yeah."

"I have a whole suitcase devoted to notebooks, you know."

"I know, I lifted that thing. I think I have a hernia now."

"Oh, hush." Emma paused. "Really?"

"Nah, I'm fine." Jacob chuckled.

"It's all so confusing. I really, really want to find Manuelita's daughters, but we might not be able to find anything."

213

"I wish we could just sit around a crystal ball and call them." Emma giggled. "Maybe we should try it."

"You have a crystal ball?"

"As a matter of fact, I still have the one my dad bought me for my Halloween costume," Emma informed him. "But, you know—not with me."

"I'm surprised you still have that," Jacob said.

"I still have the whole costume. My mom did a beautiful job on that dress; my dad went out of his way to find that ball. My bad memories have nothing to do with the costume, and I hope Ami will want to wear it someday."

"You're amazing, Em."

"Why, thanks!" Taking note of a big road sign, she added, "Welcome to New Mexico! It became a state in 1912."

"January 6th." Jacob grinned. "You and your tourist books."

"They come in pretty handy. We are now in 'The Land of Enchantment'."

"I guess we'll see tomorrow," Jacob remarked. "I can't see a thing right now."

"We should be there within the hour—if I'm calculating the map correctly."

It turned out she was close enough. It took just over an hour to enter Santa Fe and find a hotel. They weren't picky, and a Best Western was as good a choice as any. After they checked in, they hit the nearest convenience store for snacks and drinks and decided to call it a night; their late lunch was holding them over quite well enough to forgo dinner. They brought in their overnight bag and the suitcase full of notebooks and settled in for an evening of reading and snacking.

And...etc.

Chapter Fourteen

The Land of Enchantment

Emma's last act of the evening—before the snacks and the reading and the etc.—had been a phone call home to check on Avram and Amalia.

It had not been the first call that day, of course—not every stop along the way had been for bathroom breaks and gas-ups.

Naturally, the babies were fine. Of course, they were; Jill and Jack were perfectly competent caregivers!

Still, it was a rough night.

"So much for sleeping through a whole night," Jacob muttered at around two a.m.

"Yeah," Emma agreed. "At least you've gone to sleep. I've just been lying here."

"I figured so." Jacob got up and got them each some water.

"I'm sorry if I woke you."

"No, no," Jacob assured her. "You cry very quietly."

Right. Rough night.

Emma had known she would miss her babies; she'd been dreading the trip at least as much as she'd been looking forward to it. Still, it was worse than she'd anticipated. Especially now, in the middle of the night, when she would normally be cuddling and nursing them.

"Well, here we are," Jacob said, "in the heart of the land your father's family settled. I'm almost expecting to see ghosts myself on this trip."

"It would be a welcome distraction," Emma remarked. "They never show up when you want them, though."

"You know, I expected it to be different here," Jacob admitted. "It's every bit as desert-y as it is at home. Just brush and scrub."

"Yeah, I'm surprised Spain was so insistent on regaining the place after the Indians drove all the Spaniards away."

Jacob chuckled. "Look at us, getting to be history buffs!"

"Ugh!" Emma groaned. "I know! How did this ever happen to me?" She rolled over and sat up. "Gotta pee," she announced, and trotted off to the bathroom.

When she came back, she was crying again. "I miss my babies!" she wailed as she crawled back on the bed. Jacob folded her into his arms and rocked her gently. "God, Jake, how do people do it? How do people send their kids to camp, or boarding school? We've been gone one day, and I can hardly stand it! I mean, they're going to grow up and go away to college! They're going to move away and get married and travel and stuff! I'm a mess!"

Jacob sighed. "Poor Manuelita," he said.

"I know!" Emma sobbed. "And here I am, bawling my eyes out, when I know where my babies are, and that they're safe and loved. I'm an ungrateful wretch."

"Of course, you're not!" Jacob cried. He gave her a squeeze. "You're a great mom," he said. "I mean, imagine how hard this trip would be on Ami. I think Abe would have been fine, but Ami would be miserable. Instead, they both get to be spoiled by Grandma."

"True," Emma agreed. "And if I can quit crying and enjoy it, I can be a little spoiled too." She sniffed dramatically.

Jacob pulled the blankets up over them and snuggled them down into the pillows. "Try to sleep, babe," he whispered, and kissed her forehead.

"'Kay," Emma muttered.

No one should ever lose their children, they agreed. The very idea was just too horrible to comprehend. If they were this distraught being away from their children—who were safe and happy—it was impossible to imagine what Manuelita Gonzales had gone through after her daughters were stolen from her.

Through her research in Salt Lake City, Emma had been able to track down a certain Juan Gonzales who had been reported killed by Apaches in June of 1782. His wife was listed as Manuela Baca. Emma was nearly certain she was on the right track with this couple, but so far had been unable to find any information about any kidnappings related to Juan's death.

They discussed their plans to visit the library and the local museums. They'd figure out where to see public records—most likely the local courthouse would have information.

Finally, they were able to drift off to sleep, and for a wonder, they both managed to sleep late.

1.

The first visitor arrived while Jacob was showering that morning. Emma had really been expecting Manuelita to appear, so she was quite surprised to encounter a stranger.

Manuelita was a tiny woman, but this new person was even smaller. She had thick black hair that flowed to nearly her knees, wide warm brown eyes and eyelashes that would make fashion models green with envy. She stood about four feet eight, Emma guessed, and was probably in her late twenties, although she looked to be around sixteen. Emma greeted her with a smile.

"I am Tomasa," she told Emma, her smile revealing startlingly white teeth. "Maria Manuela is my daughter."

"I'm honored to meet you," Emma said.

"The honor is mine," Tomasa said. "You have given my daughter hope; she has spent so much time in distress. There was nothing I could do for her, you know; she barely remembers me; I was gone from this world when she was very small. But as you know, we watch. I watched."

"And now?" Emma asked. "Do you see her now?"

"I do," Tomasa replied. "But the relationship is difficult for her, Emmaline. She continued to live, to grow, to age, long after I was gone. I watched over her whenever I was able to—she was never gone from me. But she was a very young child, and for her, Mama was gone. At first, she missed me, but as she grew older, her memories of me faded.

"In truth, I am a stranger to her. She knows who I am—her mother—but she does not know me."

"How sad for you!" Emma cried.

217

"It is sad," Tomasa agreed. "I had but thirty years in your world; she lived more than twice as long. Her experiences in the world far surpassed my own. How does one mother an older woman?"

Emma considered the situation, and had no idea what to say.

"I would like to help you," Tomasa said, "but I don't know where my granddaughters were taken. I saw them dragged away...but I stayed with my daughter." She stared at Emma with tears in her eyes. "I should have followed them!"

"How did you come to be there?" Emma asked. "How did you even know? I mean...uh..."

Tomasa wrung her hands. "Oh, dear child," she said. "This existence is a most confusing state! Truthfully, I don't choose where I go, or when...at least, not most of the time. But in times of danger, or distress, or even times of great happiness—then I would find myself with her. I was there when she married that Griego Indio."

"That—what?" Emma frowned. "Was she married twice?"

"No, no. Juan Gonzales. He was part of the Griego family. Mestizos. Oh, how she loves that man!"

"She told me she misses him very much."

"Yes." Tomasa frowned. "I believe they will find each other again. I pray it will be so."

"Me, too."

"I have not seen him. Which, of course, means nothing. He is here—somewhere."

"I'm told it is vast, where you are," Emma said.

"I'm sure of it." Tomasa looked thoughtful. "I cannot say for certain." She shook her head. "In any case, I have no real control of my movements. I go where I go; that is all.

"On the day my son-in-law was murdered by those Apache savages, there was screaming and crying, and suddenly, I was there. Juan Gonzales was dead on the floor, throat slashed and blood still flowing, and my Manuelita was huddled with her children and grandchildren, trying to keep a little baby well hidden. The braves rushed them and grabbed the young girls and dragged them, kicking and screaming, from the house!

"I should have followed them! So many times, I have cursed myself for my failure to do that!"

"Please," Emma said. "Don't feel that way."

"I should have followed them!"

"Could you? Could you have followed them?"

"I—I don't know…" Tomasa wrung her hands again. "But if only I had, I could have told her—or you—where they went!"

"But you just told me, you don't usually get to choose where you go—or when. So, what do you believe, dear Tomasa? Do you really think you could have followed them?" Emma felt a great need to discover the answer to this question. Tomasa was carrying a great burden of guilt that Emma felt she didn't deserve.

"I don't know," Tomasa admitted. "I—probably not. My thoughts were only for my daughter—she was devastated. And so, I stayed with her for a time."

"I believe that was where you needed to be," Emma said. "Don't feel badly for it. There was nothing you could have done."

"It is very frustrating to be an observer only," Tomasa remarked.

At that point, Jacob opened the bathroom door, stark naked and drying his curls with a towel. Tomasa turned bright red and vanished.

"Well, dang!" Emma said.

2.

"I embarrassed a *ghost?*" Jacob cried. "How about a ghost embarrassed *me?*"

Emma was rolling on the bed, giggling madly. "Oh, my God, I wish you could have seen her face!" she laughed. "I'm going to hell for this, I just know it—but I can't stop laughing!"

"Oh yes you can," Jacob ordered. "Any time now, Em."

"Aw! But you looked so good, Jake!"

"Apparently not so good, if she just up and disappeared," Jacob groused. He'd snatched the towel down and wrapped it around his waist, and now he looked like he didn't know what to do next—take it off and get dressed, or just stand there, covered up.

No wonder Emma couldn't stop laughing.

"Get dressed, Jake, it's fine," Emma said.

"Oh yeah? How do I know she's not right here, waiting to get another look at my sweet patootie?"

Emma shook her head, still giggling. "I guess you don't—but I don't see her anywhere. She lit out pretty darn quick, I'll tell you that!"

"Damned ghosts," Jacob muttered. He grabbed up his briefs and jeans and went back in the bathroom, still mumbling under his breath.

Emma went on giggling for a couple more minutes, and when he came back out she gathered her things and went in for her shower.

As far back as she could remember, she'd never had a naked encounter with a spirit—that she knew of. This had been purely accidental, and it probably shouldn't have been as funny as it turned out to be. But—oh! The look on that tiny woman's face!

"She'll probably never visit me again as long as I live!" she called to Jacob through the door.

"I'm having a little trouble caring at the moment!" Jacob called back.

Emma dropped her t-shirt on the floor and called, "Oh, stop! You know you look fabulous naked!"

"Your granny didn't think so!"

"Or did she?" Emma giggled again and stepped into the shower, effectively cutting off whatever retort Jacob might have shot back.

When she emerged from the bathroom, Jacob was dressed and had gone out to fetch them coffees. "She'll be back," he told Emma as he handed her a Styrofoam cup.

"Yeah," Emma agreed. "Who could resist that sweet patootie?"

"Shush, you!" Jacob switched on the television. "It's probably too late for the news," he added. "But so far, the weather looks great. It's chilly out there, but nothing we can't handle."

"Was there a local map in the lobby?"

"Uh..." Jacob looked slightly abashed. "I was blushing so hard I forgot to look?" he suggested.

Emma shook her head. "Are we staying here tonight, too?" she asked.

"Yeah, I already paid for another night," Jacob replied. "Nothing we need to see is far from here, really. I mean, I want to see Bernalillo and Corrales, but we might be able to research everything right here. I'm kind of hoping when we get to Albuquerque we can just relax, visit and act like regular tourists."

Emma nodded her agreement. "I just want to— "

"—check on the babies. I know," Jacob said. "I wish they were talking, I want to hear their voices."

"Me, too. Unless they're crying."

They weren't. Jill answered the phone and told them that both babies were doing great. She agreed to hold the phone for each of them, so Emma and Jacob could talk to them, and they all had a good laugh when the babies stared at the receiver but refused to so much as grunt. "Oh, gosh, Mom!" Emma cried. "We miss them so much!"

"I know you do," Jill said. "But they're just fine."

"They won't even like me anymore when I get home."

"Don't be silly." Jill was firm. "Get to work!"

"Love you!"

"Love you, too. Bye! Say bye-bye, babies!"

Nothing. Not even a grunt.

3.

"Okay, we're going to get through this day without crying," Emma declared. "Feed me."

"I hope we're not too late for breakfast," Jacob said. "I really want some French toast."

"Yum."

There were plenty of restaurants to choose from, and with so many authentic Mexican dishes! Jacob was in a bit of a quandary, however, because nothing much could be considered kosher. "Let's just find an I-Hop or something and get your French toast," Emma suggested.

Jacob grinned at her. "I'm sure I can find something like that anywhere," he said. "I can get home fries and a tortilla if I have to."

"Why didn't we think about this?" Emma cried. "Or did you?"

"No, I was totally gonzo," Jacob admitted. "And honestly, Em, I don't think I'll go to hell—or whatever you think will happen to me—if I eat a cheeseburger. I'll just do the best I can. Don't worry!"

There certainly didn't seem to be any kosher restaurants in Santa Fe. As far as they knew so far, there wasn't a synagogue, either; they'd have to do some exploring.

"Ah, the old West," Jacob said. "I'm almost positive Jewish people settled here. Lots of them must have converted or something."

Emma shrugged. "I think this whole area was settled by Spaniards who converted the natives to Catholicism. I mean, I'm sure there were some Jewish people, too, but it must have been really hard for them in a Catholic- dominant area."

"Honey, no matter where we go, it's hard for us," Jake told her. "That's just the way it is."

"Well, crap. That sucks."

"'That sucks'?" Jacob grinned. "Been hanging out with your mom much?"

Emma laughed. "I can't even blame Freddie anymore. Mom uses that expression more than he does!"

They decided on a place called the Plaza Café, which they learned was the oldest restaurant still open in Santa Fe. It was owned and run by a local couple and their family, and offered a wide variety of foods. Breakfast was served until eleven a.m. To his great surprise, Jacob discovered a treat on the menu— Santa Fe Smoked Salmon, a toasted bagel with cream cheese, topped with sliced tomatoes, smoked salmon, pickled onions, capers and chopped green chili. "Oh, boy, that's for me!" he cried.

"I'm going to go totally un-kosher and have the huevos rancheros with green chili," Emma announced.

Reasonable prices, delicious food and great service. It was a wonderful way to start their day.

While they were eating, Jacob asked the waitress if it was possible to see the dinner menu. There were plenty of foods Jacob could eat without feeling too guilty, and they decided to return that evening.

They were nothing if not faithful customers when they were treated well and fed right.

As they were paying their bill, Emma asked about genealogy research in the area. "I'd start at the Palace of the Governors over on the corner of Washington Avenue and Palace Avenue," their cashier told them. "There's a ton of information there, and lots of people to talk to."

"Thank you!" Emma said. "And thanks for a great breakfast."

"Thank you for coming. I hope we see you again."

"You will," Jacob smiled.

Chapter Fifteen

Juan Baptiste the Apache

"Wow!" Jacob and Emma gasped in unison.
The Palace of the Governors was quite a sight. Emma consulted her tourist book and said, "This is the oldest building in continuous use in the United States."
"Yeah? How old is it?" Jacob asked. They had remained parked up the street by the Plaza Cafe and just walked over; it wasn't far, and the day was cool but pleasant. The Plaza itself—the town square, so to speak—was bustling with people, and quaintly lovely.
"Constructed in 1610," Emma read, "for the first governor, Pedro de Peralta. This was back when it was a Spanish territory. It's changed hands many times over the centuries, and now it's the historical museum. And, hey, check it out! It was named a national historic landmark the year I was born!"
"1906?"
"*Funny.* There will be a witty retort in your future, buddy."
"I await it with bated breath."
"You're cruisin' for a bruisin'."
"Yeah, I know."
Out front there were several members of the local Pueblo tribes selling hand-made art, and they spent a good amount of time perusing the wares and choosing small items as Christmas gifts. "Yay!" Emma said. "Now I don't have to shop later."
"Oh, sure," Jacob chuckled. "Like that will stop you."
"Oh, shush." Emma grinned at him, undaunted.
There were so many wonderful things to see, and Emma was delighted that every gift she selected was completely unique.
As they wandered under the portico, Emma noticed a man dressed in period clothing watching her. The venders under the portico were in Native dress, but it was decidedly more modern, so he stood out a bit in his flowing, cropped pants and serape. He was hatless, his hair shiny blue-black and

curly, and he seemed taller than average. His eyes were emerald green, and he was incredibly handsome.

When their eyes met, Emma smiled at him. He nodded and softly said, "Good afternoon to you, Senora."

"And to you, Senor," Emma replied.

Jacob looked at her questioningly, and Emma, knowing for sure now that the man was a spirit, nodded acknowledgement.

"Your husband?" the man asked.

"Yes."

"This is awkward," he smiled. "Perhaps we should walk the Plaza."

He waited until Jacob had paid for their purchases. They left the building and started walking in the square.

"You are looking for someone," the man observed.

"Yes," Emma agreed.

"My mother and her sister," the man announced dramatically.

"Your—your mother?" Emma gasped.

Jacob gasped. "What? Who?" He shook his head. "God, I wish—"

"I know, me too," Emma agreed, leaning her head toward him. "So...which one was your mother? And what's your name?"

"Maria Elena was my mother," the handsome man told her. "Juliana was my aunt. Also," he added emphatically, "my father was *not* a savage."

"Uh..." Emma didn't know what to say to that.

"My name is Juan Baptiste Martinez Gonzales," he went on, his green eyes flashing. "I was over forty years old when my grandmother Manuela died, and although she saw me a time or two over the years, she never knew I was the son of her daughter."

"Oh, this is going to be a good story," Emma declared, and Jacob sighed in frustration.

Juan Baptiste grinned good-naturedly. "It is a good story, to be sure," he said. "Let us sit, and I will tell you all that I know."

They sat on a park bench near the obelisk in the center of the square. Juan sat on the ground facing them. Jacob made a show of going through their shopping bag, showing Emma various items, as she listened and shared the story.

"You said your name is Martinez," Emma clarified, "and that your father was not a savage. I'm not sure what that means. Manuela said your mother and aunt were taken by the Apache…"

"So they were," Juan agreed. "And my father was an Apache warrior—"

"Named *Martinez?*" Emma was confused. She pulled a notebook and a pen from her purse and began to take notes.

Juan shook his head. "What you must understand, mi prima—my cousin—is that there were many marriages between the native people and the Spaniards who invaded our lands. My father's mother was one who married a Spaniard. But he lived among the People, forsaking the colonials he had traveled with from the south. My grandfather Juan Jesus Martinez learned the ways of the People. He was accepted as a member of the tribe and raised my father and uncles to be great warriors."

"Ah…" Emma said, and shared this information with Jacob, who nodded enthusiastically.

"My father, his brothers and other warriors raided various settlements in search of weapons and food. They had been pushed out of their own lands by the Spaniards, aided by the Pueblo tribes, and had become wanderers of the desert. They had no permanent place to call home; they were hunted continuously by other tribes, and moved frequently.

"On a particular raid, several women and children were taken from the settlement near Corrales. Among them were my mother and her sister. Soon they were taken as wives and became true members of the tribe. My mother was the younger of the sisters, and adapted well to tribal life. My aunt Juliana had a more difficult time. She was nearly twenty and betrothed at the time they were taken, and although a very accomplished warrior took her as his wife, she seemed unable to forget the man she had planned to marry. It caused many problems; she did not eat or sleep well. She cried. She tried to run away." Juan Baptiste shook his head. "She cared for her husband…but she was a troubled woman.

"While giving birth to her first child, she was having great difficulty. She fought the people who were trying to help her—she had difficulty with our language, and could not understand them. They were part of a small hunting party that day, away from the main tribe, and there was no one experienced enough to help her when things started going wrong. She begged my mother to send for a midwife. Of course, that was not possible. Finally, her husband loaded her onto his horse and rode with her to one of the Spanish settlements and left her there with a midwife.

"He never saw her again."

"Oh, that's terrible," Jacob cried when Emma told him this. "Do *you* know what happened to her?" He directed the question to Juan Baptiste, although he could not see him, and Emma's cousin answered him directly as if they really spoke face to face. Emma was delighted; no other spirit had made such a direct effort to communicate with anyone besides Emma, and she knew how much it would mean to Jacob. He had always wanted to talk to a ghost!

"I do, actually! She ended up right here in Santa Fe. She had found her great love and married him; he raised her oldest child as his own."

"But Manuelita—"

"Juliana was ashamed to face her—she'd been married to a 'savage' and had given birth to a half-breed."

"I don't think—"

"Ah, but you don't *know*, Prima! She was very bitter, my grandmother. She could be very judgmental; she learned it from the best."

Emma frowned. She decided to let her arguments go for the time being. "What happened?" she asked.

"My mother and father married, and my mother embraced the native life. She was different from other Spanish women. She could hunt with the best of the men, and then dress and butcher her kill faster than the native women. She was a protector of the women and children of the tribe, and she taught my sister to be the same."

"A liberated woman in the old west," Jacob remarked, grinning.

"Liberated?" Juan asked.

"Free."

"*All* our people were free," Juan declared, frowning. "Women were never discouraged from doing what they wanted to do. Our women were not oppressed by men. The white man did that."

"*Do* that," Emma added.

"Hey!" Jacob protested.

"Not you, honey." Emma patted Jacob's arm reassuringly.

"My mother once told us that if she had been allowed to learn to fight when she was young, we never would have been born, because she would have killed all the warriors who came to her settlement and killed her father." Juan Baptiste grinned proudly. "I have no doubt she could have done it.

"But she had no regrets," he added. "She loved my father very much, and he loved her. She was lonely for her sister sometimes, but she never left the tribe again for as long as she lived. She had no desire to return to the world she'd been taken from. Although she did *visit* it from time to time, as I will tell you.

"Julianna was left with the midwife in Bernalillo, very near Corrales, where she was born. She gave birth to a daughter, and then fled north to Santa Ana instead of going home to her mother.

"When her husband returned for her, she was gone. He did not search for her; he knew she was unhappy with the People, and decided it was best to let her go, although it made him very sad and he mourned her loss and the loss of their child.

"He *did* marry again, her husband; he had many sons with his new bride. He maintained a brotherly relationship with my mother, and his children were considered cousins to us, although there was no real blood relationship.

"At any rate, my mother found her sister soon afterward; she knew her sister well, and was able to figure out what she would have done. By that time Aunt Juliana had found her love; she had gone to Santa Ana in search of him, because she knew he did business there. She told my mother that he was still willing to marry her despite her marriage to the 'savage Apache', and so she was going to stay.

228

"And as I told you, they *did* marry. He raised her daughter and loved her as his own. He was a very good man.

"Over the years, my mother would make arrangements to meet my aunt, and so I grew up occasionally meeting my cousins and playing with them. They lived here in Santa Fe; their house was on the edge of town, so it was easy for my mother to come. She would dress in her sister's clothes and come here to the Plaza to sell or trade goods, and no one was the wiser.

"It amused them both, you know. It is my opinion that they were a little wicked!

"I grew up speaking the language of my people and the language of my mother's people, and when I was older, I began to seek work as a translator and guide. It gave me an inside look at the Spaniards' world, and helped us to plan our moves around the desert, and also to plan our raiding parties.

"I knew my Aunt's husband, Juan Santillanes, very well, and he often helped me find work. It was beneficial to earn the currency of the Spaniards; I was able to trade or buy many things for my own family. Plus, I was always able to lead the Spaniards away from my people while still helping them to expand their holdings.

"I played both sides for my own benefit. I am not ashamed of it; it kept my family clothed and fed. It kept my people safe from the Spaniards and other settlers who were coming to the area.

"I was known to the Spaniards only as Juan Baptiste the Apache—I never revealed my real name to anyone other than Juan Santillanes, who I always knew as my uncle.

"There were many Apache tribes in this area; some were friendly with the Spaniards and Pueblo peoples, and some were not. My appearance, I was told, was more Spanish than Apache, so no one knew I came from a tribe that would as soon kill and rob them as trade with them.

"I have told you that I am a Martinez. But my father, Miguel Nantan Lupan, never used the Martinez name. He went by Grey Wolf all his life. He loved and respected my grandfather, but refused to acknowledge any Spanish heritage. He never learned the language, speaking only the Apache tongue.

"I was the oldest son, and my mother insisted that I be named for her father, who was slain by the very people she came to consider her family. She had clung to parts of her Catholic religion despite becoming a great warrior in her own right, and so she added the name Baptiste. Martinez, she added out of respect and affection for my grandfather. My father, who refused the name for himself, did not object. He agreed that I would be able to choose for myself whether to use the name when I was grown.

"All my adult life, I traveled from camp to settlement, where I traded for goods, worked as a translator or guide and sometimes—I freely admit it—seduced the local women." He grinned sheepishly.

"I don't doubt it," Emma told Jacob. "I'm sure all he had to do was bat those emerald eyes and flash that smile, and the women climbed over each other to get to him."

Jacob gaped, and Juan Baptiste threw back his head and roared his laughter. "No, Prima, it was not that easy!" he protested.

"Sure," Emma said. "I believe you."

"Good looking, is he?" Jacob asked.

"Very," Emma confirmed.

"Huh." Jacob made a face, and Emma giggled.

"I was told I looked like my grandfather," Juan Baptiste told Jacob. "As did my father; except for his eyes—his eyes were black. It was quite a surprise to everyone when I was born green-eyed."

"Recessive gene," Emma said, and both men looked at her. "His grandfather gave him green eyes," she explained. "My grandfather gave me blue ones. Did your brothers and sisters have green eyes?"

"No; only me. And I had only one sister. My mother swore she was overrun with boys. There were six of us."

"Six boys and one girl! No wonder your mom taught her to be a warrior!"

"She was one of the best," he confirmed.

"All my pre-conceived notions of native women have been crushed," Jacob sighed. "I never knew women were allowed to be warriors."

"*Allowed?*" The handsome man chuckled. "Without the women, our tribes would have perished!" He shook his head dolefully. "The intruders were not wise, Emma. They suppressed their women and treated them like property. The women of my people *owned* property; they were included in decision making. My mother could never have done that as a *Spanish* woman.

"My mother *could* have gone to visit her people—my father would never have objected; he trusted her—but she never did, because she knew that her brothers would force her to stay, and she didn't want that. *Juliana* could have returned, but she felt ashamed that she'd married an Apache and bore his child. Her Spanish husband—a very liberal man for the times—told her she was being foolish, but still she never went back to Corrales. Her upbringing had made her feel shame over something that didn't have to be shameful."

"Her upbringing?" Emma asked.

"Catholicism." Juan Baptiste spat, and Emma jumped, shocked; *she* was Catholic, after all. She raised her eyebrows enquiringly.

"The Friars forced the natives to adapt their crazy religion," Juan Baptiste explained, "and all the people were taught to believe that every natural thing was a sin against their God. Juliana was married to an Apache man in a native ceremony; she lived with him as a *wife*; she became pregnant—a most natural thing! But she never believed herself a *truly* married woman, because she was not married in the Church. She believed that she had lived in *sin*, created a child in *sin*, and that she could *never* be forgiven."

Emma stared at him, open mouthed. "But—but that's not what the Church teaches us at all!" she protested. "Forgiveness—"

"No, no," Jacob interrupted, "that's not the way it used to be, Emma—"

"You cannot understand what it was like for them," Juan Baptiste argued. "Jacob might be closer to understanding than—"

"What? Why?" Emma demanded.

"I am not entirely ignorant of the continuing history of your world, Emma. I know about the persecution of your husband's people. Being condemned for failing to conform to the ideals of the majority—this is nothing new, not to my people, and not to your husband's people. Over time, our people have been driven from their homes, herded like animals into encampments where we would *never* choose to live, murdered by the thousands. *You* were not raised in the shadows of persecution; neither were your parents or even your grandparents. You have been free to worship as you choose, or not to worship at all if you so choose.

"That was not the world I was born into, and my Spanish relatives were slaves to the teachings of the friars in the area, regardless of their so-called 'message' of 'forgiveness of sins'. Tia Juliana felt condemned to hellfire because she had no other choice but to believe what she'd been taught—the Church practically *beat* her beliefs into her. She was not a strong woman, and it was a blessing that Juan Santillanes loved her, and that she was able to find him when she did, or she surely would have wasted away and died after her baby was born."

"Oh, my God," Emma moaned. "Poor thing!"

"Truly. And her mother, Maria Manuela, had lived her whole life as a Catholic, taught that every *thought* of sin could potentially condemn her to hell. Do you think she would be *forgiving?* Her daughters did not believe so."

Juan Baptiste flashed his white teeth in a charming smile. "My mother, now—she was not at *all* like her sister. There was a *fire* in her. She probably gave the friars nightmares when she was younger. She was a warrior long before she came to live with the People."

"How old was she when she was captured?"

"I don't really know. Perhaps at some time you will have an opportunity to ask her."

"I hope so."

"I am here to tell you about my grandmother, and her searches for her daughters. She never *did* stop trying to find them—I'll give her that; she was a determined woman--but her resources were limited. Her sons and grandsons would hear a story or two from time to time about where the People were living, and would ride out to investigate, but would find nothing.

"We were *never* where they searched. My people were not foolish; we moved frequently and kept well hidden. Any confrontations with the interlopers took place in their own settlements; no Spaniard stood a chance in hell of finding the People.

"I grew up a nomad; I knew these lands better than I knew the landscape of my wife's body; and have no doubts—I knew her well! I learned the languages of the Spaniards, the Pueblo natives, and the Navajo. A man like me was a valuable asset to the settlers; I let them use me to our mutual benefit.

"At a time when I was nearly twenty, I met my grandmother, Maria Manuela Baca, in the streets of Corrales. I had known about her all my life, but that was the first time I came face to face with that little woman.

"I was there to lead a search party who was hunting for a woman who had been taken by a number of Navajo warriors. I had no love for the Navajo and was happy to hunt for them.

"Grandmother was in the street, exhorting the search party to hunt down the 'savages', and to keep an eye out for her babies who were stolen from her years before.

"You must understand, she believed me to be a Spaniard. As you can see, I looked the part; I did nothing to contradict the belief. Of course, I knew who *she* was, because the entire family was well known in the area, and she had been searching for her daughters for many years; there were those who believed her insane with grief over her losses; people *talked* about her, you see. One could not visit Corrales and not hear about Ma Manuelita.

"I might have told her then—now I feel I *should* have—but she made me *angry*."

Juan Baptiste looked Emma in the eye, abashed. "I'm not a nice man when I'm angry," he admitted. "The more she called my people thieves and savages, the angrier I got. I nodded and smiled, and thought to myself that she didn't *deserve* to know what I knew.

"When I returned home, I told my mother what had transpired, and *she* became angry with *me*. So, I told her she should go back to Corrales with me, but she refused. She did not want her brothers or her uncles to try to force her to stay there.

"It was probable, you know. Spanish women were not able to make decisions for themselves; they were considered little more than property by their men. A woman was first controlled by her father; if her father was dead, a brother would manage her life until she married, and then she belonged to her husband.

"It was no way to live. She'd spent decades with the People as a free woman; she could not be faulted for wanting to continue to live as she pleased.

"She would never return, she told me, and I did not argue that. But it posed problems if she wanted me to tell her mother she was alive and safe.

I told her it made no sense to tell her mother *anything* if she wasn't going to go and see her. It would be unfair to raise her hopes and then dash them. Mama argued that at least her mother would *know*. That it would put her mind at ease.

"I did not agree. I felt that as a parent myself, I would never believe a stranger; I would want to see for myself.

"We traveled to Santa Fe, where she spoke with Juliana, who cried and argued about her fears of being driven from the city. She was afraid that if anyone besides Juan Santillanes knew of her past life among the Apache, her marriage to him would be declared illegal and she would lose everything. She was under the authority of the Church again, and they could cast her out.

"You see what I mean about the Catholics, Emma. They ruled by fear; a family remained divided forever because they believed in the power of a *church!*

Emma felt a bit defensive; the church he was faulting was not *her* church—she had learned from an early age that her Savior, Jesus Christ, had died so that her sins could be forgiven. But she held her tongue; she didn't know what the Church had been like in the 1700s. But she intended to find out.

"They argued for hours, Emma. My mother wanted to put her mother's mind at ease; Tia Juliana wanted there to be no chance of being found and punished. They decided at last that it might be better for their mother to believe they were *dead*, rather than knowing they had chosen not to return to Corrales.

"It was distressing. It seemed to me there was no good answer."

Emma was quiet. "It *still* seems like there's no good answer," she said at last.

Juan Baptiste nodded. "She was a very old woman when she died," he said. "Almost one hundred years old, I believe. I came to Corrales many times over the years; I kept track of her. She had made me angry, but she was my grandmother. And I understood her, Emma. She had no way of knowing that her daughters had found lives that made them happy. All she knew was that they were taken away from her."

He shrugged. "I sometimes tracked for her grandsons; since I knew the Navaho and Pueblo languages, I was in the area a great deal. They never knew I was their cousin. I was simply whoever they chose to believe I was; a Spaniard, a Mestizo, a talented translator and guide. It didn't matter to me, as long as I was paid.

"My mother and her sister sometimes made things for their mother; I would leave them for her in the night. Sometimes I saw her wearing a shawl my mother had made—she wore it often, never knowing it was a gift from her daughter."

"Wow," Emma said.

"I left food. Blankets. She was well taken care of." He sounded defensive.

"Okay. *Good*." Jacob said. "You did what you could—it's not like your mother and aunt left you any other choice." He looked at Emma. "I wish I could see him," he added.

"He's nodding," Emma told him.

"As I said, I understood her. She grieved for her husband. She grieved for her children. She was angry. If my children had been taken away, I would have felt the same. The difference is, I could have found them; Ma Manuela could not so much as ride a horse. She was dependent on the men of her settlement to help her, and in reality, those men were useless. They were farmers and shepherds; they couldn't track their way out of a valley with only one pass."

"Come now," Emma protested. "Isn't that a bit unfair? They were explorers! They found their way to New Mexico."

"Oh, no! Not *those* men! Perhaps their fathers and grandfathers had returned from El Paso during the re-conquest; I do not know. But I do know my grandmother's sons and grandsons were born and raised in the settlements, and there they stayed, for the most part. They lived within fortress walls. They were 'civilized'. They raised their food, rather than hunting for it.

"I admit," Juan added, "that there were attempts made to find the lost sisters. The men mounted their horses and rode out, often becoming lost and confused. They tried." He shrugged. "They failed."

"And you chose not to help them," Jacob observed.

"That is correct," Juan Baptiste acknowledged.

"But it was *their* choice? Your mother's and your aunt's?"

"It was." The handsome man shook his head. "I honored my mother, and her wish was to spare her mother the knowledge that her daughters chose not to return to her.

"I know that Ma Manuela has enlisted your aid in finding my mother and my aunt; I know that you will speak to her of these things when, in due time, she returns to see you. Therefore, I would request that you assure her that her daughters loved her and looked after her all their lives. But because they knew that their return to the settlement would result in serious disruptions in their own lives, they chose to love her from a distance."

"Wow," Emma breathed. "I have no idea how she's going to take this."

Jacob looked like he could be blown off the park bench by a mere breeze. "If it were my mother, she'd be furious," he remarked.

"Mine, too."

"If I am honest," Juan Baptiste said, "I would say that both my mother and my aunt would be furious as well. I cannot justify the decisions they made—perhaps someday they will speak to you, and better explain their motivations."

"I would welcome that," Emma said. "I would welcome a chance to speak with them and their mother together. But I have no way of making that happen; these things are not up to me."

Juan Baptiste the Apache smiled brilliantly. "You would not have called me; you would never have known to *seek* me. But we watch, Emma. We watch the living. And sometimes, we are moved to speak to those who are called to listen.

"Somehow, my grandmother found you; because I have managed to watch her occasionally since my crossing, I found you as well.

"I don't claim to understand these things; it is as much a mystery to me as anything I've ever encountered. But I have watched you and awaited my time to speak, and I know you seek understanding.

"I hope you can find it. But I don't believe in my heart that you will find the *records* you seek here," he added. "It may be that someone recorded the passing of my grandmother, but the others in this story passed into places where no written record was ever kept. There were lies and cover-ups involving my aunt and her baby; Juan Santillanes was a meticulous and intelligent man; I am certain his wife was never recorded as a member of the Gonzales family, and the child was always referred to as his own.

"I wish you luck, Prima, in your searches. Perhaps I am wrong. I learned to speak many languages, and I learned every acre of land in this area, but I did not read or write very much; what would I know of records, except what was told to me from time to time?

"Blessings to you, my cousins," Juan Baptiste said, and then he was gone.

"Well, dang!" said Emma

Chapter Sixteen

Santa Fe

Emma and Jacob remained on the park bench, stunned. Finally, Jacob grinned at her. "I talked to a ghost," he gasped.

"Yes, you did," Emma agreed.

"Thanks for being the interpreter."

"No problem." Emma sighed. "Thank God we took those Spanish classes."

"I know."

"I'm exhausted," Emma admitted. "Thinking in another language is hard work!"

"Not to mention doing the listening and retelling for my benefit," Jacob agreed. "But I'm so damned happy right now!"

"Because you talked to a ghost?" Emma asked.

"Well, yeah," Jacob replied. "And because he talked to me. But also, because we know what happened! Finally!"

Emma sighed and looked troubled. "We do," she said. "But I'm not sure what to do about it. I mean, it's going to be painful telling Manuelita these things."

Jacob nodded. "I think we should still go inside and see if we can find out anything concrete."

"I wonder if there might actually be anything documented about Juan Baptiste the Apache," Emma mused. "It sounds like he really got around."

"That's what I was thinking," Jacob agreed. "We might not be able to get details about his birth or death…"

"Probably not."

"But if he was kept as busy as he says, someone probably mentioned him."

"You'd think so. Juan Baptiste Martinez Gonzales—in the Spanish custom, the mother's surname is last." Emma consulted her notes. "I suppose if nothing else, we could research this Juan Santillanes who married Juliana. He was obviously a man of means around here."

Jacob nodded his agreement. He was repacking their shopping bags, and held up a beaded purse. "Is this the one we got for Mama?"

"Uh..." Emma frowned. "Let me see the other one?"

Jacob dug through the bag and pulled out a similar purse. "Oh," he said. "I think it was this one."

The two purses were similar styles, with beads forming star formations, but one had more blue colorings, and the other had more orange and yellow. He was holding up the blue now, and Emma said, "Yes, that one's for Mama. My mother is a sunshine-colors person."

"They're going to love these," Jacob grinned. "Let's go see what else we can find. Get Christmas out of the way!"

"Yay!"

In the end, their shopping trip necessitated a trip back to the hotel room; they didn't want to carry their purchases through the museum. Emma was particularly excited about some of the necklaces and bracelets they had found. She didn't wear much jewelry herself, but they both had sisters and aunts who would enjoy additions to their collections. Purses, medicine bags and belts, knife sheaths and wallets—they had certainly contributed to the local economy!

After packing their goodies into cloth bags—also purchased from the local artists—they walked back to the Plaza, stopping at a Panadería for baked goods and coffees. Large sweet breads made a perfect afternoon snack, which they ate while window shopping around the Plaza.

Once they finished their food and beverages, they went back to the Palace of the Governors and paid admission to the museum.

"Do we have any idea what we're looking for?" Jacob asked.

"Nope."

"So, this is just a sight-seeing trip?"

"Yep." Emma grinned. "I don't think we're going to find anything here, honestly. We might have better luck at the library. But I want to see this place, anyway."

"Me, too," Jacob agreed. "There's been nothing here so far that wasn't interesting."

"I'm curious about the Jewish population," Emma told him. "I read somewhere that some families immigrated to this area after being exiled from Spain."

"I suppose there's no place we haven't been exiled from." Jacob sighed. "If they came here from Spain, though, they'd have been in just as much trouble—it was Spanish ruled, after all, and Catholicism was forced on everyone; Juan Baptiste said it himself."

"I know," Emma agreed. "There were families here that were under investigation, accused of being Jews-in-hiding. What were they called? Uh—"

"Crypto-Jews."

Emma and Jacob turned to face the man who had spoken. "Sorry for the interruption," the man continued. "I've been doing a little research about this myself."

He appeared to be in his forties, with thick black hair greying at the temples, a prominent nose and large liquid-brown eyes. Flesh and blood, not a spirit—Emma was certain of that much; Jacob could see and hear him.

"You're researching Crypto-Jews?" Jacob asked.

"I'm researching my own family tree," the man replied. "Oh! I'm sorry; you must think I'm a cretin." He held out his hand. "I'm Roman. Roman Sanchez."

Jacob shook his hand and said, "Jacob Kramer. My wife, Emma."

"Pleased to meet you. Penny?" he called, and an attractive blond turned to face him; she'd been examining a painting. "My wife," Roman added.

"Hello," Penny said.

"Jacob and Emma Kramer," Roman told her. He smiled at them all. "My father grew up in this area," he explained. "I grew up in Chicago. Recently, my father told me that his family was probably descended from the Jews who were driven out of Spain in the sixteenth century. I don't know why, but it struck a chord in me."

"I can understand that," Jacob said.

"We decided it might be fun to do some sightseeing and art shopping," Penny said, "and also, to do some detective work. I have to say, it's been fascinating so far."

"Have you been able to find anything definitive?" Emma asked hopefully.

"Oh, of course not!" Roman cried, grinning. "The records are a mess; it's going to take more time than we have on a little vacation trip to sort out all the Sanchez families in *this* area. And it seems that the Jewish population was forced to convert—or hide their ancestry completely. It's going to be tough!" He laughed. "But we really love it here, so it'll be great to come back next year and keep digging."

Emma smiled. "I imagine that's what could happen to us, too," she said. "The more I learn, the more questions I have."

Penny smiled. "I'm game," she said. "It's so beautiful in this area. Have you been to the Pueblos?"

"I'm sorry?" Jacob asked.

"Oh, there are some ruins outside of town of the old Pueblo villages," Penny said. "The homes were built right into the sides of the cliffs! It's amazing!"

"We haven't seen them yet," Jacob admitted. "We're kind of on a quest; family tree research, like you. And like Emma said, the more we learn, the more questions we have."

"Well, if you're anything like us," Penny said, "you'll be coming back sometime. If you don't make it out for a tour on this trip, you'll really want to do it someday. It's fascinating."

"I know I'd like to. "Emma said. "I saw some pictures; I'd love to take my own. But it's probably going to have to wait until our next vacation."

"Look, please tell me if I'm being nosy," Roman said. "But I heard from a friend that you can find a lot of family history information in Utah. Do you know anything about that?"

"Oh, yes!" Emma and Jacob chorused.

The two couples continued their museum tour, exchanging family tree search information and exclaiming over the many exhibits. It was exciting to make new friends with common interests.

"Wouldn't it be something," Roman said, "if we discovered that we're relatives?"

"It would," Emma agreed. "But I don't think it would be all that *surprising*, actually."

After the museum, the couples made their way to the public library—always Emma's favorite research venue, libraries were usually the *first* places she visited.

"I doubt that newspaper archives go back as far as we're searching, but there may be related articles," Jacob said. "Surely other researchers have tried to locate our families in the past, and they may have written some historical story."

"I'm sure we'll find some fascinating history regardless," Emma remarked. "But it would be so cool to find a scout named Juan Baptiste."

"There are so many Sanchez families still in this area," Roman added, "and my father promised to try and find out who around here might be related. But in the meantime, I think I might just look for the name and see what comes up."

"Sounds like a plan to me," Penny said. "My own people are from Holland, so I think I'll just find a nice romance novel to sink my teeth into." She giggled, and the others joined her. She left them, and was soon settled in an easy chair with a racy new best-seller.

Newspaper archives were on microfilm, and the librarian graciously set them up with machines. Emma asked about Indian scouts in the area in the late 1700s, and the matronly woman chuckled. "There were quite a few," she said. "It seems there was always someone hunting for someone else back in the dark ages." She grinned. "You'll have to be more specific."

"Uh...well, the name I have is Juan Baptiste Martinez," Emma said, "possibly with Gonzales added—his mother was a Gonzales." She shrugged. "He was half Apache. I don't know when he was born or when he died, but he probably was actively guiding and translating around the end of the 1700s into the 1800s?"

"Well, *that's* pretty specific!" The librarian, a sixty-something woman with steel-grey hair and an expansive bosom, looked impressed. "Family stories?"

"You could say that," Emma giggled. "This one would fill a couple of *books*, and I can't seem to find anything concrete. It's all hearsay."

Reliable hearsay, she did not add. Ghosts were perfectly believable and reliable sources for *her*, but who else would believe it without some sort of proof?

"I'm Emma, by the way," she added aloud. "My hubby, Jacob. And this is Roman."

The librarian scooted into a chair in front of a computer terminal and typed in a few commands. "Pleased to meet you. I'm Aurora," she said, glancing up quickly at Emma. "Just running a quick system search with key words to see if any news articles or other stories hit on the name you gave me." She laughed, a tinkling sound that instantly brought grins to all their faces. "We're bound to get a *lot* of matches—first name 'Juan' in New Mexico? —but hopefully we can narrow things down and find something real."

She wasn't kidding; the screen filled with references, and Aurora began to quickly scan the items that came up.

"Crazy Spanish Catholics," Aurora muttered, scanning names. She looked up and grinned. "No offense," she added. "I'm a crazy Catholic Spaniard myself! It's just that—" she indicated the screen and all the many, many references— "everyone is Jesus, Mary, Joseph and John the Baptist! Spanish versions, of course!"

Emma nodded. "I know!" she agreed. "I spent ages researching a Juan Gonzales from Corrales."

"Oh, dear Lord!" Aurora cried. "*That* must have been a treat."

"Yeah."

"Oh, my God!" Aurora gasped.

"What?"

"Unbelievable. I think...holy wow, we *found* something!" Aurora clicked a few things, and an old newspaper story appeared. She wriggled her chair over to make room for Emma to slide in on one herself and together they scanned the article dated August 20, 1828:

"New Mexico Daily Gazette

20 August 1828

*Luciana Maria Lopez, daughter of Don Miguel Lopez, owner of Lopez Cantina, has been located in the desert west of Albuquerque by her father, her brothers Alberto and Ramon Lopez and Constable Abel Francisco Diego of Santa Fe. Constable Diego had hired the **Indian scout Juan Baptiste** to aid in the search for the young lady abducted by Navajo warriors last week while she was visiting her sisters in Corrales.*
*Lopez's daughter has stated that she was unharmed; Navajo plans to ransom her for arms and food was thwarted by the rescue executed by the **scout Baptiste**.*
*This reporter was unable to secure an interview with **Baptiste**, and must confess that nothing more is known of him, save this statement by the rescued woman: "A more handsome man I have never seen!"*
Although he has been of much assistance to the people of this region, none seem to know who he is or where he came from. We can only hope that he will know somehow the appreciation felt by the Lopez family and the community at large for his assistance in this case."

Jacob read the report over Emma's shoulder, and gave her a gentle nudge. "Sounds about right," he whispered, and Emma nodded.

"What do you mean?" Aurora asked, turning to face Jacob.

"Elusive in life," Jacob said. "As he has been since death. I'm *amazed* to see this article. I may dance!"

"I may join you," Emma agreed. "He was *real!*"

Roman was grinning from ear to ear. "I hope you have as much luck tracking down some Sanchez family members for me," he told Aurora.

"How many do you want to find?" she asked, smiling broadly. "I'm a Sanchez family member myself!"

"What? No way! Penny!"

The tall blond looked up from her racy romance novel. "What?" she cried. "What did I miss?"

After spending a pretty good amount of time at the library, talking and researching with Aurora, the two couples had dinner together and enjoyed a very nice visit. They were all delighted at the information they'd been able to uncover in a relatively small-town library, and Roman was pretty sure he'd just met a distant cousin in Aurora, which was nothing short of a miracle. They had exchanged phone numbers and agreed to investigate their family trees to see if they had any intertwining branches.

It had been an exciting and productive day.

Roman and Penny were leaving in the morning, so they agreed to meet again for an early breakfast and see them off. Finally, Jacob and Emma returned to their hotel.

They placed a phone call to check on the twins, who were doing fine—naturally. Then Emma called her friends Sasha and Martin. Their home in Albuquerque was very near Corrales. They had invited Emma and Jacob to visit while they were in the area and everyone was looking forward to a good visit, some sight-seeing and lots of good food.

Jacob had only gotten to meet Emma's dearest friends in the short period right before their wedding. It had been a blur of visiting in between running to hair appointments and last-minute dress fittings, mixed in with visits with the parents and grandparents, siblings, cousins and local friends. Jacob had enjoyed meeting them, but remembered very little beyond that, so he was looking forward to having time to really get to know them; any people who had accepted his wife for who she was and stood by her through all the years were, in his opinion, well worth knowing.

Emma too was looking forward to sitting with her friends and talking to them; besides Jacob and her family, they were two of the very few people who has always believed without doubt the stories Emma had to tell. It was refreshing to have someone to listen to her and share their ideas with her.

Being the sort of family historian she was, Emma had a very difficult job. Her research methodology was quite different from anyone else doing a little family tree documentation; anyone else gathered their paperwork first and constructed stories based on the facts they were able to piece together.

Emma worked backwards; she knew the stories, and then had to try to get the paperwork to back them up.

No matter what anyone might think, it was harder to do it her way; many of the stories she knew to be true had nothing whatsoever to back them up. It was frustrating to know things had happened and not be able to prove it.

They went to bed and spoke at length of all the things they'd discovered during the day. They were feeling self-satisfied and also quite tired out; they fell asleep without crying over missing the babies!

Chapter Seventeen

Albuquerque

Emma made up for not crying all night by calling her mother at six a.m. Jill was not amused; the babies had not refrained from crying during the night just because their parents had, and it had been a rough night for them all.

She did not tell Emma that, however; her daughter was on an important quest, and making her feel guilty would be counter-productive. Besides, it wasn't anything she hadn't handled before.

Emma shared with Jill everything they'd learned so far, and Jill was so excited to see the newspaper article she could hardly wait. "Fax it to Daddy at work!" she suggested. "I know he'd love to see it himself."

"Okay," Emma agreed. "I know there's a fax machine in the hotel; I saw a sign in the lobby."

Jill got the number for her, and Emma faxed a copy to her father while she and Jacob were checking out of the hotel.

1.

They drove back to the town square and met Penny and Roman at the Plaza Café. "I'm all about that Santa Fe Smoked Salmon," Jacob informed them all as they entered the café. "It is muy delicioso."

Emma giggled. "It's about as kosher as you can get," she agreed. "I watched him eat it yesterday while I went full-on 'great-unwashed' with pork chili and cheese, and he made it look so good I'm going to have to try it today."

"You won't be sorry!" Jacob promised.

Once they were seated Roman and Penny perused the menu. Penny cried, "Oh, my diet! I'll bet I've gained ten pounds on this vacation."

"Nah," Roman objected. "We've walked everywhere! You're fine! Enjoy!"

"That's what he says *now*," Penny told them. "But wait til I need a leg up into that four-by-four! Then it'll be 'Ooph, Penny, what have you been eating?' I can hear it now!"

"Who, me?" Roman cried. "Never, my love!"

"Never mind, *my* love," Penny giggled. "I'm having this Chile Relleno Omelet. Pray the chili isn't too hot for me!"

"Hmm," Roman said. "I've seen you eat chili hotter than my parents could stand. I'm not worried. I'm gonna try the huevos rancheros."

"You won't be sorry," Emma assured him. "Delicious!"

"I'm so glad we met you guys," Penny said. "I hope we'll get to see you again sometime."

"Me, too," Emma agreed. "It's so much fun to meet people who enjoy the same things you do."

"We've got your address and phone number," Roman reminded them. "You won't be able to get rid of us!"

"Good," Jacob said.

"Be sure to let us know if it turns out that our sweet librarian is your cousin or something!"

"Isn't that something?" Penny cried. "It really is a small world."

They visited and enjoyed their breakfast, and agreed to keep in touch throughout the next year; hopefully their vacations would coincide in coming years and they would be able to meet again in person.

After breakfast, Jacob and Emma walked their new friends to their Dodge Ram 4X4, and to his credit, Roman did not remark about Penny's eating habits as he helped her climb into the passenger seat—but he did toss Jacob a wicked wink and grin as he walked around to the driver's side. Emma stifled a giggle and they all waved as the couple backed out of their parking space and drove away.

"Gosh, they were fun," Emma sighed as they pulled out of sight.

"Yeah, they were." Jacob agreed.

"I wish I could meet more people like that," Emma mused. "You know, people who don't know…"

"I know what you mean, babe," Jacob told her, pulling her into a big bear hug. "You live in a small town where everyone knows about your gift...I'm sure it's not easy." He patted her shoulder. "But you have some great friends who love and trust you, and none of us can ask for much more than that!"

Emma squeezed him back, smiling. "That's true," she agreed. "It's just nice sometimes to spend time with people who have no idea about my 'secret life'."

"You mean it's good to know that your 'secret life' isn't the only interesting thing about you."

Emma looked at him inquiringly. "Huh?"

"It's not, you know. You're a very interesting person even when your little friends aren't running you ragged."

"I am, huh?"

Jacob gave her a playful swat on the rump and swung her around, so they could walk back to their car. "You are. Penny was fascinated by all the research tricks you've learned, but she was even more interested in your photography. Roman was initially interested in libraries and genealogy charts, but he was more interested in your work at the television station. And they were both interested in the twins!"

"Well, who could possibly resist those two?"

"I'm just saying," Jacob grinned, "that your gift doesn't define you. It's just that you grew up there, and everyone who knows kind of...I don't know...*reminds* you...?"

"Or maybe it's just me," Emma postulated. "Maybe because of how kids treated me when I was young, I just automatically think it's how they always see me—staring at things only I can see, answering questions only I can hear." She shrugged. "They may not even give it a thought anymore. What do I know?"

"I don't believe anyone's forgotten," Jacob sighed. "But I do hope they've grown up enough to understand that there's a lot more to you than that. And if they haven't—well, balls to them, then."

"Balls?"

"Balls."

Emma stared at her husband for a moment, bemused, and then giggled. "C'mon, ya big lug," she said. "Let's hit the road and go see my friends."

Albuquerque is only an hour from Santa Fe when traveling on Interstate 25. It's desert all the way, but beautiful. Landscapes here were reminiscent of Wyoming; it made Emma a little homesick. About ten minutes into the drive she started humming, and then singing out loud: "Point me in the direction of Albuquerque, I—"

"Really, babe?" Jacob cried. "The Partridge Family?"

"It's the only Albuquerque song I know!" Emma protested. "Do you know one?"

"Uh…no. Nope. Not me." Jacob scratched his head. "Do you suppose there *is* any other Albuquerque song?"

"How about, 'By the time I get to Phoenix'," Emma said.

"Well, it has a verse, but it's not *about* Albuquerque," Jacob protested. "It just has the name in the lyrics."

"True. But the Partridge family song isn't about it, either, really. It's about a runaway who wants to go home."

"To Albuquerque."

"Maybe."

"Maybe?"

"Well, we don't really know she *lives* in Albuquerque. Just that she lives in that *direction*."

"I think I'll turn on the radio now," Jacob grumbled, and Emma giggled.

After a few minutes of radio fuzz, Emma said, "I'm so glad we didn't fly. We would have missed so much."

Jacob nodded. "I know," he agreed. "I like taking my time. I just hope the weather continues to hold!"

Soon road signs announced turn-offs to Sandia Pueblo. "Is that a reservation?" Jacob asked.

"I don't think so," Emma replied. "But it *is* their land."

"So that's where all the Pueblo natives live?"

"Oh, no, not all of them." Emma consulted her guide book. "It says here that there are nineteen different Pueblo tribes."

"Nineteen? Do they all have different homes around here?"

"Um…" Emma looked through the book and located a map. "It looks like they do," she confirmed. "Plus, there are three big reservations in the state. Navaho Nation is the biggest one, but it's pretty far from here, in the northwest corner. There are two Apache reservations, the Jicarilla in the north and the Mescalero in the south."

"Which Apache tribe was your umpty-twelvth cousin's?"

Emma giggled. "I have no idea," she admitted. "I wonder, really, if he would even know. I mean...well, I *guess* he would." She shook her head. "It had to be confusing, right? I mean, the lands they're living on now—that's not where they lived *then*. It can't be; they were nomads. They lived wherever their hunting and raiding took them. Where the tribes are now—that's where the government put them, Jake." Emma made a sour face.

"And the Pueblos?"

"I think the lands they're living on were always theirs," Emma said. "It says here that they've lived in these places for centuries, long before the Spaniards showed up. They found a way to co-exist with the newcomers. The Apache and Navaho tried to get rid of them—*and* the Pueblo. For all the good *that* ended up doing any of them."

"I read somewhere that the Pueblo fought the Spaniards off at one point."

Emma nodded. "They did," she agreed. "The many pueblos revolted against them because they had been enslaved and taxed and forced into Catholicism and they wanted to reclaim their lands and religion. There was a plan put in action by a Taos Puebloan named Pope and they drove everyone out for about a dozen years! Everyone ran off to Del Paso. Santa Fe was the capitol then, just like it is now. It's the oldest capitol in the United States, you know. That's where the biggest battle took place; it holds the record for the biggest successful Indian Revolt ever."

"Good for them."

"Yeah. Of course, it didn't last—but it did cause the Spaniards to re-think a few things. When they finally returned to the area, they weren't as aggressive in their religious conversions. That's why there's a mixture of native and Catholic elements in a lot of the area churches and religious practices."

"Hmm. People were able to learn a lesson and compromise? That's hopeful."

"It is."

"I'm not being sarcastic." Jacob was emphatic.

"I know." Emma shook her head. "But no one has really learned that lesson well enough."

"Not yet." Jacob smiled at her. "But I still have hope."

3.

They had arranged to meet Sasha and Martin in Old Town Albuquerque in the Plaza and take a look at the area. The town had been founded in 1706. On the north side of the plaza stood the San Felipe de Neri Church, the oldest building in the city, which was built in 1793; it was the cornerstone of the plaza.

"Oh my God, look at you!" Sasha cried, running across the road to fling her arms around Emma. "You look great! Your hair is so long! I have missed you so much!" She burst into tears.

Emma joined her, also exclaiming over hair styles, clothes, missing each other. They stood in the middle of the sidewalk in front of the church, hugging and sobbing.

Jacob and Martin eyed each other with amusement and shook hands. "Good to see you again, man," Martin said. "I swear, I thought you were never going to get here fast enough for *that* one—" He nodded at Sasha. "She would have had me out here waiting at five this morning. I had to thump her in the head, so she'd sleep another hour."

Jacob laughed. "*This* one sang all the way here: 'Point me'—"

"— 'in the direction of Albuquerque'!" Martin joined him and they both laughed.

"Man, there *has* to be a better Albuquerque song!"

"Hey!" Sasha said, coming to hug Jacob. "Don't be dissing the Partridge Family!"

"Yeah," Emma agreed, flinging her arms around Martin and enjoying a huge bear hug in return. "We drooled over David Cassidy back in the day."

"Ugh," Jacob groaned, and Martin made a face.

The church, centuries old, was quite beautiful, as well as historically significant. It was still in use—not just a sight-seeing destination, but a functioning place of worship.

"This is amazing!" Emma cried, staring up at the building. "Have you gone to mass here?"

"All the time," Martin said. "The holiday masses are quite the spectacle. It's too bad you didn't decide to come for Christmas."

"I can't imagine making that drive in December," Jacob remarked. "Some of those passes are really high; I'll bet the snow is outrageous."

"We don't get a lot," Martin said, "but when we *do* get snow, it does *not* mess around."

"We have a lot of celebrations to enjoy here, though," Sasha said. "La Posada. Luminarias. Midnight mass."

"Luminarias?"

"Everyone around here fills tons of paper bags—you know, lunch bag sized—with sand, and those little tea-light candles and line the sidewalks and roadways with them to light the way for the newborn king. It's so pretty, Emma!"

"Do you have pictures?" Emma asked.

"*Hello?* I'm Sasha—have you met me? Of *course,* I have pictures!" She laughed gaily.

"The queens of photography class," Martin remarked.

Sasha grinned and turned to Emma. "Remember how we used to try so hard to get pictures of your ghosts?" she asked.

"You *did*?" Jacob asked, surprised.

"I never told you that?" Emma said.

"No."

"Well, it never worked," Emma admitted. "Not so much as a shadow or a fog."

"Nope," Sasha agreed. "Whenever I see photos of so-called spirits, I just shake my head. I mean, we knew they were *right there.* Emma knew *exactly* where they were. And we got zip. Zilch. Nada."

Emma nodded. "One of them even posed, Jake. I swear, she was all for it! Sat there so pretty, smiled—the whole nine yards. We had a great time. It was like a slumber party—"

"It *was!*" Sasha agreed. "That's the only time any of Emma's visitors acknowledged me in any way!"

"One talked to *me* yesterday," Jacob offered casually.

"No way!" Martin cried. "You can—"

"No, no, nothing like that. But he actually directed some conversation my way; *included* me. It was awesome!"

"It was," Emma agreed.

"I *get* it!" Sasha cried. "Because, you know, I felt so special being included that night, when usually we just get to listen in."

"Anyway, when we developed the film," Emma added, "there was nothing there! Just my room: the wall, the bed, the dresser. We were bummed."

"Wow," Jacob said. "I never even thought to try it." He shook his head disbelievingly. "What's wrong with me?" He laughed.

Sasha sighed. "Well, if you *do* try and have some success, Jake, my hat's off to you. Because—wow! —we really wanted it to work."

"Nada," Emma said, shaking her head.

"That's why we get such chuckles over some of the things we run across," Martin said.

"What do you mean?" Emma asked.

"I've been working at the museum the past couple of years," Sasha said, "and Marty volunteers there from time to time. People bring in the oddest things."

"We've seen pictures of ghosts—seriously," Martin told them. "Some of them are obvious fakes—"

"*So* obvious!" Sasha added.

"And some of them are just plain weird."

"What do you mean?"

"Just—well, we'll show you some of them later. I can't explain," Martin said. "We know they aren't *real*, but…"

"We just don't know how…" Sasha and Martin exchanged a look.

"Color me intrigued," Jacob said, frowning.

"Me too," Emma agreed.

"We're going to show you," Martin promised. "Later."

"In the meantime, let's go inside and see this church," Sasha invited. "It's so interesting."

It really was. Outside they found a sign that declared it the oldest church in Albuquerque. It said it had been in continuous use since 1706, but Emma knew that the building now at that location had been built on the foundations of the original, which had been destroyed by torrential rainfall—a really strange thing to have happened in the desert of New Mexico!

Inside, the church was long and rather narrow, with a central aisle and pews on each side. The Stations of the Cross hung high up on the walls, and the alter area featured not the Savior on a cross, but a trio of men Emma assumed must be former Priests of the Parish. The building was an adobe structure with walls about five feet thick, and everything was breathtaking.

"Wow!" Jacob breathed. "The *history* this place has seen! Centuries, Emma, imagine it."

"I am imagining it. It's amazing," Emma agreed. "My ancestors could have been married right here; baptized their children; had funerals. Wow!"

Back outside, the two couples strolled around the Plaza, taking in the adobe architecture and enjoying the sunshine.

"This place just feels so...*old!*" Emma said. "I always thought Wyoming felt like the old west, but there are no 300-year-old buildings back home. I don't think so, anyway."

Sasha shrugged. "Beats the heck out of me," she admitted. "I'm a native New Mexican; I know nothing about Wyoming that I didn't find out in school while I was there. Which was basically nothing, by the way. Um, I'm sure someone must have told us when it became a state? Maybe?"

Martin said, "I should know that; I'm going to look it up ASAP, I swear. I know I used to know that! I was *born* in Rock Springs, and I couldn't tell you how old a single building is there or anywhere else in Sweetwater County!" He shrugged. "When you're a kid, you don't care much about things like that, I guess. I do know that a lot of Chinese coal miners were murdered there. White people said they stole all the jobs, or something."

"Weren't there some mine cave-ins that killed a lot of miners there, too?" Jacob asked. "I'm pretty sure one of my crew told me that was in Rock Springs."

"Beats me," Martin admitted reluctantly. "We moved out to the valley when I was in grade school, and then to Green River for Junior High. I don't remember much about Rock Springs." He grinned mischievously. "Except K Street."

"Martin!" Sasha cried, scandalized.

"K Street?" Jacob asked. "Where that Chinese restaurant your folks like is?"

"Uh...yeah," Emma said, evasively.

Martin guffawed uproariously, and Sasha slapped his arm.

"What?" Jacob demanded. Clearly, he had missed something potentially good.

"Well...back in the seventies..." Emma began.

Martin broke in, much to Emma's relief. "There was a boost in the economy back in the day," he told Jacob. "Lots of out-of-town workers, a bunch of construction in Green River and Rock Springs. Good money. It was short-lived, but it brought in a certain...*element*. K Street became Hooker Haven for a while."

"Hooker Haven? What—?" Dawning came suddenly, and Jacob snorted laughter. "Oh! Ha ha! Really?"

Emma made a face. "My mother didn't believe it," she said. "We ate over there all the time; after shopping, sometimes after church. She made my dad drive over there after dark one night, and sure enough—hookers! Wow, did we get out of there fast." Emma burst out laughing. "That is probably the only time my father ever could have gotten a speeding ticket, he's so law-abiding."

"Wow, my parents drove over there, too," Sasha said.

"So did mine," Martin added. "They went with some friends, because no one believed it."

"Someone ended up getting killed over all that, didn't they?" Sasha asked. She pulled the group into a small art gallery, and they wandered about admiring the art work as they talked.

"I don't remember all that," Emma admitted. "We were teenagers—Seniors, I think—and I was so busy trying to get through my own life, I didn't pay much attention. Then I moved to Denver for school, came home and got married and had the twins. Oh! This is beautiful!"

They stopped and admired a portrait of a Native woman done in oils; her shining blue-black hair was so realistically rendered that Emma wanted to stroke it.

"Amazing work," Jacob agreed.

"Anyway," Emma continued, "since then, I have paid more attention to the history here in New Mexico than I ever have to anything back home." She shook her head and added, "I think I'm a little ashamed of myself."

Sasha put an arm around her. "I don't remember much of that, either," she said. "And I don't have the excuse of hunting down family mysteries and fielding ghosts in study hall, either. With all you had going on, I'm amazed you made it through High School at all!"

Jacob grinned. "Well, I'm giving myself a pass," he said. "I'm the newcomer there; I'm instantly pardoned for my ignorance. So sayeth I."

"Get outta here!" Emma cried, and gave him a playful shove. "No, don't. Feed us, Jake. I'm hungry."

"We had a huge breakfast," Jacob grinned, "but I feel like it was days ago. Where's a good place to—?"

"Oh, no you don't!" Sasha argued. "I've got tamales and green chili all ready for us when we get to the house. It's all made with chicken, Jacob," she added. "I hope that's kosher?"

"How far is your house?" Jacob demanded. "I'm starved!"

4.

Their house wasn't far, and they soon had Jacob and Emma moved into the guest room.

It was Saturday, so Sasha and Martin were both enjoying their weekend off work. They had planned a little road trip for the four of them for Sunday morning, so for the rest of the day the plan was to hang out, visit and nosh.

"When do we get to meet the kids?" Emma asked as she and Sasha set the table.

257

"They're at Grandma's house," Sasha said. "She's going to bring them by for a while later this evening, so everyone can see you, and then they're spending the night with her, so we can get an early start in the morning."

"And what are we up to in the morning?"

"It's a surprise."

Smothered tamales are a treat, and Sasha was a pro at making them. By the time they'd finished their meal, Emma felt like she might explode.

"Oh, man!" she sighed. "Why, oh, why can't my tamales ever turn out this good? Sasha, that was the *best!*"

"I can't move," Jacob groaned happily. "But I'll do the dishes as soon as I can."

"The heck?" Sasha cried. "You will not!"

"The heck? Yes, I will!" Jacob promised. "That was amazing, and I know you guys have lots of catching up to do."

"I'll help him," Martin said. "But—" he added, grinning— "don't get used to it!"

Sasha giggled. "He helps in the kitchen all the time," she confided. "Just don't tell his buddies at the lab."

"Shhhh!" Martin darted his eyes about furtively. "Spies are everywhere, just waiting to rat me out!"

"Pictures," Emma demanded.

"Wait—" Martin began.

"We'll start with the ones of the Plaza, the luminarias," Sasha cut in. "Don't worry; we won't look at ghosts without you."

"Thank you!"

The women wandered into the living room, where Sasha pulled a few photo albums from a shelf. "These are from our first Christmas here," Sasha said, handing the first book to Emma. "I'd seen similar displays growing up in Carlsbad, but nothing like they do here."

Emma flipped through the pages of photos, night scenes of the plaza with paper-bag lanterns lined up along sidewalks and on fences and window ledges. They lit the way along paths and around courtyards, and led up to the church doors. It was quite beautiful.

"My gosh, that must take hours!" Emma exclaimed.

"It does," Sasha agreed. "We put out lights last Christmas, just the front walk and the path up to the door. Sheesh! I couldn't believe all the work that goes into it."

"It's sure pretty, though."

"Yeah. Michael was a great help, blowing out every other candle," Sasha laughed, talking about her youngest child. "His birthday is a week before Christmas, and he was sure it was time to make some more wishes."

Emma laughed. "That's hilarious," she giggled. "I can just see you, trying to get all that done and Mikey right behind you!"

"Yeah, go ahead and laugh," Sasha told her. "Your turn is coming!"

Emma sobered. "I'm enjoying this trip so much," she told her friend, "and at the same time I feel guilty that I'm not home taking care of my kids. Plus," she added, tearing up a little, "I just miss them so much!"

Sasha patted her shoulder. "I know," she said. "I think it's hardest leaving them when they're this little. When they get older and brattier, it's not so difficult to take Grandma up on offers to give you a break."

"Is that true?"

"No." Sasha giggled. "Mine have been gone for a few hours and I'm already anxious to see them. It's a good thing you've been so busy every day; it would be harder, I think, if you were just laying out on a beach somewhere."

"Who, me?" Emma grinned. "Yeah, Emma on a beach—that'd be a sight to see, alright. Tomato face."

Sasha, who had never had a sunburn in her life, shook her head sympathetically. "Yeah, bad example."

"I know what you mean, though," Emma said. "This has been a work trip, in a way. And I can't believe all the things we've learned!"

"Spill."

"I think—"

"Never mind; if we don't wait for Marty, he'll kick my patootie."

"It's a long story," Emma said. "Plus, I want to see these ghost pictures."

"You know, Em, there are some weird people around here," Sasha confided. "I mean, I don't think anyone believing in *ghosts* is weird, obviously, but cursed dolls and haunted vases? I don't know…I find that a little beyond, uh…believability?"

"Haunted vases?" Emma raised her eyebrows dramatically. "Is that a thing?"

"Yeah! This old lady brought a vase into the museum and wanted to donate it because it was haunted, and she didn't want it in her house anymore."

"Uh…"

"I know!" Sasha shook her head. "She really believes it, though. She said it's been causing trouble in her family, making them fight with each other and lose things."

"Did you take the donation?"

"My boss did. He's a little scared of it; he put it in a glass case and stuck it in the back room instead of displaying it. And it's beautiful, Em. It should be displayed."

Emma thought that over. "Are there a lot of things like that in the museum?"

"A few, I guess. There's a cursed doll, like I said. And, Emma?"

"Yeah?" Emma studied her friend, who suddenly didn't look amused. "What is it?"

"That doll creeps me out!"

"*All* dolls kind of creep *me* out," Emma admitted. "I never played with them when I was a kid. I had a couple; they are still sitting on a shelf in my old bedroom. Maybe Amalia will play with them someday."

"This one, though? She's…she's really creepy, Em. I put her in a cardboard box, and put the box in a glass case and locked it. I didn't even want to see her through the glass; that's why I put her in a box."

Emma frowned. "That's not like you, Sasha," she said. "What is it about her?"

"I don't *know*. It's a porcelain doll…big, brown eyes; hair in ringlets. She should be pretty. I guess she even *is*, but…it's like she's just watching… everything. I could not *wait* to get that thing out of my sight. I don't know if she's really *cursed*, but I do know that I never want to set eyes on her again." She shuddered dramatically. "I could hardly stand to touch her, and I must have washed my hand thirty times after I put her away."

"Well, brrr!" Emma cried.

"Yeah. For sure." Sasha shook her head. "I never had anything bug me like that before. You know, I've seen you talk to *ghosts*, and I was never scared."

"I don't think any of them have ever frightened me," Emma admitted. "Some of their *stories* have scared me, but not because they were ghosts; because scary things really happened to them."

"Exactly. I have just always considered them *people*— which they are—that I couldn't see, but whose stories I really wanted to know. But that doll? It *scares* me. I don't know why, but she does. And that bugs the crap out of me!"

"Are you talking about the doll?" Martin asked as he entered the room, closely followed by Jacob.

"Yes."

"What doll?" Jacob asked, and Sasha filled him in on the story. When she'd finished, he said, "One of my mother's family—an aunt, maybe? —said dolls could be infested with evil spirits. None of her daughters was ever allowed to have one."

"Ugh!" Emma said. "Maybe Amalia won't play with my old dolls after all."

"*You* don't really believe that, do you?" Jacob asked.

"I don't know! But I never have liked dolls, personally."

Jacob shrugged. "I don't know why this woman thought that," he said, "but my *mother* thought she was full of hot air."

"That's comforting," Sasha giggled. "But I wonder if she'd change her mind if she saw *this* doll."

"Don't even think about it, Sasha," Emma cried. "I am not going to go see that doll!"

"Oh, never!" Sasha said. "No, no, no."

Martin looked grim. "No," he agreed. "I hope no one *ever* unlocks that case."

Emma and Jacob exchanged glances. "Okay. What's the story with that doll?" Jacob asked.

"We don't *know*," Sasha breathed. "She just…showed up. We don't know who sent her…or left her. It really freaked us all out."

"Yeah," Emma drawled. "Lock her up and throw away the key."

"No problem."

Martin went to a desk in the corner and pulled a large envelope out of a drawer. "We brought these photos home from the museum," he said. "Kind of without permission," he added sheepishly. "But they haven't been catalogued yet, and we knew you were coming." He handed the envelope to Emma, who took it eagerly. "I wanted to know what you think."

Emma opened the envelope and extracted several photographs. Most were in black and white; the few in color were the first she decided to look at, and after perusing one she'd pass them to Jacob.

"Huh!" Jacob said, looking at a photo of a small child with what was supposed to be a spirit hovering behind her. It was clearly a double-exposure, and badly done at that. "Someone went to a lot of trouble to do a bad job, didn't they?"

Martin grinned. "Either that," he agreed, "or it was a complete accident; one of those times you forget to advance the film? Still, someone must have decided it was spooky-looking enough to try to pull the wool over our eyes, because it was mailed to the museum with a note that a ghost had been caught on film watching over this little girl."

Sasha added, "Look on the back."

Jacob flipped the photo over and read, "'Guardian angel'. Okay…"

"Change that caption to 'bad photographer'," Emma said, now looking at a 5 X 7 black and white photo. "But…this one, now…"

"Yeah, creepy, isn't it?" Sasha agreed. "I can't figure out how that could have been staged…"

The photo was of a small, dilapidated adobe house with a crooked fence behind it. The door was hanging half off its hinges, and the window was broken. Just to the left of the doorway, and in front of the window, there appeared to be a small, stooped woman, in profile, leaning on what might be a crooked cane. She was proportionally the correct size compared to house and fence, but was transparent and indistinct. The broken window could be quite clearly seen behind her bent head.

Emma stared at the photo. "If it's a double-exposure," she said quietly, "how come the house and fence are so...hmm."

"The woman would have had to have been photographed against a screen or something..." Martin added helpfully.

Jacob sat down next to Emma and studied the photo. "It looks...really *real*, doesn't it?"

"Yeah," Emma agreed. "But *how?* I mean, we really tried! And we got nothing!"

"Maybe it doesn't work when they *know* they're being photographed," Martin suggested. "I mean, she isn't looking at the photographer at all."

"What—if they pose, it won't turn out? That seems...I dunno, kind of silly!" Sasha said.

"Trying to take pictures of ghosts seems a little silly to me." Martin shrugged.

"People do it all the time," Sasha remarked, stung.

"Shut it," Emma ordered. "Marty, we were, like, fifteen? And it seemed like a good idea at the time."

"Who was it?" Jacob asked.

"A cousin," Emma replied. "You know, just visiting to visit. Not every ghost has a compelling mystery to solve or something to clarify. Some just pop in and say hello."

"She was someone close to our age who just wanted to check us out," Sasha added. "Until then, I never considered that they might get lonely..."

"Anyway, like we said, it didn't work. But it was fun."

"That wasn't the only time we tried, either," Sasha mused. "It was just the only time we...um, you know, *asked.*"

"We tried off and on all that year we took photography and journalism," Emma informed the men.

They had set up timers; they had cameras on tripods and cameras in closets; they'd set them up on the school stage, in their front yards, in classrooms. They'd aim them at Emma, wherever they might be, and hope a visitor might show up.

They'd gotten a lot of pictures of empty rooms, and even more of Emma, animatedly engaged in conversations with no one. Well, no one visible, at any rate.

"We quit when we didn't have access to the photo lab anymore," Emma giggled. "We'd already spent a ton on film; if we had to pay for processing too, we never would have had money for anything else!"

"Lucky for us," Sasha added, "Mr. Dunlap found a lot of our shots 'creative'."

"We did get a couple of spooky shots of the stage," Emma said, "but it was because of the lighting, not because any ghosts showed up. One of them is in the yearbook."

"I remember that one," Martin said. "It made me think that if there was anyplace haunted in town, it would be the High School."

"Apparently," Jacob said, "it's the new library."

"Really?" Both Martin and Sasha leaned forward in expectation.

"Built over the original cemetery," Emma said.

"Do tell!"

"Well, a lot of people have reported seeing and hearing strange things." Emma grinned, remembering her younger brother Freddie's story. "I guess when they put in the landscaping, they found a few bodies they'd missed when the library was built. They've been moved, but...who knows? Personally, I haven't seen anything."

Jacob added, "It does feel tres creepy in there, though. I sometimes feel...watched."

"Cool!"

Emma continued to stare at the photo in her hand. "*This* is cool," she said. "If it is a fake, it's a good one!"

"If it's real," Sasha said, "I sure would like to know how they got it."

"Me, too." Emma grinned. "I'm a little jealous, honestly."

Sasha nodded. "I know!"

Most of the other photos were either so obviously fake as to be laughable or at least easily debunked, but Emma found two more that she could not explain away. She waved them at

Sasha and demanded, "Where did these come from, anyway?"

"People bring things in all the time," Sasha said. "Sometimes just to show us, but more often to donate. Some things have been in storage or with other family members for years. Some were found at estate sales or shops. Those three don't have any information attached; I have no idea who sent or brought them in."

"Too bad," Emma said. "It would be interesting to know if anyone had any stories about them."

"We just wanted you to see them," Martin said. "They'll go back to the museum on Monday, and hopefully some of them will make it into a display of some kind."

"My curiosity is piqued," Emma admitted. "Mostly because I think they might be authentic. And it bugs me! Why couldn't *we* get any pictures?"

"Maybe we'll have another chance to try someday," Sasha suggested hopefully.

"Maybe." Emma felt a childish urge to kick a rock and watch it tumble down the street.

Oh well. Sasha's living room did not come furnished with rocks.

"Now tell us all about your trip so far," Martin said, settling into his recliner.

"Yes!" Sasha agreed. "What have you learned?"

Jacob leaned back on the sofa and put his arm around Emma, who settled herself comfortably against him. "It's a long story with no ending yet," she told them. Beginning with her first visit from Maria Manuela Baca de Gonzales, she told the story she knew so far, ending with the talk with Elena's son the day before in Santa Fe.

It took a good while.

"You could have left out the part where her old mama saw me nude," Jacob remarked dryly, setting off a fresh spate of laughter.

"God, no," Martin chuckled. "That was the best part!"

"Not for me," Jacob grinned. "For me the best part was the Plaza. I really liked being included in the conversation with Juan Baptiste."

"Made you feel special, didn't it?" Sasha asked.

"It sure did," Jacob admitted.

"I haven't been to Santa Fe in a while," Martin remarked. "We'll have to get over there before Christmas."

"Our moms love pottery," Sasha added. "We always find so much around the holidays."

"We probably spent more than we should have," Emma said. "But everything was so beautiful and special. And now I don't have to shop for Christmas!"

"You will anyway," Jacob said.

"You hush." Emma giggled. "No dolls for the girls, though. Not from me!"

"I think a little kitchen set for Maggie," Sasha agreed.

"What are you going to do next, Emma?" Martin asked. "I mean, it's very cool that you found a newspaper article that backs up part of what Juan Baptiste said, but is there anything more you're looking for?"

"I'd like to find some records on Manuelita," Emma said. "We're going to Corrales on Monday, before we head home. As far as we know, she pretty much lived and died there."

5.

The doorbell rang and then the front door burst open and Sasha and Martin's children ran giggling into the front room, followed by a harassed-looking older woman. "Whew!" she panted. "I'm getting old; they've run me ragged!"

"Mama, look, remember Emma?"

"Of course, I remember Emma!" Sasha's mother slipped out of her jacket and hung it on the coat tree by the door. "She practically lived at my house for five years! She very wisely praised my peanut butter cookies to the skies, knowing full well that as long as she kept the compliments coming, the cookie supply would never run out." As she spoke she made her way to Emma, who had stood in anticipation, and wrapped her in a warm embrace.

Emma kissed her cheeks and cried "Hi, Mom!"

"Hi yourself!" She turned to Jacob. "And this is your young man, is it?"

"Clara," Emma said, "meet my husband, Jacob."

"I'm very pleased to meet you," Jacob said.

"Hmph!" Clara said. "Well. Let's get a look at you!" She gave him a very thorough once-over. "You look pretty damned good!" She grinned. "I'm glad to meet you, too. It's about time someone snagged this wonderful girl. I hope you're taking good care of her!"

"Yes, ma'am," Jacob smiled.

"He is, Mom," Emma assured her.

"And you gave her twins, I hear?" Now Clara was positively beaming.

"Yes ma'am," Jacob agreed.

"Well? Where are the pictures?"

"Well?" Emma countered, "Where are those heavenly cookies?"

Clara giggled. "Oh, you saw that, eh? Mikey!" she called.

Jacob was digging in his wallet and Emma was groping through her purse when the children skipped into the room holding the Tupperware bowls they'd been trying—without much success—to hide when they'd come in. "Cookies!" Michael cried, holding his bowl out.

"We maked 'em!" Little Maggie beamed with pride. "We was Gamma's liddle he'pers."

"You certainly were," Clara agreed. She took the wallet and the small photo album Emma was holding out to her.

"We maked cookies for Nantie Em," Maggie cried happily, and offered a Tupperware bowl to Emma, who took it eagerly.

"And Unca Jake," Michael added, handing his bowl to Jacob.

Emma grinned. "The world's best peanut butter cookies," she declared.

"Better than your mom's?" Jacob asked.

"Just try one," Emma suggested.

Jacob opened the bowl, extracted a cookie, and bit into it. "Oh, man!" he sighed. "Heaven, melting in my mouth!"

"Told ya." Emma selected her own cookie, bit into it and sighed dramatically. "Mmmm. Mmmm, mmmm, mmmm!" She grinned happily. "Oh, man! Yeah, Jake, my mother's cookies are good, but they don't melt into your taste buds like these do. Fantastic!!"

Clara smiled contentedly. "Good," she said. "Take some home with you."

"Try and stop me," Jacob cried.

"We gots more at Gamma's," Maggie informed them.

"We *have* more," Sasha corrected.

"No, you don't. *We* do." Maggie glared at her mother. "You gots the ones we gibbed you right there."

Emma clapped a hand over her mouth to keep from giggling, and Sasha shook her head at her helplessly. "You just wait," she threatened, and Jacob burst out laughing.

"No doubt," Emma agreed. She took another bite of her cookie and groaned with pleasure.

Clara was going through the photos of the twins, smiling. "They are beautiful babies, Emma," she said. "You must be so proud!"

"Oh, yeah," Emma agreed.

"I'm surprised you didn't bring them with you," she remarked.

"Me, too," Emma said. "But it would have been a disaster, really. Our little Amalia bellows constantly the minute she's buckled into a car seat."

"And she can keep it up, non-stop, for hours," Jacob added. "Avram, on the other hand, couldn't care less. He can sleep right through her screaming."

"But *we* can't." Emma sighed. "It was so hard to leave them, though. I miss them so much." Right on cue, the waterworks started.

"Oh, I'm sorry!" Clara cried. "I'm just sad that I didn't get to see them; I didn't mean to make you feel bad!"

"It's okay," Emma assured her. "I just miss them; I have cried a lot this trip."

Jacob passed her his handkerchief and she wiped her eyes.

"So, tell me," Clara said. "Business or pleasure?"

"Both," Jacob said. "Even if the trip had started out as purely a vacation, Emma really never gets time off from her business."

"Business, ftt!" Emma groused. "You talk like it's a career choice. If I only had a dime—"

"You'd have a lot of dimes," Sasha cried.

"Well...a few, anyway," Emma said. "But no one's gonna pay me for this; and I would never expect it, at any rate."

"There are people in this world who would *try* to get paid for what you do, Emma," Clara said.

"I'm sure there *are* people who make a fortune doing similar things," Emma said. "But those people, if they truly have a gift, must be able to choose who to talk to and know what to ask for. I have never been the one to choose; I merely respond."

"And then you proceed to do wonderful things," Jacob said.

"But not for profit."

"Your family profits. I profit. You do, too."

"Well, that's true," Emma conceded. "I meant monetary profit."

"Oh, Emma," Clara said. "If I was able to ask questions about my family and actually have a chance of learning the truth about some of the mysteries they left behind, I would find that priceless."

"It *is* priceless," Emma agreed. "Although I have days when I feel pressured and a little put-upon, most of the time I am just so grateful for all the wonderful stories and for being able to research and discover physical evidence that I can pass on to my family. It's quite amazing, really. Exhausting and frustrating, but amazing." She shook her head. "What drives me crazy," she added, "is when I *can't* find physical evidence. It's not that I don't believe what I'm *told*," she added, "but having tangible evidence adds weight to the stories when I pass them on."

Jacob grinned. "This has been an ordeal," he confided. "Native Americans didn't keep birth and death records, and quite frankly, the Spanish didn't do so well with that, either."

"I'll say," Emma agreed.

Martin said, "I'm always amazed when we find records. So many people were uneducated, unable even to sign their own names. Real records before the census began are treasures."

Sasha chuckled. "Even the censuses are a pain in the neck. Birth dates that say, 'born *about* 1776' or names spelled crazily. It's a wonder anyone can make sense of most of them."

Clara laughed. "Sasha's father's people didn't come from this area. The last name has been mangled so much over the last eight hundred years! I don't know how anyone arrived at the final product."

"'Young'?" Sasha asked. "How do you mangle 'Young'?"

"Your ancestors originally spelled it I-U-N-G-E," Clara told her. "Although that's just one variation of the name. No matter the spelling, though," she added, "it always *meant* 'young' or 'younger'."

"Okay, well," Sasha said, "you're a New Mexican Martinez. I've seen 'Martin' in your family tree. What's up with that?"

Clara grinned. "Prepare to be stunned," she said.

"Why?"

"My people actually came from France," Clara declared.

"What? Get outta town!"

"It's true. The name was originally Martineau. Some great-great-great-great something or other grandfather moved to Liverpool way back when, and it got changed to Martin. Then some other great-great etcetera guy came to the New World and it stayed Martin until that guy or one of his kids ended up in Texas somewhere and married a Spanish-mix woman and it gradually got changed to Martinez. Their *kids* were Spanish, but until then, there was no Spanish in my family on my father's side."

"There are some Martinezes in my family," Emma said.

"Maybe we're cousins," Sasha cried.

"Could be," Emma agreed, grinning.

"I wouldn't be a bit surprised," Martin said. "Personally, I'm a little scared to explore my relatives; I might find out I'm related to everyone in the room!"

They all laughed, but they also looked a little uncomfortable. At last, Jacob said, "Well, I'm not worried. No one in *my* family has been west of the Mississippi until me."

"That you know of," Emma added.

"Um...yeah," he conceded. "That I know of."

Clara shook her head. "If you trace it back far enough, we're all related," she declared firmly. "Adam and Eve. And the pyramid begins." She giggled wickedly. "Good luck with that! And," she added, "we really must go. We're going to the movies."

"What are you—"

"Disney. What else?" Clara laughed. "Come on, kiddies!" she called. "Grammy's off to see a cartoon! Who's coming with me?"

"Me! Me!" the children chorused, racing to her side.

"Hugs and kisses?" Sasha asked, and the kids happily complied, hugging and kissing them all before skipping off to the cinema with their grandma.

"Adam and Eve, huh?" Martin said, watching out the window as his mother-in-law loaded his children into her car.

"Plausible," Jacob agreed.

"Hmmm."

Sasha and Emma exchanged looks and giggled.

Adam and Eve! What a concept!

Chapter Eighteen

Sandia Peak Tramway

"Oh, Mom, I can't begin to tell you how much I'm enjoying myself in the midst of my guilt!" Emma said. The morning phone call had become a very important part of her days. Also, the evening phone call. And of course, any chance for a phone call during the day.

"The babies are fine. We're all doing fine. You have important things to do, Emma, and you don't need to feel guilty."

"But babies need their mothers."

"Your confidence in my abilities is stunning, Em," Jill replied dryly.

"They don't even miss me, do they?" She ignored the confidence thing; if she hadn't had complete confidence in her mother, she wouldn't even be on this trip.

"Don't be silly; of course, they do!"

Emma brushed away her tears, and lamented, "I wish they could talk!"

Jill laughed. "Be careful what you wish for," she said. "I couldn't wait for you to talk, and now I can't shut you up!"

"Thanks a lot, Mama!" Emma giggled, and felt better. "I guess I'm just grateful that I've been so busy; it makes the time pass faster."

"Well, it sounds like you've discovered quite a lot so far. It's only a couple more days, and you'll be loving on these little ones."

"I know. I love you, Mom. Thank you!"

1.

Despite their efforts to get to sleep at a decent hour, Emma and Sasha had stayed up quite late, talking and laughing and just catching up on each other's lives.

Morning came too soon, as it often does. The two couples climbed into Martin's extended cab pickup, the women in the back seat. They headed northeast to Sandia Heights, and soon arrived at their destination.

Emma stared out the window.

"Oh, gosh, what is this place?" Emma exclaimed.

"Sandia Peak Tramway," Martin told her. "We're going up."

"Oh, hell no!" Emma cried.

"Oh, hell yeah!" Jacob enthused. "This is amazing!"

Emma quaked.

Sasha gave her a squeeze. "You'll be fine," she said. "It's great!"

"Yeah," Emma moaned. "Great."

Martin chuckled. "If Sasha—who is scared to climb a footstool, by the way—can do this, you'll be fine, Emma."

"I am not scared to climb a footstool!" Sasha cried indignantly.

"Yeah, whatever," Martin grinned.

Emma took a deep breath. "Okay," she said. "I guess I'm game."

As they climbed the steps to the entrance, Jacob asked, "How much is the ride?"

"My treat, man," Martin replied.

"Only if we treat for breakfast."

"Done!" Martin grinned. "There's a great restaurant at the top. We'll eat and sight-see a little."

"Isn't there a way to—like—*drive* up?" Emma suggested meekly.

Sasha laughed. "You're going to love it," she insisted. "I promise!"

Emma grimaced. "If you say so," she said.

They purchased their tickets, and the agent invited them to enjoy their flight. Emma wasn't so sure how she felt about that; she'd opted against a flight on this trip, after all.

They had lucked out and the place wasn't crowded. Very soon they had   boarded the tram, which rather resembled a box car, Emma thought. It was designed to hold about fifty passengers, but there were fewer people aboard this time.

The tram was wall-to-wall windows, and peeking out the front, she had to admit that the view was likely to be astounding.

Still, when the tram started to move, she clutched Jacob's arm and asked, "Are we sure this is safe? We have twins, you know!"

Martin grinned at her. "Our kids love it!" he told her. "If they had their way, we'd be on this ride every week."

Well, if little kids weren't scared, Emma thought, she should probably just get a grip on herself.

But—oh! —how she hated heights!

And away they went!

As the tram began its assent, Emma's grip on Jacob's arm loosened, and she soon found herself leaning on the rails in front of the window and gaping at the scenery. She watched as the parkway slowly dwindled in the distance.

"Dang!" she gasped. Sasha took her arm and led her to the front, so they could look ahead.

"The ride up takes about fifteen minutes," Martin said. "When we reach the top, we'll be—"

"Wait!" Emma interrupted. "If you're going to tell me how high we're going, please wait until we're back on the ground."

Everyone laughed, including several strangers around the little group, and Emma giggled grudgingly.

The view was spectacular; there was no denying the overwhelming feeling of looking out on vistas that remained unchanged since the time her ancestors roamed the land. Emma was preternaturally aware of every intake of breath and the heavy thud, thud, thud of her heart.

The first part of the trip was very much a desert view, with lots of rock and scrub. Of course, Emma was not spared the details of height; there was a guide aboard who happily announced their arrival at the first tower, which he said was at an elevation of about 7500 feet. The car swayed and bumped a bit as it approached and passed. Emma gasped as the passengers around her cried. "Whoooo-eee!"

They were flying over Cibola National forest. Emma gazed out and down in wonder. The terrain included sand and boulders, a scattering of trees and scrub. Far below she was able to see a large herd of some animal or another moving across the valley floor.

She looked back over her shoulder and could see Albuquerque in the far distance.

"Can you imagine all the work involved in building this?" Jacob murmured close to her ear. Emma nodded.

The guide informed them that the trip was a total of 2.7 miles, which they were traveling at about 13.7 miles per hour.

As they continued to climb, the terrain grew stonier, but there were also more trees. In the distance they could see a huge boulder balanced on top of some other boulders. The guide announced the name, but Emma missed it; a little girl had burst into wild giggles at about the same time as the announcement.

"What did he call that?" Emma asked Jacob.

"Cannon rock."

"Ah." That made sense; as they passed, it did indeed look like a cannon aimed at the distant mountains.

Soon enough the guide pointed out another rock formation, this one called Totem Pole Pinnacle, and Emma wished she had a pair of binoculars to get a closer look at that one. Erosion had apparently carved it into a rather totem-pole like structure.

Many of the larger boulders and most of the mountain rock faces were deeply cracked. The guide explained that the cracks would fill with water during rainstorms, attracting lightning strikes that could literally cause the rock to explode. Areas of obvious landslides were visible.

Emma looked out and up. The sky was brilliantly blue and nearly cloudless. They arrived, with some swinging and swaying, at tower two: 8750 feet. She was grateful for Jacob's comforting arm around her shoulder. Although she was now enjoying herself, she still felt shaky.

"Lots of places to hide down there," she remarked.

"That's what I was thinking."

"I can't imagine anyone actually living down there."

Sasha frowned. "Do you think they did?"

"I have no idea," Emma admitted. "But if Apaches were raiding in the area, it would make sense to hide out around here, wouldn't it?"

It was certainly something to ponder.

Emma could imagine the many dangers of traveling on the ground. Mountain lions and black bears; rock slides and lightning strikes; spiders and snakes.

They were over Big Canyon at this point and at 996 feet above the ground. It was, their guide informed them, about an eight second drop; just "for your information". Emma shuddered, thinking that it was information she could have done without.

They then flew over Echo Canyon, where the trees, they were informed, grew to be about 200 feet tall. There was a natural spring providing water to the area, and it was by far the greenest, lushest area they had seen.

As they flew ever closer to the mountain range, their guide pointed out the color of the rock faces. A potassium-feldspar crystal mineral gave the range a distinct pink hue, which at sunset would glow. It is believed by many that the Spaniards who settled the area had named the range "Sandia", meaning "watermelon" because of the resemblance from a distance to a slice of the gourd.

They arrived at the dock and disembarked from the tram car. Slowly they made their way around a redwood walkway, pausing often to stare at the view. From here they had a 360-degree view of about 11,000 square miles of New Mexican landscape. Albuquerque lay before them in a patchwork quilt of tiny roads and buildings. Mountain ranges, trees and brush surrounded them.

It was breathtaking.

They had just spent fifteen minutes flying from 6559 feet to 10,378 feet. Emma was feeling amazed and a little overwhelmed. Jacob had unpacked the video camera from his backpack and was filming the area and lamenting that he hadn't thought to film the trip up. "Everyone say hello," he instructed the little group. Emma, Sasha and Martin waved and smiled accommodatingly.

"You can film the trip down," Martin told him comfortingly. "You wouldn't have wanted to miss that first trip."

"You're right," Jacob agreed. "It was amazing."

"It was," Emma admitted. "Even if my knees *are* still wobbly!"

Sasha giggled. "I don't understand you," she said. "You'd climb every tree you could find when we were kids, and you like flying around in little dinky airplanes. What's the deal with the tram?"

Emma shrugged. "I don't know," she replied. "I guess—well, if a plane goes down and you have a decent pilot, there's a chance that a crash landing can end well. But if a cable breaks at ten thousand feet, it's straight down with no possibility of a good outcome."

Jacob, Sasha and Martin stared at her, slack-jawed. So did a few other people who had just disembarked the tram. "Uh...thanks for sharing, Em," Sasha said. "The return trip just got a lot more interesting."

"Didn't you *hear* the guide say it was an eight second trip straight down?" Emma demanded.

"Well, yeah," Jacob shrugged. "But I guess I just took it as a...er...joke?"

"Yeah. Funny."

Sasha shook her head. "Enough of this happy crappy," she said. "I'm starved. Feed me."

"I need coffee," Emma informed the group.

"Follow me to a very nice place to eat and drink," Martin invited, and they made their way to the restaurant.

"Okay, obviously there are other ways up here," Emma observed. "I can't imagine people trekking up the mountainside with the building materials for all this." She gestured at the buildings housing the restaurant, a welcome center and gift shop. Wooden walkways and observation decks were strategically built along the edge of the mountain.

"Oh, sure," Martin agreed. "But the tram is the best and fastest way to get up here."

Emma nodded.

The restaurant was indeed a very nice place, and they enjoyed a delicious breakfast. "I thought we'd do a little hiking, but not too far," Sasha suggested.

"Sounds great to me," Jacob said. "Em, did you bring your inhaler?"

"Yes, Mom," Emma giggled.

"So much for outgrowing it, huh?" Martin asked.

"Yeah, that was a bust," Emma muttered in disgust.

"The trails are reasonably easy," Sasha said. "And none of us are in a big hurry."

"Nope," Emma agreed. "I'd like to see the area. Imagine it, Sash! My ancestors could have been right here on this mountain. Yours, too."

Sasha grinned. "I'm still trying to wrap my head around being French," she said. "I never heard that before."

"I guess it can all be pretty mixed up," Emma agreed, giggling. "My dad calls us Heinz 57s."

Martin burst out laughing. "Oh, that's rich!"

"I'm a Jew." Jacob offered, and they all laughed.

"We'll probably find out that we all are," Emma giggled. "Adam and Eve?"

"Boy, that'd piss some people off, wouldn't it?" Martin asked.

Jacob sighed. "Unfortunately, that's probably true," he agreed.

"Some people suck," Sasha declared, and Emma nodded.

2.

It had been warmer in Albuquerque than it was on Sandia Peak, and the group pulled sweaters out of their backpacks and put them on. Emma loaded her camera with a fresh film pack and hung it around her neck. Jacob checked the VHS cartridge on his camera and decided it didn't need changing just yet.

They headed down a trail marked "La Luz". It wasn't particularly steep, at least starting out. "The Light," Jacob remarked, translating the trail's name. "Does it go all the way down?"

"All the way back to the tram station," Martin replied. "Do you want to try it?"

"That's pretty much a whole day's trip," Sasha added hastily.

"Jacob?" Emma asked nervously. It was all downhill from here—supposedly—but she didn't know if it was a good idea.

"We don't have water or food," Jacob answered reasonably. "Or proper shoes, either, I don't think."

"True!" Emma and Sasha chorused, clearly relieved.

Martin laughed heartily. "Surrounded by chickens," he chuckled.

"Maybe next time," Jacob grinned. "But we'll plan for it properly."

"Deal," Martin agreed.

They meandered down the trail for about half an hour, taking pictures and shooting video, chatting and laughing. Then they ran into something—God alone knows what—that started Emma sneezing.

"Oh, God," she moaned after about the twentieth sneeze. "Gotta get out of here!"

"Can you even see?" Sasha demanded, alarmed. "Your eyes!"

Emma could feel them swelling. Tears streamed down her face. Jacob grabbed one arm, Martin took the other, and they began rushing her back up the trail with Sasha hurrying behind them. They stopped several yards later and Emma took a pull on her asthma inhaler to ease the wheezing that had begun in her chest.

"I think we're doing that future hike by ourselves," Martin told Jacob, trying to lighten the situation a bit.

"Yeah, we'll send these two shopping," Jacob agreed.

"Deal," Emma gasped.

Her sneezing had slowed down, but the men dragged her on up the trail. She coughed a few times, hard; she was sure she might actually end up losing her lunch. Finally, her breathing began to ease into a more natural state. However, her heart rate was up due to the effects of the inhaler plus the mad dash uphill. "Okay, I have to slow it down," she begged.

They stopped and eased her down onto a large boulder. Sasha sat beside her and rubbed her back as she sat, head down, taking increasingly slower and deeper breaths. "Whew!" Emma cried. "So...*that* was fun."

"Yeah, a real laugh riot." Jacob frowned. "What *was* that?"

"I don't know," Emma admitted. "According to my mother, I'm allergic to everything."

"That was intense," Martin said, and Sasha nodded. "I haven't seen you that bad since Junior High."

"What triggered that?" Jacob asked.

"Some flowering bush behind the school building," Sasha replied. "At least, that's what we *think.*"

"Are you feeling better, honey?" Jacob asked.

"Yeah," Emma said. "My eyes feel all puffy, though. Do I look like a pug puppy?"

"No!" Sasha insisted, too quickly.

"Of course not," Martin added.

"Yay," Emma groused. "I guess I do."

"It's not that bad," Jacob told her comfortingly. "We'll get some ice. That'll take the swelling down."

"Swell," Emma said. Then she giggled. "Oh, I am so, so funny!"

"You need to stop that!" Sasha scolded, also giggling.

They made their way back up the trail to the top of the crest. Emma and Sasha went to sit on the deck overlooking the incredible vistas while Jacob and Martin went to find some ice. They found a picnic table and slid onto benches facing each other across the table. There was plenty of room for their husbands to join them, and several other tables were scattered about around them on the observation deck.

"Do you need to use your inhaler?" Sasha asked.

"Oh, no," Emma assured her. "If I use it too often, my heart gets all hyped up and I get jittery. That's no fun at all!"

"I wish they'd find something better to treat you," Sasha said. "The cure's almost as scary as the attack."

"Sometimes," Emma agreed. "But that one was pretty scary."

"Yeah, it was," Sasha sighed. "I wonder if the guys should go back down and try to figure out what triggered it. So we'll know."

"Oh Sash," Emma said, "Thank you! But did you see all the different plants? How would they even know?"

"Yeah, I guess," Sasha admitted. "It would turn out to be some tiny little flower we could barely even see!"

Emma grinned. "Probably." She took a deep breath, coughed, and slapped her chest. "Ugh!" She looked up, over Sasha's shoulder, and jumped, startled. "Oh!"

"What?" Sasha turned quickly, then turned back to Emma. "Who is it?" she asked, nodding knowingly.

"Someone new," Emma acknowledged. She greeted the newcomer: "Hello."

"Hello," the woman replied, and smiled warmly. "I've learned that you have been looking for me. I am Maria Elena Gonzales."

"Good," Emma said, now speaking in Spanish. "Will you sit with us?"

"I will." She sat next to Sasha, which was a bit frustrating to the woman who could not see her seatmate. But it put her across from Emma, so they could speak face to face.

"May I share your story as we go along?" Emma asked.

The woman smiled again. "Of course!" she replied. "Why not?" She leaned toward Emma and confided, "This is all rather amazing to me!"

"To me, as well," Emma admitted.

Jacob and Martin returned at just that moment, and Sasha informed them of the presence of their visitor.

Jacob had made a makeshift icepack with his handkerchief, and handed it to Emma for her eyes. She took off her glasses and covered one eye, then peered nearsightedly at her many-times removed aunt. "We are looking forward to hearing this," she said.

"I am looking forward to this myself," the woman told her, and began her story.

Chapter Nineteen

Elena

"So, you have spoken with my son," she said. She was a small woman, and very much resembled her mother, Manuelita Gonzales.

"Juan Baptiste Martinez Gonzales?" Emma clarified, although she had little doubt.

"The very same. Such a *scoundrel*, my son!" She smiled, and her warm brown eyes sparkled. Scoundrel he may have been, but she clearly adored him. "I am Elena. Maria Elena Gonzales, daughter of Juan Gonzales and Maria Manuela Baca. But you already know that." Elena cocked an eyebrow at her mischievously.

Emma nodded.

"He can carry a tale, that one," Elena acknowledged, "but there are many things he doesn't know. And so," she cried, flinging her hands out expressively, "here I am at last, ready to tell my story."

She sighed then, and gave a small shrug. "You may think badly of me, Emma," Elena began.

"No, I—"

"It's fine; I was never a picture of perfection; I am quite used to having people think me inappropriate."

"I assure you," Emma interjected defensively, "that I have made no judgements of you one way or the other. I would just very much like to hear your story!" Emma passed on what had been said so far, and everyone nodded enthusiastically.

"And so, you shall." Elena bowed her head majestically, and then looked up and grinned. "I do not know when I was born, Emma, or when I moved on. The dates, the years—they meant very little to me then and nothing at all to me now. I can only tell you that I *lived*—and I lived well and happily.

"I was young the day the Apache warriors came to the hacienda and broke into the cosina where we were preparing the evening meal. I had perhaps fifteen years; I had passed the time of childhood, certainly, and attained womanly status, but my father had not yet chosen a suitor for me."

Emma and Sasha looked appalled at the thought of having suitors "chosen" for them, but they both knew it was a fact of life for women in those times.

"My sister was older; she was in love with a man whom my father despised, and she intended to marry him with or without permission; it was the one and only thing I ever remember her taking a stand on in her life!" Elena grinned as Emma shared this information. "Maria Juliana Gonzales was not a strong woman. Julia, as I called her, would be led around by her nose her entire life, if left to her own devises. Except when it came to her love for Juan Santillanes. For that alone, she would fight!"

Everyone nodded their understanding. Juan Baptiste had made clear in his own storytelling that Juliana had truly loved this man.

Periodically throughout the tale Elena told, Emma passed the information on to her companions, and Elena graciously waited while those listeners were filled in.

Elena continued: "Anyway, the Apache came, and they killed my father. Of course, that was a most terrible thing, to see our dear Papa bloody and lifeless. Yes, Julia fought bitterly with him over her love; still she loved Papa more than life itself, and she was distraught. She screamed and flung herself to the floor beside him.

"There were small children in the cosina with us, nieces and nephews, you know. The grandchildren of my parents.

"My mother grabbed up the tiny baby—that was a great-grandchild, actually! Mama hid her under her skirts to keep her safe, and used her own little body to shelter the smaller children. I tried to pull Julia away from our father, so we could run. Instead, Julia and I were taken forcefully by warriors from the house! Although we screamed and kicked and fought, the warriors were much bigger and stronger than we were; they easily overpowered us. They threw us belly down over the back of a horse and tied our hands to our feet under the horse's belly, and we rode away!

"Oh, the misery, Emma! A horse's back is not a soft place, and tied as we were, we took quite a pounding. We screamed for a short time, and then we cried. Julie became sick and vomited violently, which made the horse spook and buck. I was quite certain that our ribs would break, and we would die.

"The warriors were angry, but they would not untie us. They slowed the pace a bit, but that was all. We could hear children crying, and spoke of that and our hope that they had not tied little ones the way they had done to us.

"At daylight, we stopped in an Apache village, and Julia and I were cut loose. An Indian woman came out of a tepee to see us, and became very angry with the men we were with. We could not understand her words, but it was clear that she was displeased with the treatment of the captives. Soon all the women who were tied belly down on the backs of horses as we had been were released from their bonds. The warriors took them onto the horses in front of them, now seated, and rode away.

"The children had already been carried in such a manner; they had not been punishingly treated as we had been, thank goodness! I don't know how many children or women were taken that day. I do know that a small boy was left there with us before the Apaches rode off into the sunrise. I did not recognize the child, so I cannot say which family he may have come from.

"We never again saw the men who stole us away from our home, nor the man who killed our father. They rode away to their own homes, and did not return to see us again.

"The Indian woman surprised us by speaking to us in Spanish. She told us her name was Estrella de la Manana— Morning Star. She told us that it was not the name given her at birth, but the name given to her by her husband, a warrior who had crossed big waters and traveled great distances before finding a home with The People.

"Julia asked her how we were to get home, and Morning Star laughed and told her she was home already. There were many warriors seeking wives, she said. The interlopers had stolen many people from them, and killed many others, and there were now few women amongst them.

"Women, she told us, were very important members of the tribe. Who, she asked us, could be expected to raise families and own property and make important decisions, if not the women? Men, after all, only wanted to hunt and fight!

"I found her quite amusing—and *interesting*—but Juliana was terrified. She wanted to go home.

"I asked Morning Star about the little boy she'd chosen from among the children. She told me that the interlopers had stolen her own little boy; she was returning the favor.

"Well! There was nothing I could say to that. Was there?"

"No," Emma agreed, and the others shook their heads.

"We were cargo, I suppose," Elena continued. "Bought and paid for by Morning Star. She wanted wives for her son and his friend, and she wanted a child to replace the one who had been taken from her.

"She was not unkind to us in any way. Not ever. We had been taken from our home by force, but not one of the warriors had beaten us or harmed us; other than the rough ride on the horse, of course. *That* was miserable, but hardly life threatening.

"Julia cried and cried, and refused to accept that she would marry anyone but Juan Santillanes. She said we would be sinners if we did not marry in the church. If a Friar did not perform the ritual ceremonies, we would burn in hell!

"She *believed* this, Emma. To her dying day, she believed this. Yet, here I am—not in hell, but *here*, wherever this may be." Elena shook her head, and looked mildly confused. "This is not to say that she was wrong—perhaps one day I *will* be in hell," she conceded. "Who knows? All I really know is that I am not there now! How do I know this? Well, I am not suffering; I am not afire; I am content."

Elena looked at them all expectantly as Emma relayed this information. No one was inclined to discuss or debate the issue of hell, so she continued with the story.

"After several days, men returned to the camp. They were not the men who had brought us—their dress was not similar; yet they too were Apache. I later learned there were many different tribes, with different customs and manner of dress, with different enemies and friends. Many were friendly to each other; many were friendly with the Pueblos and the Spaniards; but many more would as soon cut all our throats!" Elena's eyes were wide when she said this, and Emma gulped, picturing the fierce tribes who would go to war with all others around them rather than give ground and go along.

"The first man I saw up close was older," Elena continued, "and fair of skin with light brown hair and very green eyes. He spoke perfect Spanish, and we soon learned why: he was from Spain! Old Spain, where there ruled an actual King and Queen. He had traveled from there on a ship, then crossed all the land from the south—New Spain, he called it—on horses.

"When they came to this area, he met The People and stayed with them, learning the language and the ways of survival in this land. He met Morning Star and married her, and never returned to his companions, forsaking them and all his old ways for her.

"He told me that he had come to believe that his companions were wrong to invade and conquer the People and their lands; he was right about that, of course. The People had always been here. The conquistadores came and stole everything, demanding payment from the People for the right to continue to live where they and their fathers before them had been born. The came with their Friars and their precious *book* of rules that taught that every pleasure they enjoyed was a sin and would condemn them to eternal fires!"

Elena laughed hard for at least a minute, and Emma stared at her, aghast, as she quickly translated. She would be revisiting her Bible soon, she thought, a little frightened. She and Sasha exchanged uneasy looks; Jacob looked thoughtful, but Martin grinned. He had days when God the "concept" left him dubious. Sasha gave him a nudge, but he couldn't manage to wipe the grin off his face completely, and she shook her head at him with a disapproving scowl.

"Oh, Emma, I am sorry!" Elena gasped. "I am almost certainly going to end up in hell. But I grew up believing those very things myself—or at least *thinking* I believed them. And isn't it silly? Think of it! What loving God would condemn me to hell fire for loving a man and marrying him and living with him

286

in his home simply because I did not go into a certain building and take a vow in front a certain kind of *man*? Is it logical?

"Perhaps it was because I was younger; perhaps it was because I was always more inclined to get into trouble; I don't know why, but it didn't take much to persuade me that the ways of The People were better.

"Of course, it didn't hurt that the *next* man I met was the son of Morning Star and the Spaniard, Juan Jesus Martinez. His given name was Miguel Nantan Lupan Martinez. Grey Wolf. He never used the Spanish part of his given name: Miguel. And he never used the surname Martinez. *Never*. He was always and forever only Grey Wolf.

"He loved and respected his father. He had his father's face, but his was a darker skin, and his eyes were black as night! The first time we looked upon each other, those eyes sparkled like stars in a night sky. And then he smiled—his teeth were perfectly straight and so white! I had never seen anything like that smile before in my life.

"I promised myself then and there that if he was looking for a wife, I would do everything in my power to be the woman he chose to marry. I would have stood on my head or licked his feet just to see that smile!"

"Wow!"

"Emma, he was beautiful! Men *can* be beautiful, you know."

"I know." Emma looked fondly at Jacob, and Sasha grinned at Martin. They both looked pleased but bashful. Whether or not anyone else thought them beautiful, it was good to know that their wives did!

"My son looks just like him, except for the curls and the green eyes. The curls he got from me; the eyes he got from his grandfather. But that smile—oh, that smile is from his father, Emma, and it was a smile to make a woman burn with desire!"

Emma, who had seen that smile earlier in the week, could not argue.

"I was very lucky," Elena added. "Grey Wolf never seemed to know how handsome he was; he had eyes only for me! We fell in love quickly, and never fell out of love. That is a blessing too few know.

"My son, though—he was indeed a scoundrel! He married a sweet Apache girl and gave her many children, but he *knew* his beauty and used it. I am sure he has many a descendent from his assignations, the scamp."

Emma shook her head; Elena didn't sound particularly ashamed of her "scoundrel" son. It was almost...pride! "Er...congratulations, grandma?" she said.

Elena gaped, and then giggled. "Oh, stop it," she said, flapping a hand at Emma. "One cannot control a man who chooses not to be controlled. He took good care of his wife and children; he worked very hard. They wanted for nothing. And," she added defensively, "not one of the women he enticed with his smile resisted in any way! Of that I am sure."

Emma giggled herself; she couldn't help it. "I'm sure of it, too," she admitted. "I'm not blind!"

Jacob glared at her and shook his head. "And there I was," he said, "feeling so cute, just a second ago!"

"Well, there you go." Elena nodded decisively.

"Okay, Tia, tell me more," Emma demanded, giving Jacob a playful nudge and swollen-eyed wink.

"We married, Grey Wolf and me. We had many children. Six boys. One girl. Her name was Dahlia Light Wolf. Her eyes were amber. She was a great warrior.

"And so was I!"

"Juan Baptiste told us so," Emma said.

"Oh, the women of The People, Emma! If only Julia could have embraced the life she was offered, how strong she would have become! But no!

"Julia was weak. Weak!

"She married Running Deer; she *liked* him. He was good to her, very gentle. She told me once she did love him— *'but'!* She told me she was 'happy enough' with him— *'but'!*

"It's the 'buts' in life, Emma. 'I love him, *but* I love someone else more. I'm happy enough, *but* I could be happier'.

"She couldn't forget Juan Santillanes. She cried for him. Running Deer tried very hard to make her happy; poor man! And I will give her *some* credit—she tried to keep her unhappiness from him. She worked hard, made things easy

288

for him in their home, cooking and cleaning, sewing his clothing. She smiled at him.

"But she did not *really* love him, and he *did* love her; it hurt him to know she pined for another man. Well," Elena shrugged. "It would hurt anyone!"

Elena was quiet for a moment even after Emma quietly shared the story.

Finally, she said, "I've had much time to ponder these things, Emma, and in the end, I know my sister did what she *had* to do. It is one thing to love a little, but quite another to love a man completely, totally. To love with every breath you draw, with every beat of your heart. Yes, one can be happy *enough*, but when you have the chance to be *completely* happy? Well! I believe we should all hope for—and strive toward—complete happiness. Don't you?"

Emma nodded. "Yes," she agreed. "I certainly do."

"They were married; they lived the life of a married couple, and so in time she became pregnant. When she went into labor with their child, she was certain God would punish her for marrying outside the church. The child would be deformed. The child would die. *She* would die and go straight to the hell fires! She was terrified.

"She fought her labor with every breath, and we all became frightened that all her dire predictions would come true just because she believed it so firmly.

"We'd been on a raiding party, and I was the only other woman in camp. I had given birth to one child, but I knew nothing of childbirth beyond that experience. I was no help at all; I was frightened for my sister's life! Finally Running Deer put her on his horse and rode off with her to Bernalillo; we were camped in an arroyo nearby, away from prying eyes; but close enough to steal a sheep or two, you know.

"Running Deer knew people; he often traded with the settlers in Bernalillo—he had family there. It was common in those times for the Spaniards to take an Indian bride. They told him where to find a midwife, and he left Julia there and came back to camp, so we could pack up and move further west. It would be just like the Spaniards to come looking for us once a Spanish woman had been delivered to them for medical attention!

"The next day Running Deer went back to the midwife's house, but Julia was gone! She had begged a ride from a traveler, the midwife told him, and had left mere hours after giving birth.

"Running Deer was bereft; *I* was *furious*! But he chose not to track her down; he knew she was unhappy. Her unhappiness made him unhappy. He told me he wished her the best, and went off with a hunting party. He was gone for days, and the entire time he was gone, I fumed with anger at my sister for being such a coward, and for hurting such a fine man.

"Grey Wolf told me I must let go of the anger and try to understand that my sister was a victim of her upbringing. I could not argue with that—had I been of a similar nature, that upbringing would have led me astray as well.

"But Emma—I was *strong*. I was happy with The People. I loved my husband and I loved my life with him. I loved the freedom I enjoyed with the Apache, who trusted their women with property and decision making. I loved to hunt, and I was good at it. No one tried to keep me from doing what I wanted to do, not ever.

"I believe it was at that time when I realized I could never go home; not if I wanted to continue to live in freedom. If I showed my face in Corrales, my brothers and uncles would try to force me to stay there; I could never live with that.

"Even so, I started searching for my sister."

Emma sat up straighter. After filling the others in on the story so far, she asked, "How did you know where to start?"

Elena giggled. "Unlike my mother, I was *very* aware of my sister's love life," she said. "I suppose we were very much like girls everywhere, giggling together over boys, talking about the first kisses and the first attempts at seduction. Our sisters and brothers were quite a bit older than we were; by the time we became interested in finding husbands, they were long married and had children. We were the youngest, and truly the children of our parents' old age. We did everything together and told each other our deepest secrets.

"Juliana met Juan Santillanes in the marketplace; he was a businessman, an *older* man, already in his thirties. He was very handsome, but he kept to himself; he was not a womanizer; he had been married and had lost his wife when she gave him his son, and for the most part he busied himself with his business and with raising his child.

"When they met, Julie was captivated at once; he ignored her, which only added to her infatuation with him. She offered to watch his son while he conducted business in Corrales, and he accepted the offer. Oh, how she loved that little boy! And Miguelito loved her, too. It was *that* love that caught Juan Santillanes's attention, and he began noticing my sister as a woman for himself and as a mother for his child.

"Our father objected strenuously; he felt that Juan Santillanes was too old. In my opinion, this only added fuel to the fire of my sister's desire. Soon enough, my parents had reconciled to the inevitable: she would marry him, come what may, and they were unwilling to lose the affections of their daughter over it. After all, it was not as though he was a man with no means to support her.

"Santillanes had businesses in Corrales, Bernalillo, Santa Ana and Santa Fe. He had regularly scheduled times to be in each place to oversee transactions and such, and to pay his employees. Julia was well aware of his dealings; she knew where to find him once she was free to seek him out, and a promise of payment from him for transporting her to Santa Ana was all it took to obtain a ride.

"Once we knew that she had fled with her baby, it was no problem figuring out where she would go. I had only to discover the date in order to know where he would be; I knew his schedule as well as Julia did. For all the time leading up to our capture and all the time following, she never ceased talking about him and longing for him."

Elena shook her head. "It was not difficult for me to find my sister, Emma. It took me several months to do it, but only because I needed to deal with my own anger and disappointment in her.

"Grey Wolf was by turns frustrated or amused with me. I was lonely for her and would cry; he would offer to take me to the settlements to see her. I was angry and would rant; he would shake his head and speak of forgiveness and understanding. I would complain; he would laugh and remind me that all I needed to do was take that first step.

Elena paused, thoughtful. "You know," she said, "we were raised in a religion that taught us to love one another and forgive one another, and that all things were possible if we believed. Yet *within* that religion we saw people banished from the church and sometimes from the settlements for committing a sin. We saw people thrown into jail; we saw them beaten or hanged.

"I do not recall ever *seeing* forgiveness; only judgement.

"But my husband, Emma—*there* was a man who knew the power of love, and the healing of forgiveness; healing not just for the forgiven, but for the one who forgives as well. He knew in his *heart* what we were told but *never* taught by example.

"And my mother would have called him a *savage!*"

There was silence for a time. After sharing with the others, Emma watched her many-times great aunt as she regained her self-control; this memory of her mother's disdain for the Natives clearly made her angry.

At last Elena sighed. "You must understand why I loved him so," she said. "And you must understand why I could never explain that love to my mother. To her he would never be a man; he would forever represent for her the abductor; the thief who stole her child. He was not there on that day, but that would not matter.

"And how can I blame *her?*" Elena shook her head, conflicted. "My own mother-in-law arranged the raid to collect wives for the men, didn't she? And my father was killed…

"There are so many sides to this story!"

Emma could do nothing but agree that it was a conundrum. She wished it was possible to give Elena a hug or squeeze her hand. Instead, all she could do was nod her understanding and wait for the story to continue.

"I love my husband, even now, and that was the thing that drove my decisions. My mother couldn't have understood." Elena sighed sadly.

"Years later she would ask my *own son* to track down the savages who stole me; she would never have accepted Grey Wolf as a son-in-law. You see that, don't you?"

Elena stared at Emma imploringly. It was important to her that they all understand her choice to stay away.

Emma shrugged. "I believe that *may* have been her state of mind throughout her lifetime," she said. "But perhaps not. She once told me she prayed that you and your sister had been taken as wives; then you would be safe, at least. And I don't know if any of those things would still matter to her today. So many things have changed; so many things have happened. And I have no way of knowing—unless she comes to me and tells me—if she has seen or heard any of the visitors I've had during this trip. But Elena, I pray that she has."

Elena stared at Emma, frowning. "If it could be so, I would pray for that, too," she agreed.

"I believe that forgiveness can be given or received at any time," Emma continued. "I believe that knowledge and understanding can lead to healing."

Elena nodded thoughtfully. "I agree."

"Surely you can understand the pain of her loss, and her fears."

"I am a mother, too!" Elena cried, defensively. "I *do* understand."

"Good. Now, I would love for you to go on and tell me about finding your sister."

Elena smiled, mollified. "Naturally, it was Grey Wolf who initiated things," she admitted. "I would have wrestled with my indecisiveness forever!

"When we first came to the People we had only the clothes on our backs," she continued. "Morning Star quickly remedied the situation, making us clothing that was well-fitting and comfortable and more suited to our lives in the desert.

"Until Grey Wolf came to me with our dresses one morning, I had no idea that Morning Star had kept them. It was good fortune that she had kept *both*; much time had passed, and I had grown; by this time, I had two children. My own dress was now too small for me!

"We went out with a raiding party and detoured near Santa Ana. I donned Juliana's dress and took an ass loaded with trade goods and walked into town. There I traded with the locals, showing many of the women little infant items hand-made by women of my tribe, and asking if there were any new mothers in the area who might be interested in trading for them."

Elena leaned in closer to Emma and lowered her voice conspiratorially. "Understand that it was very common for the Spaniards, Mestizos, Pueblo and other tribes to trade and trade again, and that none among the townspeople would have just assumed that I was a member of the Apache tribes. They would only assume that I was an Espanola or Mestizo who had been brave enough to *trade* with them.

"Within hours I had obtained several goods for my people and had met a few women with infants. By late that afternoon, I had also found Juliana.

"You see, I had never been to Santa Ana before that day. I knew of Juan Santillanes's dealings there, but I didn't know where he lived when he was there; his real home was in Santa Fe. I really did have to trade in goods and gossip to find my sister; but who doesn't love to talk, Emma? If you ask the right questions, you will learn much.

"I followed the trail given to me by my dealings with various people, and soon enough I arrived at their home. I assumed Julia would be surprised to see me. Instead; she asked what had taken me so long!" Elena laughed heartily, remembering. "I should have known!

"That day I learned that I had a niece; she was beautiful! Her name was Alicia. She had amber eyes, Emma, as my own daughter would have. The People called her 'Golden Eyes', and soon enough, Julia started calling her Goldie.

Elena shook her head. "Do you know, it was the cause of a very stupid rumor later."

"What do you mean?" Emma asked. Jacob was already nodding, though. He had a feeling he knew where this was headed.

"Languages can be very strange," Elena replied. "Translating can be really confusing. Julia called her daughter

294

Ojitos de Oro—little eyes of gold. A salesman who came from back east—a white man who spoke English, a man who traded with her husband—told her that in English 'oro' is 'gold'. From there her nickname went from 'Eyes of Gold" to 'Goldie' because there were many traders coming from the East. The children of the wealthy were sent to schools in the East, and English was becoming more commonly used all over the lands. Besides, it was a pretty name. Don't you think so?"

Emma nodded, also now understanding what this was leading to.

"Apparently the name 'Golda' is a Jewish name," Elena continued. "'Goldie' was close enough to 'Golda', at least in the eyes of certain trouble-makers who bowed to the Spanish crown, and Goldie was accused of being a Jewess and thrown in jail! She was by that time a married woman, having met and married an Englishman from the colonies. He was a man of some means, and secured lawyers, so of course it was proven that she was not a Jew. But the damage was done; she and her husband left the area after that and ended up returning to the Eastern settlements. It broke Julia's heart!"

Emma gasped. To think she and Jacob had been discussing the Crypto-Jews with their new friends earlier that week, and now she was learning that Jews had been *jailed* here in those times! She and Jacob exchanged a meaningful look.

"Was there any chance—?" Emma asked.

"*No!*" Elena cried, scandalized. "Of *course* not! The Jews—they came to this area from the north and the east. Our people all came here from Spain, and from the south through Old Spain, Emmaline. You should *know* this."

"That doesn't exactly prove anything," Emma argued. She was more than a little appalled that Elena could be so adamant. The woman's extreme prejudice was blatantly apparent.

"Don't be foolish, child!" Elena chided. "There were no Spanish *Jews*! According to my father, they had all been cast out of Spain by the queen many, many years before any of his people came to this land."

"Yeah," Emma agreed, nodding knowingly. "And where do you suppose they all *went?*"

"I—well, I am sure I do not know," Elena sputtered, frustrated with the interrogation. "But we were Catholic. *Catholic.*"

"Where *did* they all go?" Sasha whispered.

"We'll figure that out later," Emma promised. Jacob nodded, and Martin pursed his lips thoughtfully.

Emma shook her head. She felt a perverse desire to argue with her aunt over the possibilities and logistics, but she knew it was useless; Elena would never accept such a wild idea. She held to her beliefs as strongly as her mother held to her own, certainly. She'd feared her mother's reaction to her life's choices due to her beliefs so strongly that she'd never gone home. These were not particularly open-minded individuals she was dealing with, and so she held her tongue.

However, she did exchange a couple more meaningful looks with her husband. It was so interesting to think of the possibilities!

"I understand that it is not a consideration in *these* days," Elena told her hastily. She paused and considered Jacob. "You have a lovely husband, Emma, and it is of no concern to me that he is a Jew. In time, you will discover that it is the *least* important thing about a person—religion, color, sex. But in those times, it could get you *killed!*"

Elena was glaring at her, as if daring her to argue. Emma sighed deeply, and told herself it wasn't worth it. Elena *now* said it wasn't an important matter, but it clearly had been important at the time, and there would be no changing deeply-seated beliefs and fears even at this point in time when Elena knew better. What the woman knew now could not penetrate the centuries of distrust that had been instilled in her since birth. It appeared that even death and hundreds of years of disembodiment could not erase the lessons of childhood.

What a shame.

Emma shook her head again and smiled gently. "Go on with your story, dear," she said.

Elena eyed her suspiciously for a moment, and then smiled. She was a ghost; she was no longer bound to the world. She understood that her prejudices were unfounded, but were still grounded within her; she also understood that Emma would not pursue the matter; she'd have to deal with it on her own, and that was fine.

She decided to resume her story. "Well," she said, "once we had met again, my relationship with my sister continued as my son told you.

"It was a wild world then, Emma. You would think that in small settlements, people would know each other well, but that wasn't always true. There were many who were sociable, who attended fiestas and visited the cantinas, but the gentlewomen stayed at home. I feel completely sure in saying that most of the men who searched for us never really knew who we were or what we looked like.

"In Corrales, we likely would have been recognized; we drew water, we planted and harvested crops and shopped or traded amongst the townspeople. But in other settlements, even those less than a few hours' ride away? No. We were gentlewomen and stayed close to home.

"So, it was easy. No one in Santa Fe knew that the wife of Juan Santillanes was one of the missing women from Corrales; therefore, no one guessed that the sister who visited from time to time was also taken hostage by savages.

"Our children grew up together, and Julia's husband was kind enough to help my son find the work he desired. Of course, no one ever knew that Juan was Julia's nephew; that would have raised too many questions."

"How did you manage to get the children together?" Sasha asked. It seemed unreasonable to assume that they all just showed up in town and visited in the Santillanes home.

"We would arrange meetings when Julia's husband traveled for work. We would meet in the desert and share a meal. The children would play together. Over the years we both had more children. There was never any enmity amongst them; even as adults, the children remained close cousins, although of course there were difficulties staying in touch. All those years Grey Wolf and Juan Santillanes got along well and often traded goods. My father-in-law would many times visit with him as well, to discuss Spain and their interference in the area.

"It was a strange set of relationships, certainly. But we made it work."

Emma wondered aloud if they could not have somehow included their mother in the alliance, but Elena did not answer her.

"As I told you, Juan Santillanes helped Juan Baptiste to find many different jobs in the area. All the children were taught to speak Spanish, and all learned to read and write. My other sons—they had no interest in scouting. Like their grandfather, they used only their tribal names. They knew that Juan Baptiste would always lead the Spaniards astray as far as the People were concerned. Because of the dealings between those brothers there was much prosperity among the People for many years. During my lifetime, none of our party went hungry, even in winter."

"Yet Juan Baptiste managed to also help the Spaniards prosper," Emma commented.

"Oh, yes; that is true. He was sly; he was intelligent, and he was *very* charming." Elena beamed proudly. "He could have done anything he chose. He chose to care for all his people in the best way he knew how."

Elena studied Emma shrewdly. "I will tell you something, Emma," she added. "He had every opportunity to leave us, attend the local schools, perhaps even go east to study. He could have been a learned man. Julia's husband offered him the chance, but he refused to leave the People." She shook her head. "I often wondered if he regretted his decision."

"I seriously doubt it," Emma assured her.

Elena nodded. "You're probably right; he seemed content."

Emma giggled, but refrained from saying that Juan Baptiste seemed quite a bit more than content; he was pleased as punch with himself! The man led the Spaniards on wild goose chases and took their money for it. He was often helpful to them as well, leading them to enemy camps or showing them where they could find fresh water or game to hunt; but only when it did not interfere with his People and their needs. He also slept with their women and left them to raise his bastard children. He informed his tribe of the movements of their enemy and kept his family fed and clothed.

He was a pioneer double agent!

He regretted nothing; Emma had no doubt of that.

"Did none of your children attend the schools?" Emma asked. "You said they learned to read and write."

"Their cousins taught them; they taught Julia and me as well. We had learned very little growing up. Our mother did not read, and our father did not think that women needed to learn.

"My brother-in-law sent all their children east to be educated. His family had come from the East, and his first wife was an English woman. His son Miguel was quite a bit older than the other children; he was already returning from college around the same time Goldie was sent to begin her education. He was very intelligent; he became an educator in the area and was an ally to all children.

"My sister's husband was a wealthy man, Emma, and very generous. He would have sent any of my children east for schooling had they wanted to go. They chose to learn what they could from their cousins, especially from Miguel, and to stay with the people. I would have let them go; they chose for themselves."

"Tell us about your mother," Emma requested quietly. "How could you leave her all those years wondering about you and fearing for your lives?"

Elena had the decency to blush and look shamefaced. "I fear I can never justify my actions to you—or to anyone," she admitted. "Were we afraid? Yes, it is true that we were. Juliana held to the Catholic faith more strongly than I, but we both knew the penance we were sure to face should we return as the wives of Natives who were not converted. There would have been demands for immediate conversion of my husband; otherwise it would be as if I had borne bastard children while living in sin. And as an unmarried and sullied woman, I would be condemned to live wherever I could find work as a servant; my children might be taken from me to be raised among a Catholic family, and I would have nothing! No home, no family, no life! It is doubtful that my own mother would have even been allowed to take us in, were the Church to become involved—and the Church involved itself in everything! It is even more doubtful that I would have been allowed to return to the People; it was almost a certainty that I would be forced to remain if I returned.

"And if it were that bad for me, what of Juliana? She fled her life with the People and found her love, Juan Santillanes. He married her and claimed her child as his own. There were repercussions from the Church even in *that* case, as they deemed the infant a bastard, the product of an illicit affair, and for a few months they were required to be in confession every morning and evening; that is why I was still able to find them in Santa Ana; penance for their sin. Once the required penance and penalties were satisfied, they moved to Santa Fe, a legally married couple with a legally begotten child.

"Naturally, Juliana was terrified that going to our mother would negate everything she had been through to gain a marriage and legitimate child in the eyes of the Church, for how could they not then learn of the deception she and her husband had constructed? My mother so feared the fires of hell that she would likely have confessed everything if she learned the truth from us.

"She was our mother; we both knew that if we saw her again we would be unable to lie to her about the many things we'd gone through. She was our *mother.* We loved her. You don't lie to those you love.

"And she could never lie or withhold from her confessor. It wasn't in her to be able to hide the truth.

"So, you see, there were things we had gained being away from Corrales that we were sure of losing had we returned. Were we being selfish? Yes, I believe we were. *Certainly,* we were." She stared off in the distance for a time, pensive.

Emma exchanged glances with Sasha, and they waited.

"Oh, the religious nonsense!" Elena snarled suddenly, making Emma jump. "There was no way to know one way or the other if we might burn in hell for the decisions we made—or the ones made for us. And here I am, as I said before, not a hell in sight! No heaven, either! What does it mean, Emma?"

Emma stared at her, wide-eyed. "I'm sure I don't have a clue!" she protested. "Your mother thinks heaven and hell are yet to come, if that's any help."

Elena glared at her. "It's not!"

"Yeah, I didn't think so."

"It makes me angry," Elena admitted. "All the things we were so afraid of—excommunication from the Church and having her marriage declared illegal frightened Juliana so much that she begged me not to let Juan tell Mama about us. She had a comfortable home; she loved her husband, and he loved her. They had children and a profitable business. She had much to lose.

"For me it was fear of losing a life of freedom and independence. Once I had lived among the People, I realized that within the community of Spaniards I was raised in, I was little more than a slave. I would have been forced to do the will of whatever man put himself in charge of me; I could never have tolerated it!

"And over and above all of those fears, we feared hellfire. Julia ran from it. I ran toward it, in spite of my fear. Every choice I made was a choice counter to the teachings I grew up with. As I was leaving your world and entering this one, I swore to all who would listen that my choices were worth it! I had lived my life at the side of a man I loved, a man who loved me in return. We raised healthy children. We lived to see grandchildren. I owned our teepee and learned to trade profitably with the settlers and other tribes. I was a councilor to many, and my advice was actively sought by men and women alike. I was a respected member of the society! That was *huge*, Emma."

"I understand that," Emma assured her.

"And we took *care* of our mother; do not forget that!"

"I didn't forget," Emma said.

"We made her gifts. We sent vegetables and meat. Juan took them and left them for her. He kept track of her, you see. We had older brothers and sisters, so she was looked after once our father was dead. We didn't have to do it; she would have been fine! But even though no one ever knew, Juliana and I did our part to take care of her as well."

301

"I think she would love to know that, Elena."

"You tell her. Tell her, Emma."

Emma took the ice pack off her eye and laid it on the table. She put her glasses back on and realized they'd attracted a small audience; several people sat at nearby tables, listening to her as she recounted the story.

She sighed. She looked up and smiled at Elena. "You need to tell her yourself," she said. "You and Juliana."

"How?"

"Do you see Juliana?"

"From time to time, of course; I see all my family."

"But not your mother?"

"Well..."

"You've been gone from this world for nearly three centuries. Are you aware of that?"

"I don't—I suppose...in some ways—really? Three hundred years?"

"In all that time, she has *never* stopped looking for you!" Emma realized that her tone had turned scolding, but she didn't care; it pissed her off. "Three *centuries*, for the love of God! Not only that—she can't find your father, either. She's alone, and all because she can't get over losing you and never knowing the end of the story. If there is a Heaven, how can she move on without knowing the truth? If there is a Hell, she is in it now!"

Jacob put a hand on her arm, but Emma ignored him.

"I don't know how to call her here," Emma said. "I can only hope that she is somehow listening to me right now and chooses to come."

"Emma?" Sasha looked worried.

"Can you call your sister?" Emma demanded.

Elena stared at her, slack jawed. "I—I think so," she said. "But—"

"Then *do* it." Emma put her head down, wiping away tears of frustration—and possibly residual allergy effects. No, probably just frustration, she decided. "Come on, Manuelita," she muttered despairingly. "Just for once, show up when I want you."

Chapter Twenty

Reunion and Reconciliation

Emma sat with her elbows on the table and her head in her hands. Her eyes were leaking profusely, and not entirely from the effects of her allergy attack. They still felt puffy, the skin of her eyelids uncomfortable tight, but they were mostly open now, thanks to the ice pack.

Angrily, she brushed the tears away and put her glasses on. When she looked up, she was once again aware that besides Jacob and their friends, there were several people around them at other tables. They all watched her anxiously, and she blushed furiously.

Her lips tightened. She whisper-growled, "Why didn't you tell me we had an audience?"

Jacob, Sasha and Martin looked around, surprised. "I didn't even notice," Jacob admitted.

"Me, neither," Martin added, and Sasha shrugged apologetically, shaking her head.

"Great. The weirdo strikes again," Emma groused.

"Let it go," Jacob advised.

Emma sighed. What else could she do?

Jacob looked around again; yeah, it was an audience, all right. Truly, she had them eating out of her hand. He sighed, too, and looked back at his wife. "Anything?" he asked.

"No. I don't know if she'll come. Shit, if she's been listening at all, why would she even *want* to? Poor woman!" Emma glared meaningfully at Elena, who flinched. "Where's Juliana?"

"I don't know!" Elena cried. "It is not as if I know how any of this works, Emma!"

Emma frowned at her, and as she did, Juan Baptiste materialized behind his mother. Emma switched her glare to him and demanded, "Where is she?"

"She does not wish to come," Juan told her.

"Tough titty, said the kitty," Emma said. "I don't care if you have to drag her here kicking and screaming. She needs to face up to the things she's done just the same as everyone else."

"Prima—" Juan began.

"Nope." Emma shook her head. "You stubborn people need to move on with your lives—or deaths—or afterlives." Emma sighed again. "Or whatever the hell this is!"

Martin and Sasha exchanged nervous glances. "Is that what this is all about?" Martin asked. "Moving on?"

"How should I know?" Emma cried. "No one tells me anything!"

"But—" Sasha said.

"Nothing that makes sense," Emma elaborated. "I don't know why I've been chosen to see, to listen. I don't know why or what to explain, or to whom." She barked a laugh. "If this is supposed to resolve something, I need to be able to get everyone together and finish the story! But no one ever cooperates!"

She looked across the table at Elena and her handsome son. "I didn't ask for this," she said. "I was just trying to have a life. Go to school, be a regular, normal kid. Have some friends. You know?"

"Emma," Juan Baptiste said beseechingly, "we don't know how this has happened, either."

"Maria Manuela came to me," Emma said. "She begged for help. God knows I have tried to help her. But you people must work with me. Where is your sister, Elena?"

"I don't—"

"I am here."

Emma started violently, and looked to her left, where a woman was now seated next to her. "Juliana?" she asked.

"I am," the woman replied. She patted Emma's hand comfortingly, but of course Emma felt nothing. "Here I am at last—the selfish one."

"I never—" Emma protested.

"Of course, you did!" Juliana interrupted her. "I know it; Elena knows it; everyone knows it!

"It is true; I have been very selfish. I wanted what I wanted, and I got it. I paid a heavy price, and then I paid it again. And then I brooded about it and prayed over it and made excuses to justify it." She lifted her chin defiantly. "And I would do it all again."

"Julia," Elena said.

"No, sister. You have told your tale; you have included part of mine, but not the most important part."

"Juan Santillanes," Emma said quietly.

"Yes!" Juliana agreed. "He was always the most important part of *my* story."

"Indeed, he was," a new voice interjected.

Emma sagged with relief. "Manuelita," she sighed.

"Mama!" Juliana and Elena chorused.

"For you *everything* centered on Juan Santillanes," Manuelita accused her daughter.

"Mama, you have no idea—" Juliana began.

"I did not," Manuelita agreed. "But now I believe I do."

The little woman came forward and stood beside her grandson. "So," she said to him. "You lied to me!"

"I never—" he protested. "I wanted to tell you!"

"You lied by omission," she clarified. "Because you both told him to!" she scolded her daughters.

Elena stood and held up her arms, palms lifted skyward in supplication. "Oh, Mama!" she cried. "How I missed you!" She began to cry.

Manuelita and Juliana joined her in tears and soon enough the three women were embracing and sobbing loudly.

Juan Baptiste watched, bemused. "Would that this could have happened in life," he sighed. He looked at Emma. "It was my dream," he added.

Emma looked at him for a long moment and then nodded. Tears stood in his brilliant emerald eyes; he was sincere. "I believe you," she said.

"My mother had a happy life," he said. "But she was also sad and full of regrets. The same was true of my aunt."

"I hurt so many people," Juliana cried. "I'm so sorry!"

"What's your story, Juliana?" Emma asked. "You said there's more than what Juan Baptiste has told me, and what Elena has told me. Now, here is your mother—three hundred years later! Why? Please, tell us why."

Emma motioned Jacob to slide over on the bench, and Elena sat next to her. Taking their movement as a cue, Sasha and Martin moved as well, and Juliana and Manuelita sat on that side of the table across from Emma. Their hands were clasped, and Manuelita reached across to grasp Elena's hand as well.

Emma looked up at Juan Baptiste, who had remained standing. There was room for him to join his grandmother, but he shook his head and stood.

Emma shrugged and looked expectantly at Juliana.

"Elena has told you that I was not a strong woman," Juliana began. "I was one to be led about by the nose my whole life long. I surely would have agreed to marry whoever Papa chose, and lived my life in Corrales contentedly until I died, and I never would have known the difference between settling and true happiness.

"But I met Juan Santillanes, and all that changed! He was...*magnificent*. Oh, he was not so handsome as Grey Wolf. He was not even so handsome as my first husband, the Apache Running Deer. But even so, he was a most magnificent man, Emma."

Emma had heard nothing but good things about this man, so she was inclined to agree. The others nodded their acceptance as well.

Juliana continued: "For once in my life, I pursued what I wanted. I chased the poor man shamelessly. I cared for his son, Miguelito, and I loved that little boy as my own. I believe that is why Juan finally took notice of this crazy woman you see before you now—that I could love his child as my own. But it was easy, you know. Children are life! They were made to be loved.

"I stood up to my father, who had as yet no other man in mind for me, but disliked Juan Santillanes."

"He was an old man," Manuelita interjected.

"He was not so old," Juliana objected.

"Perhaps not; you were simply too young," Manuela said.

"But I was not so young that I didn't know what I wanted!"

"Settle down," Emma said.

Manuelita giggled like a youngster. "Such an old argument!" she agreed. "And Julia won—her father finally agreed to let them marry. We did not want to lose our daughter."

"But you lost her anyway," Juan Baptiste stated softly.

"Mama," Juliana said. "We were afraid. Afraid of so many things that seem very stupid now."

"I know," Manuelita said. "About many of those fears, you were right! Your uncles *would* have demanded that you stay in Corrales, Elena. I would have agreed with them; I was blinded then by hate. I am sorry it was so, but I cannot deny it."

"I know I hurt you," Juliana said. "I defied you both, and then I was stolen away before real amends could be made. And Papa was dead, and there was nothing I could do for him!

"Then I was forced to marry Running Deer." Juliana was pensive. "Oh, how I resented that! I did not resent *him;* that resentment was directed at your mother-in-law, Elena."

"I know this well," Elena acknowledged. "And so did Morning Star. She blamed herself when you fled."

"I blamed her, too." Juliana smiled ruefully. "But it was all my doing. I never stopped loving Juan Santillanes.

"Do you know," she continued, "that it is possible to love two men at the same time?"

"I suppose so," Emma said, and Sasha shrugged. Several of the women in the uninvited audience exchanged knowing glances, but the little group ignored them.

"I did not plan for that to happen," Juliana cried. "In fact, I tried very hard not to care for Running Deer at all. But he was a good man, very gentle and kind. It breaks my heart that I hurt him so.

"It breaks my heart that he didn't know his daughter; it breaks my heart that I chose never to tell her the truth of her parentage.

"I couldn't do it, of course—Juan took her into his home and accepted her as his own. Never, never did we speak of how she came to be, or of any of the details of my marriage to Running Deer.

"We told a story of an adulterous affair which produced a baby born out of wedlock and confessed it to the Friars and

307

never, ever recanted. We went to the chapel daily to confess, over and over, this lie.

"Juan Santillanes was a saint of a man, willing to give his eternal soul up to damnation in order to marry me and claim my child as his own! How could I ever go home and take the chance that any of the truth might come out? He had suffered greatly in doing the things he did for me. His reputation suffered for quite some time! He lost business dealings when the church made known some of the details of our marriage while we were detained in Santa Ana.

"The women in town shunned me; I had no friends there; I was a wanton woman. It made no difference to anyone that he had married me. If the church labeled you a sinner, all must turn their backs and stay away until such time as you were deemed forgiven.

"It was amazing to me that anyone was helpful enough to my sister so that she could find me!"

"You were surprised I hadn't come sooner!" Elena objected.

"Surprised at *you*, yes!" Juliana agreed. "Stubborn as you are, you would have managed to find me sooner or later. I thought it would be sooner; I underestimated your anger at me." She laughed and shook her head. "Oh, the wrath of my sister!"

"You had it coming."

"I did." Juliana stared down at her hands, entwined with those of her mother and her sister. "I know I hurt Running Deer terribly. I loved him." She shrugged helplessly. "I loved Juan *more*. I could not live without him; I could feel myself dying inside, day after day. And so, I did what I had to do: I ran away from one love and into the arms of *true* love."

She looked up and stared at her mother. "I regret many things in my life, but I do not regret choosing to be with the man I love. I know Papa did not like him, but—"

"You misunderstand, Juliana," Manuelita interrupted. "Your father did not dislike the man; he merely thought him too old for you. We were resigned to the marriage; he was a good man, a kind man; we knew this. We had hoped you would marry a man closer to your own age; that is all. Life is short enough; widowhood is hard! We didn't want to see you alone."

Juliana began to giggle. "Oh, Mama! Is life for everyone just a series of misunderstandings, mistakes and regrets? Juan outlived me! Such a delicious irony, no?"

"Oh, for heaven's sake!" Emma burst out. "That's not funny!"

In spite of that, she too began to giggle, and soon enough everyone was having a bit of a laugh.

"Oh, God, shut up!" Emma gasped, finally. She shook her head, smiling. "I'm sorry, I'm sorry. Look—" she added. "Are we at the end of this story, then? Manuelita, your daughters were never very far from you. They took care of you until the end of your days."

"I am grateful to know this at last," Manuelita said. "And more grateful still to be finally reunited with them."

"Good!" Juan Baptiste gave a decisive nod, winked at Emma and vanished.

"Good-bye to you, too, cousin," Emma said, shaking her head.

"That is my son!" Elena cried. "He does not say goodbye; even as a child, he would never do so! It frightened him..."

"Oh." Emma couldn't think of anything to say. "Okay, then."

"Emma," Manuelita said. "I can never repay the kindness you've shown me! Thank you! Thank you for finding my daughters!"

"I don't think I had much to do with it," Emma said.

"It would never have been possible without you," Elena assured her. Juliana nodded her agreement. "We are together at last! Oh, Mama! I'm so glad!"

The women rose and embraced, and faced Emma with tears in their eyes. Emma rose, too.

"We will not say goodbye, either, Emma," Juliana said, "because there are no real goodbyes. We will be together again."

"I know," Emma agreed.

"Oh!" Manuelita cried, her face alight with joy. "My Juan Gonzales! Oh, mi amor! Where have you been?"

Emma turned, expecting to see her many-times-removed great grandfather, but no one was there. When she turned back, Manuelita, Elena and Juliana were gone.

"Well, dang!" Emma cried.

2.

There is nothing like being the center of attention, Emma thought. For the first time, she acknowledged the little audience she'd attracted.

She didn't have much choice, really; they were applauding her!

"What'll I do?" she asked Jacob, barely moving her lips.

"I don't know...take a bow?" Jacob suggested.

Emma stifled an urge to slug him.

A woman approached her, gushing, "That was amazing! I thought the Tram guide was entertaining, but your story was just—we didn't know this was one of the attractions here!"

"It's not an—" Emma started to protest, then gasped as the woman dropped a ten-dollar bill on the table in front of her. "What—no, you don't have to—"

"Great show!" A large fellow with an enormous growth of white whiskers scattered some ones on the table.

"Wait!" Emma cried. "I don't want—"

"That was fantastic," another woman cried. "Your troupe should be so proud! It was just as if someone from the past was talking to you! I could practically see them!" And she, too, put money on the table.

"Somebody stop them!" Emma cried. "Wait! I don't need—"

No one was paying any attention to her protests, and after dropping money and complimenting the "show", the people dispersed, chatting among themselves about the wonderful storyteller and her old wild-west tale.

Emma stood watching them go, her eyes stinging and still streaming with tears, her mouth agape. Jacob reached out and gently pushed her chin up, and she turned to stare at him. "Why didn't you stop them?" she demanded.

"How?" he countered.

Martin threw back his head and roared laughter. "Oh, my God!" he gasped. "That was rich!"

"Marty!" Sasha cried.

"Someone go catch those people and give them their money!" Emma cried.

"Don't be silly, Emma!" Sasha said. "What would we say? That there really was someone there telling the story?"

"I—what? No! But—"

"Just hurry up and pick up the money, and let's get out of here," Martin chuckled. "Quick, before they send another group down to listen to a story."

Emma's jaw dropped. She grabbed Sasha by the hand and hurried up the walkway.

Martin started laughing again, and gathered up the scattered bills while Jacob also began to laugh.

"At least," he told his friend, "there was a happy ending!"

"Yeah," Martin agreed. "And money, too!"

"Shut up."

Emma and Sasha were nearly back to the Tram loading area when Emma tugged her friend off in the direction of the restrooms. "Oh, good idea," Sasha said.

"I just want to hide in a stall for a bit," Emma whispered urgently. "My God, what if we end up riding back with some of those people?"

"Maybe you should just roll with it," Sasha suggested easily.

"They left me money!" Emma hissed, scandalized.

"Do you want to explain?"

"No!"

"Gas money," Sasha shrugged. "Buy your mom a gift for babysitting. Whatever. Or...track them all down and tell them the truth."

"Sasha! It feels...wrong!"

"It's not like you asked them for it," Sasha argued reasonably. "It's not like you even invited them to listen."

"Well...that's true."

"Leave it be. You can go home and tell your mom you actually got paid for your talents. People do it all the time."

Emma glared at her, and then closed the bathroom stall door, leaving Sasha giggling outside. "Sash, don't make me punch you," she threatened.

"Yeah, right, tough guy."

Emma sat on the toilet, urinating and resisting the urge to join Sasha's giggling.

Ah, what the heck, she thought and started to laugh. Everyone else was amused, and there was nothing she could do about it. "I really hate this stuff," she said.

Sasha giggled harder. "Shut up, you!" she called. "Damn, it's a good thing we're in the bathroom."

3.

They snuck around a bit, purposely avoiding anyone they recognized from the deck, and finally boarded the Tram.

"I guess I don't care," Emma sighed, staring at the scenery stretched out before them. "Manuelita has found her daughters."

"And her husband," Jacob added. "Don't forget about that."

"I won't."

"Gosh, I love a happy ending," Martin grinned happily. "And money."

"Hush up, Marty!" Sasha hissed, trying not to giggle any more. "And by the way—how much?"

"Are you for real?" Emma demanded, scandalized.

That started the laughter again, and they couldn't quite get it under control until they were almost back to their starting point.

In the end, it wasn't a fortune, but it certainly did amount to decent gas money, and Emma decided to be grateful for it rather than fret about it. Like Sasha had said, she hadn't asked anyone for it.

And happy endings don't happen every day, after all.

She would take what she could get!

Epilogue

It had been a long day and Emma was very tired. They had plans to visit the genealogy museum the next day and then it would be time to head home again.

She could hardly wait to hold her babies! She had missed them so much.

Emma snuggled into Jacob's arms and in one of those rare times in her life, slipped into sleep almost immediately.

A few hours later, her eyes flew open. Had someone called her name?

"Emmaline." A whispering voice.

"Hmmm?" It was dark; she couldn't see.

"Emma? You need to wake up, sweetie."

She knew that voice. But...no, it couldn't be...

"Grandma?" Emma leaned over the edge of the bed, groping for the lamp.

"Wake up now, Emma."

"I'm awake." Her blood ran cold. "Grandma?"

It's not her!

No, of course not! She was in New Mexico, at Sasha's. She was dreaming. It was Sasha. It had to be Sasha!

She found the lamp switch and twisted it. The light came on.

Nothing.

Okay...good. I was just dreaming, that's all.

But she was shaking. Her nerves were jangling.

She sat up and swung her legs over the side of the bed. She sat staring at her bare feet, trying to calm her nerves.

It was just a dream!

Finally, she got up and crossed the room to the doorway. She stepped out into the hall, and slowly made her way to the bathroom.

She groped along the inside wall of the bathroom, her body only halfway through the door, her fingers searching for and locating the light switch.

She took a deep breath, then another.

313

She flipped the switch.

Her grandmother was sitting on the edge of the bathtub. She was dressed in a flowing white gown—a nightgown, from what Emma could discern. It had a square neckline, lined with lace. It was flannel, most likely.

She looked comfortable. Cozy, even. "Emma," she said, smiling. She reached out her hand beckoningly.

"No," Emma moaned, shaking her head in vehement denial.

"You need to call your mother now," Grandma said. "Before Grandpa wakes up."

"Oh, Grandma. No!" Her lower lip began to tremble, and she shook her head again.

"Call your mother now," Grandma whispered gently. "I love you, sweetheart. You need to call your mom."

"Grandma, *no!*" Emma started to cry.

Down the hall in the bedroom, Jacob sat up, startled. He could hear Emma's voice: "Oh, no, Grandma!"

Jacob, all too aware of what was happening, jumped from the bed and sped down the hall to the bathroom. He found his wife standing in the doorway, and pulled her into his arms.

"Oh, no," Emma sobbed. "No, Grandma. No. *No!*"

Jacob gently led her back to their room.

To the phone.

Emma had a call to make. A story to tell. Things to explain.

"Grandma," she sighed as she removed the receiver from the cradle. "Dang!"

End

Author's Note

I am not Emma.

People who know me, who know the history of my family and the town where I grew up might disagree, up to a point.

But no, I am not Emma.

The people who populate this small Wyoming town are not the people I grew up with. I never knew any honestly mean girls, and no one ever treated me badly—even though I really am a little weird.

Not as weird as Emma, though. Emma sees ghosts—lots of ghosts—and they talk to her. The ghosts I have seen never bothered to explain a single thing to me. They appear and disappear and except for my own great-grandmother, I don't know who they are or why they even bother to drop in.

No one talks to me.

How annoying.

The story you've just read is more the result of my own wishful thinking. I'd love some explanations, as it happens. I'd love to be able to ask questions of my ancestors and get the whole story behind the meager histories I've managed to find while doing family tree research.

There really was a Juan Gonzales who was killed by Apaches.

There really was an uncle killed in a train collision, but his name wasn't Joel.

There really was a great-great-great grandmother who lost a child at sea. Her name was not Janette, but she really did have a sister-in-law with the same given name who also lost a child at sea. It took me weeks of research to finally determine that there were two children lost on that voyage.

And all I wanted was to just have someone I could ask, you know? Hey, Grandmother, did your baby die, or was it someone else's baby?

Out of this desire to find answers, Emma was born in my imagination.

So, I really am not Emma, but she is a part of me, the part who can find answers without making things up. The part of me who can explain.

But me? I'm just Paula, that chick with all the questions who decided to make up some answers for herself and in the process further confuse herself during those times when she is doing actual research and can't for the life of her find information about the daughters who were abducted by Apaches.

You know, the ones who exist only in my imagination.

I want you to know that the ending was not my idea. My Great-Grandma told me the ending. Honest. I was barely awake, and had to get up and change the original ending to this one.

By the way, she died when I was four years old.

I don't know what she was thinking. I guess it means I must write another book. But she's not answering any of my questions.

So... to be continued?

Acknowledgements

Special thanks to my first reader, Alison Barker Bennett, who has been a great cheerleader when I was feeling too timid to give this a shot. She is also a wonderful nurse, by the way. Thank you, Alison!

Thank you to my family, for the real stories we've shared and for encouraging me to use my imagination to embellish those stories into the fictions I weave.

Thank you to my children, just for being mine. I kind of dig you guys. And I'm awfully grateful for all the grandchildren. They light up my life.

90079894R00177

Made in the USA
San Bernardino, CA
14 October 2018